"*The New Black* ought to be the New High Standard for dark fiction anthologies. It's loaded with intelligence and talent. Every one of the pieces in this extraordinary compilation is worthy of your full attention."

— Jack Ketchum, author of *The Girl Next Door*

"*The New Black* is a great collection of incredibly unique fiction. I honestly liked every story in here, and I usually don't say that about an anthology. It was also nice to encounter so many authors with whom I was unfamiliar. A strong compilation of talent—very strong."

—Shock Totem

"There's depth to darkness, a richness waiting for those who have the patience to let their vision adjust to it. Rembrandt knew that; it's there in the voluminous shadows that wrap around the figures in his paintings. So did Poe: it's the note sounding underneath the stories his narrators tell us. And so do the writers Richard Thomas has assembled for *The New Black*. At this point in our shared history, it's no secret that those things closest to us, our family, our memory, may be full of night. What is remarkable is what the writers in this book succeed in telling us about that darkness, what shapes they discern within it. A showcase of some of the most exciting writers at work today, *The New Black* is not to be missed."

— John Langan, author of *The Wide, Carnivorous Sky and Other Monstrous Geographies*

Dark House Press PRESENTS

The
NEW

BLACK

Edited by RICHARD THOMAS

FOREWORD BY LAIRD BARRON

PUBLISHED BY DARK HOUSE PRESS, AN IMPRINT OF CURBSIDE SPLENDOR PUBLISHING, INC., CHICAGO, ILLINOIS IN 2014.

FIRST EDITION
COPYRIGHT © 2014 BY RICHARD THOMAS
LIBRARY OF CONGRESS CONTROL NUMBER: 2014935338
ISBN 978-1-940430-04-1

EDITED BY RICHARD THOMAS
ILLUSTRATED BY L.A. SPOONER
DESIGNED BY ALBAN FISCHER

MANUFACTURED IN THE UNITED STATES OF AMERICA.
WWW.THEDARKHOUSEPRESS.COM

CONTENTS

LAIRD BARRON Foreword: Eye of the Raven i

RICHARD THOMAS Introduction vii

STEPHEN GRAHAM JONES Father, Son, Holy Rabbit 2

PAUL TREMBLAY It's Against the Law to Feed the Ducks 14

LINDSAY HUNTER That Baby 36

KYLE MINOR The Truth and All Its Ugly 44

CRAIG CLEVENGER Act of Contrition 66

MICAELA MORRISSETTE The Familiars 80

BENJAMIN PERCY Dial Tone 104

ROXANE GAY How 122

ROY KESEY Instituto 140

CRAIG DAVIDSON Rust and Bone 154

REBECCA JONES-HOWE Blue Hawaii 180

JOE MENO Children Are the Only Ones Who Blush 192

VANESSA VESELKA Christopher Hitchens 210

CRAIG WALLWORK Dollhouse 226

NIK KORPON His Footsteps are Made of Soot 236

TARA LASKOWSKI The Etiquette of Homicide 254

MATT BELL Dredge 260

ANTONIA CRANE Sunshine for Adrienne 288

RICHARD LANGE Fuzzyland 300

BRIAN EVENSON Windeye 332

ACKNOWLEDGMENTS 343

EYE OF THE RAVEN

I.

At heart, I prefer the bleak and the horrific. Horror with a capital H. Doesn't matter whence it springs. Nonetheless, I was weaned on the hard stuff. Jim Thompson. James M. Cain. John D. MacDonald. Stephen King. Shirley Jackson. The Brothers Grimm. Noir, horror, and fairytales are all bound together with barb wire and blood, you see.

If I may be so gauche as to quote an essay I once wrote about a fabulous author of noir named Pearce Hansen:

"There is a peculiar synergy between noir, crime fiction, and horror. It wouldn't surprise me, were I to analyze it more thoroughly, that John D. MacDonald, Donald Westlake, and Robert Parker tales of hard boiled modern day knights, treacherous scoundrels, and sloe-eyed vamps and the assorted skullduggery sum and sundry found themselves enmeshed within had as much or more to do with my becoming a horror writer than the bloody works of King or Barker."

As a kid, I loved crime and westerns, the real deal fairytales, and the authentic myths. Not the sanitized, abridged, vetted iterations we were dosed with at school. The unvarnished ones where Snow White burned the Queen's feet in red hot iron shoes, where heroes were betrayed by their lovers before dying awful deaths, or the gods went down in smoke and thunder and left Man alone in a cold, remote part of the cosmos. The secret to my fascination with noir is that as a tradition it cleaves so close to horror that it might've hatched from the same egg. Horror and noir are as mercurial as vast oil slicks upon the ocean—solid, primitive objects that nonetheless flow and shift with the currents.

In order to get a handle on the icepick that is the new black, it's instructive to look at the old black. The old black is a tradition that extends at least back through the mists to the gaslight era and Edgar Allan Poe. Classic noir shines like the moon in an austere nightscape, as cold and cruel as a raven's eye.

Noir: a dark, bitter seed that blooms into strange and cold life. It is associated with crime and starkness. Sexual deviance. Frequently, it has served as the mantle of the hardboiled and the hard cases of film and literature. Again, mirroring conservative horror, noir often functions as a filter of dark, dark morality. Its tropes and leitmotifs are legendary. Honor among thieves; double-crosses; femme fatales; skullduggery; the betrayal of lovers; the inversion of polite society's code. Good or evil, you get what's coming and what's coming is dreadful. Because the sad fact is, the universe is a dreadful place.

There's a thousand ways to die in the naked city. And more ways being invented every day.

2.

One night during the spring of 1995, James Ellroy stepped into the living room of my brain and made an adjustment to the television set. He clicked the dial to a notch between the engraved numerals, and the snowfield resolved into a psychedelic horror show. Its imprint remains permanently branded upon my imagination. At the time, I'd taken berth upon a salmon processor traveling the Bering Sea. We'd shut down the machinery and dimmed the lights in the hold after the eight consecutive fifteen hour shifts. Our vessel weighed anchor and began to chug along a forty-eight hour vector toward the next rendezvous with the fleet. When not comatose in their bunks, the majority of crew entertained themselves with booze, endless tournaments of gin rummy or dominoes, and marathon VCR sessions in the lounge. A deckhand from Seattle, among the two or three bibliophiles lurking aboard the ship, knew of my interest in Joseph Wambaugh and Martin Cruz Smith, and that sort of thing in general. He went into his stacks and loaned me a beat to hell copy of White Jazz. I wolfed it down. After that, it was, as they say, on.

White Jazz is a knockout crime novel, but also something new and strange, just as Patrick McGrath's *Spider* and Stewart O'Nan's *Speed Queen* and *A Prayer for the Dying* took the genre in strange and terrifying directions. We're witnessing a refinement of the ever-replicating mutation in the works of Donald Ray Pollack, Craig Davis, Kaaron Warren, and Gillian Flynn. And of course, new black or old black, masters such as Tom Picirrilli, Joe Lansdale, and Jack Ketchum prove with every new book that they never went anywhere. They are alive and well and spinning webs in the dark, just like the new bloods.

3.

The darkness has built like nightfall thickening and clotting at the edge of the horizon. What's here between these covers has been on its way for years. Literature is a process of assimilation. Authors are always in conversation with themselves and with those who came before. Authors push back and redefine. It is punch and counterpunch.

There's a subtle distinction between neo-noir and the tradition it has inexorably transformed. Or, perhaps, we're witnessing an iceberg calving from the great central mass that has accreted over the decades. If you've followed the genre, the trend is unmistakable. Otherwise, what's awaiting you in this anthology might come as a bracing splash of ice water. In either case, you're in for a treat. Crime is not necessarily the molten core of this contemporary machine. Nor are the characters necessarily of the hardboiled variety. Indeed, the contemporary narratives are far from hidebound. When you get down to brass tacks, neo-noir simply means dark fiction, and even within that niche, there's a hell of a lot of territory to cover. Here in this new century, ideas and plots of neo-noir have picked the locks and run amok. It's a fascinating time to be a fan.

From the mouth of Harry Angel in *Angel Heart*: "Today is Wednesday, it's anything can happen day." That's neo-noir twenty-odd years down the road—a snarling ball of tragedy, absurdity, and menace. It's a southern gothic, and it's a bloody mystery set in the wilderness, or a Peckinpah-worthy massacre among the stars. Anything can happen, and it can happen to anyone. Certainly the criminals and the cads will find themselves more readily subsumed by the forces of darkness. Provenance is always a prime consideration in these matters of the human heart. Even so, you don't have to be a bank robber or an embezzler; you don't need to be an adulterer or a con artist. Not in the multiverse of the new black. You simply have to draw breath. All it takes is a misstep, an honest miscalculation, the injustice of being in the wrong place at the right time. Then X marks the spot and you are in the soup.

It bears reiterating: The noir universe has always been a dreadful place. Baby, with neo-noir the neighborhood just took a turn for the worse. Rules are out the window, the physics of morality, ethics, and fair play smashed to powder and in the wind. Reality is on a permanent vacation. This universe is more about guidelines in sand, passwords that are randomly overwritten, splinter cells and half-enunciated shibboleths. Maybe this particular cosmos is a yearning, sentient thing that longs to right its scales. Maybe it understands nobody is truly innocent. Blood pays for blood. We all get what we paid for in the end. Maybe that's what matters. Maybe that's what we need to hold onto when we're navigating through the dark.

4.

Richard Thomas has assembled a hell of a rogues' gallery. These writers cover a spectrum of genre and lit fiction. Some of these names are familiar—Paul Tremblay has written crime novels about a narcoleptic P.I. knocking around the mean streets of Boston, horror collections, and a dystopian masterpiece. Brian Evenson recently penned a magnificent collection of surreal horror called *Windeye*. Evenson, long championed by no less a literary light than Peter Straub, will blow your doors off with his high-powered writing. Much of his work is steeped in the kind of psychological darkness that would make the aforementioned McGrath and Ellroy flinch. His weapons of choice are allegory and symbolism and magic realism that shrills a reed of bones with echoes of Kafka and Borges. Stephen Graham Jones owns a bibliography that a giraffe could wear as a floor-length stole. I consider him among the best living genre writers. No one captures the jaded innocence of youth nor the laconic expressiveness of the disaffected better than Jones, and no one surpasses his command of a Dali-esque stream of conscious delivery. Meanwhile, Benjamin Percy is bringing the fang and fur set back to prominence with his novels that blend pulp and literary sensibilities in a way that has ignited his career like a rocket.

However, keep your eye fixed upon the rising stars herein— Tara Laskowski's clinically macabre narration, the mounting dread that radiates from Matt Bell's icy miracle girl, or the pedal to the metal horror brought you by Micaela Morrissette and her little...friend. There's more, of course. A lot more of the dark side of the imagination waiting to spike you in the eye, and it will. But it's not my remit to spoil the pleasure of discovery.

So, now it comes to this, the hour of the wolf, the tap of the raven at the sill. In a few moments you will descend upon a dark odyssey into a realm of exquisite derangement. Turn the page and behold a panoply of the macabre, the sinister, and the inexplicable in all its grotesque splendor.

— Laird Barron
 October, 19, 2013
 Rifton, New York

INTRODUCTION

I f you've read Laird Barron's brilliant foreword and aren't in the mood to hear me gush about the twenty authors in this collection and my personal stories of inspiration, failure, and fulfillment, then by all means, skip ahead to the first story and dig right in. I totally understand, and won't hold it against you, my friend. But, if you'd like to hear how this collection came to be, and why I selected these specific stories and authors, then read on. You might find it interesting.

A strange series of events brought me back into the world of writing, editing, and teaching at the age of 40 years old. I remember seeing the movie *Fight Club*, and then later, discovering that there was a book by some guy named Chuck Palahniuk. After working my way through all of his books, excited by his fresh, transgressive voice, I ran across a website called The Cult. It was there that I discovered a community of fans and writers that seemed to be of a similar mindset. That got me to The Velvet and a trio of authors that were writing something called "neo-noir" fiction. As you may (or may not) know, neo-noir simply means "new-black." I fell in love with the written word all over again, and it inspired me to start writing.

One of the first classes I took at The Cult was with Craig Clevenger. I'd read both of his books, *The Contortionist's Handbook*, as well as *Dermaphoria*, after having worked my way through Palahniuk, and the trilogy by Will Christopher Baer (*Kiss Me Judas*, *Penny Dreadful*, and *Hell's Half Acre*). Craig was a brilliant instructor, and I learned a great deal from him. At the end of the class he encouraged me to send out one of my stories, "Stillness," and I hesitated. He said it was done, perfect, good to go—do it, already, he said. So I did. And I sent it to all of the wrong places, *The Paris Review* and *The New Yorker*, a ton of literary journals that were totally inappropriate, but eventually I sent it to *Cemetery Dance*. They said the magazine was backed up, but they'd like it for *Shivers VI*, an irregularly published anthology. I was disappointed—I'd never heard of the anthology, but I knew the press, so I said yes, of course, sounds great. Six months turned into a year, and the book finally came out—and my story was published alongside two of my heroes, Stephen King and Peter Straub. I think I may have cried. (This will be a recurring theme.) I was hooked. I'll always owe Craig for this start to my writing career, and his voice, his inclusion in this anthology was essential—not because I need to pay him back, but because his writing has inspired me for years. "Act of Contrition" is a dark, layered story that packs a punch.

Over time, I got more involved in writing communities, and attended my first AWP conference in New York City. It was overwhelming, and beautiful, and daunting. Stephen Graham Jones was the third member of the Velvet trio, so when I saw he was on a panel with another author I'd just started reading, Brian Evenson, I knew I had to attend. Both of these authors have been blending the best of literary and genre fiction for as long as I've been reading them, starting with Stephen's *All the Beautiful Sinners* and Brian's *The Wavering Knife*. Both of these gifted authors write with an attention to the language, a sense of unfurling tension, and the ability to let the terror slowly sink in until the epiphany of resolution is almost debilitating. "Father, Son, Holy Rabbit" was the first story that I thought of when building this collection, and "Windeye" immediately came to mind as well. Both stories have endings that are earned and unexpected, not twists, but dark understandings that have now become truth.

At about the same time, I started attending readings here in Chicago. One of the first that I went to was the Quickies! series, run by Lindsay Hunter and Mary Hamilton. The night that I read, with gifted voices such as Blake Butler, Amelia Gray, Jac Jemc, and Ben Tanzer, I also learned that Lindsay was not just the host, but an author. This was October of 2009. I would start my MFA the following January. Later, when *Daddy's* came out, Lindsay's first collection, I realized how gifted she really was. Her story "That Baby" will always stay with me, the final words about nipples and lit matchheads forever burned into my brain.

Also at that first AWP, I heard a man named Roy Kesey read a story. I was so blown away that I picked up his collection, *All Over*. He spoke about his struggles, how he tried for years to get into an elite literary journal, the *Kenyon Review*. The rejections piled up and he was about to stop submitting to them, when he finally broke in. They took his story, "Wait." When he told them that he didn't think they liked his writing, they responded by saying that they'd been fans for years. Just goes to show you how fickle and subjective this business can be. That story was later selected by Stephen King for the *Best American Short Stories 2007* anthology. His story in this anthology, "Instituto" is my favorite of his—funny and dark and original.

It was in my MFA program that a good friend of mine Drew McCoy introduced me to "Refresh, Refresh" in *The Paris Review*, by Benjamin Percy. I picked up the collection, and have been a fan ever since. Another author who isn't afraid to write horror with a literary voice, I selected "Dial Tone" because I think it's a little less known than some of the other stories in that collection, and it has a tension throughout that I love. *The Wilding* and *Red Moon* are his two novels, and both are innovative works. When I heard that he was taking on werewolves (called lycans) I wasn't sure how it would turn out, but *Red Moon* is simply amazing.

Early in my career I can remember reaching out to Matt Bell, asking him for advice, and he always took the time to respond. As I became a fan of Dzanc Books and the work they were doing there, I got to know him better. But it wasn't until *Cataclysm Baby* that I was sold—such a surreal, powerful and touching dark novel. I knew that Matt needed to be in here, too, and his story "Dredge" is a bit of contemporary noir that fit perfectly.

When I started writing book reviews for The Nervous Breakdown, one of the first books I read was *In the Mean Time* by Paul Tremblay. It was a fascinating mix of short stories— science fiction and horror, neo-noir and fantasy, a perfect blend of the kind of writing I was starting to get into. If he didn't make me aware of the genre (or sub-genre) of magical realism, he at least primed me for the voices that I would read later—Aimee Bender and Kelly Link, for example. His story "It's Against the Law to Feed the Ducks" is one of the few stories I've ever read that made me cry. And I'm not ashamed to admit that. Maybe it was being a new father at the time, maybe it was the honesty of the story, but his original look at a post-apocalyptic world has stayed with me for many years.

Around this time I can remember running across *PANK* at an AWP, probably here in Chicago. I met Roxane Gay for the first time, and once I got over how exciting the magazine was, I realized she was a gifted author as well. I was still struggling to get my work accepted, and when she took my story "Splintered," a contemporary "choose-your-own-path" bit of neo-noir adventure, it gave me a huge dose of confidence. As I started to see her name more and more often, in other publications I was chasing, I realized that I hadn't read a story of hers that was anything close to average or expected—she was a slugger, hitting them out of the park every single time. I was so thrilled to see her get into the *Best American Short Stories 2012* anthology with her story, "North Country." It was very difficult to select just one of her stories, but "How" filled a niche in this collection—maybe you'd call it rural noir, but whatever you label it, it's a powerful, touching story that holds back nothing.

As I continued to dig into neo-noir voices, mixing in the literary voices of my MFA program, I picked up new work by Craig Davidson, and realized he was slowly becoming one of my favorite authors. It started with the collection *Rust and Bone*, and then his novel *The Fighter*, followed by *Sara Court*. To hear that he just made the Giller long list for his novel *Cataract City* (which isn't even OUT yet in the U.S.) makes me even more impatient to get my hands on it. And being allowed to include the title story "Rust and Bone" from his debut collection in this anthology is a bit of a gift as well.

About this time I traveled to St. Louis (where I grew up) to be a part of the Noir at the Bar reading series, run by Scott Phillips and Jed Ayres. It was there that I first met Kyle Minor. I'd been aware of his writing, but hadn't read that much of it, just one collection, *In the Devil's Territory*. Later, I would run into him again at the release party for Frank Bill down in Corydon, Indiana, celebrating *Crimes in Southern Indiana*. After getting over the thrill of meeting Donald Ray Pollock, I reminded myself to read more of Kyle's work. When I ran across "The Truth and All Its Ugly," I was floored. I guess I have to admit that this may be the second story in this collection to make me cry—I'm turning into a real faucet here. As Kyle continues to gain attention, I'm again grateful to Sarabande Books for letting us include this story, as his new collection, *Praying Drunk*, is about to hit the streets.

It was at another AWP, Denver 2010, where I heard Joe Meno read, following Dorothy Allison, I think, which is a nearly impossible feat. I'd actually published a story of his in a little rag I guest edited, *Colored Chalk*, but Joe was on fire that night, and it spurned me to pick up more of his work, such as *Hairstyles of the Damned* and *The Boy Detective Fails*. He provides some much needed humor in this collection, but underneath the jokes and uncomfortable laughter is a sadness that really got to me, in "Children Are the Only Ones Who Blush."

As my writing continued to expand, I started writing my first novel, and joined a group called Write Club. It's a private community of like-minded authors who have been striving to publish and break out. It's been thrilling to see many of our group get agents, book deals, and break into elite magazines and journals. Two authors, Nik Korpon, and Craig Wallwork, have done exactly that. Both write gritty narratives, with Nik often focusing on the Baltimore streets, and Craig on rural English country sides. But I selected stories from these two emerging authors that are closer to the fantastic and horrific, slipping in and out of realities, asking us to suspend our disbelief, and open our minds to the possibilities. Where Nik makes me fear a possible future where our dreams can be stolen, Craig scares me to death with a haunting that feels all too possible. Nik's story "His Footsteps are Made of Soot," and Craig's "Dollhouse" were two voices that I knew immediately needed to be in this collection.

Rebecca Jones-Howe is another author that has emerged from one of my writing communities—LitReactor, where I write a column, Storyville. When I compared Lindsay Hunter to

Mary Gaitskill, in an article I wrote for Flavorwire, "10 Essential Neo-Noir Authors," Rebecca's voice is another one that came to mind, reminiscent of the heady mix of sex and violence that Gaitskill so eloquently writes. In the workshops over at LitReactor, I always enjoyed her writing. When she won the first War, a competition pitting some 60+ authors against each other in an NCAA-style series of brackets, I knew I wasn't the only person to recognize her gifts and formidable abilities. Her story "Blue Hawaii" was my favorite of that competition.

My book reviews continued over at The Nervous Breakdown. I ran across a little book called *Zazen*, one of the first Red Lemonade titles. Richard Nash has always had his thumb on the pulse of the writing community, so it was an easy sell. What Vanessa Veselka did with that narrative struck me as being very original, a literary mind dealing with heavy political issues, layers of tension stacking one upon another, a story that slowly gets under your skin. That same lyrical and haunting quality is evident in her story, "Christopher Hitchens."

As I started to fill up this anthology, I dug deeper for voices that I may have missed, searching for those last few authors to fill the collection. It's difficult to put a finger on what neo-noir is, my definition differing than someone schooled in noir vs. horror vs. dark literary fiction. I've been a fan of Akashic Books for a long time, and as I picked up book after book, *The Heroin Chronicles* got my attention. Antonia Crane is another unique voice, tapping into her past experiences to write alluring, complicated, and touching stories that often show the underbelly of the various sex worker industries. But what makes her story, "Sunshine for Adrienne" so powerful is not the titillation, but the humanity, desire, hope and fear that rests behind it.

Another name that kept popping up on my radar was Richard

Lange. Maybe it was *Dead Boys* back in 2008, or *Angel Baby*, that just came out, but I dug in deeper and found another voice that explored the world of neo-noir, the new black, with authority and depth. The subtle knowledge and unease that descends on the reader in "Fuzzyland," is a hypnotic read, leaving behind sadness, frustration, and understanding.

I wanted more weirdness, and as I looked around my office, I didn't have to go that far to trip over the tome that is *The Weird*, edited by Jeff and VanderMeer. If you've ever read the magazine *Weird Tales*, you know about Ann (now at Tor). And to miss the body of work that is Jeff VanderMeer, is to ignore a powerful voice in fantasy and crime (e.g., *Finch*). So their names on the cover of this 1,152-page monolith meant only one thing—quality. Micaela Morrissette's story "The Familiars" taps into every horror that a parent and child can conjure up—something under the bed, noises in the dark, abduction, possession, and the unknown.

Which leaves Tara Laskowksi and her story "The Etiquette of Homicide." What made this story a must-have for this collection was the unique formatting—a recipe for disaster, you could say. A strong voice in the crime and dark fiction arenas, Tara makes you pay attention, and mix up all of her ingredients to create a compelling story that builds on the classic noir staples.

Each and every author in this collection has been an inspiration to me—as an author, a reader, and a student of the imagination. These are the stories that stay with me when I close my eyes at night and try to go to sleep. These are the voices that push me to take more risks with my own writing. These are the authors you should keep an eye on, pick up at bookstores, garage sales and libraries, making them your own personal teachers of the macabre.

XIV

I wanted to take a moment to thank Victor David Giron, Jacob Knabb, Ben Tanzer, Alban Fischer, and everyone else at Curbside Splendor, as well as Carrie Gaffney and Nik Korpon at Dark House Press for their support—I couldn't do this without them. I hope you enjoy this collection and come back for more. I can't call you my Dear Constant Readers yet, as Stephen King likes to say, but I hope I can in time.

— Richard Thomas
  October 23, 2013
  Chicago, IL

The New Black

×

FATHER, SON, HOLY RABBIT

STEPHEN GRAHAM JONES

By the third day they were eating snow. Years later it would come to the boy again, rush up to him at a job interview: his father spitting out pieces of seed or pine needle into his hand. Whatever had been in the snow. The boy looked at the brown flecks in his father's palm, then up to his father, who finally nodded, put them back in his mouth, turned his face away to swallow.

Instead of sleeping, they thumped each other in the face to stay awake.

The place they'd found under the tree wasn't out of the wind, but it was dry.

They had no idea where the camp was, or how to find the truck from there, or the highway after that. They didn't even have a gun, just the knife the boy's father kept strapped to his right hip.

The first two days, the father had shrugged and told the boy not to worry, that the storm couldn't last.

The whole third day, he'd sat watching the snow fall like ash.

The boy didn't say anything, not even inside, not even a prayer. One of the times he drifted off, though, waking not to the slap of his father's fingernail on his cheek but the sound of it, there was a picture he brought up with him from sleep. A rabbit.

He told his father about it and his father pulled his lower lip into his mouth, smiled like the boy had just told a joke.

That night they fell asleep.

This time the boy woke to his father rubbing him all over, trying to make his blood flow. The boy's father was crying, so the boy told him about the rabbit, how it wasn't even white like it should be, but brown, lost like them.

3

His father hugged his knees to his chest and bounced up and down, stared out at all the white past their tree.

"A rabbit?" he said.

The boy shrugged.

Sometime later that day he woke again, wasn't sure where he was at first. His father wasn't there. The boy moved his mouth up and down, didn't know what to say. Rounded off in the crust of the snow were the dragging holes his father had made, walking away. The boy put his hand in the first footstep, then the second, then stood from the tree into the real cold. He followed the tracks until they became confused. He tried to follow them back to the tree but the light was different now. Finally he started running, falling down, getting up, his chest on fire.

His father found him sometime that night, pulled him close.

They lowered themselves under another tree.

"Where were you?" the boy asked.

"That rabbit," the father said, stroking the boy's hair down.

"You saw it?"

Instead of answering, the father just stared.

This tree they were under wasn't as good as the last. The next morning they looked for another, and another, and stumbled onto their first one.

"Home again home again," the father said, guiding the boy under then gripping onto the back of his jacket, stopping him.

There were tracks coming up out of the dirt, onto the snow. Double tracks, like the split hoof of an elk, except bigger, and not as deep.

"Your rabbit," the father said.

The boy smiled.

That night his father carved their initials into the trunk of

4

the tree with his knife. Later he broke a dead branch off, tried sharpening it. The boy watched, fascinated, hungry.

"Will it work?" he asked.

His father thumped him in the face, woke him. He asked it again, with his mouth this time.

The father shrugged. His lips were cracked, lined with blood, his beard pushing up through his skin.

"Where do you think it is right now?" he said to the boy.

"The—the rabbit?"

The father nodded.

The boy closed his eyes, turned his head, then opened his eyes again, used them to point the way he was facing. The father used his sharp stick as a cane, stood with it, and walked in that direction, folded himself into the blowing snow.

The boy knew this was going to work.

In the hours his father was gone, he studied their names in the tree. While the boy had been asleep, his father had carved the boy's mother's name into the bark as well. The boy ran the pads of his fingers over the grooves, brought the taste to his tongue.

The next thing he knew was ice. It was falling down on him in crumbly sheets.

His father had returned, had collapsed into the side of the tree.

The boy rolled him in, rubbed his back and face and neck, and then saw what his father was balled around, what he'd been protecting for miles, maybe: the rabbit. It was brown at the tips of its coat, the rest white.

With his knife, the father opened the rabbit in a line down the stomach, poured the meat out. It steamed.

Over it, the father looked at the son, nodded.

They scooped every bit of red out that the rabbit had,

swallowed it in chunks because if they chewed they tasted what they were doing. All that was left was the skin. The father scraped it with the blade of his knife, gave those scrapings to the boy.

"Glad your mom's not here to see this," he said.

The boy smiled, wiped his mouth.

Later, he threw up in his sleep, then looked at it soaking into the loose dirt, then turned to his see if his father had seen what he'd done, how he'd betrayed him. His father was sleeping. The boy lay back down, forced the rabbit back into his mouth then angled his arm over his lips, so he wouldn't lose his food again.

The next day, no helicopters came for them, no men on horseback, following dogs, no skiers poling their way home. For a few hours around what should have been lunch, the sun shone down, but all that did was make their dry spot under the tree wet. Then the wind started again.

"Where's that stick?" the boy asked.

The father narrowed his eyes as if he hadn't thought of that. "Your rabbit," he said after a few minutes.

The boy nodded, said, almost to himself, "It'll come back."

When he looked around to his father, his father was already looking at him. Studying him.

The rabbit's skin was out in the snow, just past the tree. Buried hours ago.

The father nodded like this could maybe be true. That the rabbit would come back. Because they needed it to.

The next day he went out again, with a new stick, and came back with his lips blue, one of his legs frozen wet from stepping through some ice into a creek. No rabbit. What he said about the creek was that it was a good sign. You could usually follow water one way or another, to people.

The boy didn't ask which way.

"His name is Slaney," he said.

"The rabbit?"

The boy nodded. Slaney. Things that had names were real.

That night they slept, then woke somehow at the same time, the boy under his father's heavy, jacketed arm. They were both looking the same direction, their faces even with the crust of snow past their tree. Twenty feet out, its nose tasting the air, was Slaney.

The boy felt his father's breath deepen.

"Don't . . . don't . . . " his father said, low, then exploded over the boy, crashed off into the day without his stick.

He came back an hour later with nothing slung over his shoulder, nothing balled against his stomach. No blood on his hands.

This time the son prayed, inside. He promised not to throw any of the meat up again. With the tip of his knife, his father carved a cartoon rabbit into the trunk of their tree. It looked like a frog with horse ears.

"Slaney," the boy said.

The father carved that in a line under the rabbit's feet, then circled the boy's mother's name over and over, until the boy thought that piece of the bark was going to come off like a plaque.

The next time the boy woke, he was already sitting up.

"What?" the father said.

The boy nodded the direction he was facing.

The father watched the boy's eyes, then nodded, got his stick.

This time he didn't come back for nearly a day. The boy, afraid, climbed up into the tree, then higher, as high as he could, until the wind could reach him.

His father reached up with his stick, tapped him awake.

Like a football in the crook of his arm was the rabbit. It was bloody and wonderful, already cut open.

"You ate the guts," the boy said, his mouth full.

His father reached into the rabbit, came out with a long sliver of meat. The muscle that runs along the spine, maybe.

The boy ate and ate and when he was done, he placed the rabbit skin in the same spot he'd placed the last one. The coat was just the same—white underneath, brown at the tips.

"It'll come back," he told his father.

His father rubbed the side of his face. His hand was crusted with blood.

The next day there were no walkie-talkies crackling through the woods, no four-wheelers or snowmobiles churning through the snow. And the rabbit skin was gone.

"Hungry?" the boy's father said, smiling, leaning on his stick just to stand, and the boy smiled with him.

Four hours later, his father came back with the rabbit again. He was wet to the hips this time.

"The creek?" the boy said.

"It's a good sign," the father said back.

Again, the father had fingered the guts into his mouth on the way back, left most of the stringy meat for the boy.

"Slaney," the father said, watching the boy eat.

The boy closed his eyes to swallow.

Because of his frozen pants—the creek—the father had to sit with his legs straight out. "A good sign," the boy said after the father was asleep.

The next morning his father pulled another dead branch down, so he had two poles now, like a skier.

The boy watched him walk off into the bright snow, feeling

8

ahead of himself with the poles. It made him look like a ragged, four-legged animal, one made more of legend than of skin and bone. The boy palmed some snow into his mouth and held it there until it melted.

This time his father was only gone thirty minutes. He'd had to cross the creek again. Slaney was cradled against his body.

"He was just standing there," the father said, pouring the meat out for the boy. "Like he was waiting for me."

"He knows we need him," the boy said.

One thing he no longer had to do was dab the blood off the meat before eating it. Another was swallow before chewing.

That night his father staggered out into the snow and threw up, then fell down into it. The boy pretended not to see, held his eyes closed when his father came back.

The following morning he told his father not to go out again, not today.

"But Slaney," his father said.

"I'm not hungry," the boy lied.

The day after that he was, though. It was the day the storm broke. The woods were perfectly still. Birds were even moving from tree to tree again, talking to each other.

In his head, the boy told Slaney to be closer, to not keep being on the other side of the creek, but the boy's father came back wet to the hip again. His whole frontside was bloodstained now, from hunting, and eating.

The boy scooped the meat into his mouth, watched his father try to sit in one place. Finally he couldn't, fell over on his side. The boy finished eating and curled up against him, only woke when he heard voices, scratchy like on a radio.

He sat up and the voices went away.

On the crust of snow, now, since no more had fallen, was

Slaney's skin. The boy crawled out to it, studied it, wasn't sure how Slaney could be out there already, reforming, all its muscle growing back, and be here too. But maybe it only worked if you didn't watch.

The boy scooped snow onto the blood-matted coat, curled up by his father again. All that day, his father didn't wake, but he wasn't really sleeping either.

That night, when the snow was melting more, running into their dry spot under the tree, the boy saw little pads of ice out past Slaney. They were footprints, places where the snow had packed down under a boot, into a column. Now that column wasn't melting as fast as the rest.

Instead of going in a line to the creek, these tracks cut straight across.

The boy squatted over them, looked the direction they were maybe going.

When he stood, there was a tearing sound. The seat of his pants had stuck to his calf while he'd been squatting. It was blood. The boy fell back, pulled his pants down to see if it had come from him.

When it hadn't, he looked back to his father, then just sat in the snow again, his arms around his knees, rocking back and forth.

"Slaney, Slaney," he chanted. Not to eat him again, but just to hold him.

Sometime that night—it was clear, soundless—a flashlight found him, pinned him to the ground.

"Slaney?" he said, looking up into the yellow beam.

The man in the flannel was breathing too hard to talk into his radio the right way. He lifted the boy up, and the boy said it again: "Slaney."

"What?" the man asked.

The boy didn't say anything then.

The other men found the boy's father curled under the tree. When they cut his pants away to understand where the blood was coming from, the boy looked away, the lower lids of his eyes pushing up into his field of vision. Over the years it would come to be one of his mannerisms, a stare that might suggest thoughtfulness to a potential employer, but right then, sitting with a blanket and his first cup of coffee, waiting for a helicopter, it had just been a way of blurring the tree his father was still sleeping under.

Watching like that—both holding his breath and trying not to focus—when the boy's father finally stood, he was an unsteady smear against the evergreen. And then the boy had to look.

Somehow, using his poles as crutches, the boy's father was walking, his head slung low between his shoulders, his poles reaching out before him like feelers.

When he lurched out from the under the tree, the boy drew his breath in.

The father's pants were tatters now, and his legs too, where he'd been carving off the rabbit meat, stuffing it into the same skin again and again. The father pulled his lower lip into his mouth, nodded once to the boy, then stuck one of his poles into the ground before him, pulled himself towards it, then repeated the complicated process, pulling himself deeper into the woods.

"Where's he going?" one of the men asked.

The boy nodded, understood, his father retreating into the trees for the last time, having to move his legs from the hip now, like things, and the boy answered—Hunting—then ran back from the helicopter they were dragging him into, to dig in the snow just past their tree, but there was nothing there. Just coldness. His own numb fingers.

"What's he saying?" one of the men asked.

The boy stopped, closed his eyes, tried to hear it too, his own voice, then let the men pull him out of the snow, into the world of houses and bank loans and, finally, job interviews. Because they were wearing gloves, though, or because it was cold and their fingers were numb too, they weren't able to pull all of him from the woods that day. They couldn't tell that an important part of him was still there, sitting under a blanket, watching his father move across the snow, the poles just extensions of his arms, the boy holding his lips tight against each other. Because it would have been a betrayal, he hadn't let himself throw up what his father had given him, not then, and not years later, when the man across the desk palms a handful of sunflower seeds into his mouth all at once, then holds his hand there to make sure none get away, leans forward a bit for the boy to explain what he's written for a name here on this application.

Slade?

Slake?

Slather, slavery?

What the boy does here, what he's just now realizing he should have been doing all along, is reach across, delicately thump the man's cheek, and then pretend not to see past the office, out the window, to the small brown rabbit in the flowers, watching.

Soon enough it'll be white.

The boy smiles.

Some woods, they're big enough you never find your way out.

Stephen Graham Jones

is the author of eleven novels and three collections. Most recent are *The Last Final Girl*, *Growing Up Dead in Texas*, and *Zombie Bake-Off*. Up soon are *Zombie Sharks with Metal Teeth*, *The Least of My Scars*, and *The Gospel of Z*. Jones has some hundred and fifty stories published, many collected in best of the year annuals. He's been a Shirley Jackson Award finalist, a Bram Stoker Award finalist, a Colorado Book Award finalist, and has won the Texas Institute of Letters Award for fiction and an NEA fellowship in fiction. He teaches in the MFA programs at CU Boulder and UCR–Palm Desert. More at demontheory.net or twitter.com/SGJ72.

IT'S AGAINST THE LAW TO FEED THE DUCKS

PAUL TREMBLAY

Saturday

Ninety plus degrees, hours of relentless getaway traffic on the interstate, then the bumps and curves of rural route 25 as late afternoon melts into early evening, and it's the fourth time Danny asks the question.

"Daddy, are you lost again?"

Tom says, "I know where we're going, buddy. Trust me. We're almost there."

Dotted lines and bleached pavement give way to a dirt path that roughly invades the woods. Danny watches his infant sister Beth sleep, all tucked into herself and looking like a new punctuation mark. Danny strains against his twisted shoulder harness. He needs to go pee but he holds it, remembering how Daddy didn't say any mad words but sighed and breathed all heavy the last time he asked to stop for a pee break.

Danny says, "Mommy, pretend you didn't know I was going to be five in September."

Ellen holds a finger to her chin and looks at the car's ceiling for answers. "Are you going to be ten years old tomorrow?"

"No. I will be five in September."

"Oh, wow. I didn't know that, honey."

Tom and Ellen slip into a quick and just-the-facts discussion about what to do for dinner and whether or not they think Beth will sleep through the night. Danny learns more about his parents through these conversations, the ones they don't think he's listening to.

It's dark enough for headlights. Danny counts the blue bug-zappers as their car chugs along the dirt road. He gets to four.

"Daddy, what kind of animals live in these woods?"

"The usual. Raccoons, squirrels, birds."

"No, tell me *dangerous* animals."

"Coyotes, maybe bears."

Their car somehow finds the rented cottage and its gravel driveway between two rows of giant trees. Beth wakes screaming. Danny stays in the car while his parents unpack. He's afraid of the bears. They don't celebrate getting to the cottage like they were supposed to.

Sunday

They need a piece of magic yellow paper to go to Lake Winnipesauke. Danny likes to say the name of the lake inside his head. The beach is only a mile from their cottage and when they get there Danny puts the magic paper on the dashboard. He hopes the sun doesn't melt it or turn it funny colors.

Danny runs ahead. He's all arms and legs, a marionette with tangled strings, just like Daddy. He claims a shady spot beneath a tree. He doesn't know what kind of tree. Ellen and Beth come next. Beth can only say 'Daddy' and likes to give head butts. Tom is last, carrying the towels and shovels and pails and squirt-guns and food. Danny watches his parents set everything up. They know how to unfold things and they know where everything goes without having to ask questions, without having to talk to each other.

Danny likes that his parents look younger than everybody else's parents, even if they are old. Danny is a round face and big rubber ball cheeks, just like Mommy. Ellen has a tee shirt and shorts pulled over her bathing suit. She won't take them off, even when she goes into the water. She says, "You need sun screen before you go anywhere, little boy."

Danny closes his eyes as she rubs it all in and everywhere. He's had to wear it all summer long but he doesn't understand what *sun screen* really means. *Sun screen* sounds like something that should be built onto their little vacation cottage.

✕

Danny is disappointed with the magic beach because there are too many other people using it. They all get in his way when he runs on the sand, pretending to be Speed Boy. And the older kids are scary in the water. They thrash around like sharks.

Lunch time. Danny sits at the picnic table next to their tree, eating and looking out over Winnipesauke. The White Mountains surround the bowl of the lake and in the lake there are swimmers, boats, buoys, and a raft. Danny wants to go with Daddy to the raft, but only when the scary older kids are gone. Danny says Winnipesauke, that magical word, into his peanut butter and jelly sandwich. It tastes good.

A family of ducks comes out of the water. They must be afraid of the older kids too. They walk underneath his picnic table.

Ellen says, "Ducks!" picks up Beth, and points her at the ducks. Beth's bucket hat is over her eyes.

Tom sits down next to Danny and throws a few scraps of bread on the sand. Danny does the same, taking pieces from his sandwich, mostly crust, but not chunks with a lot of peanut butter, he eats those. The ducks get mostly jelly chunks, and they swallow everything.

Tom stops throwing bread and says, "Whoops. Sorry, pal. It's against the law to feed the ducks."

He doesn't know if Daddy is joking. Danny likes to laugh at his jokes. Jokes are powerful magic words because they make

17

you laugh. But when he's not sure if it's a joke or not, Danny thinks life is too full of magic words.

He laughs a little and says, "Good one, Daddy." Danny is pleased with his answer, even if it's wrong.

"No really, it says so on that sign." Tom points to a white sign with red letters nailed into their tree. Danny can't read yet. He knows his letters but not how they fit together.

Ellen says, "That's weird. A state law against feeding the ducks?"

Danny knows it's not a joke. It is a law. The word *law* is scary, like the older kids in the water.

Danny says, "Mommy, pretend you didn't know it was against the law to feed the ducks."

"Okay. So, I can just go order a pizza and some hotdogs for the ducks, right?"

"No. You can't feed the ducks. It's against the law."

Danny eats the rest of his sandwich, swinging his feet beneath the picnic table bench. The scary older kids come out of the water and chase the ducks, even the babies. Danny wants to know why it's not against the law to chase the ducks, but he doesn't ask.

Their cottage has two bedrooms, but they sleep in the same bedroom because of the bears. Danny sleeps in the tallest bed. There's a ceiling fan above him and after Daddy tells a story about Spider-man and dinosaurs, he has to duck to keep from getting a haircut. That's Danny's joke.

Beth is asleep in her playpen. Everyone has to be quiet because of her.

18

Danny is tired after a full day at the beach. His favorite part was holding onto Daddy's neck while they swam out to the raft.

Danny wakes up when his parents creep into the bedroom. He is happy they are keeping their promise. He falls back to sleep listening to them fill up the small bed by the door. He knows his parents would rather sleep in the other bedroom by themselves, but he doesn't know why.

✕

Danny wakes again. It's that middle-of-the-night time his parents always talk about. He hears noises, but gets the sense he's waking at the end of the noises. The noises are outside the cottage, echoing in the mountains. He hears thunder and lightning or a plane or a bunch of planes or a bunch of thunder and lightning and he is still convinced you can hear both thunder and lightning or he hears a bear's roar or a bunch of bears' roars or he hears the cottage's toilet, which has the world's loudest super-flush according to Daddy or he hears a bomb or a bunch of bombs, bombs are something he has only seen and heard in Spider-Man cartoons. Whatever the noises are, they are very far away and he has no magic words that will send his ears out that far. Danny falls back to sleep even though he doesn't want to.

Monday

The beach lot is only half full. Ellen says, "Where is everybody?"

Tom says, "I don't know. Mondays are kind of funny days. Right, pal?"

Danny nods and clutches the magic yellow paper and doesn't

19

care where everybody is because maybe this means Daddy and him can spend more time out on the raft.

They get the same spot they had yesterday, next to the tree with its against-the-law sign. They dump their stuff and boldly spread it out. Beth and Ellen sit at the shore. Beth tries to eat sand and knocks her head into Ellen's. Tom sits in the shade and reads a book. Danny takes advantage of the increased running room on the beach and turns into Speed Boy.

By lunch, the beach population thins. No more young families around. There are some really old people with tree-bark skin and a few older kids around, but they are less scary because they look like they don't know what to do. The lake is empty of boats and jet-skis. The ducks are still there, swimming and safe from renegade feeders.

Tom swims to the raft with Danny's arms wrapped tight around his neck. Somewhere in the middle of the lake, Tom says, "Stop kicking me!" Danny knows not to say I was trying to help you swim. Danny climbs up the raft ladder first, runs to the middle then slips, feet shooting out from beneath him, and he falls on a mat that feels like moss. Tom yells. Don't run, be careful, watch what you're doing. Danny doesn't hear the words, only what's in his voice. They sit on the raft's edge, dangling their legs and feet into the water. Daddy's long legs go deeper.

Tom takes a breath, the one that signals the end of something, and says, "It is kind of strange that hardly anybody is here." He pats Danny's head, so everything is okay.

Danny nods. Commiserating, supporting, happy and grateful to be back in Daddy's good graces. He's also in his head, making up a face and body for a stranger named "Hardly Anybody." He can't decide if he should make Hardly Anybody magical or not.

They wave at Mommy and Beth at the shore. Ellen's wave is

tired, like a sleeping bird. Ellen wears the same shirt and shorts over her bathing suit. Danny wonders how long it takes for his wave to make it across the water.

They leave the beach early. On the short drive back, Tom makes up a silly song that rhymes mountain peaks with butt-cheeks and it's these Daddy-moments that make Danny love him so hard he's afraid he'll break something.

Back at the cottage. Beth is asleep and Ellen dumps her in the playpen. Danny sits at the kitchen table and eats grapes because he was told to. Tom goes into the living room and turns on the TV. Danny listens to the voices but doesn't hear what they say. But he hears Tom say a bad word, real quick, like he is surprised.

"Ellen?" Tom jogs into the kitchen. "Where's Mommy?" He doesn't wait for Danny's answer. Ellen comes out of the bathroom holding her mostly dry bathing suit and wearing a different set of tee shirt and shorts. Tom grabs her arm, whispers something, then pulls her into the living room, to the TV.

"Hey, where did everybody go?" Danny says it like a joke, but there's no punch line coming. He leaves his grapes, which he didn't want to eat anyway, and tip-toes into the living room.

His parents are huddled close to the TV, too close. If Danny was ever that close they'd tell him to move back. They're both on their knees, Ellen with a hand over her mouth, holding something in, or maybe keeping something out. The TV volume is low and letters and words scroll by on the top and bottom of the screen and in the middle there's a man in a tie and he is talking. He looks serious. That's all Danny sees before Tom sees him.

"Come with me, bud."

Daddy picks him up and plops him down in a small sunroom at the front of the cottage.

Tom says, "Mommy and Daddy need to watch a grown-up show for a little while."

"So I can't see it?"

"Right."

"How come?"

Tom is crouched low, face to face with Danny. Danny stares at the scraggly hairs of his mustache and beard. "Because I said it's only for grown-ups."

"Is it about feeding the ducks? Is it scary?"

Daddy doesn't answer that. "We'll come get you in a few minutes. Okay, bud?" He stands, walks out, and starts to close sliding glass doors.

"Wait! Let me say something to Mommy first."

Tom gives that sigh of his, loud enough for Ellen to give him that look of hers. They always share like this. Danny stays in the sunroom, pokes his head between the glass doors. Ellen is to his left, sitting in front of the TV, same position, same hand over her mouth. "Mommy, pretend you didn't know that I could see through these doors."

Mommy works to put her eyes on her son. "So, you won't be able to see anything in here when we shut the doors?"

"No, I can see through them."

Tuesday

It's raining. They don't go to the beach. Danny is in the sunroom watching Beth. His parents are in the living room watching more grown-up TV. Beth pulls on Danny's shirt and tries to walk, but she falls next to the couch and cries. Ellen comes in, picks up Beth, and sits down next to Danny.

He says, "This is boring."

"I know, sweetie. Maybe we'll go out soon."

Danny looks out the front windows and watches the rain fall on the front lawn and the dirt road. Beth crawls away from Ellen and toward the glass doors. She bangs on the glass with meaty little hands.

Danny says, "Mommy, pretend you didn't know we were in a spaceship."

There's a pause. Beth bangs her head on the glass. Ellen says, "So, we're all just sitting here in a cottage room, right?"

"No. This is a spaceship with glass doors."

Beth bangs on the glass harder and yells in rhythm.

Ellen says, "If we're in a ship, what about Daddy?"

"We'll come back for him later."

"Good idea."

✕

Ellen and Beth stay at the cottage. Tom and Danny are in the car but they don't listen to the radio and Daddy isn't singing silly songs. Danny holds the magic yellow paper even though he knows they're going to the supermarket, not the beach.

They have to travel to the center of Moultonborough. Another long and obviously magical word that he'll say inside his head. There isn't much traffic. The supermarket's super-lot has more carts than cars.

Inside, the music is boring and has no words. Danny hangs off the side of their cart like a fireman. He waves and salutes to other shoppers as they wind their way around the stacks,

23

but nobody waves back. Nobody looks at each other over their overflowing carts.

The line isn't long even though there are only three registers open. Tom tries to pay with a credit card. Danny is proud he knows what a credit card is.

"I'm sorry, sir, but the system is down. No credit cards. Cash or check." The girl working the register is young, but like the older kids. She has dark circles under her eyes.

Danny points and says, "Excuse me, you should go to bed early tonight."

Tom has a green piece of paper and is writing something down on it. He gives it to the register girl.

She says, "I'll try," and offers a smile. A smile that isn't happy.

In the parking lot, Danny says, "Go fast."

Tom says, "Hey, Danny."

Danny's whole body tenses up. He doesn't know what he did wrong. "What?"

"I love you. You know that, right?"

Danny swings on those marionette arms and looks everywhere at once. "Yeah."

Then Tom smiles and obeys and runs with the full cart. Danny melts and laughs, stretching out and throwing his head back, closing his eyes in the brightening haze. There are no other cars between the cart and their car.

Wednesday

They spend the day in the cottage. More sunroom. More grown-up TV. When Tom and Ellen finally shut off the TV they talk about going out just to go out somewhere anywhere but the TV room and sunroom and maybe find an early dinner. Danny says, "Moultonborough." They talk about how much gas is in the car. Danny says, "Winnipesauke." They try to use their cell phones but the little LCD screens say *no service*. Danny says, "Pretend you didn't know I say magic words." They talk about how much cash they have. Everybody in the car. Tom tells Danny it's his job to keep Beth awake. There are no other vehicles on the dirt road and more than half of the cottages they pass are dark. Beth is falling asleep so Danny sings loud silly songs and pokes her chin and cheeks. They pass empty gravel driveways and the blue bug-zappers aren't on. Beth cries. Danny is trying not to think about the bears in the woods. Ellen asks Danny to stop touching his sister's face and then says it's okay if Beth falls asleep. They don't have to look left or right when pulling out of the dirt road. Danny still works at the keep-Beth-awake job Daddy gave him and there's something inside him that wants to hear her cry and he touches her face again. They're into the center of Moultonborough and there's less traffic than there was yesterday. Beth cries and Ellen is stern but not yelling she never yells telling Danny to stop touching Beth's face. Maybe the bears are why there aren't as many people around. Beth is asleep. There's a smattering of parked cars in the downtown area but they don't look parked they look empty. Danny gently pats Beth's foot and sees Daddy watching him in the rear view mirror. The antique stores gift shops and hamburger huts are dark and have red signs on their doors and red always means either stopped or closed or something bad. Tom yells did you hear your mother keep your hands off your sister! They pass a row of empty family restaurants. Ellen says Tom like his name is sharp like it hurts and she says I only asked him to stop touching her face I don't want him to be freaked out by his sister he's being nice now why are you yelling when he was just doing what you asked him to do you have to be consistent with him and she is stern and she is not yelling. They pull into a lot that has one truck another empty restaurant this one with a moose on the roof and they stop. Then Tom is loud again this time with some hard alrights and then I hear you I get it okay I heard you the first time. Tom gets out of the car and slams the door and an older man with white hair that could mean he's magic and a white apron walks out the restaurant's front door. Danny waves. The older man waves them inside. Ellen gets out of the car and whispers but it's not a soft whisper not at all it's through teeth and it has teeth she says don't you dare yell at me in front of the kids. Beth wakes up and points and chews on her rabbit. They go inside. The older man says they are lucky he was just cooking up the last of his non-frozen food so it wouldn't go to waste and it was on the house. Danny thinks about the moose on the house. They walk by the bar and there's a woman sitting on a stool staring up at a big screen TV. Tom asks if they could shut that off because of the kids. The old man nods and uses a big remote control. Danny doesn't see anything again. The old man serves some BBQ chicken and ribs and fries and then leaves them alone. The lights are on and nobody says anything important in the empty restaurant.

On the way back to the cottage they see a lonely mansion built into the side of a mountain. Looking dollhouse-sized, its white walls and red roof surrounded by the green trees stands out like a star even in the twilight.

Danny says, "What is that?"

26

Tom says, "That's called the Castle in the Clouds."

"Can we go see it?"

"Maybe. Maybe we'll even go and live there. Would you like that?"

Danny says, "Yes," but he then he thinks the Castle is too alone, cloaked in a mountain forest, but too open, anyone can see it from this road. He doesn't know what's worse, being alone alone or a watched alone. Danny doesn't change his answer.

It's past Danny's bedtime but his parents aren't ready to put him to bed.

Ellen is on the couch reading a magazine that has a tall, blonde, skinny woman on the cover. Tom sits in front of the TV, flipping channels. There's nothing but static. The TV is like their cell phones now.

Tom says, "Well, at least they've stopped showing commercials for the *War of the Worlds* remake."

Danny wants to laugh because he knows it's what Daddy wants. But he doesn't because Mommy isn't. Danny has a good idea what 'war' means even though no one has ever explained it to him. Tom shuts off the TV.

There are pictures of other people all over the cottage. Now that Danny is allowed back in the TV room, he's looking at each one. Strangers with familiar smiles and beach poses. He looks at the frames too. They have designs and letters and words. Maybe magic words. Danny picks up one picture of a little girl and boy hugging and sitting on a big rock. He doesn't care about those kids. He wants to know what all the letters etched onto the wooden frame say. Those letters wrap all the way around the photo.

"Read this please, Daddy."

"'Children are the magic dreamers that we all once were.'"

"Mommy, pretend you didn't know I was a magic dreamer."

"So, you dream about boring, non-magical stuff, right?"

"No. I'm a magic dreamer. Are you a magic dreamer?"

Ellen sleeps with Beth in the small bed next to the bedroom door, Danny sleeps in his Princess-and-the-Pea tall bed. Tom sleeps in the other bedroom. Alone alone.

Thursday

A perfect summer day. The corner Gas 'N Save is open. The pumps still work. Tom fills up the car's tank and five red, two-gallon containers he took from inside the market. Danny is inside, running around the stacks. No one tells him to stop. He climbs onto an empty shelf next to some bread, though there isn't much bread left, and he lies down, breathing heavy from all the running.

Tom makes multiple trips from the market to the car. On the last trip, he plucks Danny off the shelf. He says, "Hmm, this melon doesn't look too ripe." Danny giggles and squirms in Daddy's arms. "But I'll take it anyway."

The older woman behind the counter is smoking a cigarette and has a face with extra skin. She looks like the girl from the supermarket but one-thousand years older. Tom extends a fistful of money and asks, "Is this enough?"

She says, "Yes," without counting it. Danny thinks she is lying and that she just wants them gone like everyone else.

Tom buckles Danny into his seat. Danny says, "What would you do if you were a giant?"

"A giant? Well, I'd use a mountain as my pillow and the trees as a mattress."

Danny thinks about a Giant Daddy lying on a mountain, crushing all the trees and bears and other animals and the Castle in the Clouds with his back and arms, and his legs would be long enough to crush Moultonborough and the other towns too, maybe his feet would dangle into Winnipesauke and cause huge waves, drown the poor ducks, flood everything.

Danny says, "That would hurt."

At night the electricity goes out, but it's okay because they have two lanterns and lots of candles. They sit in the back yard around a football-shaped charcoal grill eating hotdogs and holding sticks with marshmallows skewered on the tips. The smoke keeps the bugs away. They sing loud to keep the bears away. Danny sits on Mommy's lap and tells stories about magic and the adventures of Speed Boy and Giant Daddy. Then Tom carries him to bed and Ellen carries a candle. They kiss him goodnight. Danny closes his eyes. He almost knows why they are still here when everyone else is disappearing, but he can't quite get there, can't reach it, like the night he tried to send his ears out to the noises.

Danny tries to send his ears out again and this time he hears his parents in the hallway. They speak with one voice. He hears words that he doesn't understand. They might be arguing and they might be laughing and they might be crying but it doesn't matter, because Danny knows tonight was the best night of their vacation.

Friday

Danny wakes up before anyone else and goes into the sunroom. There's morning mist and a bear on the front lawn. The bear is black and bigger than Danny's world, although that world seems to be shrinking. Danny thinks bears, even the dumb-looking Teddy bears, always know more about what's going on than the other animals and it's part of what scares Danny. He's scared now but he wants a better view so he opens the front door and stands on the elevated stoop, his hand on the door, ready to dash back inside if necessary. The bear runs away at the sound of the door and it disappears. Danny hears it crashing through some brush but then everything goes quiet. Why would a bear be afraid of him?

Now that it's gone Danny steps outside, the wet grass soaking his feet. He says, "Hey, come back." He wants to ask the bear, where are all the people? The bear must know the answer.

Danny and Ellen sit out back, playing *Go Fish* at the picnic table. Tom went shopping for supplies, a phrase he used before leaving, by himself. He's been gone most of the morning.

Danny loses again but Ellen calls him the winner.

Danny says, "Mommy, pretend you didn't know it was a beautiful day."

Ellen shuffles the cards. "So it's really rainy and cold out, right?"

"No. There're no clouds. And the sun is out and super hot. It's a beautiful day."

They play more card games. They play with Beth. She's

almost ready to walk by herself but she still falls, and after she falls, she rips out fistfuls of grass and stuffs it in her mouth. They eat lunch. They nap.

Tom comes home after the naps. Supplies fill the car, including a mini-trailer hitched to the back. Tom gets out of the car and gives everyone an enthusiastic kiss and puts Danny on his shoulders. Ellen shrinks as he goes up.

Ellen says, "Did you see anybody."

Tom whispers an answer that Danny can't hear because he's above Daddy's head.

Ellen says, "What you got there in the trailer?"

"A generator."

"Really? You know how to set one of those up?"

"Yup."

Danny comes back down.

"Where'd you learn how to do that?"

"I just know, okay?"

Ellen goes back to the picnic table with Beth. Tom to the trailer and the generator. There are no more enthusiastic kisses.

Danny watches Tom setting up the generator. He says, "Daddy, pretend you didn't know this was a beautiful day."

"It's not a beautiful day."

"No, it is! There're no clouds. And the sun is out and super hot. It's a beautiful day, Daddy. I just know, okay?"

Saturday

They leave the car at the cottage and walk the mile to the beach. They don't carry much beach stuff. Beth is asleep in the stroller. Danny has on his swimming trunks but his parents are wearing shorts and tee shirts. The trip to the beach is for him. His parents don't know it, but Danny has the yellow magic paper folded up in his pocket.

Danny asks, "Is today supposed to be the last day of vacation?"

Ellen says, "I think we're going to stay here a little while longer."

Tom says, "Maybe a long while longer."

Ellen says, "Is that okay?"

"Sure."

Tom says, "Maybe we'll go check out that Castle in the Clouds tomorrow."

Danny almost tells them about the bear. Instead he says, "Mommy, pretend you didn't know we were still on vacation."

They pass empty driveways of empty cottages. Danny, for the first time, is really starting to feel uneasy about the people being gone. It's like when he thinks about why and how he got here and how are his parents his parents and how is his sister his sister, because if he thinks too much about any of that he probably won't like the answers.

The beach lot is empty. They stake out their regular spot next to the tree and its duck sign. There are ducks on the shore scratching the sand and dipping their bills in the water. It's another beautiful day.

Tom says, "I don't get it. I thought this is where everyone would want to be."

Ellen finishes for him. "Especially now."

The ducks waddle over. They don't know the law. Tom pulls out a bag of Cheerios, Beth's snack, and tosses a few on the sand. The ducks converge and are greedy.

Ellen pushes the stroller deeper into the shade away from the ducks and says, "Are you sure we can spare those, Mr. Keeperof-the-Supplies?" It walks like a joke and talks like a joke but it isn't a joke.

Danny says, "Daddy! Don't you remember the sign? It's against the law to feed the ducks." Danny looks around, making sure the people who aren't there still aren't there.

"It's okay now, buddy. I don't think anyone will care anymore. Here, kiddo."

He takes the Cheerio bag from Daddy. Daddy pats his head. Danny digs a hand deep into the bag, pulls it out, and throws Cheerios onto the sand. The ducks flinch and scatter toward the water, but they come back and feed.

Paul Tremblay

is the author of the novels *The Little Sleep*, *No Sleep Till Wonderland*, and *Swallowing a Donkey's Eye*, and the short story collections *Compositions for the Young and Old* and *In the Mean Time*. He has published two novellas, and his essays and short fiction have appeared in the *Los Angeles Times*, *Five Chapters.com*, and *Best American Fantasy 3*. He is the co-editor of four anthologies including *Creatures: Thirty Years of Monster Stories* (with John Langan). Paul is the president of the board of directors for the Shirley Jackson Awards (www.shirleyjacksonawards.org). He lives outside of Boston, Massachusetts, has a master's degree in Mathematics, and has no uvula.

THAT BABY

LINDSAY HUNTER

The baby was normal when it came out. Daddy snipped the cord like nothing, the baby screaming silently till the nurse sucked out whatever bloodsnot was stuck in his throat, then there was no turning back, it was there, his voice, his mouth wide and wider, that baby was all mouth, his cries like a nail being driven into rotten wood. Normal.

Daddy said, let's name him Levis, we always liked Vs in names, and I'd heard the name Levis before but couldn't place it, and besides, that baby was a Levis, it was obvious.

We took Levis home and he sucked me dry within an hour. Daddy went to the store for some formula and Levis ate that up too. I made a pot of mashed potatoes for me and Daddy and the baby did his best to stick his face into it, his neck nothing more than a taffy pull, his big head hanging so I could see the three curls he'd already grown at the base of his neck, sweaty, looking for all the world like pubes lathered with baby oil, and I shuddered looking at them and chalked that feeling up to postpartum.

Levis wouldn't let Daddy sleep in bed with us, he was clever that way, soon as Daddy slid under the bedcovers Levis would start screaming, that nail torturing that rotted wood, that endless nail, then when Daddy would get up for a glass of something the baby would quiet down, and Daddy and I aren't stupid so soon we figured Daddy could get familiar with the couch for a while if it ensured Levis acted peaceful, and I gave Daddy permission to tend to himself in that way as much as he needed to since I was busy with Levis and couldn't do my wifelies.

Levis grew at night and plenty of mornings I'd wake up to see him laying there with his diaper busted open. Other ladies I've known who have given birth had always chittered on about their babies' growth spurts, but here Levis was 40 pounds within a week and 60 midway through the next, hair on his knuckles and three block teeth scattered amongst his jaws, then when he was one month old he called me Honey, his first word, fisted my breast, his nails leaving little half-moons in my flesh when I pried his hand from me, his grinning mouth showing a fourth tooth, a molar like a wad of gum wedged way back.

Daddy and I had heard of ugly babies, of unnaturally big babies. We'd seen a show once where what looked like a 12-year old boy was in a giant diaper his mother had fashioned out of her front-room curtain, sitting there with his legs straight out in front of him like he was pleased to meet them, his eyes pushed into his face like dull buttons, and the mother claiming he wasn't yet a year. But Levis wasn't on the TV, he was right there, his eyes following Daddy across the room, those eyes like gray milk ringed with spider's legs, and at two months Levis had chewed through a wooden bar in his crib, splinters in his gums, him crying while I plucked them with a tweezer, me feeling that nail in my gut, me feeling something less than love.

We took the baby to the doctor, Daddy explaining that there was something off about Levis, he was big, he didn't look like other babies, he had teeth like a man, and Levis quiet and studying Daddy like he understood, twirling his finger in his nostril, around and around, pulling it out tipped with blood. The doctor weighed Levis and he was up to 75 pounds and his third month still a week away, the doctor asking what on earth we were feeding him, warning us babies his age shouldn't be eating table food, and me and Daddy scared to say that the night before Levis had lunged for a pork chop, screamed until we let him suck on the bone, Levis making slurping noises like he was a normal baby, like the bone was his momma's nipple, his cheeks like two halves of a blush apple. The doctor sent us home, told us to watch what Levis ate, get him a jumpy chair for exercise. The doctor reaching out to pat Levis' head, then thinking different when Levis grabbed his wrist, the doctor blanching at the thick hair on Levis' arms, Levis giggling like a normal baby playing, just playing.

During bath time that night Levis' baby penis stiffened and poked out of the water, Levis saying HoneyHoneyHoneyHoney in his husky baby voice. I called Daddy to finish the bath so I could lay down but Levis screamed until I came for him, wrapped him in a towel, him freeing an arm to reach up and stroke my cheek, for all the world like I was his, like he had me, and there was that stiffy again when I was fitting him with his diaper.

At six months Levis walked into the kitchen at breakfast and tried to open the fridge himself, Daddy stunned and dropping scrambled eggs from his mouth, and Levis speaking his next word, Pickles. Pickles, Honey, he said, pounding on the fridge door with his hairy chunk fists, and I sliced some bread and butter pickles up for him and that's what he had for breakfast, a whole jar, me noticing that he was only a foot shorter than the fridge door, could almost reach the freezer where Daddy kept his vodka.

One night Daddy turned to me and we began our special time, I let Daddy do what he would since it had been so long, but soon enough I noticed Levis standing in the doorway watching, that finger in that nostril, and when I made Daddy stop Levis climbed into bed between us and began feeding, something he hadn't done in months, falling asleep with my breast in his mouth, like any other sweet baby, I told myself, like any other sweet baby boy, Daddy going back to his couch for the night, his shoulders hanging heavy, like the pillow he carried was a stone.

39

At eight months Levis opened a drawer and found a paring knife, held it to Daddy's gut and giggled, a sheen of drool on his chin, finally pulling the knife away when he got distracted by the ladybugs printed on his T-shirt. Then Daddy left, saying Levis wasn't right, saying he needed to get away, saying he'd be back, driving away while Levis watched him from the window, his baby man hands flat to the window, like everything he saw could be touched that way, me watching Daddy's headlights cut the dark and then the dark crowding right back in behind them, Levis saying Honey? to whatever he saw out that window, maybe even to himself.

Levis came to bed with me, molding his body to mine, rubbing his face on Daddy's pillow sleepily, his breath like garlic, like garlic and meat, didn't even open my eyes when he reached for my breast in the early hours and fed himself. In the morning he woke me, whispering Honey, Honey, smearing the sheets in elaborate patterns with fingerfuls of poop from his diaper, twining his fingers in my hair, Honey.

Normal. Later I bathed Levis and dressed him and we went to the park. For a while I pushed him on the swings, waited for him at the bottom of the slide, did the seesaw with him. When Levis was playing in the sandbox another mother came and sat beside me on the bench, said Your boy is quite large, me saying Yes, me saying Thank you. The woman's son got into the sandbox with Levis and they started building something and the woman went on, said I'm a producer for the local news and we'd love to have your boy on if you're interested, as kind of a feature on local unnaturals, and Levis looking up and showing his teeth, his eyes slitted at the woman, like he heard her, like he understood.

Maybe, I told the woman, when Levis is a little older, the woman saying Fine, fine, smoothing her jeans like she was

48

peeved at the color of the wash, and her son getting up to bring his fat little shoe down on Levis' sandpile, over and over, saying Unh Unh Unh, Levis letting him for a while before grinding a fist of sand into the boy's face, the boy just blinking for a minute like his second hand had stopped, Levis taking the opportunity to grab the boy by his ankle and bring him down to where he could pound on his abdomen with his fists, like any baby with a toy drum, like any baby figuring out how hard to pound to get just the right sound, the boy going Unh Unh Unh.

The woman said, My Lord, do something, he's flattened my Jared, her running over like her legs were breaking out of concrete molds, her boy saying Unh a little quieter now and me more proud of Levis than I'd ever been and so getting up and walking to the car, Levis saying Honey? Levis standing up to see better, saying Honey, stepping over the boy and out of the sandbox, me getting into the car and locking the doors, key in the ignition, Levis just standing there, the late afternoon sunlight giving him a glow, just standing there with his fists at his sides, looking like a fat little man more than anybody's baby, a little fat man beating his chest now, me pulling out onto the road, Levis wailing Honey, wailing Pickles, getting smaller and smaller in the rearview until I took a turn and he was gone, my heart like a fist to a door and my breasts empty and my nipples like lit matchheads.

Lindsay Hunter

lives in Chicago and is the author of the story collections
Daddy's and *DON'T KISS ME*. Her novel is forthcoming on FSG in
the fall of 2014. Find her at lindsayhunter.com.

THE TRUTH AND ALL ITS UGLY

KYLE MINOR

The year my boy Danny turned six, my wife Penny and me took him down to Lexington and got him good and scanned because that's what everybody was doing back then, and, like they say, better safe than sorry.

He was a good boy and never got out of hand until he was seventeen years old and we got out of hand together. Around this same time Penny kept saying she was going to leave and stay with her sister in town. She said it enough that we stopped believing her, but the last time she said it, she did it. I remember the day and the hour. Friday, September 17, 2024. Quarter after five in the afternoon, because that's what time her grandmother's grandfather clock stopped when I kicked it over.

Danny heard all the yelling, and he came running downstairs and saw her standing there with her two suitcases and looked at me like I ought to do something. "Goddamn it, I'm not going to stop her," I said.

"It's your fault she's going," he said.

Penny hauled off and slapped his mouth. "I didn't raise you to talk to your father that way," she said, and at that moment I was of two minds, one of them swelled up with pride at the way she didn't let him mouth off to me.

It's the other one that won out. I reached back and gave her what she'd had coming for a long time now. I didn't knock her down, but I put one tooth through her lip, hit her just hard enough so she would come back to us when she was calmed down.

She didn't come back, though, and she didn't go stay with her sister, who claimed not even to know where she was. One week, two, then on a Saturday me and Danny had enough. We hauled

Penny's mother's pink-painted upright piano out the front door and onto the porch and then we pushed it off and picked up our axes from by the wood pile and jumped down on it. "You got to be careful, Danny," I said. "There's a tension on those strings that'll cut you up bad you hit them wrong."

It was pure joy, watching him lift that axe and drive it into that piano. Up until then his head was always in books or that damn computer. Dead trees, I'd tell him, got not one thing on milkweed and sumac, horsemint and sweet William. But now I wasn't so sure, and now he'd caught on. "It's what you do with the dead trees," he said, like he was reading my mind.

I don't know what came over us after that, and it's not enough to blame it on our getting into the whiskey, which we did plenty. Penny had a old collection of Precious Moments figurines handed down from her own mama and grandmom. Children at a picnic, or playing the accordion to a bunch of birds, or hands folded in prayer, and nearly every little boy or girl wearing a bonnet. At first Danny said we ought to shoot at them—we had everything from assault rifles to a old Civil War service revolver that I'd be afraid to try firing—but then one Tuesday morning—by now it was November, and the old dog pens were near snowed under— he found some of the yellowjackets I had caught in glass Mason jars and forgot about. He found them dead in there and I saw him looking at them and he saw me watching but didn't say anything, just went upstairs and came down with my old orange tacklebox, which was where Penny kept her scrapbooking things.

"You gonna scrapbook those yellowjackets, buddy bear?" I said.

He said his plan was to shellac them, but I could see he couldn't near do it right. I said, "Here, let me show you how," and showed him how to thin the shellac with turpentine and dab

46

it on soft with the paintbrush bristles, which was something I knew from when things were better with Penny and I'd help her with her scrapbooks just so we could sit with our legs touching for a while.

He got good at it fast, and then we caught more yellowjackets and did what Danny had in mind all along, which was shellac them stiff, wings out like they were ready to fly, and set them on the Precious Moments figurines in a swarm.

After a while that stopped being fun, and it kind of took the shock away when every Precious Moment in the house was swarmed like that, plus we were running out of yellowjackets. "We got to get more minimal," Danny said, and I could see what he meant. It's like when I served my country in the African wars. You get to see enough dead bodies and before too long you get used to seeing them, and then you see another and it don't mean one thing to you. But you run into one little live black girl with a open chicken wire wound up and down her face and maybe three flies in her cut up eye, that gets to you.

So after that, we got strategic. We'd put three yellowjackets right by a brown marbly eye, eye to eye. Or one, stinger first.

Nobody but us had got to see what we had done to the Precious Moments until a few days later when Benny Gil, our postman, came by with the junk mail, and Danny saw him and invited him in for a glass of water, and he saw what it was we were doing with the wasps, and he said, "Son, that's sick," but he was smiling when he said it, and it was then I knew he was a person who could be trusted. Up until then, he'd always been asking about my methadone, which I got regular from the pharmacy at St. Claire's Hospital in town, on account of my back pain. He wanted to get some off me because he could trade it for other things he wanted.

41

This day I asked him, "Why is it nobody writes letters anymore?"

"It's a general lack of literacy," he said, and we started laughing because everybody knew that wasn't why.

"It's the government," Danny said, but he was just repeating what he always heard me say, and I wished he wouldn't get so serious in front of Benny Gil.

"They're spying," Benny Gil said, "listening in on us right now," but he wasn't serious.

"Best be careful," I said, because now was a time to keep it light. "Benny Gil here is on the government teat."

Benny Gil took a sip of his water and smiled some more. "That one," he said, "and maybe a couple two or three others."

Danny caught on. "It's you we saw across the creek there, in the tall grass."

"I been watching," Benny Gil said. He leaned back in the wooden chair, put all his weight on the back two legs. I could see by the look on Danny's face he was still thinking about how Penny would say not to lean back like that because it could put another divot in the wood floor, which was the kind of not-important thing Penny was always worried about. There was a thousand or more divots in the wood floor, and by now another one just added a little extra character.

Benny Gil leaned forward again, put his elbows on his knees so his face was closer to mine. "I know where Penny can be found," he said.

Danny's ears perked up at that.

"She wants to be found," I said, "and I don't care to find her."

"Irregardless," Benny Gil said.

"Where is she?" Danny said, and I shot him a look.

"Maybe," Benny Gil said, "me and your Dad ought to go out back and have a smoke."

Danny watched us through the window, and I wonder what it is he was thinking and wonder to this day whether whatever it was he thought had anything to do with what he did later. Surely he saw something changing hands between me and Benny Gil, and he must have seen us shaking hands, too.

What he didn't hear was Benny Gil saying, "God didn't invent thirteen-digit zip codes for nothing," or me saying, "How many?" or him saying, "Sixteen," or me talking him down to six. Six, I could spare, by careful rationing, and by grinding the white pills into white powder with my pocketknife, and snorting them instead of swallowing, which meant I could stretch out the supply until it was time for a new scrip.

Danny didn't hear any of it, but maybe he knew something of it, because after Benny Gil left, he said, "You get to hurting again, I know somebody who can get you what you need."

"Who?"

"Ben Holbrook," he said.

"That's the case," I said, "I don't want to hear of you talking to Ben Holbrook ever again."

I meant it when I said it, but the problem was the methadone got better after I started grinding it up, and once I knew how much better it could get, I had a harder time rationing it, and ran out a week early.

Believe me when I say I know a thing or two about pain. I was wounded twice in Liberia, and got radiation poisoning from the Arabs in Yemen. Once in Minnesota I split a fourteen-point buck in half on a old fossil fuel motorcycle and broke nearly every bone in my body and knocked one eye crooked, and it stayed that way until I could afford to get it fixed. But, son, you don't know pain until you get what I got, which is a repetitive stress injury in my back from solar panel installations up there on roofs in the heat or the cold. So when the methadone ran out, I forgot about what I said before, and told Danny maybe if he knew somebody he ought to give him a call.

Ben Holbrook was a skinny son of a gun, no more than maybe eighteen years old, pimple-faced, head shaved bald so you could see its lumps. Money was not a problem for us. Benny Gil wasn't the only one on the government teat, he just had to work for his. Still, I didn't like the way this bald zitty kid came into our house thinking he was the only one who could set prices in America.

"Who do you think you are," I said, "Federal Reserve Chairman Dean Karlan?"

He was cool as a cucumber. "Supply and demand," he said, "is the law of the land in Kentucky, U.S.A."

Much as I didn't like it, I knew he was right, and I paid what he asked, which was considerable, and he handed over three brown-orange plastic bottles, which was supply enough for my demand and then some.

Soon as Ben Holbrook left, I went into the bathroom with my pocketknife and dropped two tablets on the sink counter and chopped them to powder and made a line. Then I put my nose low to the Formica and closed off my right nostril with a finger and snorted the line through my left.

I must have left the door open a crack, because I saw Danny there, just outside, watching. He knew it was a thing I was doing, but I don't think he ever saw me do it before.

I knew good and well that wasn't the type of thing I wanted him to see. Any other time I would have thrown a shoe at him if I caught him spying like that. But when you take your medicine through your nose, it hits your bloodstream fast and hard. That's why you take it that way. So my first thought was to throw a shoe, but before that first thought was even gone the juice hit my bloodstream, and there was my boy, his eyes looking at mine through the crack in the bathroom door, and if I ever loved him I loved him more in that now than in any ever, and right alongside that first thought was the second, which came out my mouth the same time it came into my head, even though I knew it was wrong as I thought it and said it. "Boy," I said. "Come on in here and try a line."

Some things you see like from outside yourself and from above, and that's how I see what happened next. Right there, below, there's big old me, and there's my boy Danny, and I'm coming around behind him, putting my arms around him like I did when I showed him how to line up a cue stick at Jack's Tavern or sink a putt at the Gooney Golf, and he's got the open pocketknife in his hand, and I've got his hand in my hand, pushing down on it, showing him how to crush without wasting anything, how to corral the powder, how a good line is made. That's me, leaning down, pantomiming to show him how. That's him, fast learner, nose to the counter, finger to nostril. There's the line, gone up like the rapture. Danny, standing up too fast because he don't know any better, and the trickle of blood down his lip and chin, and me, tilting his head back, cradling it in the crook of my arm, putting the old Boy Scout press on his nose with a wad of toilet paper, saying, "Hold still now, baby boy," and his eyes bright, and his cheeks flushed, and his voice like from a hundred miles away saying, "Lord, have mercy," then, "Weird," and us lying back, then, on the cold tile, his shoulder blades resting on my chest, both of us waiting for the hit to pass so we could take another.

The days and nights started going by fast after that, and sometimes there was no cause to tell one from the other. One morning or afternoon or midnight, for all I know, I went into my room and found Danny half-naked underneath the bed I shared for all those years with Penny, and when I asked him what he was doing under there, he said, "She's been after us all this time," and I said, "Who?" and he said, "Her," and hauled out a stash of scented candles his mother must have left under there, cinnamon and jasmine and persimmon-lemon.

At first I thought he was talking crazy, but then he pulled himself out from under the bed and walked real close and put the purple jasmine one under his eye and struck a blue tip match and lit the wick, and soon as it started to burn his eye went all bloodshot and swelled up. Even still, I wanted to take up her case.

"How was she to know?" I said, but he was looking at me hard. "Turn around," he said, "and look in that mirror." And sure enough, my eye was tearing up and swelling and all the blood vessels were turning red.

"Benny Gil," he said, "told you where she is."

"That's not strictly true," I said, except it was.

"The general area, then," he said.

"The general neck of the woods," I said.

He went into me and Penny's bathroom, then, and for some reason, even though we had being doing it together, I couldn't go in there just then and do it with him. I could hear him, though, and then I heard a few more sounds I knew but hadn't expected to hear, which were the sounds of him loading my old Browning 9mm, which I kept under the sink in case of emergencies. When I heard that, I got scared, because for a while now I had been feeling, like I said before, like things were getting out of hand, but now, him stepping out of the bathroom, hand around the grip of that nine, I had the kind of proof that makes it so you can't look the other way anymore.

"Killing," I said, "isn't a kind of thing you can take back."

"I don't mean to kill her," he said. "I just mean to scare her a little."

That was more sensible talk than the talk I had been expecting from him, but still not altogether sensible. He was angry, I knew, after finding those candles, and I can't say I wasn't angry, either, but when you're young and full of piss and vinegar, caution is not a thing you take to naturally, and, besides, neither one of us was going through life in any kind of measured way at that particular point.

"I'm not saying she don't deserve a little scaring," I said. "When the time comes you'll see me front and center, taking the pleasure you and me both deserve after everything. But what I'm saying is that the time isn't come. Not yet."

"Look around," Danny said, and all around us was eighteen kinds of mess, some we'd made, and some that had just kind of grown while we weren't paying attention. "Sheila," he said, which was the name of a dog we'd had once who had abandoned her young before it was time, and all five of them had died, and who I had taken out back and shot because there wasn't one good thing about a dog who would go and do that.

"We're grown," I told him.

"Not me," he said.

There wasn't much I could say to that, because it was true, but I got him to hand over the Browning, and then he went upstairs and didn't come down for the rest of the night, and I figured he'd be down when he got hungry enough.

I went into the kitchen and made some pancakes and made

some extra and wrapped them in foil and put them in the refrigerator so he could have them later. Then I put some butter and maple syrup over mine and ate them and drank some milk and fell asleep in front of a old Wesley Snipes movie and figured when I woke up I'd see if he didn't want to put on his boots and go out into the Daniel Boone National Forest and hike for a while and get cleared out the way the cold air will do you.

When I woke up, though, the car was gone, and the extension cord for the battery charger was running from the living room out the front door, and I followed it on out to the side of the house where we parked the car, which was sure enough gone, and with juice enough to go to Lexington and back probably. That's when panic kicked in, and I ran back into the house, toward me and Penny's bathroom, knowing the Browning was going to be gone, but hoping it wasn't, and when I got there and didn't find it where it should have been, I figured there wasn't any way I was going to see Penny alive again, but I was wrong.

2.

It was Penny who found him. It took some time, but after a while the authorities pieced together what had happened. Around six in the evening, they said, must have been the time I fell asleep. When the house got quiet enough, Danny went out to the shed and brought in the long extension cord and ran it to the car battery. While it was charging he loaded up three assault rifles, including the Kalashnikov 3000, the one made to look like a AK-47, but with the guts of a MicroKal, laser gun and flamethrower and all. He took the Browning, too, and my Bowie knife, and his old play camo war paint, and a cache of armor-piercing bullets, although he never did use any of it except the 9mm. Then he sat down and ate the pancakes I had made, and washed the plate and knife and fork he had used to eat them off, and left them out to air dry.

By time he got to Benny Gil's house, he had worked himself up into something cold enough that Benny Gil didn't argue, didn't even need to be shown knife or gun to know it was in his best interest to give up Penny's location and get Danny on his way. I don't know what that means, exactly, except to say that Benny Gil is not a person I've ever known or heard of to be afraid of anyone or anything.

What Benny Gil told Danny was that Penny was staying with her sister's husband's nephew Kelly, a bookish boy we never knew well because he never came around to family things, probably because he, or more likely his mother, thought he was better than us, from what they call a more refined stock.

Kelly was, by then, well to do, UK law degree in hand, specialty in horse law. He even had a office at Keeneland and another at Churchill Downs, and if he thought as highly of himself as he seemed to every year on the television, sitting there next to some half-dead Derby owner who needed a oxygen tank just to breathe, sipping a mint julep, then I'm sure him and Penny made a fine pair.

There's no way to know it now, but my guess is that Danny, when he heard of it, came to the same idea I did when I first heard of it, which was that something not-right was happening between Penny and that boy, but I put it out of my head at the time because it was too horrible a thing to look at directly.

At any rate, what happened next is the part of the story that got out into the world. Danny drove east on Interstate 64, stopped at the Sonicburger in Mt. Sterling and ordered and ate a egg sandwich, then headed toward the big expensive stone houses by the airport, where Penny and Kelly was shacked up.

When he got there, he rang the doorbell three times—that's what Kelly's security company came up with later—and nobody was home, and I guess he didn't want to wait, and I guess he knew well enough what ended up being true, which was that there was something worse for a mother than to be killed by her son.

At the funeral, the preacher and everyone else said that wasn't the case, that Danny was sick in the head and that these things happen in the brain, something trips or snaps or misfires, and then somebody is doing something they wouldn't do if they were themself. But I think that's the kind of thing people say when what they want to do is make themselves feel better instead of look straight ahead at the truth and all its ugly. Because what I think and pretty near to know happened goes like this:

When he got there, he rang that doorbell three times, and nobody was home, and he got to thinking, and what he was thinking about was clear enough to him, and what he was thinking was that he had come all this way to hurt his mother, and his stomach was full from that egg sandwich, and that Browning 9mm was in his hand, and what if instead of killing her and just hurting her that one time, what if instead he did himself right there where she would have to come home and find him, and wouldn't that be something she would have to live with, and go on living and living and living? And wouldn't that be the way to hurt her again and again, the way she had hurt him and us by running off?

So that's what he did. He sat down in front of Kelly's front door, and put the muzzle to his right temple, and turned his head so his left temple was to the door, and when Penny came home that night, what she found was the worst thing you can ever find, and when I heard about it, I couldn't hate her the way I wanted to anymore.

At the funeral, they sat us both on the front row, but far apart from each other, with a bunch of her brothers and other male relatives between us so I would know clear as daylight that I was meant to stay away from her. But before the service got started, the preacher came over and asked if there were things each of us needed to say to the deceased, and we both said yes, but for me it wasn't because I had anything to say to Danny. He was dead and gone and wherever it is he ended up, and that was hard enough to bear without making a show of telling him something he wasn't ever going to hear. It was Penny I wanted to say some things to, and I thought maybe up there next to Danny she might in that moment have ears to hear them.

Her brothers didn't leave the room when the preacher asked, but they did go stand in the back and give what they must have thought was a respectful distance. Me and Penny went and knelt beside the casket, her near his head and me near the middle, maybe three feet separating us. She bowed her head to pray silently, and I did, too, although I didn't right then have any words to say, and then she said some things to Danny too personal for me to repeat, although I don't think it would be wrong to say that the things she said, if they were true, moved me in a way I didn't think I could be moved by her.

When she was done, she looked over at me. It seemed like she was able to keep from crying all that time until she looked into my eyes, and I was reminded that it was our looking into each other's eyes that was happening while we were about the business of getting him made in the first place, and maybe that's what she saw that finally broke her down when she looked over

57

at me. Maybe that, and all the years we had together, the three of us, and how there wasn't anyone else in the world who knew what those years were, and how there wouldn't ever be anyone else again.

It was right then, though I didn't say anything at the time because it didn't seem like the right time, that I decided I couldn't live in a world where Penny would go on being as unhappy as she had been made to be.

First thing the next morning I went down to Lexington again and went to the place where we had taken Danny when he was six years old to get scanned. It was gone, boarded up, the part of town where it had been now all but forgotten by people in business to make money. The only place in the storefront where the lights were still on was the WIC food stamp place, and I went inside and was told where to go on the Loop, to a part of town I remembered as Lexington Green but which was now called Stonewall.

The business had changed its name too, was now called Livelong, and occupied a building the size of a city block. The woman at the front desk said my number was A83, gave me a smartpad to fill in and told me to take a seat.

By time they called my name I had run my fingerprint and verified all my information and watched the screen that said the scan we had got was old technology, and while the guarantee we had bought was still good, the Danny we would get would eventually wear out, but would not age the way the ones they could make now could. We'd get him six years old, and six years old he would stay.

They made me meet with a kid in a suit and tie, and all he said was the same thing I had heard from the smartpad. He was looking at me funny, and I said, "All I want to get is the service

I paid for eleven years ago, near to the day," and he lowered his head for just a moment, like he was ashamed, and then he said, "You're entitled to it, and we'll give it to you if you want, but what you need to know is sometimes what you want isn't the same as the thing we can give you."

Even though he was a kid, what he was saying was true, and I knew it then, and it made me want to pound the sense out of him, and even so I wanted what I wanted.

I walked out of that Stonewall storefront that afternoon holding the warm flesh hand of a thing that moved and talked and looked for the life of me just like Danny did at six years old, and it was nearly unbearable, at first, to touch him or hear him say, "Now we're going for ice cream, Daddy?" and to remember the bargain we had made with Danny the day we took him to get him scanned. *You be good through this,* we'd told him, *we'll take you to get whatever kind of ice cream you want.*

So I said, "Sure, buddy bear," and I took him to up the road to the Baskin Robbins, and he ordered what Danny always ordered, which was Rocky Road with green and only green M&Ms sprinkled over top, and we got a high table for two, and I sat and watched him chew exactly the way he used to chew, and lick the spoon exactly the way he used to lick the spoon. He said, "Can we split a Coke, Dad?" and I said sure, and went up to the counter and ordered a large Coke, and when I forgot to get an extra straw, I regretted it the way I used to regret it, because he chewed the straw down to where you could hardly get any Coke out of it.

After that he wanted to go walk the old stone wall like we always did when we came to Lexington, so I took him down there and parked the car and got him out and hoisted him up on the wall, and held his hand to steady him as he walked on top of it, and he said, "Tell me about the slaves, Daddy," so I did what I used to do and told him about how all the black people in Kentucky used to belong to the white people, and how this very wall he was walking on had been made by their hands, one stone at a time, and the mortar mixed with probably some of their sweat and maybe some of their blood, too, still in it, and how even with all that Kentucky fought for the Union and could well have been the difference in that war. While I was saying it, I was remembering how I used to believe things like that, and the feelings that used to rise up in my chest when I said them, feelings of pride and certainty, and warm feelings toward my people I had come from. These were stories my own dad and granddad used to tell me and which I was now passing along to my own son, and this little Danny, walking along that wall, holding my hand, said the same thing the other little Danny had said in a moment a whole lot like this one but which couldn't have been, if you think about it, any more different if it was happening on the other side of the world. He said, "It wasn't right, was it, for people to keep other people to do their work for them? How did anybody ever think it was right?"

And I said the same thing I said then, which was, "People don't always do what's right, son, but you and me get the privilege of making our own choices, and we have to make good choices. That's what makes a person good, is the choices you make."

Right then is when we went off the script. Could be that something was wrong with his making, or could be that I wasn't leading him right, but right at that moment, he took a wrong step and fell. He didn't fall off the wall altogether, but he caught his shoe on a stone that was sticking up at a bad angle, and when he fell, he caught his arm on another stone, and it cut deep into his skin, and when he tried to stand up, he pulled away and didn't seem aware that his skin was caught on that rock. I guess they don't build those things in such a way that they feel pain the same way you and me do, because as he stood up, the skin of his arm began to pull away from what was underneath, which wasn't bone or sinew, but cold lightweight metal, what I now know they call the endoskeleton, and what began to drain from him warm wasn't his own blood, but somebody else's, and the reason it was in there wasn't to keep him alive, but just to keep his skin warm and pink, just to make him look and feel like someone alive.

"Danny," I said. He must have heard the alarm in my voice, and I could tell it scared him. He looked down and saw his metal arm, the skin hanging off it, and the blood pouring out in a way that wasn't natural, and then he gave me a look that sank my soul, and I realized what I should have realized before I signed what I signed, which was that I had got them to make a boy out of something that wasn't a boy. All that was in his head was all that was in Danny's head a long time ago, back when Danny was himself someone different than who he became later, and it wasn't his fault. He didn't know what he was, and the sight of it was more than he could handle.

His lip began, then, to tremble, in the way Danny's did when he needed comforting, and I lifted him down off that stone wall and took him in my arms and held him and comforted him, and then, in the car, I stretched the skin back to where it had been, and took Penny's old emergency button sewing kit out of the glove compartment and took needle and thread to it and got him to where none of the metal was showing. I didn't take him to Penny's like I had planned.

He was real quiet all the way home. He just stared straight ahead and didn't look at his arm and didn't look at me. Near

Winchester I asked him if he wanted to hear some music, and he said all right, but we couldn't find anything good on the radio. "How about the football game?" I said, and he said all right again, and we found the Tennessee Titans and the Dallas Cowboys, and I made a show of cheering for the Titans the way we always had, but when he said, "How come all their names are different?" I didn't have a good answer, and after that I asked if he wouldn't mind just a little quiet, and he said he wouldn't mind, and I leaned back his seat and said, "Why don't you just close your eyes and rest awhile? It's been a long day and I bet you're tired."

He did. He closed his eyes then, and after some time had passed and I thought he was asleep, I stroked his hair with my free hand and made some kind of mothering sounds.

It was dark when we got to the house. I parked the car by the bedroom window, then went around to his side and picked him up like I was going to carry him sleeping to bed. I held him there in the dark for a little while and thought about that, carrying him up to bed, laying him there, laying his head on the pillow, pulling the covers up around his shoulders, tucking him in. It would have been the easiest thing to do, and it was the thing I wanted to do, but then I got to thinking about Penny, and sooner or later, I knew, she would have to be brought in on this, and even though I thought I had done it for her, I could see now that I had really done it for me, like maybe if I showed up with this little Danny she would come back home and the three of us could have another go of it.

But already this little Danny was wearing out. I could feel it in his skin. He wasn't warm like he was when I had picked him up, I guess because the blood had run out of him on the stone wall. He was breathing, but he was cold, and a little too heavy compared to what I remembered. There wasn't any future for him, either. I got to thinking about how if I put him in school, everyone would get bigger than him fast, and it would get worse every year, the distance between who he was and who his friends were becoming.

He was stirring a little, so I put his head on my shoulder, the way I used to do, and patted his back until his breathing told me he was asleep again. Then I went around to the front of the house and reached up to the porch and took down my axe from the wood pile and went off into the woods, down the path I had mowed with my riding mower a few weeks back, and which was already starting to come up enough that I had to watch my step.

I kept walking, him on my shoulder, axe in my free hand, until I reached the clearing. Then, careful not to wake him, I unbuttoned my jacket and got it out from under him and took it off and laid it on the ground. Then I laid him down on it and made sure he was still sleeping. Then I lifted up the axe and aimed it for the joint where his head met his neck and brought it down. In the split second right before blade struck skin, I saw his eyes open, and they were wide, and what I saw in them was not fear but instead some kind of wonder, and then, fast as it had come, it was gone, and all I could tell myself, over and over, was *It's not Danny. It's not Danny.*

Kyle Minor

is the author of two collections of short fiction,
In the Devils Territory (2008) and *Praying Drunk.*

ACT OF CONTRITION

CRAIG CLEVENGER

She flared in the dark like some wild animal's lone eye in my headlights. White sweatshirt and ragged sunbleached hair, a ghost with her thumb to the road. I slowed to the right and stopped just ahead of her. My tires straddled the broken black edge where the dirt shoulder dropped below the asphalt, the car sloping passengerwise like a sinking boat. Its lopsided timing shuddered through the wheel and into my arms. I nursed the gas, nudged the idle back to its center and kept the engine alive. My brake lights bathed the hitcher in blood then she turned white again, stopped at my passenger side and looked back down the road. Maybe somebody else would stop. But she bent to the window and her eyes said she was long past working those odds or any other. Her sunburn ran deep, patches of skin flaking from her face. Lower lip split open and dried to a hardened hairline of blood.

How far you going? she asked.

I named some place. I lied.

Okay. She climbed in and pulled at the door but it pulled back.

Try again. Hinge is real stubborn.

She did. On her third pull I saw headlights in my mirror, a diesel rig snailing around the one-lane curve to my back. Her door was still open when I punched the gas. With no shoulder grade to the road I reckoned maybe six-inches of crumbling curb beneath my chassis. I torqued left onto the highway and scraped my oil pan across a yard of jagged blacktop. A sound I heard through my teeth.

✕

Crystal was fifteen and she was my cousin. She wore jean shorts frayed at the top of her thighs, snug like she'd cut off the legs last summer before she started looking the way she did. The way she cocked her hip and bent to scratch her bare foot or chewed a lock of hair tickling her face, oblivious to herself. She caught me looking at her once and I froze, squeezed out a smile with my mouth full of cold meatloaf. She gave no read at all, just picked up the remote and turned her back to me. She caught me a few times after that but never got creeped or let on that she did. But her spell broke anytime she opened her mouth. She was just a kid again, wanting help with a bicycle flat or a ride to the mall.

I pray every day. Crews on the job site got quiet when I came around. Work was drying up and the scarce jobs were going to friends of foremen and subcontractors first. I had to give up my place. I prayed for help. My aunt and uncle had a room and there was lots of development out where they lived. They let me slide on rent, long as I built a new railing for their deck and kept an eye on Crystal from time to time. I prayed more.

The grid went down during a heat wave so the job cut us loose early. I collapsed on the couch with a cold beer and some solitude. It was August, there was no school. My aunt and uncle were gone for the weekend. I heard the back door open and close and there stood Crystal, bronzed from her afternoons in the backyard and smelling like coconut, wearing a two-piece I could ball into my fist. She looked taller in the doorway. Legs and gold hair meeting at her hips where a more modest suit had cast a shadow of pale winter skin. She drifted toward me, strips of wet light shining from her skin and I saw her every movement in quarter time.

Got any more of those? She didn't sound like a kid this time.

No. These are my last six. Sorry.

She didn't whine or plead like she did when I turned down certain movie rentals or enforced her bedtime.

I'll help myself, she said, and stuck her tongue out. She left the room, catwalk-style and I followed the curve of her waist, the shoelace knots at her hips and the stretch of bright yellow fabric in between sliding into itself with each step. A minute passed, slow and hot. I heard the hiss of a bottle cap crimping open.

I shot to the kitchen and she tucked the bottle behind her and ran so I chased her and grabbed her before she could pour it on me and had to pin her and she wouldn't stop laughing and the beer foamed all over both of us.

I knocked that clip out of my head.

I grabbed her wrist and squeezed until the bottle hit the kitchen floor, beer foaming around the shards of brown glass. I can't remember what I said but I may have held her wrist too hard. Crystal locked herself in her room. She didn't come out and I didn't knock. At 4:30 the next morning I slipped a hundred bucks under her door with a note that said her parents would be home after the weekend. Then I left for good.

The hitcher looked older up close, hard years beneath the sun damage.

Got no radio? She spoke slowly, words from a morphine drip.

Radio works fine, was all I said.

She didn't touch the radio. No one ever does. I'm okay with just the humming road but most people need noise, the talk shows and morning deejays. They need the ad jingles, something they can hum silently to help forget their forty hours every week.

She sat frozen with her hands folded in her lap, gearing up to do whatever the ride or a few bucks called for, her body flying solo while she looked away from somewhere inside her head. I didn't want anything. The silence was enough for me, like a sleeping guard dog between us.

Crystal and her backyard tanning routine were seven-hundred miles away. I filled my tank, then blinked and found myself staring into the open back hatch of my car. A stray socket wrench, hot to the touch. A ballpoint pen with no cap, a few pennies and bits of dog kibble though I've never owned a dog. I loaded up the provisions I couldn't recall buying moments earlier. Two gallons of drinking water, a dozen granola bars and a canvas knapsack. I had a thin recollection of the air conditioner and the bored liquor store clerk, but they could have been from another stop on a different day. Whatever was clipping the time from my waking activity was getting greedy. I used to zone out for a few seconds, maybe a minute or two. Then the stretches of time got longer and longer. I'd be parked at a job site with my keys in my lap and the half-hour commute wiped clean from my morning. Lately I'd practically been leaving my body.

Hey. Can you spare any change?

Straight black hair and pale skin. She was a year older than Crystal, judging by her curves, and dressed for the heat. Gossamer skirt rippling high on her legs and a babydoll top with pink script across her breasts that I couldn't read without staring so I didn't. She was too clean to be homeless and too young to be panhandling.

Do you have fifty cents?

Sorry, I said. Can't help you.

What's your name?

The thin silver chain around her waist looked like a wire of sunlight. The cold free-fall rush blew through me and I reckoned every wrong twist of backstory before my keys hit the ground. There was a stepfather or stepbrother in the scene. She didn't know where to get help but she was learning the angles, and I could be one of them. She came through the heat, twisting a rubber band between her fingers. Her flip-flops slapped the soles of her feet but the way her hips moved made everything else quiet.

Ezekiel, I said.

For real?

Yeah.

Sounds like a Bible name.

It is.

But you don't have any money?

None to spare. I didn't look below her neck. And I didn't look around. If I wasn't doing anything wrong then it didn't matter who saw me.

Someone peeled out of the gas station and set my pulse loose like a racing dog. A matte-black Nova with a bondo patch on the driver's door screamed through the intersection. I picked up my keys and when I stood up she'd found another mark, a middle-aged business man with a map spread across his steering wheel. Her hazy skirt rode on the current of heat, flaring up to her hips in slow motion. Pale crescents of skin flexed at the tops of her thighs. The skirt settled around her again, like something cast off and drifting to the bottom of a swimming pool.

✕

71

The hitcher's fingers danced nervously on her lap and tickled the edge of my vision. They went still if I looked at them straight on. Maybe she was playing with me. Maybe she was thinking this ride was her last, that I had a rag for her mouth and a shovel in my trunk. The highway was empty one second and the next I was bearing down on a five-hundred pound elk standing on the dotted yellow divide. I hit the brakes and we swerved. The elk bolted. Big enough to take out my front end and kill us both but it darted like a squirrel, so quick I wasn't sure I'd really seen it.

The fuck was that? The hitcher had braced herself against the dashboard, elbows locked and eyes wide but she wasn't asking about the elk. The accusation was silent but clear. Maybe I hadn't seen anything.

Keep your hands still, I said. It's distracting. I was parked right where the phantom elk had been, crossways in the dead middle of the highway, a broadside collision set to go.

You fucking crazy?

You got a problem then walk, I said, then hit the ignition.

I've been good my whole life, walking that barren firebreak between feeling the rush of caving to temptation but still having the strength to resist. A girl came to my hotel room once, after I called an ad in the paper. Somewhere in west Texas. She took off her clothes and asked me what I wanted. I said I didn't know. Then she opened my door and a guy was waiting there, big guy with a tattoo on his shaved head and lots of earrings. He held out a badge but not for very long. Said he could arrest me or fine me on the spot. I asked him how much the fine was and the girl laughed. Another hitcher had offered to thank me for the ride. I stopped at a liquor store and gave her money for condoms and beer and when she got out I drove away. It was always the same. I never did anything wrong but I never stopped thinking about those things I never did.

I'd lied to that girl in the parking lot. My name wasn't Ezekiel, not yet. That was up to God.

When the girl and the big guy left, she'd stuck her business card in my Bible. The big guy laughed when she did that. The glossy pink card had a picture of her chest and a phone number. It was marking the Book of Ezekiel.

I knew a sign when I saw it.

It's easier to hear God in the desert. Fewer obstructions, so God's got a halfway decent view, plus a man's got fewer things clouding his own sight. Jesus, John the Baptist, all of them, the desert was where they heard God loudest and clearest, where they had their showdown with the Devil. I'd been driving around the desert for weeks since I'd left Crystal's house. Driving and praying, waiting for God to show me where to stop.

We hit the truck lot after midnight. A row of fueling bays the size of a city block with a cashier's booth in the middle, a coffee shop, a cheap motel on either side and a couple dozen eighteen-wheelers. Two hours since I'd picked her up and I don't think she blinked the entire trip, at least not since the elk that I may or may not have imagined, that may or may not have nearly killed us.

This is good, she said. Right here.

The cashier's booth was lit up like daylight. I could almost read the newspaper headlines from the far edge of the lot.

Just stop right here, she said.

Let me get you closer. No sense in you walking through a

parking lot this size in the dark. You want the coffee shop or just that little convenience store?

Let me out of this goddamned car.

I stopped. Probably a couple hundred yards out on a stretch of empty asphalt. She'd been so docile until now and I was nervous. I hadn't done anything wrong. Her bag strap had caught under the seat. She was fighting with it and cursing under her breath, louder and louder. She flung the door open and jumped out. Then she screamed. She hugged herself and closed her eyes and screamed as loud as she could. She stomped her feet and beat her fists against her head then pointed at my car and screamed for help.

I couldn't lift my hands or move and I felt hot all over.

She screamed that I'd tried to kill her and then she ran toward the coffee shop.

The dome light came on in a nearby semi. I reached over and closed the door and drove away as fast as I could, found the nearest onramp and doubled back toward where I'd just driven from. It didn't matter which way I went as long as I kept driving. I prayed for forgiveness, told God I was sorry, that I was ready and just needed a sign. I passed the truck lot on my left, kept to the speed limit and watched for square headlights in my mirror. After a while I was back where I'd first picked her up. At the next juncture I took the unfamiliar road.

She was the last one. No more inhaling the vapor in Hell's vestibule. I promised God, no more.

I loved cowboy movies when I was a kid. Ford, Peckinpah, Leone. But I had a weakness for the second-rate gunfighter films with cowboys and Indians and cattle barons and railroads. They hotwired the classics then stripped them down in some B-movie chop shop and recycled the good parts as their own.

14

Like when the hero walked into a saloon for the first time and everything stopped. The music went quiet, folks would stare for a minute and then go back to their whiskey or cards. But everyone had to look at the good guy.

My Sunday school teacher had taught us about life in the Holy Land. She wanted to make the Bible real for us. She taught us about the desert, how the heat wave we once had was nothing compared to life in the Middle East. We learned how they had to preserve food and how risky it was to travel. It took the Israelites forty years to make it to the Holy Land. They only survived because of miracles. John the Baptist ate insects. I'd been driving through the American desert for weeks, where all of those frontier towns from the cowboy movies used to be. The pile of maps and guidebooks in my glovebox agreed on the highways and major roads and most of the big dots but little else. The small towns and the little roads, especially the dirt ones, never matched up. They couldn't agree on exactly where the desert began, or the exact annual rainfall or average temperature. We know as much about the desert now as those people in the ghost towns did. It's hard to make a deep map of a territory that can kill you in a matter of hours.

Someone showed up in one of those Old West towns by himself, no railroad or wagon train, of course people were going to stare. Because he was supposed to be dead. That's how you knew who the good guy was.

I passed three more elk that night. No close calls but their electric Roswell eyes hovering in the dark startled me every time. It was four in the morning when I found a rest stop with an RV slumbering in the lot and four other cars parked as far apart as they could manage. A stretch of grass with picnic benches, fire pits and a brick hut split into restrooms, its curbside face a mottled black and white mural like a blown-up newspaper photograph. The collage of leaflets came into focus once I was up close.

Missing

Have You Seen Me?

Missing

Missing Since—

Last Seen On—

Missing

Missing

Missing

Young teenagers and children. Mostly Caucasian, mostly female, last seen wearing anything and everything from the Junior Miss Department.

The bathroom smelled like an outhouse and had almost as little light. The floor was wet. I held my breath long enough to take a leak then went back to my car. I passed a station wagon with expired tags and a coat hanger twisted around the loose muffler. One if its back windows covered with duct tape and a garbage bag. I locked my doors, let my seat back as far as it could go and draped a T-shirt over my eyes. Before long there came a tentative knock, the way someone knocks to see if you're awake without disturbing you if you aren't. Definitely not a cop. I sat up and saw the face fogging up my window, hands cupped around his eyes to see through the dark. If he'd needed money, gas or a jump start he wouldn't have been smiling the way he was. I gave up on sleeping, started my car and he made the looping pantomime signal for me to roll down my window. I couldn't exactly race my engine, but he got the message that I was driving off and the placement of his foot didn't worry me.

The high desert had too many elk and too much plant life.

Too many places to hide or disappear. And it was full of people hiding or disappearing. If you walked out of nowhere into a room full of strangers nobody would give you a second look. The high desert was no place for a prophet.

By 10:00 that morning it was ninety-five degrees. Nothing on either side of the road but bleached sand and brittle shrubs as far as I could see. The mountains ahead of me hadn't changed size since sunrise. An hour later my temperature gauge was reaching for the red and the bottle of water in my passenger seat was hot to the touch. I turned on the heat and rolled down my windows and the needle eased back. I drove on, eyeing the mountains and the needle but neither one moved. At the stroke of noon my dashboard blacked out and smoke billowed from my hood. I coasted to the shoulder and once the hissing and smoking stopped, I stepped out and just stood there in the desert. Heat like nothing I'd learned about in Sunday school, silence like I'd never felt in church. A short distance off the road and I'd be standing where no human being had ever walked. It was like being on Mars. A place where a man finds redemption beneath the unyielding sun that burns away his sins and what is left of that man becomes a prophet.

I opened the map and found my place, a scratch of north-south highway hardly worth printing. The nearest town of Jackdaw Flats lay forty miles due west on a faint pencil mark of road roughly parallel to mine, with neither a direct route nor an inch of shade in between. I emptied the hot bottle of water over my head then cloaked myself in a beach towel. John the Baptist didn't wear sunblock. I packed the granola bars and my Bible into the canvas knapsack, slung it over my shoulder then took up a gallon water jug in each hand. There hadn't been anyone else on the road all morning. I crossed the highway without looking, stopped at the edge of the road and prayed. The triple-digit temperatures would drop below freezing after dark. There were definitely diamondbacks, possibly coyotes and the narrow chance of a flash flood. I could be in Jackdaw Flats by morning.

When I come in from the desert, everyone will stare at me. And my name will be Ezekiel.

Craig Clevenger

is the author of *The Contortionist's Handbook* and *Dermaphoria*. He
divides his time between San Francisco and the Mojave Desert.

THE FAMILIARS

MICAELA MORRISSETTE

The boy and his mother wake late in the swampy summer mornings and sit on the edge of the porch drinking their first glass of water and spooning out their wedges of melon and picking the dead heads off poppies with their toes. They brush their teeth side by side at the kitchen sink and sometimes the mother lathers the boy's cheeks with almond soap and pretends to shave him with a butter knife, chattering in an arch accent that aspires to cockney. They fill the wheelbarrow with the boy's stuffed animals and matchbox cars and his wand for blowing bubbles and his kazoo and tambourine and truck down to the pond where the boy lies in the hammock, holding his toys in the air and swooping them up and down and crooning to them, and the mother reads paperbacks in the deep low wicker rocker, pushing the hammock gently back and forth with her foot.

For lunch there is French bread spread with soft cheese and served with purple pickled eggs and Jordan almonds. They picnic under the sycamore on one of the boy's old bed sheets, patterned with smiling clouds and pastel rainbows, too childish for him now, and suck the candy shells from the nuts, and see who can flick an ant the farthest. The sheet smells as the boy used to, hot heavy cream, slightly soured, and powdered sugar, and cough syrup, black cherry.

They put on their cleanest clothes and drift through the heat down the dirt road to town, the mother pale beneath a black umbrella and the boy's head swimming in a man-sized baseball cap. They check at the post office for their bills and catalogues and postcards of the town which the mother has sent to the boy on the sly, and they buy a wheel of licorice or a birch beer or a small wooden crate of sour clementines. They also buy a backpack, or some tennis shoes, or a lunch box, for the boy's first day of school, which is nearly upon them. With two pennies they wish in the fountain, and they walk home, carefully matching their steps to the footprints they made on the first leg of their journey.

They plant mason jars in the garden to steep their sun tea, and they blow trumpeting squeals on blades of grass. They play a game that is both tic-tac-toe and hopscotch with chalk and stones on the cement walkway, and the mother turns the hose on the boy and washes off the chalk and dust and sweat while he shrills and capers. For dinner there are drumsticks, sticky and burnt, off the old gas grill, or hotdogs charred on sticks at the fire pit. Then cold red wine with seltzer water for the mother, and warm milk with vanilla and sugar for the boy, in the swooning, exhausted armchairs of the living room, with the white gauze curtains swelling at every breath of breeze.

The mother reads to the boy in bed, adventure stories about islands or magic pools or noble lovers or gallant orphans, or the boy tells ghost stories to the mother, in which crushed faces press against the glass of windows, or trees grown over graves sigh and weep and rustle their leaves. The mother sleeps on one side of an enormous mattress, under an avalanche of pillows, and in another room the boy sleeps in a red wooden bed and his legs and arms tumble over the sides.

It's dawn and the boy has woken early when the friend appears. It unfurls from under the bed. Its features have not quite coalesced. Its skin rises up like a blush. The mouth, full of rapid shadows, comes painfully. As the boy watches, its teeth emerge and its eyes take on their hues. It's both gawky and graceful and the boy is touched by the tentativeness of its existence. Its limbs fold out with small tremblings. The boy moves over in the bed and the friend huddles gratefully into the warm depression he leaves. The boy knows not to touch the friend as it is born. Shyly, the boy indicates that the friend is welcome.

The friend begins right away to tell secrets. Some of them are astounding, and the boy giggles in nervous exhilaration. Some of them the boy already knew without knowing it. The wonderful thing is that the boy has secrets too, and the friend is fascinated, and they whisper under the covers until the mother pokes her head around the door, stirring honey into the first glass of their new batch of sun tea for the boy's good morning. The friend is under the bed so quickly that the boy has no time to feel alarm. But when the mother asks, was he talking to himself, the boy responds without hesitation that he was talking to his invisible friend. His mother smiles and asks what's his friend's name, and since the boy doesn't know, he says it's a secret.

His mother smiles and looks proud in a forlorn sort of way and brushes back his hair with her fingers and he feels the happy little pokes and tickles of his friend through the mattress, approving him, and all three are happy, and he drinks his sun tea with the honey not quite dissolved, coating his tongue and staying sweet there for some minutes. The damp smell that attends the friend, a stain of its birth, is clogging the air of the room, but the mother says nothing and the boy thinks that perhaps the friend is invisible after all.

That day it rains and the boy and his friend play in the attic. There is a trunk full of clothes and dust and the boy's friend dresses up as the princess and the boy as the minstrel without any money, or the boy dresses up as a monster of the air and the friend as a monster of the deep, or the boy dresses up as a man of the future and the friend holds over his face a helmet that carries the boy through time and space. The rain assaults the roof of the attic. They have stores of crackers and dried fruit and they plant flashlights all over the floor, the beams gaping up at the rafters. There is a box of paper houses that unfold: castles, a Hindu temple, a Victorian country-home. They set these up and populate the rooms with colored plastic figurines from sets of jungle beasts, dinosaurs, and the Wild West.

The Christmas tree is stored in the attic, still tangled in its lights. The boy and his friend creep in under the lowest fronds, curling themselves around the base, and turn the beams of their flashlights out through the strings of dead bulbs to make them glow.

Between the panes of the windows are cemeteries of moth wings and wasp heads and fly legs. The attic swells into the rain.

They find a punchbowl roped in cobwebs and fill it with water and stare in to see the silk awake. They turn off all the flashlights and haunt each other in the dark with sobs and screeches. They roast marshmallows with a butane lighter. The boy recites the alphabet backwards. The friend dances.

By nightfall the sky has cleared and the mother takes the boy out onto the slanting roof of the house and they lie on their backs on the shingles and she shows him the constellations. The dippers, the hunter, the seven sisters, the two bears. The mother tells the boy how the stars are immense balls of flame millions of miles away, and how many of them may already have been dead for hundreds of thousands of years.

Hidden behind the stack of the chimney, the friend laughs in derision and reaches out its hand and rubs the pattern off the sky. Then it draws new figures: the claw, the widow, the thief, the cocoon. The planet shudders and rocks and the boy loses his grip and skids down the plane of the roof until the mother catches his hand and pulls him to safety. She bundles him into her arms and totes him down the attic stair, soothing and scolding and breathless, while he cranes his neck to peer behind him at the lights scattering across the dark like startled starlings.

The boy and his friend play in the garden, under the sun. They play in the garden, which is on the edge of the wood, and the trees shade it, many games. They play pick-up sticks, checkers, hide-and-go-seek, and things, and the sun enacts changes in their skin and hair and eyes. They play in the garden, and smile. They smile and smile and smile and smile and smile.

The boy's mother puts an extra cookie on the plate for the friend, but the boy says the friend doesn't eat. She brings an extra pillow for the bed, but the boy says the friend doesn't sleep. What does it do all night then, she asks the boy, doesn't it get bored? Plays in my dreams, the boy tells her.

The boy and his friend make shadow puppets in the afternoon. The boy curtains the windows and holds his hands in front of the lamp and does a bird, a rabbit, a hunchback, a spider. The friend opens the curtains and crouches on the windowsill, a black silhouette against the sun. The sun pulses and shivers in the sky and the outline of the friend flickers and wavers at the edges. Its body makes an ocean wave, a spouting volcano, a hurricane, a shape-changing cloud: giraffe, dragon, whale. The boy crows and claps his hands. The friend grows huge in the window and blots out the light, making the night sky. It spreads its limbs so no sliver of sunlight peeks through and it makes the bottomless well.

The boy's mother sits on the edge of the tub and the steam clings to her; she is composed of droplets. At bath time the friend disappears, the boy says; it hates water. The mother runs the hot when the boy complains that the bath is cooling. She shampoos the boy's golden hair with the tips of her fingers. She rubs the puffs and cracks of deep pruning on his hands. When he announces that the bath is over, she starts a splashing war to make him forget.

The boy has a duck for the bath, and to play with the duck, an inflatable bear, and to amuse the bear, little pills that pop open into sponges, and to collect the sponges, a net with butterfly shapes sewn into the webbing, and to transport the net, a battleship that sprays water through its nose, and to fight the battleship, a tin rocket that rusts in the water, and the mother cuts her hand on the crumbling metal and the blood makes a blossom in the bath. The boy leaps up and shouts out that his friend is calling and he runs shivering and half drowned out of the bathroom.

The mother stays behind and bandages her hand into an enormous white paw. When she tucks the boy in that night, she brandishes the paw and growls and tickles his stomach. But he says the friend can smell the rusty blood and he insists that she leave, and she does and wonders if the boy is weary of her or protecting her from his imaginary friend, and she sits for an hour in the window seat in her bedroom, watching trees and clouds move across the reflection of her face in the pane.

The boy and his friend camp out in the tree house. They make believe there's a siege and they're starving to death. They make believe there's a war and they're hidden in a priest's hole. They make believe it's a nuclear winter and they're trapped in a fallout shelter. They make believe they're princes locked in a dungeon by the king's wicked councilor. They make believe they're hermits fasting in a mountain cave. They make believe they're stowaways in the hold of a galleon. They make believe they're magicians tied up in a chest. They make believe they're scientists in a sunken bathysphere. They make believe they've been swallowed by a giant and explore the vast cavern of his stomach. They make believe they're in a spaceship warping through black holes. They make believe they're shrunken to the size of tiny bugs, stuck in a raindrop falling to earth. Sometimes they climb through the trapdoor out into the treetop and sit astride the sturdy limbs and pretend they're galloping on white stallions in a thundering herd of wild black horses.

Sometimes they close their eyes and pretend to be blind and

they feel each other's faces and the boy is careful not to hurt the friend. Sometimes the friend grooms the boy, picking the bark and sap from his hair and licking the pollen dust from his face. Sometimes the boy curls up in the lap of the friend and the friend asks him questions. What animal would you like to be? What food would you eat if you could only eat one? How would you choose to die? What is your greatest fear? What superpower would be the best? If you could save the world by sacrificing one life, would you do it? What was your first word? What is your earliest memory?

The mother calls the boy into her bedroom and shows him the photographs she has spilled out over the white froth of tumbled linens. The scent of the soap washed into the sheets has always reminded the boy of snow, but tonight it stings his cringing nose, astringent. She shows the boy pictures in dull umbers and maroons, long-ago film, of the boy's parents before he was born. This is his mother, distracted in an itchy sweater, in a cabin on her honeymoon, lamplight the color of cooking oil shining and blurring on her face. Her hair is shorter and it looks rough and blunt and prickly. Her smile is unfamiliar. Here is his father, forehead buried in a dark navy watchman's cap, chin and nose smothered in a charcoal turtleneck, marking off a pale strip of skin out of which black eyes gape, the inverse of the bandit's eye mask.

Now pictures of the boy as a baby, with a fat lolling neck and a glazed expression, bulbous and gaping in a matted blue towel, or seemingly deserted in a flat field on a gray day. The photos get glossier and brighter as they go on. Last year on the ferry, noses and eyelids smashed flat by the wind. This past winter, roasting potatoes in foil in the fireplace here, the lighting off, their hands red and their faces smeared across the exposure. The boy and the mother on the boy's birthday at the zoo. A leather- chested gorilla with blood in its eyes stands behind them as they pose, the spit spray of its roar fouling the glass wall of the enclosure. The boy squirms on the bed, bored and truculent.

In the night the boy and the friend sneak back into the mother's bedroom and steal the box of photographs. They draw the friend into the pictures: sometimes a black zigzag of shadow at the corner of the frame behind the mother, sometimes a silvery trail the friend makes with the point of a needle, a shape hovering between the boy and the lens. With crayons, the boy draws the friend's scales and the stripes of its fur onto the face of his father, and the friend shades its own eyes within the eyes of the gorilla.

When the mother finds the pictures in the morning she cries and screams at the boy, and he takes off, kicking the ground, the corners of his mouth wrenching down despite himself, and runs to the wood, and begs the friend to take him inside, behind the tree line, and the friend does, and comforts him.

The boy and the mother make up and on Sunday they bake cookies for breakfast. They have a collection of cookie cutters and they bake pigs and crescent moons and hearts and maple leaves, royal crowns and saxophones and lighthouses and bumblebees. They sprinkle jimmies on the tops, or push in currants with their thumbs. Shivery with sugar, they bustle into town and the mother, rapid and excitable, buys suspenders and striped shoelaces for the boy's first day of school, and a set of stencils, and stickers that smell of chocolate, bubble gum, peanut butter, and green apple. On the way home she asks casually how the friend will keep busy when the boy is at school all day. It will come with me, says the boy, startled, and the mother, kind and vague, shakes her head with her eyes set on the distance.

When they reach the house, the boy tears through the rooms, but the friend is nowhere to be found. At last the boy discovers it in the basement, huddled beneath the stairs, tearing apart a daddy longlegs. I won't go! promises the boy, and any other supplication he can think of. By and by, he's able to coax the friend upstairs, where it scuttles into the boy's bedroom and under his bed. It stays there through the evening and all night, and in the morning the mother sees the boy's face is puffed and flushed as if he's been stung, and his eyes have a queer translucence.

The mother invites the boy and the friend to dance. She pushes the armchairs and ottomans to the outskirts of the living room and sweeps the floor, making an odd pile of broken dried leaves, frayed and twisted threads of gold and purple, small slivers of glass, dust clumps woven in spheres like tumbleweeds, and wasps, curled in on themselves like fetuses, their antennae shattered.

The mother wears an ivory slip and black opera gloves and, on a long chain, a cameo that chills her through the thin silk of her slip. The boy comes down in his small black suit, which still fits him perfectly. He hasn't grown. The mother rummages in the spare room for a man's dove-gray fedora, which engulfs the boy's ears and slips backward, the brim chafing his neck. Baby's breath is wedged in the band.

The boy informs the mother solemnly that the friend has sent its regrets. The mother, stymied, asks if he and she might go together to press the invitation, but the boy fuddles the needle onto the record and extends his hand without answering. The boy and the mother waltz awkwardly. Where did you learn to dance? says the mother, I thought I would have to teach you. My friend taught me, says the boy, are you jealous? The mother stares at him. No, she says, that's not it. The needle staggers into a gouge in the record. Oh, dear, the mother says, what a shame. My friend loves this song, says the boy. He puts his arms up trustingly, as if to be carried, high above his head, and his fingers curl around where the shoulders of the friend might be. They sweep about the room, the friend a confident lead, the boy swooning gracefully in its embrace. The mother forms an encouraging smile. I'll get some refreshments, she says, champagne with ginger ale, and lemon ices. Switch off the lights when you go, says the boy, still revolving. The mother hesitates, flicks the switch, and mounts the stairs. Sometime in the night the music skids to a halt.

She knows it's beautiful. She knows what kind of skin it has— blue-veined, with a thick translucence like shellfish, bruising easily in a kind of panic. She knows because it's obvious.

She knows, because her son has told her, in a voice with a reverential, primal hush, like the silence of dim morning air at ease on still water, that his friend has a wonderful facility of climbing in the trees and running in the tallest, most whipping, stinging grass. She knows that a heartbeat will slow to the rhythm of its voice. She knows its eyes are colors from another spectrum. She knows the fine golden down that covers its limbs; she just knows.

She knows the ravishable tenderness of its throat. She knows the coils of its ears can provoke a dangerous hypnosis if regarded too long. She knows the razor sharpness of its elbows and the woozy perfume of its breath.

She knows that the rays of the sun are addicted to its body and that it drinks in the moonlight with upturned mouth. She's never seen it, but she knows. She doesn't know the secrets it shares, the memories it hides, the fears it cherishes, or why it is vying for her son.

Past the tree line, just within the wood, is the skeleton of a burned-down barn, and brambles of blackberries and bushes of lady's slippers have gentled the ruins. Past the barn, a deer trail leads through a claustrophobia of clawing saplings and lashing briars, until the wood opens, and the floor is a miniature forest of tiny trees of climacium moss. Long gray vines sway from the canopy; the branches over which they're looped are lost in leaves and in the clouds of spores and insects that laze overhead. The boy grabs a vine and swings. He whoops once, then swoops silently between the trunks on the endless arc of his pendulum. The friend tugs the vine to a halt and brushes the boy's face in apology. Hurry, it says.

They trudge out of the forest of moss and down a short bank graceful with ferns and irises and ending in a stream that cuts through the wood. Water fleas flash in the current and the boy sees the velvety puffs of silt where crawfish have shot back under rocks with fear of him. Before the water, the friend pants in terror, so the boy tucks it in his pocket and hops carefully across the rocks to the opposite bank. The leaves of the wood rustle and sunshine shakes down in a brief warm muddy rain. Beyond the stream is the dank overhang of the cliff, under which round stones mark out a ring in the mud. There are some curls of burned metal, mildewed spent shells from a shotgun, and bones chewed by an animal. The friend breathes deeply here, and traces its hand against the soot smoked on the rock ceiling, and a silver skin oozes down to blind its eye. Up the back of the cliff they go, grabbing at tree trunks and clawing the dirt to ascend the incline. Then suddenly they've plunged to the top and the summer has fallen away.

The ground is covered with black and brown leaves, and the wind has shaken the treetops gray. There's a gravestone, white with chips of mica, and with a carving of an arum lily garbled and shallowed by weather, and violets growing all around. All already ready, says the friend. The boy sighs. Let's run away, he says. The friend is silent. I'm hungry, says the boy. You're never hungry now, says the friend, and that's true. The boy shrugs. The friend ruminates, and chews a sprig of poison ivy. Suddenly its hot hiss snakes out and its tongue is in the boy's ear. Poisoned you! cries the friend. The boy screams his laughter and he's running through the wood yelling, I'll find the antidote, and the friend strolls after him, smiling.

The boy and the mother sit Indian style on the boy's bed and play Cat's Cradle. The boy threads his fingers through the string to make the Cradle. The mother slips her hands into the maze. Pinching the taut cord, she whisks the boy's fingers free, and makes the Soldier's Bed. The boy snatches at the intersections, and pulls them through themselves, and the Candles shine in his hands. The mother reaches over awkwardly, and twists the string. Its bite tightens around the boy, and his skin swells and reddens. With a wrench of her wrist, she constructs the Manger between them. The boy's tiny fingers go darting among the knots. Before she knows it, he's imprisoned in Diamonds. We won! exults the mother. The boy smiles at her. His eyes are prisms for the day's light. She sees that there's something he holds in his mouth, gleaming dark and wet. A candy, a tongue, a morsel of mercury.

The mother reaches slowly for the bowl of water that stands by her son's painting set, on the night table, dips her hand in it, and with a panicked lunge, she flicks the liquid on the boy. It wrenches back on the bed with a jolt and a high-pitched moan. Her hand flies to her throat. She squeezes her eyes closed. Hey! protests the boy. What are you doing? Then he lurches for the bowl and begins to flick her back, in messy muddy splashes. The mother quavers and laughs in great gulps. The paint water soaks into the blankets, patterning her legs and hands with blurred designs, mottled markings, scaly smudges in brownish red and brownish blue and brownish green.

She lets the boy spill out the whole bowl, and although she changes the linens and blots the bed with towels to soak up the moisture, he still makes her flip the whole mattress before bedtime, so that the friend can nest there with no fear of the wet.

The boy discovers the friend hidden away in the fortress that sprawls across the living room, layer upon layer of sheets and wool blankets and towels and clothes slung between armchairs. The friend is prone, half sunk into the floor, disappearing into the wood like a ship slowly submerging below the skin of the sea. The boy throws his arms about the friend and covers it with chafing kisses. The friend coughs faintly but its eyes flash into brightness, burning the boy where the friend's gaze falls on him. What's wrong? the boy whispers fiercely. What's happened? You haven't gone, croaks the friend, you're here. I'm here, says the boy, of course I'm here.

The friend and the boy stand up and spin themselves in circles. Even when the dizziness has passed the boy can't remember what's where in the room outside the fortress. The French doors, the fireplace, the grandfather clock have all lost their places. The friend draws three doors for the boy. Where do they lead? says the friend.

The boy thinks hard. The first door, he says, a garden full of delicious fruit that feels pain when you bite it. Your turn. The friend considers. It says, the second door: a world in the center of the earth where you're turned inside out. You walk backward, talk backward, and see backward. Third door? The boy imagines. Third door, he says, somebody else. You can live in their body, but they control all your movements and your thoughts. The friend laughs. Pick a door, it says. The boy spins and spins until he doesn't remember which door is which. He opens one and falls out into darkness.

✕

In the yard, in her bathing suit and sunglasses, the mother sits rigid in the blare of the sun. Little worms of perspiration nose their way out of her skin and trail across her upper lip. Beside her is a glass of ice water; she picks it up to watch the blades of grass, pale with the cold of the glass, rise shakily from their crushing. Glossy crows settle over the lawn. She lies down but finds she can't endure the crawling of the grass across the back of her neck. A dragonfly comes crashing toward her face and she gasps. A gnat executes stiff seizures in the cold of the ice water. Her fingernails ache from the dirt packed beneath them. She puffs at a dying dandelion to make a wish, and the seeds blow back and stick to her lips and tongue. She plucks at the petals of a daisy, then beheads the whole thing summarily with a jerk of her thumb. *Mama had a baby and its head popped off!* she sings.

The boy is staring at the lion and he doesn't dare to move. The boy is in the big blue armchair in the living room, with the lamp in the shape of a dancing lady spilling light from the table beside him, but the lion only a few feet away is in darkness, a darkness that grows thicker and thinner, so the boy keeps losing sight of the lion, though neither of them is moving.

Into the boy's dream comes the friend, and the boy feels relief like the sudden release of a waterfall that's been dammed up, and with his eyes he signals the presence of the lion to the friend. The friend stays very still, and the darkness blows like wind over its face, and the boy loses and finds the friend's features for hours. At last the boy comes to wonder, in a rush of urgency, why the friend doesn't slay the lion. Kill it! whispers the boy. Please, kill it! The friend makes a sign and the boy sees that he himself is holding a long dagger. Me? I can't, pleads the boy. Please, kill it. The friend gestures to the boy to make use of the dagger. The boy stares aghast at the lion. Its eyes are mournful like the eyes of the boy's dog that had died, but there's a low growl coming from it like the moans of the tomcats that fight in the yard at night. The boy doesn't move. The lion climbs painfully to its feet and pads over to the boy and lies down beside him. Wondering and trembling, the boy places his hand on the lion's head. The friend spins around, claps its hands, and screams, and the lion's jaws hurtle open and its roar is pounding the boy like blows, and his terror is gagging his throat.

He comes awake with the friend beside him in bed, laughing and fanning the boy's face. That was a close one! says the friend, twinkling. What were you thinking? You almost got us killed, it giggles, and cuddles. The boy falls back into sleep, with his eyes screwed tight shut against dreams, and his skin smelling sour with dried crust of sweat.

The mother goes in the gloaming to the grave in the wood. She sits. Moths smack against her flashlight and are snarled in her hair. After some time, she climbs back down the cliff and wades into the stream, flinching at the bite of the water on her skin. She drops a ring, a small plastic figurine, and a gray fedora into the water. She makes three wishes. With her toe she buries the ring and the toy in the mud, and she watches the floating fedora tear against some bracken on the bank and be devoured by shadows. On the way home she bats in a fury against the thorns that snag her clothes and beat her legs.

She sits on the porch. The screaming of the mosquitoes, an incessant and furious anguish, is overwhelming; it seems to the mother that all the darkness of the lawn might be a black cloud of suffering insects; but nothing bites her. There's a damp smell and she feels her skin crawling, flinching away from her bones. Behind her, the screen door slaps against the jamb in the windless, ponderous night, and the mother stays very still, only slightly stiffening her back.

Before dawn she goes into the boy's room and lifts his body from the bed. She bears him cautiously out of the house to the car, and tucks him into the back seat. His clothes are already folded on the passenger seat. In the minute between the starting of the car and rolling out of their driveway, the mother's alarm grows so fierce that her vision is blurred. Once they gain the public road, it's vanished, and she's calm and deadened. She drives to the school and she parks.

When the sun comes up and the doors groan open and the flag struggles up into the pale air above her, she's ready. By the time the buses come marching in disciplined formation up the drive, he's awake. He doesn't seem alarmed by his abduction; just sleepy and bewildered and quiescent. They get his overalls on and his Velcro firmly strapped. He observes the patterns described by the hundreds of small milling bodies with grave interest. She holds onto his hand as far as the classroom door. For some time she sits in the car and watches, but nothing comes or goes until she does.

Alone in the house, the friend trickles from room to room, carried by a draught that floats past the curtains, through the walls, and around the doors. The molecules of the air bruise the friend's body and it suffers this.

In her car, driving, the mother thinks of the friend with shaken pity, and in his classroom the boy draws a picture with a blank face and long arms like tangled ropes and a sky full of dashes like rain falling like arrows or like shooting stars.

The friend drifts into a cobweb and clings there till its weight rends the strands and it resumes its meandering course. Where it drags along the floor, dust gathers on its skin, smothering the pores. The eyes of the friend empty and its mouth consumes itself. At last, with a sigh, it disperses.

At the end of the day, the mother watches to see that the boy files out with the others, and then in her car she shoots out ahead of the school bus to be ready to greet him when he jumps down the steps to disembark at the end of their drive. He's glowing like a new penny and he navigates the yard in a series of bounds. He has a collage for the fridge, of black horses pasted on a picture of a coral reef, and he has a caterpillar made of pipe cleaners. The mother and the boy nestle the caterpillar in the grass at the base of the sycamore to protect the tree house.

There are mimeographed lists from the teacher, of Things to Buy and Things to Do, and the boy has won a ribbon for thinking of the most words beginning with A. At lunchtime the other children had raised an outcry over the boy's purple pickled egg, and the mother promises that tomorrow he will have a white-bread sandwich cut in triangles and an apple with a leaf still on the stem. For recess they learned to jump rope while singing songs and afterward the teacher read a story that the boy had never heard, about a child who flies on the back of the wind. The boy runs about the house, visiting the attic and the basement and the bathroom, as if to see how different they've become. He told a girl in his class about the pond and the girl didn't believe that he has one and the mother says that the girl can come and see for herself, with some other of the boy's classmates, if he would like.

During dinner the boy bounces up and down, upsetting the jar of cucumber salad. He runs out twice to make sure that he has everything in his backpack that he'll need at school the next day, and three times to check that the caterpillar is still in place, guarding the tree house. He doesn't mention the friend, and his eyes are the color that the mother remembers.

By bedtime the boy is exhausted and the mother tucks him in and sings *mairzy doats and dozy doats and liddle lamzy divey* and he accompanies her in a contented blur of humming that spins around the edge of the tune. When she turns out the light and clicks closed the door he's already quite asleep.

He wakes not because of the volume of the breathing in the room or because of its horrible wet crackling and sucking, but because of the heat the breath gives off, a heat like an anvil, which crushes him into the bed. The windows are fogged over and the moon leaks through the droplets on the glass in weak smears of sickly light, like the ghosts of murdered stars.

He knows his waking has been noticed, for whatever it

is is now holding its breath. He can hear the interminable, deliberate creak of the floorboards where something is shifting its weight under the bed with infinite caution and cunning. Then a terrible quiet. The boy quakes and his spasmodic gasp is like a slap cracking across the silent face of the darkness. The longest pause. At last the bed begins to joggle teasingly and then to rock violently so he can barely keep from sliding off. Every time his hand or foot slips over the side of the mattress he sobs with terror and feels the humid wind where something has just missed its snatch at him. The earthquake in the bed is because the thing is shaking with laughter. Whatever is under the bed is laughing.

Then the laughter stops, and the smell comes up, dank and congealed, and he can feel the putrefying odor worming inside his pyjamas and bloating his skin with its stink, and the monster stretches itself. The room tilts as the monster ripples its spine, voluptuous; and the flayed leather of its body rustles and sucks as it moves, and it unfurls from under the bed, he sees its arm creep out, as if on a thousand little millipedal feet, right there before him, in the same air that's burning and lashing against his own starting eyeballs, and the nails of the thing shred whatever faint moonlight has crept through the steam in the room, and the boy knows, he knows, its head is coming out next, and he hears the cut and the thrust and the singing of its teeth as they emerge, smiling and smiling and smiling.

Micaela Morrissette

has been anthologized in *Best American Fantasy* (Prime Books),
The Pushcart Prize XXXIII (Pushcart Press), *Best Horror of the
Year* (Night Shade), and *The Weird* (Tor and Atlantic/Corvus).
Periodical publications include *Conjunctions* (where she is the
managing editor), *Tor.com*, *Ninth Letter*, and *Weird Tales*.

DIAL TONE

BENJAMIN PERCY

A jogger spotted the body hanging from the cell tower. At first he thought it was a mannequin. That's what he told Z-21, the local NBC affiliate. The way the wind blew it, the way it flopped limply, made it appear insubstantial, maybe stuffed with straw. It couldn't be a body, he thought, not in a place like Redmond, Oregon, a nowhere town on the edge of a great wash of desert. But it was. It was the body of a man. He had a choke chain, the kind you buy at Pet Depot, wrapped around his neck and anchored to the steel ladder that rose twelve hundred feet in the air to the tip of the tower, where a red light blinked a warning.

Word spread quickly. And everyone, the whole town, it seemed, crowded around, some of them with binoculars and cameras, to watch three deputies, joined by a worker from Clark Tower Service, scale the tower and then descend with the body in a sling.

I was there. And from where I stood, the tower looked like a great spear thrust into the hilltop.

Yesterday—or maybe it was the day before—I went to work, like I always go to work, at West Teleservices Corporation, where, as a marketing associate, I go through the same motions every morning. I hit the power button on my computer and listen to it hum and mumble and blip to life. I settle my weight into my ergonomic chair. I fit the headset around my skull and into my ear and take a deep breath, and, with the pale light of the monitor washing over me, I dial the first number on the screen.

In this low-ceilinged fluorescent-lit room, there are twenty-four rows of cubicles, each ten deep. I am C5. When I take a break and stand up and peer into the cubicle to my right, C6, I find a Greg or a Josh or a Linda—every day a new name to remember, a new hand to shake, or so it seems, with the turnover rate so high. This is why I call everyone you.

"Hey, you," I say. "How's it going?"

A short, toad-like woman in a Looney Toons sweatshirt massages the bridge of her nose and sighs, "You know how it is."

In response I give her a sympathetic smile, before looking away, out over the vast hive of cubicles that surrounds us. The air is filled with so many voices, all of them coming together into one voice that reads the same script, trying to make a sale for AT&T, Visa, Northwest Airlines, Sandals Beach Resorts, among our many clients.

There are always three supervisors on duty, all of them beefy men with mustaches. Their bulging bellies remind me of feed sacks that might split open with one slit of a knife. They wear polo shirts with "West Teleservices" embroidered on the breast. They drink coffee from stainless-steel mugs. They never seem to sit down. Every few minutes I feel a rush of wind at the back of my neck as they hurry by, usually to heckle some associate who hasn't met the hourly quota.

"Back to work, C5," one of them tells me, and I roll my eyes at C6 and settle into my cubicle, where the noise all around me falls away into a vague murmur, like the distant drone of bees.

I'm having trouble remembering things. Small things, like where I put my keys, for instance. Whether or not I put on deodorant or took my daily vitamin or paid the cable bill. Big things, too. Like, getting up at 6 a.m. and driving to work on a Saturday, not realizing my mistake until I pull into the empty parking lot.

Sometimes I walk into a room or drive to the store and can't remember why. In this way I am like a ghost: someone who can travel through walls and find myself someplace else in the middle of a sentence or thought and not know what brought me there. The other night I woke up to discover I was walking down the driveway in my pajamas, my bare feet blue in the moonlight. I was carrying a shovel.

Today I'm calling on behalf of Capital One, pitching a mileage card. This is what I'm supposed to say: *Hello, is this _____? How are you doing today, sir/ma'am? That's wonderful! I'm calling with a fantastic offer from Capital One. Did you know that with our no-annual-fee No-Hassle Miles Visa Signature Card you can earn 25 percent more than regular mileage cards, with 1.25 miles for every $1 spent on purchases? On top of that, if you make just $3,000 in purchases a year, you'll earn 20,000 bonus miles!*

And so on.

The computer tells me what to tell them. The bold sections indicate where I ought to raise my voice for emphasis. If the customer tries to say they aren't interested, I'm supposed to keep talking, to pretend I don't hear. If I stray too far from the script and if one of the supervisors is listening in, I will feel a hand on my shoulder and hear a voice whispering, "Stay on target. Don't lose sight of your primary objective."

The lights on the tops of cell towers are meant to warn pilots to stay away. But they have become a kind of beacon. Migratory birds mistake them for the stars they use to navigate, so they circle such towers in a trance, sometimes crashing into a structure, its steadying guy wires, or even into other birds. And sometimes they keep circling until they fall to the ground, dead from exhaustion. You can find them all around our cell tower: thousands of them, dotting the hilltop, caught in the sagebrush and pine boughs like ghostly ornaments. Their bones are picked clean by ants. Their feathers are dampened by the rain and bleached by the sun and ruffled and loosened and spread like spores by the wind.

In the sky, so many more circle, screeching their frustration as they try to find their way south. Of course they discovered the body. As he hung there, swinging slightly in the wind, they roosted on his shoulders. They pecked away his eyes, and they pecked away his cheeks, so that we could see all of his teeth when the deputies brought him down. He looked like he was grinning.

At night, from where I lie in bed, I can see the light of the cell tower—through the window, through the branches of a juniper tree, way off in the distance—like a winking red eye that assures me of the confidentiality of some terrible secret.

Midmorning, I pop my neck and crack my knuckles and prepare to make maybe my fortieth or sixtieth call of the day. "Pete Johnston" is the name on the screen. I say it aloud—twice—the second time as a question. I feel as though I have heard the name before, but really, that means nothing when you consider the hundreds of thousands of people I have called in my three years working here. I notice that his number, 503-531-1440, is local. Normally I pay no attention to the address listing unless the voice on the other end has a thick accent I can't quite decipher—New Jersey? Texas? Minnesota?—but in this case I look and see that he lives just outside of Redmond, in a new housing development only a few miles away.

"Yeah?" is how he answers the phone.

"Hello. Is this Pete Johnston?"

He clears his throat in a growl. "You a telemarketer?"

"How are you doing today, sir?"

"Bad."

"I'm calling on behalf of—"

"Look, cocksucker. How many times I got to tell you? Take me off your list."

"If you'll just hear me out, I want to tell you about a fantastic offer from—"

"You people are so fucking pathetic."

Now I remember him. He said the same thing before, a week or so ago, when I called him. "If you ever fucking call me again, you fucking worthless piece of shit," he said, "I'll reach through the phone and rip your tongue out."

He goes off on a similar rant now, asking me how can I live with myself, if every time I call someone they answer with hatred?

For a moment I forget about the script and answer him. "I don't know," I say.

"What the—?" he says, his voice somewhere between panicked and incensed. "What the hell are you doing in my house? I thought I told you to—"

There is a noise—the noise teeth might make biting hurriedly into melon—punctuated by a series of screams. It makes me want to tear the headset away from my ear.

And then I realize I am not alone. Someone is listening. I don't know how—a certain displacement of sound as the phone rises from the floor to an ear—but I can sense it.

"Hello?" I say.

The line goes dead.

Sometimes, when I go to work for yet another eight-hour shift or when I visit my parents for yet another casserole dinner, I want to be alone more than anything in the world. But once I'm alone, I feel I can't stand another second of it. Everything is mixed up.

This is why I pick up the phone sometimes and listen. There is something reassuring about a dial tone. That simple sound, a low purr, as constant and predictable as the sun's path across the sky. No matter if you are in Istanbul or London or Beijing or Redmond, you can bring your ear to the receiver and hear it.

Sometimes I pick up the phone and bring it to my ear for the same reason people raise their heads to peer at the moon when they're in a strange place. It makes them—it makes me—feel oriented, calmer than I was a moment before.

Perhaps this has something to do with why I drive to the top of the hill and park beneath the cell tower and climb onto the hood of my Neon and lean against the windshield with my hands folded behind my head to watch the red light blinking and the black shapes of birds swirling against the backdrop of an even blacker sky.

I am here to listen. The radio signals emanating from the

tower sound like a blade hissing through the air or a glob of spit sizzling on a hot stove: something dangerous, about to draw blood or catch fire. It's nice.

I imagine I hear in it the thousands of voices channeling through the tower at any given moment, and I wonder what terrible things could be happening to these people that they want to tell the person on the other end of the line but don't. .

A conversation overheard:
"Do you live here?"
"Yes."
"Are you Pete Johnston?"
"Yes. Who are you? What do you want?"
"To talk to you. Just to talk."

Noon, I take my lunch break. I remove my headset and lurch out of my chair with a groan and bring my fists to my back and push until I feel my vertebrae separate and realign with a juicy series of pops. Then I wander along my row, moving past so many cubicles, each with a person hunched over inside it—and for a moment West Teleservices feels almost like a chapel, with everyone bowing their heads and murmuring together, as if exorcising some private pain.

I sign out with one of the managers and enter the break room, a forty-by-forty-foot room with white walls and a white dropped ceiling and a white linoleum floor. There are two sinks, two microwaves, two fridges, a Coke machine and a SNAX machine. In front of the SNAX machine stands C6, the woman stationed in the cubicle next to me. A Looney Toons theme apparently unifies her wardrobe, since today she wears a sweatshirt with Sylvester on it. Below him, blocky black letters read, WITHCONTHIN. She stares with intense concentration at the candy bars and chip bags and gum packs, as if they hold some secret message she has yet to decode.

I go to the nearby water fountain and take a drink and dry my mouth with my sleeve, all the while watching C6, who hardly seems to breathe. "Hey, you," I say, moving to within a few steps of her. "Doing all right there?"

She looks at me, her face creased with puzzlement. Then she shakes her head, and a fog seems to lift, and for the first time she sees me and says, "Been better."

"I know how you feel."

She looks again to the SNAX machine, where her reflection hovers like a ghost. "Nobody knows how I feel."

"No. You're wrong. I know."

At first C6 seems to get angry, her face cragging up, but then I say, "You feel like you would feel if you were hurrying along and smacked your shin against the corner of the coffee table. You feel like you want to yell a lot. The pain hasn't completely arrived, but you can see it coming, and you want to yell at it, scare it off." I go to the fridge labeled A-K and remove from it my sack lunch and sit down at one of the five tables staggered throughout the room. "Something like that, anyway."

An awkward silence follows, in which I eat my ham sandwich and C6 studies me closely, no doubt recognizing in me some common damage, some likeness of herself.

Then C6 says, "Can't seem to figure out what I want," nodding at the vending machine. "I've been staring at all these goodies for twenty minutes, and I'll be darned if I know what I want." She forces a laugh and then says with some curiosity in her voice, "Hey, what's with your eye?"

I cup a hand to my ear like a seashell, like: Say again?

"Your eyeball." She points and then draws her finger back as if she might catch something from me. "It's really red."

"Huh," I say and knuckle the corner of my eye as if to nudge away a loose eyelash. "Maybe I've got pinkeye. Must have picked it up off a doorknob."

"It's not pink. It's red. It's really, really red."

The nearest reflective surface is the SNAX machine. And she's right. My eye is red. The dark luscious red of an apple. I at once want to scream and pluck it out and suck on it.

"I think you should see somebody," C6 says.

"Maybe I should." I comb a hand back through my hair and feel a vaguely pleasant release as several dozen hairs come out by the roots, just like that, with hardly any effort. I hold my hand out before me and study the clump of hairs woven in between the fingers and the fresh scabs jewelling my knuckles and say to no one in particular, "Looks like I'm falling apart."

Have you ever been on the phone, canceling a credit card or talking to your mother, when all of a sudden—with a pop of static—another conversation bleeds into yours? Probably. It happens a lot, with so many radio signals hissing through the air. What you might not know is, what you're hearing might have been said a minute ago or a day ago or a week ago or a month ago. Years ago.

When you speak into the receiver, your words are compressed

into an electronic signal that bounces from phone to tower to satellite to phone, traveling thousands of miles, even if you're talking to your next-door neighbor, Joe. Which means there's plenty of room for a signal to ricochet or duplicate or get lost. Which means there are so many words—the ghosts of old conversations—floating all around us.

Consider this possibility. You pick up your phone and hear a voice—your voice—engaged in some ancient conversation, like that time in high school when you asked Natasha Flatt out for coffee and she made an excuse about her cat being sick. It's like a conversation shouted into a canyon, its words bouncing off walls to eventually come fluttering back to you, warped and soft and sounding like somebody else.

Sometimes this is what my memory feels like. An image or a conversation or a place will rise to the surface of my mind, and I'll recognize it vaguely, not knowing if I experienced it or saw it on television or invented it altogether.

Whenever I try to fix my attention on something, a red light goes on in my head, and I'm like a bird circling in confusion.

I find myself on the sidewalk of a new hillside development called Bear Brook. Here all the streets have names like Kodiak and Grizzly. All around me are two-story houses of a similar design, with freshly painted gray siding and river-rock entryways and cathedral windows rising above their front doors to reveal chandeliers in the foyer of each. Each home has a sizable lot that runs up against a pine forest. And each costs more than I would make in twenty years with West Teleservices.

A garbage truck rushes past me, raising tiny tornadoes of

dust and trash, and I raise my hand to shield my face and notice a number written on the back of it, just below my knuckles—13743—and though I am sure it will occur to me later, for the moment I can't for the life of me remember what it means.

At that moment a bird swoops toward a nearby house. Mistaking the window for a piece of sky, it strikes the glass with a thud and falls into the rose garden beneath it, absently fluttering its wings; soon it goes still. I rush across the lawn and into the garden and bend over to get a better look at it. A bubble of blood grows from its beak and pops. I do not know why, but I reach through the thorns and pick up the bird and stroke its cool, reddish feathers. Its complete lack of weight and its stillness overwhelm me.

When the bird fell, something fell off a shelf inside me—a nice, gold-framed picture of my life, what I dreamed it would be, full of sunshine and ice cream and go-go dancers. It tumbled down and shattered, and my smiling face dissolved into the distressed expression reflected in the living room window before me.

I look alarmingly ugly. My eyes are black-bagged. My skin is yellow. My upper lip is raised to reveal long, thin teeth. Mine is the sort of face that belongs to someone who bites the heads off chickens in a carnival pit, not the sort that belongs to a man who cradles in his hands a tiny red-winged blackbird. The vision of me, coupled with the vision of what I once dreamed I would be—handsome, wealthy, feared by men and cherished by women—assaults me, the ridiculousness of it and also the terror, the realization that I have crept to the edge of a void and am on the verge of falling in, barely balanced.

And then my eyes refocus, concentrating on a farther distance, where through the window I see a man rising from a couch and approaching me. He is tall and square-shouldered. His hair is the color of dried blood on a bandage. He looks at me with derision, saying through the glass, "The hell do you think you're doing on my property?" without saying a word.

I drop the bird and raise my hand, not quite waving, the gesture more like holding up something dark to the light. He does not move except to narrow his eyes further. There's a stone pagoda at the edge of the garden, and when I take several steps back my heel catches against it. I stumble and then lose my balance entirely, falling hard, sprawling out on the lawn. The gray expanse of the sky fills my vision. Moisture from the grass seeps into my jeans and dampens my underwear. My testicles tighten like a fist.

In the window the man continues to watch me. He has a little red mustache, and he fingers it. Then he disappears from sight, moving away from the window and toward the front door.

Just before I stagger off the lawn and hurry along the sidewalk and retreat from this place, my eyes zero in on the porch, waiting for the man to appear there, and I catch sight of the address: 13743.

And then I am off and running. A siren announces itself nearby. The air seems to vibrate with its noise. It is a police cruiser, I'm certain, though how I can tell the difference between it and an ambulance, I don't know. Either way, someone is in trouble.

The body was blackened by its lengthy exposure to radio frequency fields. Cooked. Like a marshmallow left too long over flame. This is why the deputies shut off the transmitters, when they climbed the tower.

Z-21 interviewed Jack Millhouse, a professor of radiation biology at Oregon State. He had a beard, and he stroked it thoughtfully. He said that climbing the tower would expose a person to radio frequencies so powerful they would cook the skin. "I'd ask around at the ER," he said. "See if somebody has come in with radiation burns."

Then they interviewed a woman in a yellow, too-large T-shirt and purple stretch pants. She lived nearby and had seen the commotion from her living room window. She thought a man was preparing to jump, she said. So she came running in the hopes of praying him down. She had a blank, round face no one would ever call beautiful. "It's just awful," she said, her lips disappearing as she tightened her mouth. "It's the most horrible thing in the world, and it's right here, and we don't know why."

I know I am not the only one who has been cut off by a swerving car in traffic or yelled at by a teacher in a classroom or laughed at by a woman in a bar. I am not the only one who has wished someone dead and imagined how it might happen, pleasuring in the goriest details.

Here is how it might happen:

I am in a kitchen with duck-patterned wallpaper. I stand over a man with a Gerber hunting knife in my hand. There is blood dripping off the knife, and there is blood coming out of the man. Gouts of it. It matches the color of his hair. A forked vein rises on his forehead to reveal the panicked beating of his heart. A gray string of saliva webs the corner of his mouth. He holds his hands out, waving me away, and I cut my way through them.

A dog barks from the hallway, and the man screams a

repulsive scream, a girlish scream, and all this noise sounds to me far away, like a conversation overheard between pops of static.

I am aware of my muscles and their purpose as never before, using them to place the knife, putting it finally to the man's chest, where it will make the most difference.

At first the blade won't budge, caught on a rib, and then it slips past the bone and into the soft red interior, deeper and then deeper still, with the same feeling you get when you break through that final restraining grip and enter a woman fully. The response is just as cathartic: a shriek, a gasp, a stiffening of the limbs followed by a terrible shivering that eventually gives way to a great, calming release.

There is blood everywhere—on the knife, on the floor, gurgling from the newly rendered wound that looks so much like a mouth—and the man's eyes are open and empty, and his sharp pink tongue lolls out the side of his mouth. I am amazed at the thrill I feel.

When I surprised him, only a few minutes ago, he was on the phone. I spot it now, on the shale floor, with a halo of blood around it. I pick it up and bring it to my ear and hope for the familiar, calming murmur of the dial tone.

Instead I hear a voice. "Hello?" it says.

One day, I think, maybe I'll write a story about all of this. Something permanent. So that I can trace every sentence and find my way to the end and back to the beginning without worrying about losing my way.

The telling would be complicated.

To write a story like this you would have to talk about what it means to speak into a headset all day, reading from a script you don't believe in, conversing with bodiless voices that snarl with hatred, voices that want to claw out your eyes and scissor off your tongue. And you would have to show what that does to a person, experiencing such a routine day after day, with no relief except for the occasional coffee break where you talk about the television show you watched last night.

And you would have to explain how the man named Pete Johnston sort of leaned and sort of collapsed against the fridge, how a magnet fell to the linoleum with a clack after you flashed the knife in a silvery arc across his face and then his outstretched hand and then into that soft basin behind the collarbone. After that came blood. And screaming. Again you stabbed the body, in the thigh, the belly, your muscles pulsing with a red electricity. Something inside you, some internal switch, had been triggered, filling you with an unthinking adrenaline that made you feel capable of turning over Volkswagens, punching through concrete, tearing phone books in half.

And you would have to end this story by explaining what it felt like to pull the body from the trunk of your car and hoist it to your shoulder and begin to climb the tower—one rung, then another—going slowly. You breathed raggedly. The dampness of your sweat mingled with the dampness of blood. From here—thirty, then forty, then fifty feet off the ground—you could see the chains of light on Route 97 and Highway 100, each bright link belonging to a machine that carried inside it a man who could lose control in an instant, distracted by the radio or startled by a deer or overwhelmed by tiredness, careening off the asphalt and into the surrounding woods. It could happen to anyone.

Your thighs trembled. You were weary, dizzy. Your fillings tingled, and a funny baked taste filled your mouth. The edges of your eyes went white and then crazy with streaks of color. But you continued climbing, with the wind tugging at your body, with the blackness of the night and the black shapes of birds all around you, the birds swirling through the air like ashes thrown from a fire. And let's not forget the sound—the sound of the tower—how it sounded almost like words. The hissing of radio frequencies, the voices of so many others coming together into one voice that coursed through you in dark conversation.

Benjamin Percy

is the author of two novels, *Red Moon* (Grand Central/Hachette, 2013) and *The Wilding*, as well as two books of short stories, *Refresh, Refresh* and *The Language of Elk*. His fiction and nonfiction have been published in *Esquire* (where he is a contributing editor), *GQ*, *Time*, *Men's Journal*, *Outside*, *The Wall Street Journal*, *Tin House* and *The Paris Review*. His honors include an NEA fellowship, the Whiting Writer's Award, the Plimpton Prize, the Pushcart Prize and inclusion in Best American Short Stories and Best American Comics. He is the writer-in-residence at St. Olaf College and teaches at the low-residency MFA program at Pacific University.

HOW

ROXANE GAY

How These Things Come To Pass

Hanna does her best thinking late at night when all the usurpers living in her house are asleep. If it isn't winter, which is not often, she climbs out onto her roof with a pack of cigarettes and a lighter. She smokes and stares up at the blue black night sky. She lives in the North Country where the stars make sense. Hanna shares her home with her unemployed husband, her twin sister, her sister's husband, their son, and her father. She is the only one who works—mornings, she waits tables the Koivu Café and nights, she tends bar at Karpela's Supper Club. She leaves most of her tips at her best friend Laura's house. Hanna is plotting her escape.

The most popular dish at the Koivu is the *pannukakku*, a Finnish pancake. If Old Larsen, is too hung over, Hanna will heat the iron skillet in the oven and mix the batter—first eggs, beating them lightly, slowly adding the honey, salt, and milk, finally sifting the flour in. She enjoys the ratchet sound as she pulls the sift trigger. She sways from side to side, and imagines she is a Flamenco dancer. She is in Spain where it is warm, where there is sun and beauty. Hanna likes making *pannukakku* with extra butter so the edges of the pancakes are golden and crisp. Sometimes, she'll carefully remove the edges from a pancake and eat them just like that. She's still in Spain, eating bread from a *panadería*, perhaps enjoying a little wine. Then she'll hear someone shout order up and she is no longer in Spain. She is in the middle of nowhere, standing over a hot, greasy stove.

Peter, Hanna's husband, comes in for breakfast every morning. Hanna saves him a spot at the counter and she takes his order. He

123

stares down her uniform, ogling her cleavage and waggling his eyebrows. She feigns affection, smacks his head with her order pad, and hands his ticket to Old Larsen who growls, "We don't do any damn substitutions," but then makes Peter three eggs over easy, hash browns with onions and cheese, four slices of bacon, white toast, and two *pannukakku*, slightly undercooked. When his food is ready, Hanna takes a break, sits next to Peter, watches him eat. His beard is growing long. A man without a job doesn't need a clean face, he tells her. She hates watching Peter eat. She hates that he follows her to work. She hates his face.

Her husband thinks they are trying to have a child. He wears boxers instead of briefs though he prefers the security of the latter. Peter once read in a magazine that wearing boxers increased sperm motility. He and Hanna only have sex when the home ovulation kit he bought at Walmart indicates she is fertile. Peter would prefer to have sex every day. Hanna would prefer to never have sex with Peter again, not because she's frigid but because she finds it difficult to become aroused by a perpetually unemployed man. Two years ago, Hanna said she was going on vacation with Laura downstate and instead drove to Marquette and had her tubes tied. She wasn't going to end up like her mother with too many children in a too small house with too little to eat. Despite her best efforts, however, she has found herself living in a too small house with too many people and too little to eat. It is a bitter pill to swallow.

When she gets off work at three in the afternoon, Hanna goes home, washes the grease and salt from her skin, and changes into something cute but a little slutty. She heads to the university the next town over. She's 27 but looks far younger, so she pretends she's a student. Sometimes, she attends a class in one of the big lecture halls. She takes notes and plays with her hair and thinks about all the things she could have done. Other days, she sits in the library and reads books and learns things so that when she finally escapes she can be more than a waitress with a great rack in a dead Upper Michigan town.

Hanna flirts with boys because at the Michigan Institute of Technology there are lots and lots of boys who want nothing more than to be noticed by a pretty girl. She never pretends she's anything but smart. She's too old for that. Sometimes, the boys take her to the dining hall or the Campus Café for a snack. She tells them she's in mechanical engineering because Laura is a secretary in that department. Sometimes, the boys invite her to their messy dorm rooms littered with dirty laundry and video game consoles and roommates or their squalid apartments off campus. She gives them blowjobs and lays with them on their narrow twin beds covered in thin sheets and tells them lies they like to hear. After the boys fall asleep, Hanna heads back across the bridge to Karpela's where she tends bar until two in the morning.

Peter visits Hanna at the supper club too, but he has to pay for his drinks so he doesn't visit often. Don Karpela, the owner, is always around, grabbing at things with his meaty fingers. He's a greedy man and a friend of her father. Even though he's nearing sixty, Don is always breathing down Hanna's neck, bumping up against her in the cramped space behind the bar, telling her he'd make her damn happy if she'd leave her old man. When he does that, Hanna closes her eyes and breathes easy because she needs her job. If Peter is around when Don is making his moves, he'll laugh and raise his glass. "You can have her," he'll slur, as if he has a say in the matter.

After the bar closes Hanna wipes everything down and washes all the glasses and empties the ashtrays. She and Laura, who also works at the supper club, will sit on the hood of Hanna's car in the back alley and hold hands. Hanna will lean against Laura's shoulder and inhale deeply and marvel that her friend can still smell good after hours in that dark, smoky space where men don't hear the word *no*. If the night is empty enough, they will kiss for a very long time, until their cold lips become warm, until the world falls away, until their bodies feel like they will split at the heart. She and Laura never talk about these moments but when Hanna is plotting her escape, she is not going alone.

Hanna's twin sister Anna often waits up for Hanna. She worries. She always has. She's a nervous woman. As a child, she was a nervous girl. Their mother, before she left, liked to say that Hanna got all the *sisu*, the fierce strength that should have been shared by both girls. Hanna and Anna always knew their mother didn't know them at all. They were both strong and fierce. Anna's husband worked at the paper mill in Niagara until some foreign company bought it and closed it and then most everyone in town lost their homes because all the work that needed doing was already done. When Anna called, nervous as always, to ask if she and her family could stay with Hanna, she had not even posed the question before Hanna said, "Yes."

Hanna and Anna are not openly demonstrative but they love each other wildly. In high school, Anna dated a boy who didn't treat her well. When Hanna found out, she put a good hurting on him. Hanna pretended to be her sister and she took the bad boy up to the trails behind the county fairgrounds. She got down on her knees and started to give him head and she told him *if he ever laid a hand on her sister again* and before she finished that sentence, she bit down on his cock and told herself she wouldn't stop biting down until her teeth met. She smiled

126

when she tasted his blood. He screamed so softly it made the hairs on her arm stand on end. Hanna still sees that boy around town once in a while. He's not a boy anymore but he walks with a hitch and always crosses to the other side of the street when he sees her coming.

On the nights when Hanna and Laura sit on the hood of Laura's car and kiss until their cold lips warm, Anna stands outside on the front porch, shivering, waiting. Her cheeks flush. Her heart flutters around her chest awkwardly. Anna asks Hanna if she's seeing another man and Hanna tells her sister the truth. She says, "No," and Anna frowns. She knows Hanna is telling the truth. She knows Hanna is lying. She cannot quite figure out how she's doing both at the same time. The sisters smoke a cigarette together, and before they go in, Anna will place a gently hand on Hanna's arm. She'll say, "Be careful." Hanna will kiss her twin's forehead, and she'll think, "I will," and Anna will hear her.

How Hanna Khonen knows it is time to get the girl and get out of town

Hanna and Anna's father Red lives in the basement. He's not allowed on the second floor where everyone sleeps. When Peter asks why, Hanna just shakes her head and says, "It's personal." She doesn't share personal things with her husband. Her father used to work in the mines. When the last copper mine closed he didn't bother trying to learn a new trade. He started holding his back when he walked around, said he was injured. He collected disability and when that ran out, he lived with a series of girlfriends who each kicked him out before long. Finally, when there was no woman in town who would give him the time of day, Red showed up on Hanna's doorstep, reeking of whiskey, his beard long and unkempt. He slurred an incoherent apology for being a lousy father. He begged his daughter to have mercy on an old man. Hanna wasn't moved by his plea but she knew he would be her problem one way or the other. She told him he could make himself comfortable in the basement, but if she ever saw him on the second floor, that would be that. It has been fifteen years since the mine closed but Red still calls himself a miner.

The whereabouts of Hanna and Anna's mother, Ilse, are unknown. She left when the girls were eleven. It was a Thursday morning. Ilse got the girls and their brothers ready for school, fed them breakfast—steel cut oats topped with sliced bananas. She kissed them atop their pale blonde heads and told them to be good. She was gone when they returned home from school. For a while, they heard a rumor that Ilse had taken up with a shoe salesman in Marquette. Later, there was news of her from Iron Mountain, a dentist's wife, with a new family. Then there was no news at all.

Hanna and Anna have five brothers scattered throughout the state. They are mostly bitter, lazy, indifferent and unwilling to have a hand in the care and feeding of their father. When Hanna organized a conference call with her siblings to discuss the disposition of their father, The Boys, as they are collectively known, said it was women's work and if The Twins didn't want to do that work, they could let the old man rot. One of the brothers, Venn, offered to send Hanna or Anna, whomever shouldered the burden of caring for Red, twenty dollars a month. Simultaneously, The Twins told him to stick it up his ass and then they told The Boys to go fuck themselves. After they hung up, Hanna called Anna and Anna offered to take care of Red until he drank himself to death but Hanna worried that death by drink would take too long. Anna had a child to raise, after all.

It is an ordinary Tuesday when Hanna decides to go home after working at the café instead of heading across the bridge to the Institute to play make believe with college boys. She can feel grease oozing out of her pores and what she wants, more than anything, is to soak in a clean bathtub, in an empty house. When she pulls into her driveway and sees Anna pacing back and forth in front of the garage, Hanna knows there will be no bath or empty house today. She parks the car, takes a deep breath and joins her sister who informs Hanna that their mother is sitting on the Salvation Army couch in the living room drinking a cup of tea. Hanna thinks, "Of course she is."

How Hanna met and married Peter Lahti

Anna fell in love when she was seventeen. His name was Logan, and he lived on the reservation in Baraga. She loved his long black hair and his smooth brown skin and the softness of his voice. They met at a football game and the day after graduation, they married and moved. When Anna left, Hanna was happy for her sister, but she also hoped beyond all hopes that her sister and her new husband would take her with them. She could have said something. Years later Hanna realized she should have said something, but she became the one who stayed. She got an apartment of her own and started hanging out at the university sitting in on the classes she couldn't afford. Peter lived in the apartment next door and back then, he worked as a truck driver hauling lumber downstate so dating him was fine because he wasn't around much.

After a long trip where Peter was gone for three weeks, he showed up at Hanna's door, his hair slicked back, beard trimmed, wearing a button down shirt and freshly pressed jeans. In one hand, he held a cheap bouquet of carnations. He had forgotten that Hanna had told him, on their first date, that she hated carnations. He thrust the flowers into Hanna's hands, invited himself into her apartment and said, "I missed you so much. Let's get married." Hanna, elbow deep into a bottle of wine at that point, shrugged. Peter, an optimist at heart, took the gesture as a response in the affirmative. They married not long after in a ceremony attended by Anna and her husband, Red, and three of The Boys. No one from Peter's family attended. His mother was scandalized her boy would marry any child of Red Ikonen.

How Red Ikonen got his reputation

Red Ikonen had mining in his blood. His daddy and his daddy's daddy had been miners up in Calumet when mining was something that mattered up there and the town was rich and every Sunday the churches were full of good folks grateful for the bounties of the hard earth. As a boy, Red loved his father's stories about the world beneath the world. By the time it was Red's turn to head underground, there wasn't much mining left to do and that was a hell of a cross to bear. He was as a soldier without a war. Red started drinking to numb his disappointment. He married a pretty girl, had five handsome boys and two lovely girls and continued drinking to celebrate his good fortune. The pretty girl left and he drank so he wouldn't feel so lonesome. Finally, drinking was the only thing he knew how to do so that's just what he did.

He was a tall man—6'7", and he had a loud voice and no sense of how to act right. That sort of thing just wasn't in him. There wasn't a bar in town where Red hadn't started a fight or done something untoward with his woman or someone else's woman. Things had gotten so bad he needed to drive over to South Range or Chassell to drink with the old guys at the VFW who really were soldiers without a war because no one in town wanted to serve him a drink. When The Boys were still in town, bartenders would call and have one of them come get their father. By the time Red Ikonen was drinking so he wouldn't feel so lonesome he had become a mean drunk. He never had a kind word for his boys who drove miles into the middle of the night to bring their drunk daddy back home.

One by one The Boys left home, tried to get as far away from their father as possible, until it was only The Twins left and then he started doing untoward things with them and it was a small town so people talked and it wasn't long before no one at all wanted a thing to do with Red Ikonen.

How Laura and Hanna became best friends

Laura Kappi grew up next door to the Ikonens. For a while in high school, she dated one of The Boys, but then he moved away, went to college, and didn't bother to take her with him. Laura was, in fact, a friend to both Hanna and Anna throughout high school. When Anna and Logan moved down to Niagara, Laura saw how lost Hanna was without her twin. She decided to do her best to take Anna's place. Hanna was more than happy to let her. They became best friends and then they became more than friends but they never talked about it because there wasn't much to be said on the subject.

How Hanna reacts when she sees her mother for the first time in sixteen years

Before they go inside, Anna reaches for Hanna's waiting hand. They both squeeze, hard, their knuckles cracking and then The Twins go inside. Ilse Ikonen is sitting on the edge of the couch. She is a small woman with sharp features. She has always been beautiful and neither time nor distance has changed that. Her hair is graying around the scalp, her features hang a bit lower, but she doesn't look a day over forty. Red is sitting where he always sits during the day, in the recliner next to the couch staring at his estranged wife. He has tucked in his shirt, but his hands are shaking because he is trying not to drink. He wants to be clear headed but his wife is so damned beautiful that with or without the drink he doesn't know up from down. Peter is sitting next to Ilse, also staring, because the resemblance between his wife and her mother is uncanny. They have never met. Anna's husband Logan is sitting next to Peter, holding their son, half asleep, in his lap. He is deliberately avoiding any eye contact with his mother in law. He is helping his wife with the burden of her anger.

As soon as they enter the room, Hanna and Anna's stomachs churn. Beads of sweat slowly spread across their foreheads. Ilse leans forward, setting her teacup on the coffee table. She smiles at her daughters. Hanna thinks, "Why did you offer her tea?" Anna thinks, "I was being polite." Hanna bites her lip. "What are you doing here, Ilse?" she asks.

Ilse Ikonen uncrosses her legs and folds her hands in her lap. "It has been a long time," she says.

Hanna looks at all the broken people sitting in her living room on her broken furniture looking to her to fix their broken lives. She turns around and walks right back out the front door. Anna makes her excuses and rushes after her sister. She finds Hanna holding on to the still warm hood of her car, hunched over, throwing up. Anna's stomach rolls uncomfortably. When Hanna stands up, she wipes her lips with the back of her hand and says, "I mean... really?"

How Laura finally convinces Hanna to run away with her

Hanna sits in her car until Ilse Ikonen takes her leave and gets a room at the motel down the street. After her mother leaves, Hanna drives to campus and goes to the dank room of one of her college boys. She lies on his musty, narrow twin bed and stares at the constellation of glow in the dark stars on the ceiling while the boy awkwardly fumbles at her breasts with his bony fingers. She sighs, closes her eyes, thinks of Laura. Afterward, when the boy is fast asleep, his fingers curled in a loose fist near his mouth, Hanna slips out of bed and heads back across the bridge to Laura's house.

Laura smiles when she opens her front door. Hanna shrugs and stands in the doorway, her cheeks numb, still nauseous. She shoves her small hands into her pockets, tries to ignore the cold. Laura wraps her arms around herself, shifts quickly from one foot to the other. "Why don't you come in?"

Hanna shakes her head. "I can't do this anymore."

Laura arches an eyebrow and even though she is barefoot, she steps onto her snowy front porch. She gasps, steps onto Hanna's boots, slides her arms beneath Hanna's coat and around her waist. Laura lightly brushes her lips against Hanna's. Hanna closes her eyes. She breathes deeply.

How Hanna falls even more in love with Laura than she thought possible

When Laura can no longer feel her toes, she says, "We better get inside before I get frostbite and I am forced to spend the rest of my life hobbling after you."

Hanna nods and follows Laura into her house. It is familiar, has looked mostly the same for the past twenty years and in that there is comfort. Inside the foyer, amidst coats and boots, a shovel, a knitted scarf, a bag of salt, Hanna sinks to the floor and sits cross-legged. Laura sits across from Hanna, extends her legs, resting her cold feet in Hanna's lap.

"Do you want to tell me about it?"

Hanna shakes her head angrily. "My mother's back."

"I mean... really?" she says.

Hanna doesn't go home. She calls Anna and assures her sister that she's fine. Anna doesn't ask where she is. She's starting to make sense of things. Hanna lets Laura lead her up the steep staircase lined with books. She lets Laura put her into a hot bath. She lets Laura wash her clean. She follows Laura to bed and for the first time in months, she falls asleep in a mostly empty house. She thinks, "This is everything I want."

As Hanna sleeps, Laura calculates how much money she has saved, the tread on her tires, how far they will need to travel so that Hanna might begin to forget about the life she's leaving behind. It all makes Laura very tired but then she looks at Hanna's lower lip, how it trembles while she's sleeping.

How it has always been

The next morning, Laura hears the knocking at her front door. She wraps herself in a thin robe and takes one last

134

look at Hanna, still sleeping, lower lip still trembling. Laura has always loved Hanna even before she understood why her entire body flushed when she saw Hanna at school or running around her backyard or sitting on the roof outside her bedroom window. Dating one of The Boys a way to get closer to Hanna. Laura would kiss Hanna's brother and think of his sister, her smile, the way she walked around with her shoulder muscles bunched up. Being with the brother was not what Laura wanted but she told herself it was enough. For the first time Laura feels something unfamiliar in her throat. It makes her a little sick to her stomach. She thinks it might be hope. Downstairs, Anna is standing on the front porch shivering. She has a splitting headache. When Laura opens the door Anna quickly slips into the house. Anna squeezes Laura's hand and heads upstairs into Laura's bedroom. Anna crawls into bed behind her sister, wraps her arms around Hanna's waist. Hanna covers one of Anna's hands with hers. She is not quite awake yet.

"Don't make me go back there," Hanna says, hoarsely.

Anna tightens her arms around her sister, kisses Hanna's shoulder. Anna says, "You have to go back to say goodbye." There is a confidence in Anna's voice that reassures Hanna.

Hanna sighs, slowly opens her eyes. She sees Laura standing in the doorway. Hanna smiles. "You don't have to stand so far away," she says. Laura grins and crawls into bed with The Twins. Laura says, "Remember when we were kids and the three of us would lay on your roof at night during the summer to cool down?" Both Hanna and Anna nod. The three women roll onto their backs and stare at the ceiling—the cracks and water stains, how it sags. "We were miserable even then," Laura says.

now hanna finally confronts her mother

Where Hanna has always been the protector, Anna has always been the voice of reason, able to make the right choices between impossible alternatives. When they were girls and Hanna would plot retribution against anyone who had wronged The Twins, it was Anna who would deter her sister from acting thoughtlessly. When Red Ikonen would stumble into their room drunk and Hanna would try to stab him with a kitchen knife or bite his ear off it was Anna who grabbed her sister's arm and said, "It's him or Superior Home." It was Anna who would sing to her father and stroke his beard and soothe all the meanness out of him. In these moments, Hanna would feel so much anger inside her she thought her heart would rip apart but then she would let the knife fall to the floor or she would unclench her teeth because anything was better than Superior Home, the state facility where motherless children were often discarded until they turned eighteen. They heard stories bad enough to make them believe there were worse things than the stink of Red Ikonen's breath against their cheeks as he forgot how to behave like a proper father.

Anna held Hanna's hand as they walked back to their house, a bracing wind pushing their bodies through the snow. Hanna tried to breathe but found the air thin and cold and it hurt her lungs. As they climbed the porch stairs Hanna stopped, leaned against the railing, her body heavy.

"I don't feel so good," she said.

Anna pressed the cool palm of her hand against Hanna's forehead. "You get to leave soon," she said. "Hold on to that."

Hanna stared at her sister. She said, "Come with us—you and Logan and the baby."

Anna shook her head. "It's my turn to stay."

"Bullshit. We've taken our turns long enough."

The front door opened. Peter glared at The Twins. "Where the hell were you last night?" He grabbed Hanna by the elbow, pulling her into the house and she let him. She wanted to save what fight she had left.

In the living room the scene closely resembled the tableau Hanna stumbled into the previous day with Ilse Ikonen sitting on the couch, poised regally like she had never left and had no need to offer acts of contrition.

Hanna tried to squirm free from Peter's grasp and he finally relented when calmly, quietly, Anna said, "Let go of my sister." Peter held a natural distrust of twins. It wasn't normal, he thought, for there to be two people who were so identical. He also harbored no small amount of jealousy for the relationship twins shared. While he was not a bright man, Peter was smart enough to know he would never be as close to his wife as he wanted.

The Twins stood before their father, their mother, their husbands. They stood in the house where they had grown up filled with broken people and broken things. Anna thought, "This is the last time we will ever stand in this room," and Hanna suddenly felt like she could breathe again. She tried to say something but she couldn't find her voice. Her throat was dry and hollow. The Twins looked at their parents and thought about everything they had ever wanted to say to two people so ill-suited for doing right by their children.

"I'm sorry to intrude," Ilse said, her voice tight, her words clipped. She crossed her legs and fidgeted with a big diamond ring on her left hand. "I wanted to see how you girls and The Boys were doing, perhaps explain myself."

Anna shook her head. "Explanations aren't necessary," she said. "Your leaving is a long time gone."

Hanna removed her wedding ring and dropped it on the coffee table. Peter sneered and said, "Whatever," and Hanna rolled her eyes.

The Twins stood before their father, their mother, their husbands. They sucked in a great mass of air, threw their shoulders back. They had rehearsed this moment more than once but then they realized that with all the time and wrongs gone by, there was nothing worth saying.

how hanna, Laura, Anna, Logan and the baby got away

They piled into Laura's truck, their belongings packed tightly into a small trailer hitched to the back. They sat perfectly still, held their breaths, looked straight ahead.

Roxane Gay

lives and writes in the Midwest.

INSTITUTO

ROY KESEY

—Good afternoon, *Instituto de Perfeccionamiento*.

– Hi, good afternoon. Look, sorry to bother you, but I'm calling because I was reading the newspaper yesterday and I saw your advertisement, and I was wondering what, exactly, you are capable of perfecting. And also why the name's in Spanish.

– All consultations are personal and in person, sir.

– Yes, but, just in general, what sort of things do you improve?

– We improve nothing, sir. If we improved things, the institute would be called the *Instituto de Mejoramiento*. It is not. We are not. It, we, is, are the *Instituto de Perfeccionamiento*.

– Okay, but again, sorry, what exactly do you perfect?

– All consultations are personal and in person.

– I see.

– Will there be anything else today, sir?

– I guess, well, sure, why not. Could you give me the address? I read through your advertisement, read it very carefully in fact, but—

– We are located on the *avenida*.

– The... Sorry, the what?

– The *avenida*. The avenue.

– The... Which avenue would that be?

– The *avenida*, sir.

– Madam, is this some kind of joke?

– No, sir, it is not. We do not joke here at the *Instituto de Perfeccionamiento*.

– Right, okay, but this is a city, madam. A large, not a small but a large-sized city, with thousands of avenues.

– There is only one *avenida*, sir.

– Well, but—

– We are not hard to find if you are in need of our services. If on the other hand you are not in need of our services, we are quite literally impossible to locate, but then, that wouldn't be such a problem, would it?

– No, I guess not. One last thing—do you, there at the *Instituto de Perfeccionamiento*, do you speak, in general, English?

– We are speaking English now, sir, you and I.

– Right, but the others, the, um, doctors or therapists or—

– *Perfeccionadores*. Perfectioners.

– Exactly, the perfectioners, do they speak English as well?

– All consultations are—

– Yes, yes I know. Well. Very well.

He went. He left his house and got in his car and drove. He turned left, and turned left again, and turned right, and went straight ahead. He turned left and right and left and left and left, and then he hit the *avenida*. He'd never seen it before, but there it was. He turned right and drove up the avenida until it dead-ended at the bay. There was a white fence or railing along the cliff-top, and a fine view: the bay, the seagulls, the sailboats. For a time he stared at the view. Then he got back in his car and drove down the *avenida* until it dead-ended at a white fence or railing along a cliff-top overlooking the open ocean. There was a view here as well. Again the seagulls and sailboats, though fewer of both than before. After staring at this new yet familiar view for a time, he got back in his car and drove back up the avenida, and just as he was about to turn right into the maze toward home, there on the corner he saw a sign. *Instituto de Perfeccionamiento*, it said.

He parked his car and walked to the door, knocked and opened and entered. Inside was a small lobby or vestibule and to one side was a desk and behind the desk was a woman. She had large dark eyes and creamy skin and short dark hair and a pretty smile.

– Yes? she said.

– Good afternoon. You, we, I called earlier and we spoke, you and I, I believe.

– Yes, sir, we did. One hundred dollars, please.

– But—

– Each session costs one hundred dollars, sir, regardless or irregardless, both are acceptable now, of the treatment received.

– But—

He waited for her to interrupt him, and she did not.

– But... isn't that a little, I don't know, irregular? I haven't even seen the perfectionists yet. How do I know—

– *Perfeccionadores*, sir. Perfectioners. Not perfectionists, not in any sense of the word. "Perfectionist," sir, while likewise from "perfection," from the Middle English *perfeccioun*, from the Old French *perfection*, from the Latin *perfectio, perfectus*, was first used in or around 1846 to refer to or as signifier for an adherent to the ethical doctrine which states that the perfection of moral character constitutes man's highest good, or alternately b: an adherent to the theological doctrine that a state of freedom from sin is attainable on earth, or alternately 2: anyone disposed to regard anything short of perfection as unacceptable. Perfectioners are something else entirely, and no one ever sees them.

– Oh.

– I believe we will start with your skin.

– My skin? But madam, my skin... Well, okay, but it's not what I had in mind.

– Rest assured, sir, it's all part of the program, the program that has been chosen on your behalf. For now, try not to worry about the other aspects, the aspects that you did in fact have in mind. Those will be attended to in due time, insofar as they yield to our treatment—all of them, each and every one, insofar as they yield to our treatment, but in accordance with the program, and in due time. Now. Cash, check, or credit card?

He paid in cash and was shown by the large-eyed dark-eyed creamy-skinned short-haired dark-haired prettily smiling woman into a square waiting room. He sat down in the only chair, and the woman left, closing the door behind her too quickly for him to catch more than a glimpse of her splendid, better than splendid, quite genuinely ideal rump.

The walls were lined with bookshelves lined with books. After fifteen or twenty minutes of waiting he began to walk around, not in circles but in squares with sharp right angles, inspecting the books. None of them were in English. He wished he had paid more attention to his Spanish teacher in high school, just on general principles, just for the good of the thing, as none of the books were in Spanish either. After fifteen or twenty minutes of walking around in squares he sat down. After fifteen or twenty minutes of sitting he got up again and went to the door of the waiting room. There, he listened. He heard nothing. After five or seven minutes of hearing nothing he opened the door and walked out to the lobby or vestibule. Now there was no one sitting behind the desk. He waited at the desk for nine or eighteen minutes, standing rigidly though not at attention. If there had been a bell or buzzer of any kind, he would have rung or buzzed it. He called out. He shouted. He screamed. At last he rapped his knuckles firmly on the desktop. Then he walked out the door and down the walk and to his parking spot, got into his car, and drove the long drive home.

What a gyp, he thought.

✕

First thing the next morning, he stopped sleeping and awoke. He opened his eyes and stretched, closed his eyes and opened them again. He stretched again. He got up and went to the bathroom and turned on the light and removed his underpants and turned on the shower and looked in the mirror.

His skin was perfect.

It was blemishless.

His acne, the acne that had plagued him, a forty-year plague, the very acne that had served as Elizabeth Wannaker's excuse for not accompanying him to the junior prom, and she'd said it out loud and to his face and in the presence of many persons, his friends and hers, though mostly hers as his lurked a short distance away, It's those zits, Stanley, those zits, do something about those zits and then maybe I'll accompany you to a prom, though not the junior prom as it will be too late for that and anyways I'm hoping Harold Plansky will ask me. Do you know him? His friends? His phone number?

That self-same acne was gone.

As were his scars. The thin curvilinear pink line across the top of his left big toe from that time he'd dropped the paint-can, and god alone knows why he'd been painting barefoot, freshening up the trim around the front door like his dad had told him to, and what a weird accident, the can had caught him just right, opened his toe down to the bone, and paint

145

everywhere, blood-colored paint, no way to tell what was injury and what was home improvement and his whole foot hurt like a bitch—that thin curvilinear pink line was gone.

And the purple gouge in his left shin from that time he'd been running through the shopping center and had turned mid-flight to see if the bikers were still chasing him and had smacked into the low stone planter—that purplish gouge, filled in and touched up, the same color as the rest of his shin, shin-colored.

And the slight pucker in his glans from that mucked-up circumcision—vanished.

And the jagged slash down his right cheek from that time his ex-wife had come at him with the bread-knife, not that he blamed her, he'd been heavy on the sauce back then and heavy with his hands—invisible as if undone.

And the horrendous molten rippling of his left cheek and ear and part of his scalp from that time he'd gone into the JC Penney's, the whole place on fire, stacks of outerwear and racks of innerwear blazing torch-like, to save the Billingham kid trapped and cowering in the dressing room, who ended up dying anyway the following year, mowed down in a crosswalk by an unknown motorist who did not stop and was never apprehended—all that horrendous molten rippling now baby-smooth.

And the five mauve nickel-sized welts scattered irregularly across his chest from that time when RT Pickaxe had run into a whole goddamn battalion of NVA maybe ten clicks into Cambodia, unable to hold the LZ and god was it hot, the perimeter brought in tight, calling for air support, calling for extraction, and he heard a voice, the voice of Johnson, and Johnson said the chopper was delayed but air support would be there in zero-six, would lay it down thick and close and give them a chance; three minutes later there was no one to return incoming fire but Stanley and Rahlan Drot, the rest of the team KIA and broken, and Rahlan Drot, the one Montagnard left who'd been with him from the start, Rahlan Drot with a shattered femur, the gooks closing in, and Stanley had taken Rahlan Drot on his back and oh how he'd run, the brush ripping at his face and the air keening sick all around, he'd hit a trail and no choice now, up the trail he ran, three gooks in front of him and reaching but he put them down, and how he ran, he dodged them all, all but one, a short skinny dude with an SKS carbine, and the bullets opened holes across the front of Stanley's shirt, five holes, black-rimmed and loose-fringed, and he'd dropped Rahlan Drot and fallen, and old Rahlan Drot, good old Rahlan Drot had taken Stanley's CAR-15 and waxed that short skinny gook, had picked Stanley up, an unbelievable thing, Rahlan Drot losing blood, the shattered femur, but he carried Stanley to the secondary LZ that Johnson's voice guided them towards, they'd popped smoke, purple and yellow and red, and the chopper had come, had pulled them out, by god an unbelievable thing—those five mauve nickel-sized welts, they had been polished away.

And what had become of Rahlan Drot? Stanley stood staring into the mirror in his bathroom, the light on, the shower running, his underpants balled in the corner. Had Rahlan Drot made it through to the end? They'd kept in touch for a time, but then the letters had stopped. Plenty of reasons why that might have happened, though. Say he made it. Say he is even now an aging man, a smiling happy aging man, the shattered femur healed not by any *Instituto de Perfeccionamiento* but by time and the body itself, the marvelous body, and Rahlan Drot with his wife, a tiny woman she must be, tiny and lovely and kind, and the two of them tend small fields of rice, and at times in the evening their children and grandchildren come, walking the long walk up and along the ridge, the grandchildren laughing and playing and at times oddly cruel, but only in childish ways, and Rahlan Drot rests in his thatched and stilted longhouse, chats with his wife and his children, watches his grandchildren play.

Stanley stared into the mirror, stared at his perfect skin, and an old word came to him, an old and funny and appropriate word, a word his mother had often used back when the two of them were still speaking, and he smiled, and stared at himself in the mirror, and said the word:

– Gadzooks! he said, perhaps from "God's hooks," swearing by the Crucifixion nails, archaic, used as a mild oath.

Or perhaps Rahlan Drot hadn't made it.

✕

On Sunday he returned to the institute, and the institute was closed.

✕

On Monday he returned to the institute, and the institute was open, and behind the desk sat the large-eyed dark-eyed creamy-skinned short-haired dark-haired prettily smiling woman.

– Hello, she said.

– Hello, he said.

– Are you pleased? she asked.

– It is a miracle, he answered. Or at the very least miraculous. You even perfected my glans.

– Not me, sir. The *perfeccionadores*.

– Even so. A miracle, or at the very least miraculous.

– We here at the *Instituto de Perfeccionamiento* aim to please.

– But I don't understand. How—

– You are not meant to understand, sir. You are meant only to be pleased. And now, I believe, your hair. One hundred dollars, please.

– My hair?

– Your hair.

– But my hair, my hair, I like my hair. My hair is fine. Or if it's not, and okay, let's say it's not, let's say it's graying, gone a bit thin on top, but no big deal, no particularly big deal, nothing I can't handle.

– You're forgetting about the program.

– Look, okay, the program, but if I want to fix my hair I can just go to the hairdresser and get a damn haircut, can't I. And for a damn sight less than a hundred dollars.

– If that is what you wish, sir, by all means, you may. If what you wish is to get your hair fixed, you can and may just go to the hairdresser and get a damn haircut. Do not let us stop you. We here at the *Instituto de Perfeccionamiento* are neither interested in nor capable of fixing things. If we fixed things, the institute would be called the *Instituto de Reparación*. It is not. We are not. It, we, is, are the *Instituto de Perfeccionamiento*.

– Well, hell.

– Yes, she said, from the Middle English, and that from the Old English, akin to helan, 'to conceal,' the Latin *celare*, the Greek *kalyptein*, compared metaphorically and perhaps also likened literally to war by General W. T. Sherman. Have you come to a decision?

Again he paid in cash, and again he was shown into the waiting room. Again the chair and the sitting down, again only a glimpse of the ideal rump. Again the bookshelves and books and the fifteen or twenty minutes and the walking around and the sharp right angles and the inspection and the wish. Again the sitting, the getting up, the walking to the door, the listening, the hearing of nothing, the five or seven minutes, the opening of the door, the walking, the lobby or vestibule. Again the nine or eighteen minutes, the lack of bell or buzzer, the calling out, the shouting, the screaming, the firm rapping of the knuckles, the opening and closing, the walking, the long drive home.

He awoke in the morning with perfect hair. Movie-star hair. Thick and wavy and lustrous, unlike it had ever been. He did not have to open his eyes or stretch or get up or go to the bathroom or turn on the light or remove his underpants or turn on the shower or look in the mirror. He awoke and simply knew: he could feel its perfection against his scalp. He would never have to rinse or shampoo or condition ever again.

And so it went. Skin, hair, refrigerator, eyesight, wardrobe, gastrointestinal tract, sofa, car, unicycle, hearing, pogo-stick, flooring, plumbing, prostate, wiring, fingernails, and so on. Drive, walk, knock, open, enter, chat, pay, walk, sit, glimpse, wait, inspect, wish, sit, get up, walk, listen, hear, wait, open, walk, wait, stand, call out, shout, scream, rap, walk, drive, over and over.

Then she said, Your program, sir, is complete.

– What?

– Your program is complete.

– No, I don't, it can't be, I'm, we're just getting started, just getting going, just getting into the groove.

– No, sir, I'm afraid we're not doing any of those things. Your program is complete.

- Well, okay, but surely there are, there must be, aren't there other programs?

- Not for you, sir. I'm sorry.

- But— But what about my fear of heights? My fear of lows? My nightmares? My echolalia?

- Sir, you do not suffer from echolalia.

- But I can feel it coming on right now at this very moment! "Sir, you do not suffer from echolalia." You see?

- I'm sorry, sir. Your program, your only program, the one and only program for you, it is finished.

- But what about Rahlan Drot? I'd give anything just to know if he made it, and if he did, to get back in touch, to know that he's okay, doing well, being happy. And what about my mother? She's old, extremely old, ancient and kind-hearted and courageous but we haven't spoken in years—she's never forgiven me for allowing my ex-wife to get away. And my ex-wife, speaking of my ex-wife, beautiful woman, I don't blame her a bit for what happened, and she, well, yes, she remarried, but I heard she's since redivorced, so she's free now, reunattached, and there's nothing in the world I want more than to have her as my ex-ex-wife, to try again, to do right by her this time.

- I'm afraid that none of those things fall within our purview, sir. That is to say, none of those things yield to our treatment. Your program is complete.

- But—

Again she did not interrupt him. He sought a way to end his sentence. He found it nonendable.

- So I guess this is goodbye, he said.

- Yes, she said, an alteration of "God be with you," 1573, a concluding remark or gesture at parting; see also "*adios*," 1837, from the Spanish *adiós*, from *a*, from the Latin *ad*, and *Dios*, from the Latin *Deus*, used to express farewell.

Back to his car, his perfect car, back to his house, his perfect house. He walked immortal in circles and squares, one perfect room, and then the next. He ran his fingertips across his perfect skin. He ran his hands through his perfect hair. He ran across his perfect carpeting, stumbled over his perfect roller-blades, slammed headlong into a perfect wall, and there was no mark upon it, no mark at all, and his head was also still perfect, no pain, no swelling, no blood, and he ran from his living room to his kitchen to his hallway to his bedroom and the three pictures framed on his dresser: his mother, her apron stained, the rolling pin held up for show, the flour on her cheek, her laughter caught and held; and Rahlan Drot standing next to Stanley, the small brown man and the large white man, their arms interlocked, Rahlan Drot's earlobes pierced and stretched, Stanley's tigersuit faded but clean, this one moment permitted, friendship and trust, this one moment of grace before the next descent; and his ex-wife, the first day of their honeymoon in Cabo San Lucas, behind her the ocean stretched out calmly and bluely, the low white wall of the terrace, the orchid in her hair, he'd told her how beautiful she looked, he'd raised the camera and she'd smiled and averted her eyes.

Roy Kesey

is a writer and translator living in Maryland. His latest book is the short story collection *Any Deadly Thing* (Dzanc Books 2013). His other books include the novel *Pacazo*, the short story collection *All Over*, the novella *Nothing in the World*, and two historical guidebooks. He has received an NEA creative writing fellowship, the Paula Anderson Book Award, and the Bullfight Media Little Book Award. His short stories, essays, translations and poems have appeared in more than a hundred magazines and anthologies, including *Best American Short Stories* and *New Sudden Fiction*.

RUST AND BONE

CRAIG DAVIDSON

Twenty-seven bones make up the human hand. Lunate and capitate and navicular, scaphoid and triquetrum, the tiny horn-shaped pisiforms of the outer wrist. Though differing in shape and density, each is smoothly aligned and flush-fitted, lashed by a meshwork of ligatures running under the skin. All vertebrates share a similar set of bones, and all bones grow out of the same tissue: a bird's wing, a whale's dorsal fin, a gecko's pad, your own hand. Some primates got more—gorilla's got thirty-two, five in each thumb. Humans, twenty-seven.

Bust an arm or leg and the knitting bone's sealed in a wrap of calcium so it's stronger than before. Bust a bone in your hand and it never heals right. Fracture a tarsus and the hairline's there to stay— looks like a crack in granite under the x-ray. Crush a metacarpal and that's that: bone splinters not driven into soft tissue are eaten by enzymes; powder sifts to the bloodstream. Look at a prizefighter's hands: knucks busted flat against the heavy bag or some pug's face and skin split on crossing diagonals, a ridge of scarred X's.

You'll see men cry breaking their hand in a fight, leather-assed Mexies and Steeltown bruisers slumped on a corner stool with tears squirting out their eyes. It's not quite the pain, though the anticipation of pain is there—mitts swelling inside red fourteen-ouncers and the electric grind of bone on bone, maybe it's the eighth and you're jabbing a busted lead right through the tenth to eke a decision. It's the frustration makes them cry. Fighting's all about minimizing weakness. Shoddy endurance? Roadwork. Sloppy footwork? Skip rope. Weak gut? A thousand stomach crunches daily. But fighters with bad hands can't do a thing about it, aside from hiring a cornerman who knows a little about wrapping brittle bones. Same goes for fighters with sharp brows and weak skin who can't help splitting wide at the slightest pawing. They're crying because it's a weakness there's not a damn thing they can do for and it'll commit them to the second tier, one step below the MGM Grand and Foxwoods, the showgirls and Bentleys.

Room's the size of a gas chamber. Wooden chair, sink, small mirror hung on the pigmented concrete wall. Forty-watt bulb hangs on a dark cord, cold yellow light touching my clean-shaven skull and breaking in spears across the floor. Cobwebs suspended like silken parachutes in corners beyond the light. Old Pony duffel between my legs packed with wintergreen liniment and Vaseline, foul protector, mouthguard with cinnamon Dentyne embedded in the teeth prints. I've got my hand wraps laid out on my lap, winding grimy herringbone around the left thumb, wrist, the meat of my palm. Time was, I had strong hands—*nutcrackers*, Teddy Hutch called them. By now they've been broken so many times the bones are like crockery shards in a muslin bag. You get one hard shot before they shatter.

A man with a swollen face pokes his head through the door. He rolls a gnarled toscano cigarillo to the side of his mouth and says, "You ready? Best for you these yahoos don't get any drunker."

"Got a hot water bottle?" Roll my neck low, touch chin to chest. "Can't get loose."

"Where do you think you are, Caesars Palace? When you're set, it's down the hall and up a flight of stairs."

I was born Eddie Brown, Jr., on July 19, 1966, in San Benito, a hard-scrabble town ten miles north of the Tex-Mex border; "somewhere between nowhere and *adiós*," my mother said of her adopted home town. My father, a Border Patrol agent, worked the international fenceline running from McAllen to

Brownsville and up around the horn to the Padre Island chain off the coast. On a clear July day you'd see illegals sunning their lean bodies on the projecting headlands, soaking up heat like seals before embarking on a twilight crossing to the shores of Laguna Madre. He met his wife-to-be on a cool September evening when her raft—uneven lengths of peachwood lashed together with twine, a plastic milk jug skirt—butted the prow of his patrolling johnboat.

"It was cold, wind blowing off the Gulf," my mother once told me. "*Mío Dios.* The raft seem okay when I go, but then the twine is breaking and those jugs fill with water. Those waters swimming with tiger sharks plump as hens, so many *entrangeros borricos* to gobble up. I'm thinking I'm seeing these shapes," her index finger described the sickle of a shark's fin. "I'm thinking why I leave Cuidad Miguel— was that so terrible? But I wanted the land of opportunity." An ironic gesture: shoulders shrugged, eyes rolled heavenwards. "I almost made it, Ed, yeah?"

My father's eyes rose over a copy of the *Daily Sentinel.* "A few more hours and you'd've washed up somewhere, my dear."

The details of that boat ride were never revealed, so I'll never know whether love blossomed or a sober deal was struck. I can picture my mother wrapped in an emergency blanket, sitting beside my father as he worked the hand-throttle on an old Evinrude, the glow of a harvest moon touching the soft curve of her cheek. Maybe something stirred. But I can also picture a hushed negotiation as they lay anchored at the government dock, maiden's hair slapping the pilings and jaundiced light spilling between the bars of the holding cell beyond. She was a classic Latin beauty: raven hair and polished umber skin, a birthmark on her left cheek resembling a bird in distant flight. Many border guards took Mexican wives; the paperwork wasn't

157

difficult to push through. My sister was born that year. Three years later, me.

I finish wrapping my hands and stand, bobbing on the tips of my toes. Tug the sweatshirt hood up, cinch the drawstring. Half-circle to the left, feint low and fire a right cross, arm cocked at a ninety-degree L to generate maximum force. Torque the hips, still bobbing slightly, three stiff jabs, turning the elbow out at the end. A lot of people don't like a jabby fighter, a pitty-patter, but a smart boxer knows everything flows off the jab: keeps your opponent at a distance and muffles his offense, plus you're always in a position to counterpunch. And hey, if the guy's glass-jawed or thin-skulled, a jab might just knock him onto queer street.

My father once took me on his evening rounds. August, so hot even the adders and geckos sought shade. We drove across the dry wash in his patrol Bronco, past clumps of sun-browned chickweed and pokeberry bushes so withered their fruit rattled like hollow plastic beads. He stopped to show me the vents cut through the border fence, chain-link pried back in silvery flaps.

"Tin snips stashed in a plastic bag tied to an ankle. Swim across the Rio Grande, creep up the bank and cut through." A defeated shrug. "Easy as pie."

The sky was darkening by the time we reached the dock. Walking down the berm to the shoreline, we passed a patch of agaves so sickly even the moonshiners couldn't be bothered. Our boots stirred up clouds of rust-hued dust. Stars hovered at the eastern horizon, casting slivers of metallic light on the water.

My father cycled the motor, pulling into the bay. Suspended between day and night, the sky was a tight-sheened purple, shiny as eggplant skin. The oily stink of exhaust mingled with the scent of creosote and Cherokee rose. To one side, the fawn-colored foothills of west Texas rolled in knuckled swells beneath a bank of violet-edged clouds. To the other, the Sierra Madres were a finned ridge, wedges of terra cotta light burning though the gaps. A brush fire burned distantly to the north, wavering funnels of flame holding the darkness at bay. Stars stood on their reflections at the Rio Grande's delta, a seam of perfectly smooth water where river met ocean.

My father fired a flare into the sky. As the comet of red light arced, he squinted at the water's surface lit by the spreading contrail.

"They don't understand how dangerous it is," he said. "The pulls and undertows. Fighting a stiff current all the way." He pulled a Black Cat cigar from his shirt pocket and lit it with a wooden match. "Shouldn't feel any responsibility, truly. Not like I make them take the plunge. Everyone thinks it's sunnier on the other side of the street." I snap off a few more jabs as my heart falls into pre-fight rhythm. Sweat's coming now, clear odorless beads collecting on my brow and clinging to the short hairs of my wrists. Twist the sink's spigot and splash cold, sulfurous water on my face. A milky crack bisects the mirror, running up the left side of my neck to the jaw before turning sharply, cleaving my lips and continuing north through cheek and temple. Stare at my face split into unequal portions: forehead marbled with knots of sub-dermal scar tissue and nose broken in the center, the angle of cartilage obtuse. Weak fingers of light crawl around the base of my skull, shadowing the deep pits of my sockets.

Thirty-seven years old. Not so old. Too old for this.

On my fourteenth birthday my father drove me to Top Rank, a boxing gym owned by ex-welterweight contender Exum Speight. I'd been tussling at school, and I guess he figured the sport might channel that aggression. We walked through a black door set in a flat tin-roofed building, inhaling air cooler but somehow denser than the air from the street. The gym was as spacious as a dance hall and dim, vapor lamps set in the ceiling. The ring erected in the center with a row of folding chairs in front. A punching bag platform stood between two dusty tinted windows on the left. An old movie poster hung on the water-stained wall: The Joe Louis Story. *America's Greatness was in his FISTS*, the tagline read, *The Screen's Big Story in his HEART!* A squat black man worked the speed bag in a ponderous rhythm while a Philco radio played "Boogie Oogie Oogie," by A Taste of Honey.

A short thin man in his early forties exited the office. He wore a checkered blazer with leatherette elbow patches and a brown fedora with faded salt stains peaking the hatband. "How you doing, fellas?"

"You Speight?"

"Exum's up in Chicago with a fighter," the man told my father. "Jack Cantrales. I mind the shop while he's gone."

Jack made me skip rope for a few minutes, then quoted a monthly training fee. My father shook his hand again and said, "Be back in a few hours, Eddie."

For the next two years I spent every free minute at Top Rank. As Exum Speight busied himself with the heavyweights, my training fell to Cantrales. Jack was an amiable bullshitter, always joking and free with advice, but later I came to realize he was one of the milling coves known to haunt boxing clubs, the "gym bums." Gym bums were pugilistic has-beens or never-wases—Cantrales's pro record stood at 3-18-2, his sole attribute an ability to consume mass quantities of red leather—who hovered, wraithlike, around promising fighters.

Gym bums were also known to squeeze a penny 'til it screamed, and Contrales was typical of the breed: he once slid his foot over a coin a kid had dropped, shrugged, and told the kid it must've rolled into the sewer.

It was a *dime*.

Near the end of high school Cantrales booked my first fight at Rosalita's, a honkeytonk border bar. My parents would've never allowed it had they known, so I squeezed through my bedroom window after lights out and met Cantrales at the end of the block. He drove a Chevelle 454 SS—car had get-up like a scalded cat.

"You loose?" he asked as we fled down the I-38 to Norias. June bugs hammered the windshield, exoskeletons shattering with a high tensile sound, bodies bursting in pale yellow riots.

"Yeah," I said, though I couldn't stop shaking. "Loose."

"That's good." Cantrales had recently switched his fedora in favor of a captain's hat of a style worn by Captain Merrill Stubing on *Love Boat*. Dashboard light reflected off the black plastic visor, according his features a malign aspect. "You'll eat this frito bandito up."

Rosalita's was a clapboard tonk cut out of a canebrake. Acres of cane swayed in the wind's grip, dry stalks clashing with a hollow sound, bamboo wind chimes.

Inside was dark and fusty. Hank Snow growled about some woman's cheatin' heart from a heat-warped Wurlitzer. Off in the corner: a canted plankboard ring, red and blue ropes sagging from the ring posts. I bent between the ropes and shuffled to the four corners, shadowboxing. A rogue's gallery of bloodsport enthusiasts swiveled on their bar stools. Someone called, "Looking sharp, kiddo!" My opponent was a whippet-thin Mexican in his mid-thirties. White sneakers, no socks, a clean white towel around his neck. His hair plastered to his skull in black ropes. He looked exhausted. Mexican fighters often hopped the border on the night they were to fight, winding up at Rosalita's soaked from the swim and gashed from razor wire, sometimes pursued by feral dogs roaming the lowlands.

I took a hellish beating. The fight was a four-round smoker, each round three minutes long. Those twelve minutes stretched into an eternity, especially the final three, eyes swelled to pinhole slits and gut aching from the Mexie's relentless assault. The guy knew things about momentum and leverage I'd never learned in sparring sessions, how to angle a hook so it grazed my abdomen and robbed my breath, leaving slashes of glove-burned flesh. It was as though he possessed secret information about the exact placement of my organs, finding the kidneys and liver, drilling hard crosses into my short rib. I pissed red for days. Between rounds the bartender—who doubled as cutman— tended to my rapidly expanding face. He wore a visor, the kind worn by blackjack dealers, Vaseline smeared on the green plastic brim. He'd reach up and scoop a blob to grease my cheeks.

"You're breaking him down," Jack lied. "Stick and move, Eddie."

By the final round the Mexican looked slightly ashamed. He ducked punches nimbly, sticking a soft jab in my face or tying me up in close. A chorus of boos arose: the shadowy bar patrons were anticipating a KO. The only damaging shot I landed all night was a right hook to the Mexican's crotch. It wasn't on purpose: my eyes were so swelled I couldn't see what I was punching. He took the foul in good spirit, pulling me close until our heads touched, whispering, "*Cuidado*, lo blo, *cuidado*."

Afterwards I sat on the trunk of Jack's Chevelle pressing an icepack to my neck. There was a tinny ringing in my ears and the moon held a wavering penumbra. I concentrated on not throwing up. Contrales handed over my fight purse: five dollars, management fee and transportation surcharge deducted.

"You were tight. Gotta let go with a few bombs or you get no respect. He laid your ass on the canvas five or six times, but you stood up.

Counts for something, right? Little bastard was sharp," Jack admitted. "A dead game fighter."

I nodded vaguely, not paying much attention, more concerned with how I'd explain my state to my folks.

"You fight, you lose. You fight, you win. You fight," Jack suggested, heading back inside for a fifth of off-sale Johnny Red.

The Mexican exited Rosalita's. He moved out into the cane, clearing the razor-edged stalks from his path with still-taped hands. Spokes of heat lightning flashed behind a bank of night clouds, whetting the foothills in crimson light. The fighter walked gingerly, no wasted movement. He stopped at a grove of palmettos and glanced up at a low bronze moon, orienting himself to the land before melting into the trees. I thought about the coming hours as he hiked to the border and scaled the fence, where perhaps a boat was moored amidst the cattails. He'd battle the Rio Grande's currents as they bore him to the far shore, then another hike would bring him to an adobe house in one of the fringing settlements. I pictured his wife and children: his wife's oval face and fine-boned hands, shafts of dawn sunlight slanting low-angled and orange through an open window to touch his daughter's sleeping eyes. The fantasy may've stood in sharp contrast to the abject reality—perhaps the man had nothing worth fighting for—perhaps all that waited was a lightless room, a bottle of mescal.

Looking back now, I do not believe that was the case. Reach a certain experience level, you don't fight without reason. You've seen too many boxers hurt, killed even, to treat matches as dick-swinging contests. Fighting becomes a job, stepping into the ring punching a clock. It's a pragmatic pursuit, opponents' equations to be solved using the chimerical physics of reach, height, spacing, leverage, heart. You'd no more fight outside the ropes than a factory lineman would work a shift for no pay. I entered my first fight for no other reason than to see if I *could*, testing what I thought I'd known against the unknown reality.

I lost because I was green, yes, but also because nothing was really at stake: my life wouldn't've been substantially better or worse, win or lose. The Mexican stepped between the ropes with the subdued air of a man entering an office cubicle. When he realized it was going to be an easy day he leaned back in his chair, kicked off his shoes. He didn't give the crowd what they wanted, didn't hurt me without cause. His job was to defeat his opponent, and he did. But he wouldn't be there without reason. He fought for the money, and for those he loved.

A family waited on the other side of that river. I know that now. I know what it means to fight for a reason.

The hallway's lit by forty-watt bulbs set behind meshed screens. The cement perspires, as do the oxidized copper pipes overhead. Rivulets of brown water spill from the joists. The place is a foreclosed steelworks factory. Corkscrews of drilled iron crunch beneath my boots. The air smells of mildewed rock and ozone. Up through the layers of concrete and wires and piping the crowd issues a gathering buzz that beats against my eardrums.

We fight bare-knuckle, or nearly so. A nostalgic few see it as a throwback to the days when barrel-chested dockhands brawled aboard barges moored off the New York harbor. It's not throwback so much as regression. A dogfight. No referees. No ten count. The winner is the man left standing. Rabbit punches and low blows, eye gouges, headbutts—I once saw a fishhook tear a man's face open, lip to high ear. Fighters score their hand wraps with sandpaper, soak them in turpentine, wind concertina wire around their knuckles.

I fight fair. Try to, anyhow.

I graduated high school in the spring of 1984. Excelling at English and Languages, I was accepted to Wiley College on a scholarship. That August I moved north to Marshall and spent three years living in my sister Gail's basement, studying and continuing to box. Gail's husband Steve was a journeyman carpenter and drywaller; he converted the unfinished basement into an apartment: bedroom and kitchenette, a small training area to skip rope and practice footwork. I'd squirrel myself away during midterms and finals, but otherwise spent my time reading in the family room, shooting hoops on the driveway net, or raiding the fridge. Gail occasionally tripped over my gym kit or spied a pair of hand wraps laid over the armrest of her favorite chair and pitched a fit, but for the most part we got along. Steve was a long-haul trucker circuiting between San Antonio and Sioux Falls. On my twenty-first birthday he bought a case of Lone Star and we sat on the back porch until the flagstones were littered with empties and we were howling at the moon.

With Steve hauling and Gail landing a teller job at Marshall First Trust, babysitting duties fell to me. My nephew Jacob was ten months old when I moved in. An inquisitive boy with a sweet temperament. The kid was forever crawling out of sight, disappearing around corners or behind curtains, knees pumping so quickly I was sure friction would singe the carpet. We'd play this game where Jake stuck his fingers in my mouth and I'd curl my lips over my teeth and bite down gently, growling; Jake would shriek—a garbled string of syllables, "eep-ooo-*ap!*" or "yee-*ack!*" or "boo-*ta*-tet!"—and pull his hand away. This went on for hours, until I became slightly nauseated by the taste of Jake's hand, a blend of sweat and mucus and the residue of whatever bacterial micro-sites he'd investigated that day. I remember the way Jake's gaze locked with mine, fingers inches from my mouth, his eyes glowing, positively *aflame*, as though to say—

"Look at the runt. Gonna get *creamed!* Run along find your daddy, peckerwood!"

The spectators hurl other insults, but these two I pick up clearly. There looks to be a hundred or more, ranged around a barricade of sawhorses stolen from a construction site: bright orange, flashing halogen discs screwed to the horizontal beams. The intermittently blinking lights brighten the spectators' faces in ghostly yellows: a pack of blood hungry crazies waving dollar bills. Moonlight pours through holes rusted in the roof, silver shafts gilding the crossbeams and glossing feathery shapes roosting in the latticework. A hypnotic sound underlies the hollering crowd: a distant, nearly sub-audible clash and cycle, the sound of long-derelict machinery shuddering uneasily to life.

My opponent is a dreadlocked kid two inches taller and forty pounds heavier than me. Goes by Nicodemus. Bare-chested, his arms are swelled, monstrous. Tribal tattoos crisscross the ribbed muscula- ture of his stomach; ornate curlicues encircle his extruded bellybutton, giving it the look of a sightless eye. He turns to his cutman and says, "Who this, the shoeshine boy? Mus' be my birthday."

We meet in the center of the ring, where the cigarillo-smoking promoter runs down the stakes: a thousand cash to the winner, five hundred to the loser.

166

Nicodemus dry-gulches me while the guy's still laying out the stakes, a hard sucker punch glancing off the high ridge of cheek, splitting bone. The blow drops me to my knees. Chill static wind pours through my skull, electric snakes skating the bones of my arms and legs. Nicodemus shrugs and smiles, as though to say, *Hey, you knew the score when you stepped up,* then wades in swinging. Guess the fight's started without me. It's not uncommon.

I graduated in '87 and moved north to Pennsylvania. Having trained and fought steadily through college, I'd amassed a Golden Gloves record of 13-1. Teddy Hutch, an Olympic boxing coach, caught one of my fights and invited me to his training facility in Butler. The welterweight division was thin, he said; I could earn a berth on the qualifying squad. The program covered food and accommodation. His prospects worked at a local box factory.

I arrived in Butler late September. The trees and water, even the sky: everything was different. The Texas sky was not completely blue; its colour, I've come to realize, was more of a diffuse lavender. The skies of Pennsylvania were a piercing, monotone blue; they pressed down with a palpable weight. The tattery, see-through clouds I'd known since childhood were replaced with thick cumulus formations. And the *cold*—me and a Hawaiian boxer named David Tua bundled ourselves in sweaters and jackets on the mildest of fall days, much to the amusement of the Minnesotans and Dakotans in training.

The prospects were billeted in a ranch house. The land behind fell away to a lake ringed by hemlocks and firs, rising to a wooded escarpment. We roused at five o'clock each morning and ate breakfast at long tables before donning road gear to run a three-mile circuit around the lake. Afterwards we herded into a school bus bound for Olympia Paper, where we spent the next nine hours ranged along canvas belt lines, driven half-mad by the pneumatic hiss of the fold-and-stamp machines. When the shift whistle blew we were driven to the Cyclone, a downtown boxing gym. We trained until eight o'clock before dragging ourselves to the bus, bolting dinner, and flopping into bed for lights out.

It was a rough life, and a lot of fighters couldn't stomach it: prospects came and went with such frequency Teddy considered installing a turnstile. But the regimen yielded results: I packed on ten pounds of muscle in eight months, and my cardiovascular endurance shot through the roof. My sparring partner was a Dixieland welter- weight named Jimmy Carmichael. Jimmy had a peacemaker of a left cross; we beat each other black and blue in the ring but spent our days off together, catching the Sunday matinee and wolfing thick wedges of pecan pie at Marcy's on Lagan Street.

Jake visited that March. Steve was hauling a load up to Rochester and brought Jake along to visit. Steve dropped him off mid-morning, and we arranged to meet later for dinner. I was surprised how much Jake had grown. His cheeks, framed by the furred hood of a new winter jacket, were flush and rosy.

"How ya been, jellybean?" I said.

"I been fine, pal o' mine," he said, repeating the greeting I'd taught him.

Jake was antsy following the long drive. We walked down to the lake. A low fog rolled across the frozen water, faint ripples thickening into groundmist at the tree line. We held hands. Every fir looked dusted in powdered sugar. Jake's hand slipped from mine as he ran ahead. He said, "I've never seen so much *white*."

The lake was a flat opaque sheet. A murder of crows congregated on a tree shattered under a weight of snow. The northern boys skated here on weekends; I saw the ruts their blades had left in the ice. Jake ran out, falling, sliding, getting up, running faster.

"Hey," I called. "Hey, slow 'er down, big guy."

I was raised in a part of Texas where the only ice was of the cubed variety. I'd only seen snow in Christmas movies. I mean, what did I know of ice? I knew it felt good pressed to the back of my neck between rounds. My five-year-old nephew ran heedlessly, hood tugged down around his shoulders, fine sandy hair and clean tanned skin brightened by the sun. What did he know of ice? Perhaps that it melted quickly on a summer sidewalk. Did he even know that much? We were both ignorant. But I should've known.

Nicodemus rushes across the ring, jackhammering his fists. He throws a series of haymakers so slow he might as well have telegraphed them last week; I feint from a kneeling position and hammer a left hook into his ass, nailing the sciatic nerve. Shrieking, he limps back. I struggle to my feet and bicycle into the open ring. From time to time someone shouts Nicodemus's name, and under that the distant hum of machinery.

He throws a looping right that I duck, rising with a short-armed cross to the midriff. He bulls me into a corner. I juke, try to circle clear, but he steps on my foot and hits me with an overhand right. Lips flatten against teeth, mouth filling with the taste of rust and bone. The air shimmers, shards of filigreed light raining down like shiny foil in a tickertape parade. I go down heavily under a sawhorse, staring up at a dark forest of legs.

I can no longer consciously recall the sound that ice made as it broke. Sometimes I'll hear another noise—the low crumple of a beer can; the squeal of an old nail pried from a sodden plank—similar in some way, timbre or pitch or resonance, and realize it lives somewhere inside me now. I remember the fault line racing out to meet him, a silver crease transecting the ice like a cracked whip. It seemed to advance slowly, a thin sluggish snake zigging and zagging; it was as though I had only to holler "Step back!" and it would rip harmlessly past.

Water shot up in thin pressurized needles from hairline cracks under Jake's feet. He lurched sideways, outflung arms seeking balance. The ice pan broke in half, plates levering up, a V of frozen water with Jake plunging through the middle.

I laughed. Maybe Jake looked silly going down, mouth and eyes wide, hands clutching at the broken border of ice that crumbled like spun sugar in his grasp. Maybe I could not conceive the danger: I pictured the two of us sitting before the fireplace in the big safe house, a blanket wrapped around his shoulders, a mug of hot chocolate, tendrils of steam rising off Jake's wet pants as they dried.

"Hold on, big fella," I said. "Do the eggbeater!"

My boots skidded along the ice. I overbalanced, fell down. Jake churned foam, clothes plumping with water. Everything seemed all right until I saw the fear and confusion, deep thin creases out of place on a face so young; I saw, with the dreamlike clarity that colors all memories of the event, molecular beads of water clinging to his cheeks and nose. I crawled forward, outspread hands distributing my weight. Jake splashed and kicked and called out in a reedy whisper, nose and mouth barely above water. Ice crackling under my hands and chunks of ice floating on the water and the trees of the near shore wrapped in transparent icy layers. So much *ice*.

He stopped struggling abruptly, just hanging there, eyes closed, water trickling into his mouth. Only his chin and the tips of his fingers floated clear. I reached the edge and extended a hand. The supporting ridge broke away and my chest and head slipped below the surface. Cold black water pressed against my eyeballs. I caught movement through the brown water and grabbed something—smooth and slim, perhaps a jacket sleeve—but the cold made my fingers clumsy and it slipped through. The lake shoved me back and forth, currents stronger than I'd imagined. Sinewy shapes turned over in the murk, shapes like seal pups at play.

I broke the surface snorting streams of water, wiping away cords of snot. I stared into the swirling blackness in search of movement, a leg kicking, fingers grasping. I plunged my arm in, stirring around, hopeful: a few strands of eelgrass draped over numb fingers. Not knowing what to do, I called his name. "Jake!" The word echoed uselessly across the flat expanse.

When my voice died away I heard it: a sustained resonant thump. I couldn't tell where it came from. The ice trembled. A dark form was pressed to the chalky sheet a few feet to the left, trapped beneath the surface. It twisted and thrashed, beating the ice.

I crawled towards the shape—crawled on my hands and knees like a fucking *infant*. Ice pocked with craters and boils from thawing and re-freezing. I saw a dim outline down there, a creature of crude lines and angles. The ice shuddered; fresh-fallen snow jumped off the surface, resettling. My fingers spread across the milky whiteness and ears plugged with frozen lake water, a frantic buzzing between.

I made a fist with my right hand and brought it down. The ice buckled, splintered, but held. Pain shot up my arm to the shoulder, a white-hot bolt. I raised the right again—my lead hand, the dynamite right—smashing the ice. It broke and my fist plunged into the darkness, grasping frantically, closing on nothing. A powerful current caught hold of Jake and he drifted sideways, beyond my grasp. Something passed through my fingers—a bootlace?

I tracked the shape beneath the ice. The freezing water on my arms crackled like dull metal. My teeth chattered and I called his name. Maybe I was screaming.

Passing beneath a patch of perfectly clear, glasslike ice, I caught his face through the scalloped sheet. Lips and nostrils robin's egg blue, the rest a creamy shade of gray. Cheek flattened to the ice, the buoyancy of flesh pushing him up. Eyes so blue, luminously blue, pearlescent air bubbles clinging to the dark lashes. A sinuous white flash below, silky curve of a trout's belly.

My right hand was badly broken: knuckles split and flesh peeled to the wrist, a lot of blood, some bones. I slammed my left hand down. The ice fractured in a radiating spiderweb. Water shot up through the fissures. My hand shattered like a china plate. Didn't feel a thing at the time. Jake stopped clawing, stopped thumping. His eyes open but rolled to the whites beneath the fine network of cracks. I hammered my left hand down once more, breaking into the icy shock of the lake. I snagged his hood but the hole was too small so I clawed with my free hand, breaking off chunks, razored edges gashing my fingers to the bone.

Finally the hole was wide enough for me to pull him through. A long swipe of mud on Jake's forehead, hair stuck up in rapidly freezing corkscrews. His nose broken and me who'd done it, smashing ice into his face. I gathered him in my arms and stumbled uphill to the house. "Please," I remember saying, over and over, a breathy whisper. *"Please."*

Ernie Munger, a flyweight mending a broken rib, had spent a few summers as a lifeguard. He administered CPR while the cook rang for help. Munger's thick hands pumped the brackish water from Jake's lungs, pumped life back into him. Jake was breathing by the time the paramedics arrived. They snaked a rubber tube down his throat. Afterwards I stood by a large bay window overlooking the lake. The hole, the size of a dime from that distant vantage, was freezing over in the evening chill; tiny red pinpricks represented my bloody handprints on the ice. The splintered bones pulsed: I'd broken forty-five of fifty-four.

I push off the floor and lean against a sawhorse, waiting for the teeth to align and the gears to mesh again. Nicodemus circles somewhere to the left, dancing side to side, weaving through blue shafts of shadow like animate liquid. Some bastard kicks me in the spine, "Get up and fight, you pitiful son of a bitch." Standing, I wonder how long was I down. Eight seconds? No ref, so nobody's counting. A pair of hands clutch my shoulders, shoving, the same voice saying, "Get out there, chickenshit." I strike back with an elbow, impacting something fleshy and forgiving. A muted crack. Those hands fall away.

Nicodemus advances and hits me in the face. He grabs a handful of hair and bends me over the sawhorse, pummeling with his lead hand. The skin above my eyes comes apart, soft meat tearing away from the deeply seamed scar tissue. Blood sprays in a fine mist. I blink away red and smack him in the kidneys. He pulls back, nursing his side. Knuckling the blood out of my eyes, I move in throwing jabs. Nicodemus's skull is oddly planed, a tank turret, deflecting my punches. His fists are bunched in front of his mouth, arms spread in an invert funnel leading to the point of his chin: a perfect opening, but not yet. Reaching blindly, he entangles my arms, pulling me to his chest. He rubs his hand wraps across my eyes and I wince at the turpentine sting. I snap an uppercut, thumping him under the heart.

The hospital room walls were glossy tile, windows inlaid with wire mesh. Jake lay in an elevated hospital bed, shirtless, chest stuck with EKG discs. Outside a heavy mist fell, making a nimbus around the moon and stars. Teddy'd visited the emergency ward earlier, taking one look at my hands and saying I'd never box again. I was on Dilaudid for pain, Haldol for hysteria. My mind was stark and bewildered. A machine helped Jake breathe. His father sat beside the bed, gripping his hand.

"Is he—will he be all right?" "He's alive, Ed."

Steve'd never called me that before. Always Eddie. "Is he... will he wake up soon?"

"Nobody can say. There was...damage. Parts shutting down. I don't know, exactly."

"We were...holding hands. He broke away. He'd never done that before. It was so strange. We were holding hands, then he didn't want to do that anymore. It's only human. I let him go. It was okay. I thought, He's growing up, and that's okay."

Steve smoothed the white sheets over Jake's legs. "The golden hour. It's...a period of time. Three minutes, three-and-a-half. The amount of time the brain can survive without oxygen. Only a few minutes, but the doctor called it the golden hour. So...stupid."

"I'm so sorry."

Steve didn't look at me. His hands smoothed the sheets.

I stalk Nicodemus, keeping left, outside his range. His eyes shot with streaks of red, their wavering gaze fixated on the darkness beyond me. I stab forward, placing weight on my lead foot and twisting sharply at the hip, left hand rising towards the point of his chin.

When I was a kid, a rancher with a lizard problem paid a dime for every one I killed. I stuffed geckos in a sack and smashed the squirming burlap with a rock.

When my fist hits Nicodemus it sounds an awful lot like those geckos.

The punch forces his jawbone into his neck, spiking a big bundle of nerves. My hand shatters on impact, bones breaking down their old fault lines. Nicodemus's eyes flutter uncontrollably as he falls backward. He falls in defiance of gravity, body hanging on a horizontal plane, arms at his sides, palms upraised. There's a strange look on his face. Not a smile, not exactly, but close. A peaceful expression.

Jake's twenty years old now. Comatose fifteen years. Were it not for a certain slackness of features he'd be a handsome young man. He grows a wispy beard, which his mother shaves with an electric razor. I've visited a few times over the years. I sat beside the bed holding his hand, so much larger than the one I held all those years ago. He smiled at the sound of my voice and laughed at one of our shared jokes. Maybe just nerves and old memories. Every penny I make goes to him. Gail and Steve take it because they can use it, and because they know I need to give it.

There are other ways. I know that. You think I don't know that? This is the only way that feels right.

Nicodemus rises to one knee. He looks like something risen from its crypt, shattered jaw hanging lopsidedly, bloodshot eyes albino-red. Pain sings in my broken hand and I vaguely remember a song my mother used to sing when I was very young, sitting on her lap as she rocked me to sleep, beautiful foreign words sung softly into my hair.

He makes his way across the ring and I dutifully step forward to meet him. We stand facing each other, swaying slightly. My eyes swelled to slits and he moves in a womb of mellow amber light.

And I see this:

A pair of young-old eyes opening, the clear blue of them. A hand breaking up from sucking black water, fist smashed through the ice sheet and a body dragging itself to the surface. A boy lying on the ice in the ashy evening light, lungs drawing clean winter air, eyes oriented on a sky where even the palest stars burn intensely after such lasting darkness. I see a man walking across the lake from the west, body casting a lean shadow. He offers his hand: twisted and rheumatoid, a talon. The boy's face smooth and unlined, preserved beneath the ice; the man's face a roadmap of knots and scar tissue and poorly knitted bones. For a long moment, the boy does not move. Then he reaches up, takes that hand. The man clasps tightly; the boy gasps at the fierceness of his grip. I see them walking towards a distant house. Squares of light burning in odd windows, a crackling fire, blankets, hot chocolate. The man leans down and whispers something. The boy laughs—a beautiful, snorting laugh, fine droplets of water spraying from his nose. They walk together. Neither leads or follows. I see this happening. I still hold a belief in this possibility.

We circle in a dimming ring of light, feet spread, fists balled, knees flexed. The crowd recedes, as do the noises they are making. The only sound is a distant subterranean pound, the beat of a giant's heart. Shivering silver mist falls through the holes in the roof and that coldness feels good on my skin.

Nicodemus steps forward on his lead foot, left hand sweeping in a tight downwards orbit, flecks of blood flying off his brow as his head snaps with the punch. I come forward on my right foot, stepping inside his lead and angling my head away from his fist but not fast enough, tensing for it while my right hand splits his guard, barely passing through the narrowing gap and

I'm torquing my shoulder, throwing everything I've got into it, *kitchen-sinking* the bastard, and, for a brilliant split second in the center of that darkening ring, we meet.

Craig Davidson

has written four books: *Rust and Bone*, *The Fighter*, *Sarah Court*
and *Cataract City*. His nonfiction and fiction has appeared in
Esquire, *GQ*, *The Walrus*, *Salon*, *Nerve*, *The London Observer*, *The
Cincinatti Review*, *Avenue*, *Agni*, *Event*, *The Fiddlehead*, *Prairie
Fire*, *SubTerrain* and elsewhere. His first book was made into a film
directed by Jacques Audiard, starring Marion Cotillard. Graduate of
the UNB Creative Writing Program and the University of Iowa's
MFA program. Currently jobless.

BLUE HAWAII

REBECCA JONES-HOWE

The wheels of the jogging stroller squeak with every turn, timing the anxiety in my chest, making me think of rum rushing from the bottle to a glass. Cold and refreshing. It's the sort of thought that jogging can't push away.

Every run uphill makes me feel like I'm starting over.

My calves throb. There's a heat wave in my throat, making every exhale a cough. I wipe at the sweat on my face, smearing the cover-up on my lip.

"Shit."

The baby starts crying. Leaning over the handle of the stroller, I reach out and touch her cheek. Her eyes close tight and her mouth gapes. Her screeches fill my ears.

"Please stop," I gasp.

She doesn't. I turn the stroller around, the summer heat bearing down on my walk back home. The squeaking wheels and the baby's wails force me to shut my eyes. Even the speed bump at the entrance to the townhouse complex feels like a burden.

"Hey, there. Hey!" It's a male voice calling.

I turn around and the new neighbour jogs past. He's wearing a navy blue shirt and white jogging shorts. A sweatband pushes his brown hair back. "Hey," he says again, jogging on the spot. "You okay? You don't look so great. You look beat, just totally beat."

He's tall, lean. He scratches at his beard. His pupils are dilated, but I can still see that his eyes are the colour of Blue Hawaii, the first drink I ever had. All I can think of is the chilled pineapple sweetness as my gaze trickles down. He's sweating, and the fabric of his shirt clings to his chest.

My fingers tense around the stroller.

He's got a water bottle. He rotates it in his grasp, spinning circles so fast that the water clings to the sides. "You live right there, right?" he asks, pointing. "I know because I saw you. You were in the window with that other girl. You were watching me move all my shit."

"That was my sister, Marie," I say. "I live with her and her baby. She just went back to work after her maternity leave."

"You should come in," he says, paying no attention to the crying infant in the stroller. "You're not busy, right? I can show you my place."

"I don't know," I say, looking at him.

"Come on." He jogs backwards, his smile too nice, eyes so intense like Blue Hawaii vacation excitement. "Come on," he urges. "You can have a glass of water. I promise I'll make it cold and relieving. I promise. I guarantee, even."

There's an ant's nest beside his front door, a swarm of black spots crawling around my feet. Inside, his place is barren, the boxes still taped up, stacked beside his kitchen counter. There's a couch in the living room. The suede clings to the sweat on my thighs when I sit down.

He gets me a glass of water and he sits beside me, watching me while I drink. "You had a cleft lip," he says.

"What?"

"You did at one point, didn't you?" He rubs at his nose, sniffing. "I mean, it doesn't look like it, but I can see the scar."

My hand flinches, touching the uneven skin. He catches my wrist, his palm hot, sweaty. I jerk my hand away.

"I'm sorry," says. He laughs, reaching out again, rubbing his thumb over the scar. "I've seen all those pictures of babies with cleft lips. It's crazy that those kids can look so normal, isn't it?"

"I guess," I say. The scar throbs and I stare down at the floor, thinking like ants are crawling around my feet, flashbacks of my first memories: learning to speak without slurring or spewing spit, trying to explain to classmates why my mouth was so ugly, all that social withdrawal sewn up inside my restructured upper lip. It's hard to breathe. I turn my head and take a drink. The water's cold but it doesn't provide the right kind of relief.

"Do you want to do something?" He leans forward, hands shaking, edging toward my leg. "Do you want to fuck?" he asks.

My fingers slip against the condensation on the glass.

"Sex is just the best when I'm high," he says. "It feels so fucking good."

I shift, feeling his grasp on my thigh. "What are you high on?"

His lips curl into a smile. "It's coke," he says. "It makes me want to fuck you so fucking hard." He fingers at the leg of my shorts, pinching the fabric.

My gaze drifts to the baby, now asleep. Her head's slumped forward. Her eyes are closed and her mucus-filled nose makes sounds every time she breathes in and out, dazed, dreaming.

He leans in. I can smell his cologne, mixed with perspiration, sweet and salty, something new, something different. I set the glass down on the floor. "You have to be quiet," I say. "You can't wake her, okay?"

He's got a face beyond my league, but he kisses me, eager. His tongue probes past the scar, slipping in deep. A gasp slips up my throat and my limbs go loose, veins running hot, heart throbbing. This is what everything used to feel like when I first started drinking. No tension, just a black hole to fill with anything.

"My name's Ian," he says, climbing over me on the couch. His shaking fingers slide under my shirt, tickling my stomach. He stares me down, his big eyes just dark holes with blue edges. He's somewhere else, somewhere better. He kisses me again, thick saliva in my throat, taking me with him.

He pulls at my clothes, pulls his shorts down so he can shove his dick between my legs. "You're so fucking wet," he says, grabbing my knees, pushing himself in. "Fuck," he says, his voice forced, shouting. "You fucking like me, don't you? You fucking want me, don't you, baby?"

He wakes the baby. The cries squeal like the stroller wheels.

I shut my eyes as I smooth my palms over his chest, feeling the rapid pace of his heartbeat, the pulsing throbs. Under him, everything else is hard to hear.

When Marie comes home from work, I sit up straight in the couch, holding the baby, pretending there's nothing to hide.

"I met the new neighbour today," I say.

"Oh yeah?" She sets her purse down on the table.

"His name's Ian," I say. "He's really nice. He showed me his place."

She looks at me. My lip itches and I rub it with my wrist, sniffing. I can still smell the sweat on my skin.

"How was Emma today?" she asks, taking the baby.

"Fussy," I say. "I don't think she likes jogging, the motion of it. I don't think it does anything for her."

At night Ian follows me, chases me through the dirt trail beside the highway. The sun beats down on my skin. I can barely run, and he tackles me into the sagebrush, the dirt scraping my knees. There's an ant's nest beside my face.

"What did your mouth look like?" he asks.

"I don't remember," I say. "My mom never took pictures of me."

"It was probably a hole you could slip right into," he says. He slides two fingers into the nest and the ants crawl out. I realize he's naked, that I'm naked. I wince, arching myself against his hard-on. He enters me, invades me, and I gasp, the ants finding a new home in my mouth, crawling inside.

I wake up in my bedroom. There's nothing but black outside the tiny window, and I lay there, looking at the shadows, the comfort of them.

I put the baby in the stroller, her little mouth filled with a pacifier so she's quiet, non-existent. I walk across the parking lot and knock on Ian's door. He's shaved off his beard and his face is marked with little red nicks. His skin looks sallow. He looks at me with empty blue eyes. There's a plastic bottle of white powder clutched in his hand. I push the stroller in and close the door.

"I just want to do another line," he says. "That's all I ever want to do. That's all I can think about." His voice is low, quiet, the way mine used to sound when going out stopped being about blended drinks and partying, when it became solely about booze, its influence feeding my veins.

"It's better to talk than to keep it all in," I say.

"What does it matter to you?"

"I was an alcoholic," I say. "I know what it's like."

He stares.

"It's still hard, trying not to think about drinking, knowing it's not an option. Everything's harder now." My gaze drops and I lean my head against his chest, breathing in, inhaling the scent of him.

His fingers curl around the bottle. "The first time I did it, I felt like angels were in the walls, talking to me, giving me energy and powers. Now the highs never last as long. I never know what to do. Every time I come down, I can't even...I can't do anything."

"You can't be in denial," I say, "You're only going to feel worse." My lip twitches. He watches me rub at the scar. "I tried to cut it open once," I say. "Marie found me in the bathroom with a knife. I told her there was nowhere else for the bullshit to go. The hole had to get bigger. She started crying then. She didn't know what to say. Nobody ever did."

His hand starts shaking, clutching the bottle like a tiny martini shaker. The powder inside looks like drink froth.

"There's no point taking it out on yourself," I say. "It's better when you're not alone."

He pours a bump on his wrist and he snorts it back. His chest heaves in and out. He looks at me, his lips tight, eyes wide, hot. He smiles. Blue Hawaii vacation relief.

I want it. I want him.

Marie wakes me up, walking into my bedroom with the baby wailing in her arms. "Where's Emma's pacifier?" she asks. "You had it this morning. She can't fall asleep without it."

"I don't know" I say. "Maybe it fell out at Ian's place."

"What?" Her face is blurry in the dark. "You went there again?"

"I was talking with him. What's wrong with that?"

"You're supposed to be looking after Emma," she says.

"I get bored sometimes," I say. "What do you expect, that I'm just going to sit by myself all day trying to get her to talk?"

Marie groans. "I'm not having this argument now," she says. She slams the door, but it doesn't mask the sound of the baby's colic cries.

Ian never unpacks. He tells me that he's started selling stuff to pay for more cocaine. He's so high, so excited, stubble on his face. He lets his beard grow back.

I buy pacifiers. There's a bag of them on his kitchen counter. The baby cries and I pop one in. Her mouth is so pretty, so perfect. Her lips close around the pacifier and she falls asleep like a normal person. Then Ian does another line.

Every climb up to his bedroom makes me feel like I'm starting over. Blue Hawaii vacation refreshment.

He doesn't have a bed. There's just a mattress on the floor, and it squeaks like the baby's stroller when he fucks me on it. He's shaved again. The scabs are thick, dark, almost black, like tiny ants are crawling on his face. His nostrils are lined in red.

His room smells like sweat and bile and aftermath. Sickness.

His dick slips in, going hard, fast, deep, until I'm moaning, feeling cramps in my abdomen. He groans, pulling out, gushing all over my torso. He rubs his hands over the sticky white, slides two fingers into my mouth, making me taste him.

"Don't you like me?" he asks. "Don't you want me?"

He pries my lip up, right where the scar is. "What's it like, knowing you were born with all the ugly on the outside?" His voice is aggressive. "Don't you ever just want to cut yourself open again, make another fucking hole?"

I feel like insects are crawling in my veins.

"It used to be so different," he says, voice cracking.

I wince, but I can't shake him off. He clings to me, bearing his nails against my skin so they feel like tiny bites, stinging all over. His groan echoes, turns into a cough. My lip throbs.

"It's never like it used to be," he says, his eyes turning red, blinking, tears slipping. It's like a Blue Hawaii vacation gone awry.

He starts crying, deep moans that sound stuck in his throat. It's how I imagine my cries sounding when I was a baby, when my mouth was still a gaping open mess. I crawl away from him, his sweetness diluted on my tongue.

I watch him from the living room window, holding the baby. She cries and I rock her, watching Ian as he bends down over the doorstep, a can of aerosol can of insect killer clutched in his unsteady hand.

Marie comes home.

"Jessica, are you okay?"

I shake my head, my fingers flinching, the baby slipping.

Marie takes her, pats her back. She looks out the window.

"I'm sorry," I say. "I relapsed."

Marie looks at me.

"I'm not going back there. I just wanted to feel like I used to."

"What is going on?" she asks.

I shake my head, tight-lipped. Outside, Ian turns, looking up at the window, at me, nothing but black filling his gaze. I look away.

Emma wakes me, crying again. There's blue behind the white sheer of the curtains. Dawn. Marie's in the living room, trying to soothe the baby back to sleep. She doesn't even notice me.

"I can take her," I say.

"Huh?" Marie blinks, looking up.

"Go to bed," I say. "I can take her for you."

Emma settles in my arms, her cries fading. Her skin's warm and soft, her tiny infant fingers reaching out. In the daylight, her eyes glisten bright blue. Normal.

Rebecca Jones-Howe

lives and writes in Kamloops, British Columbia. Her work has
appeared in *Pulp Modern*, *Punchnel's* and *ManArchy*, among others.
She is currently working on her first collection of short fiction. She
can be found online at rebeccajoneshowe.com.

CHILDREN ARE THE ONLY
ONES THAT BLUSH

JOE MENO

A rt school is where I'd meet my sister each Wednesday, and then, the two of us would travel, by cab, to couple's counseling. Although Jane and I were twins, by the age of nineteen, she was already two years ahead of me in school, and because both of our parents were psychiatrists, and because I had been diagnosed with a rare social disorder, a disorder of my parent's own invention, Jane and I were forced to undergo couple's therapy every Wednesday afternoon. The counseling sessions were ninety-minutes long and held in a dentist's office. As both of my parents were well-known in their field, they had a difficult time finding a colleague to analyze their children, and so they were forced to settle on a dentist named Dr. Dank, a former psychiatrist who had turned his talents to dentistry. He was an incredibly hairy man who smoked while my sister and I reclined in twin gray dental chairs. Dr. Dank did all he could to convince me that I was angry at my twin sister for being smarter and also that I was gay.

Once I had made the mistake of mentioning to my sister that the doorman of our building was "handsome"—to me, he looked like a comic book hero with a slim mustache. She frequently brought this remark up in our sessions as evidence of my latent homosexual desires. She would leave various kinds of gay pornography for me on my bed. I would come from school and find a magazine or videotape lying there and stare at it—at the faces of the oiled, suntanned men and their arching, shaven genitals—then return the magazine to my pillow, and back out of my room like a thief. Jane was nineteen and a sculpture major in art school. She was also taking a minor in psychology through correspondence courses in the mail. Technically, I was still a senior in high school. My sister's sophistication, her worldliness and intelligence were absolutely terrifying to me.

In the taxi on the way to our counseling appointments, I would stare across the backseat at her, studying her profile. Jane had short black hair; she was skinny and there was a field of freckles on her nose which made her look a lot younger than she actually was. When she wasn't looking, that's where I'd always stare, at the freckles on the bridge of her nose. "Jack, what's happening with your gym class?" she asked me. One of the reasons my sister was two years ahead of me in school was because I failed gym, year after year. As part of my social disorder, I was paralyzed by a fear of stranger's bodily fluids, their blood, sweat, spit, urine, even their tears. If someone sneezed near me, I would begin to convulse violently. I was unable to participate in any gym activity where bodily fluids were involved. Because of this, and because my disorder was unrecognized anywhere outside our household, I had failed gym every semester for the last three years and had yet to finish high school.

"Dad told me you have a new gym teacher this year," Jane said. "Is he nice?"

"His name is Mr. Trask. He asked me why I don't participate and I told him I had a medical condition and then he told me to go sit in the bleachers. I'm supposed to meet with him tomorrow to talk about it."

"Did you give any more thought to what we talked about in therapy last week?"

"What? That the reason I'm failing gym is because I won't admit I'm gay?"

"Dr. Dank completely agreed with me, Jack. You're queer. You're living a lie. The sooner you admit it, the happier we'll all be."

I decided then, watching the Chicago Avenue traffic drizzling past, not to argue with her. For all I knew I was queer. I had never kissed a girl. Their bodily fluids seemed incredibly dangerous to me. Also, I had a poster from the musical Miss Saigon hanging in my room, a gift from Mr. Brice, my marching band instructor, the only teacher at my school who had made accommodations for my fictional disorder. Jane might be right. It was entirely possible that I was gay.

✕

A day later I met with Mr. Trask, who was a tousled-haired, thoroughly-bearded man. He sat across from me in a swivel chair, his running shorts riding up his broad hairy thighs. If I glanced long enough, I could see the dark cavity of his crotch. As disgusting as it was, it was hard not to stare.

"Why do you keep failing gym?" he asked.

"I'm afraid of bodily fluids."

"Well, they're not going to let you graduate unless you pass gym class."

"I know. I've already accepted that I won't graduate from high school. It doesn't bother me."

"Hold on," he said, leaning back in the chair, the running shorts inching even higher. "Here's what we're going to do. Your parents are shrinks right?"

"Yes."

"You get me some Valium and I'll make sure you'll graduate."

After class, I called my father. A day or so later, I gave Mr. Trask what he had asked for. From then on, I spent gym class watching the other boys my age sword-fighting with upturned tennis rackets and knew I was missing nothing.

X

The next week, I met my sister Jane for our counseling appointment in front of her art school, where a number of young men and women gathered to smoke cigarettes, looking purposeful and shabby. Jane marched up to me, said hello, and then pointed at a gawky-looking young man who was leaning against the wall, lighting a clove cigarette. "Look? How about him? Go tell him you'd like to give him a blowjob."

I looked way, shaking my head, and said something like, "I don't think so."

"You need to grow up. Part of being an adult is dealing with adult feelings. Do you want to end up an old dirty queer getting teenage boys to suck you off in bathrooms or something? Because that's what will happen, Jack. You have to deal with this openly before you sublimate it."

I had no idea how I was supposed to answer.

Just then a girl named Jill Thirby came up to us and said, "My name is Jill Thirby. My father and mother are both famous artists. You may have heard of them." Jill Thirby had a yellow dress on and long brown hair. She also had black-framed glasses and these dangly yellow earrings. "I'm working on this really intense project right now and I was wondering if you guys would like to help."

"What is it?" I asked, staring at her long yellow scarf.

"Basically, I'm trying to make things fly."

"What does that mean?" Jane asked tersely.

"I'm basically attaching hundreds of balloons to different things to see what'll fly and what won't."

"Wow. That sounds cool," I said.

"That sounds fucking stupid," Jane cursed. "That's exactly

what the world needs. More childish, performance art bullshit. Why don't you do something meaningful? Like confront what's happening in the Middle East?"

Jill Thirby looked ashamed all of a sudden, her yellow eyeshadow going red. "You don't have to talk to me like that. I was just trying to be...I'm just trying to do something nice."

"Well, why don't you do something nice somewhere else?" Jane asked.

Jill Thirby nodded, still shocked, and walked away. I looked over at Jane and asked her, "What's your problem?"

"She is my problem. I can't believe how many girls there are like her. Their fathers don't love them enough and so they go to art school and everything they make is this twee, meaningless bullshit. They don't ever deal with anything serious, you know. Like I bet that girl never even heard of the Situationists. I bet she has no idea what's going on in Palestine right now."

"What?"

"Forget it. We're late for Dr. Dank. Let's go," she said and then, unfortunately, we did.

That afternoon in therapy, Jane suggested that the real reason I was afraid of bodily fluids was because I was in denial of my own sexuality. I did not argue with her. The whole next week during gym class, I watched the other boys in class doing windsprints, their bodies virulent with overripe sweat. It was the intimacy I did not like, I wanted to tell her. The idea of sharing something vital with someone I did not know or understand.

Outside of the sculpture building the next Wednesday, while

I was waiting on my sister, I ran into Jill Thirby again. She was still dressed in yellow, this time with a yellow stocking hat, with a yellow ball on the end. She had yellow mittens on and was chewing what appeared to be yellow gum.

"Hey," I said. "I wanted to say I'm sorry. You know, about my sister, the other day."

"I don't get why some people have to be so negative. She's really, really mean."

"Have you gotten anything to fly yet?"

"Not yet," she said, itching her nose. "I've tried a chair, a pineapple, and a bowling ball. None of them even got off the ground."

"Well, if you ever need any help, I'd be happy to give you a hand."

"What are you doing right now?" she asked.

"Nothing," I said, glancing around, seeing my sister was late once again.

"Do you want to help me then? I was going to try and float a birdcage."

A few moments later, we climbed up the fire escape to the roof of the student dorm and stood looking out over the city. Jill Thirby had about fifty red helium balloons with her, which she promptly tied to an empty birdcage. "Okay, here we go," she said, and we both stepped away. The birdcage did not move, though the balloons fluttered back and forth in the wind, dancing ferociously.

"Maybe you need something smaller," I said.

Jill Thirby kneeled beside the birdcage, inspecting it, and said. "Or more balloons possibly." I thought about leaning over beside her and trying to kiss her. I think she saw me looking at her in a funny way and said, "What is it? Is there something in my teeth? It's this weird problem I have. My teeth are too far apart. I always have food stuck in them. My dad's always reminding me to brush them."

"No. I was just...it's nothing."

"Do you want to try and float something else tomorrow?"

"Okay," I said, and took her hand as she stepped back onto the fire escape.

Jane was waiting outside the sculpture building swearing to herself when I found her. She squinted at me angrily when I said hello. "Do you know what time it is? Where the fuck were you? Mom and dad pay by the hour if you didn't happen to notice."

"I was helping out that girl Jill Thirby."

"What? Why were you hanging out with her?"

"I don't know. She seems nice. I like her glasses and everything."

"Why are you in such denial? Jesus, Jack, everyone's trying to help you but you're not even trying."

"What did I do?"

"Just when we're getting somewhere with your therapy, you decide to ditch your appointment to go 'hang' with a 'girl.' That's textbook denial. Seriously."

"I just wanted to see if she could make something float."

"I guess we should just stop worrying about your severe emotional issues because, all of a sudden, you like some Jewish girl."

"What? She's not Jewish."

"She's definitely Jewish."

"So what? Mom's Jewish," I said.

"You are so completely clueless. Why don't you screw this girl and get it over with? And maybe then you'll be ready to admit what your problem really is."

"I don't want to screw anyone."

"Bullshit. You want to screw her in her little Jew butt."

"I'm going to walk home by myself now," I said and then, for once, I did.

X

The following week I did not wait for Jane to go to couple's counseling. Instead I met Jill Thirby outside the sculpture building and we walked up and down the street looking for things in the trash that we could try and make fly. We were sorting through some garbage cans when she found a small gray cat. It was undernourished and hiding under a moldy cardboard box. Jill Thirby held it to her chest and decided to take it back to her dorm, where we washed it in the common bathroom sink, and then fed it black licorice from the vending machine. "I have the perfect name for it," Jill Thirby said. "Blah-blah."

"That's good," I said. Jill Thirby leaned over and held the cat to her chest, burying her face in the animal's wet gray fur.

"Do you want to spend the night here?" she asked me suddenly. "I don't have intercourse with anyone I don't know intimately, but you can sleep here if you want."

I told her okay. Later that evening, as we were lying in bed together, Jill Thirby began to cry. I did not know what was happening at first. I laid there, holding my breath, pretending to be asleep. Her shoulders were shaking, her back trembling before me. She was holding the cat to her chest and the cat was meowing, trying to get free. I thought about putting my hand on her arm or saying something out loud, but I was afraid of what would happen if she knew I wasn't asleep. Finally, I asked her what was wrong, and she said, "I'm sick of being related to my father and mother." Then she sniffled and said, "But I miss them both a lot," and then turned away from me, the cat leaping off the bed. In the darkness, Jill Thirby became quiet and it seemed like she had momentarily disappeared.

✕

The next day I was late for school. I hurried into gym class and took my spot on the wood bleachers and watched the other poor saps running laps. Mr. Trask saw me and climbed the bleachers, and then took a seat beside me, staring off into the distance at something that I don't think existed. He turned and looked at me and said, "How old are you, Jack?"

"Nineteen."

"Nineteen. Jesus. You should have finished school a year ago."

"I know."

"Don't you want to get out of here?"

"Not really. I don't have any idea what's supposed to happen next."

Mr. Trask nodded, then fumbled through his extremely tight shorts for a pack of cigarettes. He offered me one. I shook my head, feeling pretty uncomfortable all of a sudden. He inhaled deeply and then started to cough, his rasps sounding exactly like a gym whistle, high and tinny. "I'll tell you something: I don't think anybody knows what the hell comes next. I mean, I see these kids, and some of them walk around like they got it all figured out—they're going to this college or that college or what, I dunno. I'll let you in on a little secret: if someone comes up to you and tells you they got anything figured out, you can be sure of one thing. They're full of it. Because the thing is, as soon as you figure one thing out, you see there's a whole other world of shit you don't understand. The people who think they know it all, those are the ones to beware of. And that's all I got to say about that."

I nodded, seeing two pale sophomores—in the middle of the track—begin to collapse from exhaustion.

"Do you think your dad could get me some barbiturates? I think I need something stronger. I'm having a heck of a time sorting out my thoughts this week."

"I'll look into it."

"Great." Mr. Trask nodded and then stood. He held his hands in front of his face like a megaphone and shouted, "Okay, ladies, bring it in."

After class, I waited around the art school campus all afternoon, hoping to find Jill Thirby again. It was getting dark when I saw her sneaking across the student pavilion with what looked to be several hundred red balloons. I followed her from a distance, watched her as she climbed up the fire escape, back to the roof of the dorm. Halfway up, she heard me climbing beneath her and looked down, then smiled a wide, goofy smile, holding the balloons with one hand, and her yellow stocking cap with the other.

"What are you doing?" I asked.

"Today I got a brilliant idea: I decided to try and float myself."

"That doesn't sound so good."

"I did some calculations." She scrambled into her pocket with

CHILDREN ARE THE ONLY ONES THAT BLUSH

her free hand and handed me a piece of graph paper on which was the most incomprehensible drawing I had ever seen: there were numbers and arrows and what appeared to be a cloud of some kind.

"It doesn't seem like a good idea. Maybe you should practice first."

"With what?"

"I don't know. Something not too high."

"That's probably a good idea," Jill Thirby said. "That's something my dad would probably tell me. I guess we could try it from my dorm room. I live on the second floor so if I fell, it wouldn't be so bad."

"Okay, that sounds good," I said but as soon as we got to her room, we started to kiss instead, and then Jill was pulling down her long yellow tights, and she had pale yellow underwear on, and then those were off, and I could see her thighs, the plains of her hips, the entire dark world between, and she was saying, "I usually don't have sex with people I don't know for at least three months," but then we did it anyway. For some reason, for the first time in as long as I could remember, I did not think about the danger of bodily fluids. Things were passed between us but it did not bother me. A few minutes later, we were lying in bed, and she still had her yellow stocking hat on with the yellow ball at the end, and I don't know why but I suddenly blurted out, "Jill Thirby, do you want to be my girlfriend?"

Jill Thirby's face went blank just then. "I thought you were gay. That's what your sister told me."

"I know, that's what everyone keeps telling me." I looked her in the face, her lips smudged with yellow lipstick and asked her again. "Do you want to be my girlfriend anyway?"

She smiled at me softly, blinked once, and then said: "Thanks but no thanks."

I sat in bed and watched her dress quickly. "You should probably go," she said. The cat we had found, Blah-blah, seemed to look at me anxiously, too, and so I got dressed quick and left in a hurry.

✕

When I got home, my parents and sister were there waiting for me. So was Dr. Dank. For the next two hours I sat in the gray armchair while my sister and Dr. Dank tried to get me to admit I was incredibly unhappy. I told them I had never been happier. "Jack, how can you be happy?" my sister asked, arms folded, standing over me. Her silver hairpin looked like a threat, pointing down at me. "Look at you. You spend all your time alone. You're completely disinterested in dating. You're failing high school. You have no intellectual curiosity. It's not normal, Jack. It's not even abnormal. It's subnormal or something like that."

Dr. Dank puffed out two nostrils full of smoke and I said, "I couldn't agree more. It is subnormal. And also, he hasn't been flossing. He's becoming a prime candidate for gum disease."

"Why don't you just admit you're gay so we can all just move on?" my sister groaned.

I stared at my parents, who hadn't spoken a word since I walked in. My father looked exhausted. My mother looked bored. She had a notepad in her lap, taking notes, though I think she was actually finishing a crossword puzzle. It was pretty obvious, even in their professional detachment, who they were siding with. I sat in the armchair, facing them all, my father pulling off his glasses to clean them. He did this whenever he thought a patient was lying. I knew this because he had told me several times before that psychiatry was as much performance as it was science. Taking off his glasses and cleaning them was one of his signature moves. I tried to look at my mother but she was busy scribbling down the answer to 15 across. Neither one of them would dare to look me in the eye. So I glanced over at my sister, who was still standing above me, arms crossed, her dark eyebrows looking like they had not been groomed in some time. I understood right then that, no matter what, she would always be smarter than me, more sophisticated, as would the rest of my family. I thought maybe this was the reason all of them were, on their own, pretty miserable. I decided right then to just give in and agree and try to make them all happy.

"You're right," I said, looking down at my gray plaid socks. "It's true. I'm gay. I'm really gay."

Jane grinned, tears coming to her eyes. She slid her arms around my neck and hugged me savagely, saying, "Doesn't it feel like an incredible weight has been lifted, Jack?" and I nodded because it was true in a way. She was hugging me and my father was patting me on the back and Dr. Dank was celebrating by lighting my mother's cigarette. It did feel good to have Jane feel proud of me, even for a moment, even for the absolute wrong reasons. I told everyone I loved them then and that I needed to get some sleep. Before I closed the door, I heard Dr. Dank announce that couples counseling for my sister and I would resume the very next day, and now that everything was in the open, our sessions were going to have to be bumped-up to twice a week.

×

I did not hear from Jill Thirby for almost a month, not until she called me to say that the cat we had found in the trash was dying. She asked me to come over and help her take it to the vet. I didn't have any reason to say no. When I got to her room, Jill Thirby was standing in the door with a small cardboard box: inside the cat was curled up, mewling. Its eyes were barely open and its entire body seemed to shudder. "He looks bad," I said.

"I know. He keeps crying. I don't know what to do."

"Why did you call me?" I asked.

"Because I don't want to go by myself."

Jill Thirby had looked in the phone book and had found an animal shelter in midtown. We called and made an appointment and then waited at the bus stop. Twice I thought the cat was dead, its rheumy eyes gazing up at us without any kind of life, but then it started to cry again, the sound of which made my hands feel shaky.

After we got to the shelter, after we were led down the hall to a tiny examination room, after the vet looked at the cat's scrawny stomach and weak legs and failing kidneys, he suggested Jill Thirby have it put to sleep. Jill Thirby immediately started sobbing. I had never seen anyone crying before like that. She was trying to say something but she was crying too hard and so I took her hand. She had yellow mittens on and I felt the stitches there against my palm and said, "It's okay," and Jill Thirby nodded and then the vet disappeared, taking the cat with him, and we stood alone in the tiny white room, like we were on the set of some soap opera, and Jill Thirby was still crying, and then we were waiting at the bus stop, and then we were getting on the bus, and the whole time we were sitting there, she was still holding the empty cardboard box, and we sat beside each other, watching the buildings go past in a blur, riding past my stop, past the stop for her school, past the part of the city we knew, at that moment wondering who we were, what was going to happen to us, waiting, like everybody else, for someone to tell us what to do.

Joe Meno

is a fiction writer and playwright who lives in Chicago. He is
the winner of the Nelson Algren Literary Award, a Pushcart
Prize, the Great Lakes Book Award, and a finalist for the Story
Prize. He is the author of six novels including the bestsellers
Hairstyles of the Damned and *The Boy Detective Fails*, and two
short story collections including *Demons in the Spring*. His short
fiction has been published in *One Story*, *McSweeney's*, *Swink*,
LIT, *TriQuarterly*, *Hayden Ferry's Review*, *Ninth Letter*, *Alaska
Quarterly Review*, *Mid-American-Review*, *Fourteen Hills*, *Washington
Square Review*, *Other Voices*, *Gulf Coast*, and broadcast on NPR's
Selected Shorts. His non-fiction has appeared in *The New York
Times* and *Chicago Magazine*. He was a longtime contributing editor
to *Punk Planet*, the seminal underground arts and politics magazine,
before it ceased publication in 2007. His plays have been produced
in Chicago, Los Angeles, Washington DC, and Paris, France. He
is a professor in the Fiction Writing Department at Columbia
College Chicago.

CHRISTOPHER HITCHENS

VANESSA VESELKA

yle claims he can cure faith. I asked him to do it. A year ago I wouldn't have, I would have paid to believe in anything. But Elena gets worse every night. She fell asleep in my bed and when I checked on her I thought she wasn't breathing because her little three-year-old face was so gray. It turned out to be nothing but the shadow of the quilt, though. I moved her stuffed sea lion closer to her and she rolled over on it dragging it down to the deep. Moments like those are more than I can take.

The doctors just tell me to love her. Someone else suggested I pray.

But belief of any kind at this point feels like being rocked in the arms of an insane mother—faith, that great and breaking bough—not with Elena at stake, I'm done with that.

When Lyle gave me his card, I thought it was a joke. It had a picture of a beach on it with that poem about the footsteps. He had crossed out the words and written: *You can be alone again.* According to his website, he can extract the finest strands of transcendent hope. That's what I'm counting on.

I did break down and pray last night. I thought I felt something. I told Lyle and he said that it's natural. He says faith is the only gateway to no faith. I asked what he meant and he said that beliefs, all beliefs, are like a series of tunnels.

"What we're after here is an open road."

He showed me the room where it's going to happen. The walls are covered with pictures of Jesus, Shiva, JFK, Osiris, and the Mandelbrot Set. There are big black Xs through each of them. Lining the windowsill were smaller icons—Einstein, the Dalai Lama, Elvis, Malcolm X, Christopher Hitchens, and a woman I recognized from late-night infomercials who sold

Ever Bliss™ powdered nutrient drinks. All in cheap plastic frames with the same black X over the image. Lyle had clearly snapped the shot of Hitchens off a TV screen with his phone and printed it out. The frame had no glass so I could see the streaks left by the Sharpie when he drew the X.

"Nobody is pure anything," Lyle said, "We have to get it all, even beliefs we think don't count."

"But I don't have any faith I just wish I did."

"Same thing."

But it's not the same thing because if I were capable of any real belief I wouldn't be here. I'd be gone.

"I have no faith to take," I said.

"Besides," said Lyle, "I'll bet you have more faith than you think. It just takes different shapes. In situations like yours it usually just takes different shapes."

I thought of my Wiccan high school years and flushed. Then the Marias came to mind, the ones I could only take in Spanish or Bosnian, and the candles for the dead and Mexican rosewater, the vague years of humming rocks and shells and feathers and cigarette smoke blown in all four directions—Lyle was right. Faith was in me. It was like a curtain behind a curtain. Put a gun to my head and ask me if I believe in anything and I'd point to Elena and say, I don't believe in a goddamned thing. Not if she's going to die. But take that gun away? Faith grows back in me like a field of mushrooms. Almost overnight.

"The first thing I need you to do," Lyle said, "is to write down a history of belief. Like praying you don't get caught stealing candy or calling Christians cowards when you're drunk [!]. It's all the same thing, it all has to go."

"Should I write it on anything special?"

"Write it on anything. That's the point."

I started that night and went all the way back to second grade when I thought I heard God's voice in a dream. By the time I fell asleep the bush outside my window was filled with chattering finches. I know now what Lyle means when he says faith and no faith is the same thing. I saw both sides of the coin flipping through the air. He means they come from the same place, believing and hating believers, a single tree, and if you don't pull out all the roots it grows back.

Elena goes to her Dad on Fridays. I don't get a choice in that. The worst part is that if something happens to her over the weekend, I won't be there. The idea that I wouldn't be there when it counted, that I might be out somewhere not even thinking about her when the real stuff happened it just too much. I try not to think about it but I do, all the time. I can't sleep when she's gone.

There's a revival going on down the street in a vacant lot out there in the weeds, right on the corner. They put up a tent. You can hear the preacher's voice through the PA echoing off the basketball courts in the park two blocks away. I've been hearing it every night. At first it was just annoying. Another thing like gunshots and Greenpeace knocking on your door, stuff you should care about but don't anymore because it happens all the time. All evening and into the night:

God's got it! God's got it!

And all the black voices calling it back.

God's got it! God's got it!

If they had been white I would have called the cops.

Every day I walk through the reedy lot. I see them setting up for the revival. Raking the flattened clumps of grass. Chasing the newspaper tumbleweeds. Bagging the bottles and needles and collecting grocery store circulars, holding them in their hands like garish fans.

They've been there all summer.

Fix it, Jesus! Fix it!

They yell out all the things that are wrong—

Fix it! Fix it, Jesus! Fix it!

They have a van full of clean white shirts for the converts and they come in all sizes. I saw a man that weighed over 400 pounds get saved. They wrapped him in white like a baby. No one is banned from the arms of Jesus. I imagine myself in white steeped in the smell of starch and irons and lemon water, and for a second, I'm pretty damn sure that if everybody would just get the hell away from me I could ride this feeling down into forever, this moment of grace, but they don't and I can't and it all breaks into smaller and smaller bits, even when they're already so small you think they can't, they do. Faith is like entropy according to Lyle. The heat it gives off is just from decline. It's not a closed system.

Lyle set up our second consultation at the food court tables by the Orange Julius. He has a face like Eric Clapton's; you'd never recognize him without context. Both times we met I thought it was a stranger approaching me.

This time Lyle came with diagrams. He set his smoothie down and unfolded a sheet of paper, flattening it with his hand. On it was a genderless human form with tiny lines drawn all over the body. My body.

"I'm thinking we'll put the needles here." He took a slug off his Orange Julius and pointed to a series of hash marks. "One for every belief."

I tried to see the pattern, but couldn't really. Some lines looked like sutures and others more like Amish hex symbols or asterisks. My whole history of hope before me in train trestles and broken rails.

"Will it hurt?"

"Probably," he said.

"Is that the chakra system?"

Lyle looked at me for a second then borrowed a pen and drew another set of lines on the figure. "You should have told me about that one."

Later on that night, I threw a full can of beer at someone's head. I was at a show and it was a singer of this band I knew. He was prancing around, doing the Iggy Pop thing, rolling on glass with bloody handprints and finger streaks all over his chest. When he pulled himself up on the microphone stand I threw the beer can as hard as I could. The Pabst logo spun like a ninja shuriken across the heads of the audience.

Lyle says he sees cases like mine all the time.

I punched a wall when they threw me out. When I woke up, my knuckles were swollen and there was dried brown streaks of blood on my hand. After I washed up, I snuck over to see Elena. She and Silas were eating macaroni and cheese for breakfast when I came in. Her cheeks were sticky with orange sauce. In front of her was a huge, half-drunk glass of milk.

"Is it hormone free?"

"They were out."

"I thought we had an agreement."

"I didn't ask you to come over."

215

He knows how I feel about those things. I keep Elena away from plastic and fish and she's never had antibiotics.

"That's not the point," I said, "We had an agreement."

"Yeah, and we also had an agreement about you not taking her to the doctor."

"There was something wrong with how she was breathing," I said, "I didn't take her right away, I watched her, for a long time. You would have taken her, too."

Silas looked me like I was wearing a wristband or a day pass or something. But I'm sick of seeing patience on people's faces. It doesn't affect me like it used to. You have to be an advocate. Silas will believe anything a doctor tells him. And the doctors say Elena meets all the developmental markers for her age. They say she's fine. But she's not fine. They don't know her like I do and so they can't see what's happening. She's changed. I've watched her now through countless car crashes, slips on the stairs, through terrible accidents on the playground when the bigger kids on the chain bridge pretend to shoot each other and knock her off. She's not the same. It's written all over her. She is going to die. Someday that is going to happen. And even though I don't know when, I know it will be too soon.

Later in the week, I took Elena to the doctor so they could check out her lungs again but they wouldn't see me. They just sent out a medical assistant and all she did was weigh Elena. I tried to make another appointment but they said to wait and see how she was doing in a few weeks. The scheduler in the waiting room gave Elena a rubber ball. It was the size of a plum, the color of honey and had a dolphin inside. Elena held it up to the light and showed me all the tiny flecks of glitter. I would rather have had some actual information, but I guess the glitter ball is something. Elena liked it, anyway.

When I pulled back up to the house the evangelists were testing the PA system at the revival down the street.

Check. Good afternoon. Check.

The man tapped the microphone. The sound was like a concussion grenade.

Check. Hello. Check.

A shrill squeal rang out and then a loud crack. Someone killed the sound. I tried to get Elena out of the car seat but she didn't want to put her arm through the strap because she had the dolphin ball in her fist and thought I was trying to make her give it up. Like I would take that thing from her? She can have all the glitter dolphin balls she wants.

Down the street, they raised the volume slowly and I heard the man on the microphone's clear voice arc upwards.

Hello. Check. Sisters and brothers. Family in Christ.

I know everyone dies but if I were a believer I wouldn't mind. If I were a believer, I would go like a lover to meet my girl the second she was gone.

I asked the guys on the corner to baptize me. I figured it was the only road left. I waited until Friday when Elena was at her dad's and went over right when they were setting up.

"Please," I said, "I want to be in the arms of Jesus."

"Welcome, sister. What is your name?"

"I want to be baptized."

I looked around for a pool or some kind of water.

"Where do you do it?"

He smiled. "In good order, sister, in good order."

"I live close-by. I have a kid pool. It doesn't have to look like anything special. I know it's not about that. I just need it to happen."

The man's moisturized black hands settled on mine. I touched his starched white sleeve. His oiled hair shone, light inside each follicle.

"Has the Lord called you?"

"Not really. But can't I call him?"

He patted my hands.

"Come back later. We'll have you talk to one of the sisters."

He released my hand.

In that moment I was aglow. I walked back towards the park at the end of the street then around the park and through it. It seemed to me like all the leaves were green moths that had only landed on the branch. I cut through the basketball courts and strolled under the Sugar Maple and Ginko trees. I saw Elena in a yellow field. I was beside her and there was no end.

From several blocks behind me I heard the preacher starting up and the crowd beginning to call back at him. My heart jumped because I thought I might have missed my chance to talk to the sisters and that there might be a list for those who want to be baptized and that it might fill up. I might even be told to come back the next night and I couldn't, it I had to be on it this night because I don't know how I will feel tomorrow. I turned and ran back to the revival to see if they were ready for me. They weren't, though. People were just getting started. The man on the microphone wasn't the main preacher, but another man and warming up the crowd as the dusk settled. When the last of the violet sky was gone, the street lamps along Martin Luther King Avenue turned on all at once. They cast wide circles of hazy light on the road through which cars

218

passed breaking them into shards that leapt like shamans, like sparks, and threw a net out over the world.

Sisters and brothers, are you ready to call on Jesus?

The crowd rippled with small waves of energy and began to answer back. The feeling was leaving me. Already. I moved to the back of the crowd to see if that made a difference. I thought if it was all further away, it might feel more real. But as hard as I tried, I couldn't make it stay.

I backed up and backed up until I was on the edge of the lot. Behind me was a tagged Plexiglas bus shelter and I sat down on the bench and waited. When it got darker the evangelists broke out the white shirts. One after another, men and women climbed the stairs to the platform and got saved. The preacher and the callers in their own white shirts moved over the stage like great actors. But it was Kabuki to me then. When they were done they packed the leftover white shirts into cardboard boxes and loaded them back into the van with the sound gear for the next night. I called Lyle and asked him to come and get me.

It was well past midnight when he picked me up in his Crown Victoria. He pulled into the bus stop and I got in. Lyle tapped the dashboard, "She was a cop car but I got her from a cab company. They sell them after they hit 300,000 miles. Rides like a dream but it's a little hard to get in and out of."

I rolled down the window and put my head on the vibrating door. Everybody's going to die someday, sure, but it's different when it's your daughter.

"Yeah," said Lyle, "They don't make these beauties anymore."

Lyle thinks small talk puts people at ease.

Nick Cave came on the radio and he turned it up.

"Now that guy could really benefit from this procedure. He's all over the place. A shame, too. Dualism is pretty easy to cure. Not like what you've got. A yard full of dandelions seeds with no flowers? That's a tough extraction."

Lyle turned without signaling. We pulled into the empty parking lot of a peach, two-story commercial building. His office was on the second floor. On the door was a gestural line drawing of a fat woman floating on a cloud that I hadn't noticed it before.

"I share the office with a massage therapist. She lets me use her table."

"Shouldn't we turn on the lights?"

"No, leave them off. This is the kind of thing best done in the dark."

A wave of nervous energy rippled through me and I was a teenager again. Crashing at the house of some creepy guy, not sure what I was in for. But the difference between me then and me now is that sex with someone I'm not into doesn't scare me. There are worse things. My mind, for example.

I took off my boots and left them by the door. The streetlight from the parking lot was coming through the blinds and when my eyes adjusted, I could see the room almost as I had before, the posters and photos.

"Are we going to have sex?" I asked.

"It's not that kind of thing. But I will need access to you."

I remembered the diagrams of my body covered with scratches like someone had used it to notch time.

Lyle walked over to his desk and began pulling things out of drawers while I climbed up on the massage table and unbuttoned my shirt. He set up a small tray table near the donut where you put your face when you get a massage and poured some rubbing alcohol into a glass. Walking back the desk, he pulled a chrome Newton's Cradle out of the bottom drawer.

"We're going to need this, too" he said and held it up. It was polished like a new toaster and the metal balls knocked irregularly against each other as he carried it over to the tray table. Then Lyle reached over and pulled what looked like a slim book off a shelf, but it wasn't a book. It was a purple, velvet folder full of needles. Hundreds it seemed. I saw them glint for a split second as a truck passed outside and lit the room.

I took off my bra and lay back.

Lyle tacked up a poster to the ceiling, directly above my line of sight. Krishna superimposed on a spiral of fractal patterns.

"I like to think of him as Blue Jesus," he said and wrote on the bottom of the poster: *There is no real connection but the one you make.*

Lyle put a thin cover over me. It had a satin edge like a baby's blanket. He lifted the silver ball on the Newton's Cradle then let it fall.

Click, click, click, click.

"I want you to do it like we talked about."

He picked a needle off the tray and dipped it in the alcohol. But he wasn't wearing gloves or using tweezers or anything. When I asked he said the alcohol was mostly for the burn.

"Now every time I put in a needle, I'm going to say what belief it's attached to. When I say that belief, I want you to think only of that belief and nothing else. Make sure you take your thoughts all the way to the end. Don't trail off. Faith has to run its course."

"How long do they stay in?"

"As long as it takes to break up the belief."

"How will we know?"

"Oh, you'll know."

Lyle smiled and fear hit me, the sense of what I was doing, that feeling of suddenly looking down. I wasn't so sure anymore.

"If you get distracted, focus on the sound of the ticking. It will never slow down or speed up. Everything else just bends around it. Now that's what I call real eternal."

Lyle crossed his hands and held them an inch above my body. I could feel the heat of his palms. I thought he would start at my feet or at my head and work from there but he said it doesn't matter what he does, that that's just another system of belief.

Then the first needle went in. He stuck it laterally through part of my forearm, but deeper than you'd think, like he was trying to pin me to me. But I've had tattoos and babies and cigarette and stove burns—nothing can hurt you like an idea can. Go ahead. Stick as many needles in me as you want. I barely felt the next one, only the heat as it radiated out.

He began to chant.

The part of you that believes in synchronicity, the part of you that doesn't.

I tried to imagine that each of his fingers had a fishing line coming from it and that and that on the other end were minnows of faith.

"I used to play music in the background," he said conversationally, "But too many people hid their faith in sound."

He moved his hands and put in another needle.

"People will attach to anything and for this to work there

222

has to be nothing to hang on to at all. Deep breath."

The part of you that thinks you're alive for a reason, the part of you that doesn't.

You don't know how many beliefs you have until someone tries to remove them.

Lyle said it was important not to fall asleep.

"If you fell asleep while we were doing this, we'd have to do it all again because two months later you would be trying to sleep all the time. Another deep breath, please."

The part of you that secretly hopes for a personal universe, the part of you that doesn't.

My skin was hot and my body hummed like a tuning fork. The clicking of the Newton's Cradle syncopated against his speech. I tried to hear a rhythm in it, but couldn't. There wasn't any rhythm but the one I made.

The part of you that believes in magic parking spaces or the perfect timing of ambulances or that the arc is long but bends toward justice...

It felt like a thousand fishhooks coming out of me. A tug and they went, my string of guarantees, each a pretty fly wound in bright colors around the hook, my faith. Maybe it was the pain. Maybe I was tired and making it up. I can do that too. But Elena was there and when I saw her I caved, okay, I said, okay, I will. I will give it all up. I want to see to the world again. I'll even whisper that awful thing—I want to be alone. Which was the promise, right? That I could be? Because that's what I want. I want to be alone again.

In a yellow field I saw Elena flickering behind glass that didn't curve. She wasn't bigger or smaller, just a shape in the weeds. My beautiful three-year-old girl before me, and there's nothing I can do to save her. She flickers like a firefly. God like a golden cloud around her, God not like a golden cloud around her. A reign of angels protecting her, a reign of angels not protecting her. Her choices guided by grace, her choices not guided by grace. Elena in the yellow field—but not guided by grace, not protected by angels, not clouded by god. She throws her glitter ball into the air and that dolphin just spins inside it as it rises.

Vanessa Veselka

is the author of the novel, *Zazen*, which was a finalist for the Ken Kesey Award for Fiction and won the 2012 PEN/Robert W. Bingham prize for fiction. Her short stories have appeared in *Tin House*, *YETI*, and *Zyzzyva*. Her nonfiction has been published in *GQ*, *The Atlantic*, *The American Reader*, *Salon*, and is included in the *2013 Best American Essays*.

DOLLHOUSE

CRAIG WALLWORK

The cottage where Darcy lived was set within the peaceful district of the Ryburn Valley. It stood on high grounds where heather, crowberry and cotton grass dressed the Yorkshire moorland in shades of green, purple and white. The limestone walls were cinereous in colour, becoming more charcoal when the sun settled behind the hills. The rapport between the snap and spit of burning logs, and cinder trails on the carpet from embers which had jumped from the open fireplace, were commonplace to Darcy. The autumn wind with its tortured voice baying upon every window pane had become her lullaby before bedtime and her birdsong when she awoke. Fear never exploited Darcy's mind, for as her father contested on many occasions, all things can be explained. The low thundering rumble that tore a hole in the night was not that of a monster pushing its way from one world to the next, but the nightly groans from the heifers keeping warm in the farmer's barn across the field. The unexpected squeak of a floorboard was not the heels of a ghost, but instead the yawning of wood as it waned under the heat of water pipes. The illusory evil that supposedly cowered in shadows, or became the cold breath of night that followed her from room to room, was only a mischievous current of air that fussed its way around the dank old cottage. All could be explained. Everything that is, except the dollhouse.

It was a perfect replica of the cottage in every detail. Shaped gable ends, stone quoining to front corner elevations, and detailed mullion windows with glazing were all perfectly crafted. The entire front of the cottage along with its roof opened to reveal the same three story, eight room accommodation. Stair railings, banisters and newel posts perfectly matched the deep mahogany like those her hands touched every day. The roll top bath was finished with similar gold fixtures and ornate feet, and the only noticeable difference was the absence of furniture in the rooms. But the dollhouse was beautiful in design, and would have probably remained hidden in the attic without Darcy ever seeing it had it not been for the ghost.

Darcy had awaked to a large bang. Believing it to be a door that had swung on its hinges due to the draft, she left her bed and felt the pinch of a cold wooden floor against her bare feet. The faint hue of a silver moon cast the landing in a static haze. Shadows huddled for warmth in every corner and the floorboards moaned and grumbled as each was stirred from their slumber by her tread. Darcy passed her parent's bedroom and pressed her ear to the door. The sonorous breathing of her father bled through the wooden paneling. Their door was firmly closed, as was the bathroom's. As she passed the attic she felt a cool breeze and turned to find the door was open. Crude steps made from wood ascended to a blanket of darkness beyond the staircase. Darcy approached and peered in with a quizzical, almost brazen air of displeasure. As her hand reached for the latch to close the door, she caught sight of a willowy form moving across the attic. She was not alarmed by this revelation, and assumed a car had passed outside; the light from the headlamp throwing a wayward shadow across the wall. A small light switch assured her steps as she made her way up to the attic.

Cardboard boxes of various sizes lay strewn across the floor, each labelled for every room in the house. Cobwebs hung from the apex and wooden beams like old rags and the smell in the air was like that of wet shoes and mothballs. A small window confirmed her suspicions that the ghost was only a light passing against the wall. She was about to leave when she noticed a large object covered under a dust sheet in the corner of the room. For years her parents had the habit of hiding gifts and birthday presents in lofts, attics and basements. Her ninth birthday was in three weeks and so Darcy assumed what lay beneath the dust sheet was her birthday present. She crept across the floor and lifted the sheet to reveal the dollhouse. That she had not hinted or requested one mattered little, for upon seeing it in that dimly lit room, she was completely happy to know it was hers.

Her clandestine visits became a nightly routine. Darcy would wait until her parents had gone to bed. She would then leave her bed quietly and visit the attic to see the dollhouse. An increasing number of ornamental furniture and fixtures were being added on each visit that matched perfectly those in the cottage. Her parents must have hired a master craftsman to fashion these items before placing them in the rooms every day. From the sleigh bed in her parent's bedroom to the antique Wellington chest in the living room, all the way to the Georgian oak antique chest of drawers in the dining room, the world she physically lived within had been shrunk to Liliputian size. By the first week, wallpaper had been added, and by the end of the second, the same taupe Saxony carpet covered the living room. But the biggest surprise came three days before her birthday. Darcy arrived in the attic to discover three small figurines had been placed in the dollhouse. Each resembled in the most accurate detail Darcy and her parents. She took them out and marvelled at each. Her father's figurine had the same Roman nose, designer glasses and widow's peak. Cheekbones were prominent and neck lacking in muscle. Her mother's hair was styled into the same bob that flanked a rounded face. Lips were like clam shells and eyes of onyx. Darcy's effigy wore a pretty blue flowery dress, the same she had in her wardrobe and was her favourite of all her clothes. Her auburn hair was tied into a ponytail, much the same way Darcy preferred to wear it. The nose was delicate, its bridge peppered with tiny specks of brown paint. The scar upon her chin that she had gained when she fell from a tree when five years old was etched into the wooden face of her counterpart. The house was complete.

On the eve of her birthday Darcy visited the attic to play with the house for the final time. She undid the latch and pulled back the front façade and roof. Everything was there, from the tiny furniture to the bowl of quince in the kitchen. Darcy found her wooden parents lay in their wooden bed, just like her real parents lay sleeping one floor below. To her surprise, Darcy's figurine was in the attic, knelt before a smaller version of the dollhouse, the most recent addition to the collection. Darcy moved her smaller self out of the way to get a better look of that tiny dollhouse. She did not wish to touch it in case it broke. In that moment, a noise like that of shifting feet presented itself behind her. Darcy turned, and for the briefest of moments saw an image of a man. His limbs were extended beyond that of what could be considered normal. He wore no clothes, and while shadows draped him like a veil, Darcy noted deep scars traversing his torso. The fingers of his ribcage were pressed against cyanotic skin, and a long, malformed face like that of a gnarled tree remained devoid of emotion. She had enough time to blink twice before the man disappeared. Darcy sprang to her feet and ran to the area the man had occupied, and with each step that pulled her toward the shadows, she convinced herself it was a trick of the light; a mix of fatigue and the sickly hue of the bulb. The space where he was stood was empty. Darcy reached her hand out to the blackness and found nothing residing there but a cold breeze that tightened her skin.

Darcy returned back to the dollhouse, and as she reached for the small clasp that secured the front of the cottage, she noticed the figurines of her parents were no longer sleeping in their beds. Her father was in the living room, his little wooden effigy lay suspended by a piece of brown twine; one end fixed to the wooden beam fixed to the ceiling, the other end wrapped around his wooden neck. She found her mother's figurine lay in the roll top bath, a trickle of red paint bleeding from her wrists. Both her parent's wooden faces of power pink and cream were bent by fear.

A dull thud came from the rooms below the attic, and in tandem, her heart beat out a similar sound. Darcy got to her feet and ran down the wooden stairs back to the landing. She opened the door to her parent's bedroom and found a feral landscape of bed sheets and nothing more. She called out for her mother, skewering a cry for her father to its end. More stairs. Two at a time. Down she went. The moonlight was split upon the cold slate floor of the kitchen like a gallon of milk. Darcy slipped as she rushed through it and fell on her back. Pain danced up her leg and spine, elbows throbbed. She clambered up and limped to the door that divided the kitchen to the living room and paused to catch her breath. *All can be explained*, she said like a mantra. *All can be explained*. The wind was a werewolf trapped in the walls, the moon a phantom consuming the stars. The house creaked and moaned as though the souls of the damned resided under floorboards. The door's handle cooled her sweltering palm as she twisted it slowly and pulled back, releasing a whimper from the hinges. The gap could not have been more than a few inches, but the naked heel of her father's foot suspended in the pastel shades of a lifeless night was enough to force her to not open it any wider.

She assumed it was tears. The tips of her fingers were darker after she wiped her cheek, but when Darcy felt another large drop upon her face, she looked up. A patch of water had collected on the ceiling, its colour brownish in tone. Darcy moved back and every drip that hit the kitchen floor resembled a short-lived scarlet coronet. To her knees she fell, shaking, sobbing. The bathroom was directly above her. Flashes of a naked wrist cleaved to reveal open veins flooded her fragile mind. She scampered to the sanctuary of a shadow, wrapped it around her shoulders and wept. It had to be a dream. Darcy convinced herself of this. Her parents would not end their lives. They were happy, and they would have never left her alone. The noise from upstairs suggested something, or someone was still in the attic. If it was a dream, she had nothing to fear. If it wasn't, then it was better she was with her parents than in an empty and cold cottage alone.

Her legs had turned weak. Nightgown, drenched with tears. She passed the bathroom without looking in. At the foot of the attic stairs she inhaled deeply, wiped her eyes and took the first step toward the beyond. The world slowed to a crawl. Silence overruled the clamour of what lain among the flotsam of domestic knick-knacks. Even Darcy's weight held no influence on the steps beneath her feet. It was though the whole house was holding its breath in apprehension. She arrived in the attic to find it as it was. The boxes were unmoved, the cobwebs sloth-like as they hung from corners. Shadows hugged miserably to the walls and floor. And there the dollhouse glowed like a Halloween pumpkin in the dim light, a macabre symbol of her fate. There was no change to her parent's figurines, which remained in their varying exhibition of death. But Darcy drew her attention to the small attic in the dollhouse. There was the small crafted model of herself kneeling before the miniature dollhouse, just as she was knelt before the larger one. On closer inspection she noted a red line that scored the throat of the tiny figure. The winter's breath she grew to believe was only a draft fell upon her neck in that moment, and from the corner of her eye a hand came into view. The tips of each finger were sheltered by gauze, blood seeping through as if the toil of intricacy and detail had worn the skin to the flesh. Scars as thick as leaches chartered the hand, and the rasp of failing lungs stirred her hair. The glimmer of a small whittling knife constricted her pupils, and upon her throat its cooled edge prevented the words she longed to speak.

All can be explained.
All can be explained.

Craig Wallwork

lives in West Yorkshire, England. He is the author of the short story collection *Quintessence of Dust* (KUBOA), and the novels *To Die Upon a Kiss* (Snubnose Press) and *The Sound of Loneliness* (Perfect Edge Books). His fiction has appeared in various anthologies, journals and magazines. He is the fiction editor at *Menacing Hedge Magazine*.

HIS FOOTSTEPS ARE
MADE OF SOOT

NIK KORPON

Her skin parts like wet silk under a razor, and even with a gaping hole in her face, she's quite beautiful. Marcel blots sweat from his forehead with the bandana cinched around his wrist. The scent of iodine and Pine Sol hangs so heavily in his basement, it's almost visible. At least it covers the mildew tang usually present.

"Knife," he grunts, stained palm extended.

"Filet or paring?"

He chews on the inside of his cheek, debating, then looks up at me. "What do you think?"

Adjusting the clamp light above the table, I lean over the girl, probe her opened cheek with a modified barbecue fork. After a minute, I shrug and suggest the paring knife, and say, "But you're the doctor." He mutters something in French that doesn't sound complimentary. Another brief contemplation, he snatches the paring knife and goes to work.

She came to us because her smile was uneven and it made her self-conscious. How this girl could despise her appearance is beyond my pay scale, but that's why I assist a surgeon, not a psychologist. Her name is probably just as beautiful as her lips, something that could turn your knees to water as you shout it across the bus terminal, begging her not to leave. Megan, our pseudo-secretary, keeps the clients anonymous, though. Sometimes things happen in home-surgery, and it's easier to be objective when the body doesn't have a name, an address, a way they take their coffee. Everything's easier when history is malleable.

Marcel nudges my arm. Isopropyl alcohol slops over the side of the cup in my hand.

"Eight inches of fishing line. Please." His tone says that he's asked this more than once and I was miles away.

I help him close the girl's face, holding the knot with a finger while he ties the line. It makes me glad that Mom bought me Velcro shoes as a kid, but I can't fall down that wormhole right now. For having fingers as thick as hotdogs, he's surprisingly nimble. He once told me he was a boxer, back where he came up, but I've never known if that was an inside joke.

Marcel snips the line and takes an appraising look, pursing his lips. He looks at me and raises an eyebrow. I nod.

"Wake her," he says, then carries the mixing bowl of cutlery and flatware to the laundry sink in the corner.

Her eyelashes are delicate spiderlegs. Pallid eyelids flutter as she dreams of ethereal places. I brush the back of my hand across her good cheek, warm with blood. Curls of hair pool behind the soft slope of her skull like a puddle of coffee. Lips twitching as if they're hoping for a kiss and I startle when Marcel coughs. He's bent over the sink, scrubbing at a pair of tongs.

I fidget with my hands—as if nothing unusual had happened—then move towards her feet, and, until I glance down and see her arm, she's the most beautiful creature to lie on our table. Just below the crook of her elbow sit three purple dots that could be mistaken for ticks, and if dots like these didn't turn my blood to acid, I could say they were innocuous bug bites, not trackmarks.

Two jabs on the bottom of the feet wake her, though if it was an ice-pick instead of a needle, she'd be a bloody mess. She jerks to the side, blinking away the haze. I wait for the disorientation to pass before giving rudimentary healing instructions and sending her to Megan in the other part of the partitioned basement.

"Pretty girl," Marcel says, head down into the sink.

"Mmhm." I double-check the nitrous valve and make sure

it's closed. A few months ago, I didn't twist it far enough. Marcel thought it was funny at the time, for obvious reasons, but proceeded to berate me for an hour once the drugs wore off. Clowns bounce around the tank in various joyful positions. It's a wonder people will still lay under our knife after we offer them Krusty-brand anesthetic. Then again, we're not exactly your normal HMO.

"Do you have time to get dinner tonight?"

The big hand relentlessly follows the little hand around the face of my watch. Mom will need to eat within the hour.

"Can I get a rain check?"

He's already nodding before I answer.

"Leave the clean-up for me. You'll miss your bus."

Rain collects in buckets and pots and pickle jars scattered across the floor of our house. The anonymous cheering on her gameshow trickles from upstairs. I light scented candles to cover the smell of damp smoke, then balance a glass of milk, a mug of tea, and a bowl of soup on the orange plastic tray.

"Mom," I shout. "Did Daniel drop off any bread today?'"

The crowd roars at something inanely thrilling.

"Mom?"

Someone wagered too much or bought the wrong vowel and now the crowd is disappointed. I pile a few crackers on the cracked plastic and tentatively shuffle up the steps. The rain falls with a rhythmic plink. Hung in the stairwell are prints of flower paintings, gilded frames around the edges. I remember, when I was younger, Mom would get mad because I'd leave smudges all over the glass. The colors were so vibrant, I had to touch the prints to check if they were real. Now, soaked in water and old smoke, they all look dead.

Her wheelchair is facing the wall when I walk in. 'Jesus, Ma,' I mutter.

"Henry, darling." She raises her hand, feeling for my face. "I didn't hear you come in."

Jagged lines of soot stagger along the walls like a cursed mountain range. I nudge her hand with my chin. "That's because the whole neighborhood is listening to *Wheel of Fortune* with you."

"It's *Press Your Luck*."

"Whatever." I press my foot against her wheel and turn her towards me.

Her hand flutters like an epileptic moth in the dim light. "Henry, let your mother say hello to you."

"My hands are full. Just give me a minute." I drag a table over with my foot and set her tray down. Rain drips from the roof, cloudy with insulation and ash, and lands on a towel at the foot of the bed. I toss it onto the pile in the corner and place Mom's hands on my cheeks.

"There's my boy," she sighs. Her smile is almost as cockeyed as her pupils, as if they're joined by some of Marcel's fishing line. 'How was your day, darling?'

"Fine, Mom." I wedge the edges of the tray between the armrests of her chair and wrap her fingers around the spoon, guide it to the bowl. "Eat your soup before it's cold."

The crowd roars again, and I press mute instead of throwing the TV out the cracked window. A blonde who really wants the trip they're offering beats her hands together and looks strikingly like a seal. Through the thin walls, I can hear the junkie next door playing violin. It's more seizure than concerto, but at least he's learned the concept of rhythm in the past year.

I wipe beads of broth from Mom's chin and light a cigarette. Smoke twists from the burning end and dissipates in the grey air. She pauses, spoon halfway to her mouth.

"I thought you switched from menthol."

I drop the cigarette in a soda can and thumb one from her pack. "I did."

She just smiles.

I watch game show contestants beat their hands together, silently laughing and throwing their arms up in awe. The house smells of dampness, of a dog in the river or unwashed clothing. When the wind blows, I swear to Christ it gets ten degrees colder in here. I close my eyes and visualize smoke filling my lungs, concentrate on the wet air dissolving me. The metal spoon clatters on cracked porcelain. She gives a contented sigh and extends her hand.

"You almost ready for bed?" I light a cigarette and set it in her mouth.

"Thank you, but I was reaching for your hand." She gropes my elbow, working her way down to my wrist. Squeezing my palm, head cocked and pupils floating like drowned flies in a pool of yellowed milk, she says, "Talk to me."

"I am talking to you."

"Real talk." She jerks her shoulders, trying to move her chair closer.

I light another cigarette. She slowly shakes her head. A bus passes our house, the wet whoosh making our walls shiver. Rain falls in steady droplets from the ceiling, plinks matching my heartbeat.

"I'm fine, Mom. Let's get you into bed."

I push her to her room, lay out her pajamas, and after she

calls out that she's decent, lift her into bed. I kiss her goodnight, and her forehead is cold as a forgotten hallway. She holds my wrist and I turn to leave.

"If you won't talk, please sing to me."

"Mom," I look at my watch, as if I have someplace to be, as if she could even see it.

"Please, Henry." She squeezes my hand again. I sigh and give in. Even through my pants, I can feel that the chair is wet when I sit.

"What song? Not Johnny Cash, we always do Johnny Cash."

She nestles her head into the pillow and a smile trickles across her face. "Hank Williams."

"Why do you keep asking?"

"Because your father loved it."

"Exactly." I push the chair back to leave.

"Henry." Her chin trembles despite itself, as she tries to mouth please. "For me?"

"I'll sing you something, but it won't be Hank."

She purses her lips and, eventually, nods.

I hum the opening verse of a Roy Orbison tune she used to play a lot, making up a few of the words I can't remember, and drag the covers up to her chin, pressing them around her body. Sitting on the night table is a framed picture of her with cat's-eye glasses and a pencil skirt, shaking the hand of a man in a suit that looks so expensive, I can practically smell the wool through the photo. She was young, really young. Her first real job, I think, as an assistant at Bethlehem Steel, a few months before the plant shut down. The certificate that the man is handing her used to hang on the wall in what used to be her office, before my father commandeered it and blacked out the windows with tinfoil and duct tape.

Halfway through the bridge and her breaths are slower,

longer. I ebb from singing to humming and creep away from her bed, minding the few spots that creak.

For a blind woman, she can be incredibly crafty, and before I turn off the light, I lay facedown a sheep stuffed animal my father won for her at the State Fair, back when they were dating. It holds a sign in its mouth with I Love Ewe scrawled in what I suppose is sheep-script. Every night I turn it down, and every morning, it's upright again. I tried to tell myself that it was only ghosts, that poltergeists were toying with me, trying to make me insane. Truth is, it's far worse than that.

It's love.

The unconscious boy sprawled facedown across the table poked a hole in the vacuum of my chest the minute I saw him. His arms could've passed for a January sky finger-painted by a four year-old. The cloud of bruises started around his bicep, drifting down a fading sun the color of pus. His back was less artistic; the shapes of belt buckles competed with spoons–probably wooden, if they left marks like that–and all a similar shade of scarred brown. I paced in the alley, chain-smoking four cigarettes before I could get my head together to operate.

Marcel goes to work on the back of the kid's neck. I ask him what the procedure is and he flaps his arms like a mad duck, mutters a bunch of words and the only ones I can pick up are nerve endings.

I laugh to myself. "Are you an electrician now, rewiring sensations?"

He glares at me above his safety goggles. "Deadening them."

"Oh," I say, more into my shoulder than aloud.

The surgery proceeds in forty minutes of silence, broken only by single phrases. Knife. Melon baller. Corkscrew. Hold it, not there–there. Whether he's concentrating or pissed, it doesn't really matter: all I can focus on is the pattern of scarred-brown that covers the kid's back.

When Marcel clears his throat, it's my father standing over my mother, laughing, as she's crumpled on the floor. When he re-sterilizes the knife over flame, it's the click of my father's lighter under a tarnished spoon. When he coughs, it's my father with his face in the crook of his arm, hurrying down the steps as smoke billows behind him.

A bright white spot flashes in my eyes. I startle, and Marcel's right hand is reared back to smack me again, his left holding down the boy's head.

"I said get the goddamn nitrous! He's waking up!"

I scurry to the tank and drag it over, crush the mouthpiece on the boy's face and in seconds, he's unconscious again. Marcel releases his tentative grip and exhales hard through his nose.

"Send in Megan. You need to go home."

The rain drips. The studio audience cheers. The haunting smoke lingers. My life is a crooked deck of cards: all varying slightly, but basically the same and repeated endlessly.

While Mom eats her stew, I excuse myself to the bathroom and, silent as a shadow, grab the stuffed animal from her dresser. I flush the toilet and open the window while the water is still running and throw the sheep into the alley between houses.

She's stopped eating when I return.

"Where were you?"

244

"In the bathroom, Ma. I just told you that."

"What were you doing in the bathroom?"

I light a cigarette and laugh.

"Don't laugh at me, Henry," she snaps. "What were you doing in the bathroom?"

"Christ, what do you think?" In some remote part of my brain, I'm wondering if she can hear my hands twitching. "What people always do in the bathroom."

She sits, silent but for the breathing coursing in and out of her nostrils. She takes a deep breath and crosses her arms. "I'm ready for bed."

"Okay, keep your wig on." I wheel her towards her bed and she sticks her arms up like a toddler waiting to be dressed.

"I want you to sing to me, Henry."

"I sing to you every night." I hand her a pair of pajamas. "Change your clothes first."

"You're the only one I see. I don't need to keep up airs." She's gnawing on her bottom lip, and the way her eyes float when she gets angry is almost comical. "I want you to sing."

"Jesus, fine, whatever." I start into an Elvis tune, from his gospel years, and she cuts me off.

"Hank Williams."

"We've been over this before."

"Hank Williams, Henry. Sing it."

"Damn it, Ma." I forget and crush my cigarette on the floor under my foot. It sizzles on the damp surface and the mark is indistinguishable. "I'm not singing that fucking song. I don't care if it's the only song that won't...won't make your head explode. I'm not going to sing that song."

"But it's all I have." Her jaw tightens, lip shivers. "I love it."

"He loved it."

She flinches, as if I'd hit her. As if she could see me try to strike her. "He loved you."

"He loved smack and he loved you buying it for him."

She swings her hand, swatting dust particles and drops of rain and coming nowhere near my face

"Don't talk about you father that way!"

"Why, Mom?" I pace the other side of the bed. "Tell me."

"Because he was a good man."

"He tried to burn the fucking house down!" I knock the picture of her and the man off her night table. "You're blind and you're crippled, and you're telling me he was a good fucking man!"

"Don't scream at me!" Her voice shatters into a thousand jagged pieces, chest heaving and shaking so hard the armrest falls off the wheelchair. It clatters on the floor, and I look around and the whole scene comes crashing down on me as if the roof finally gave in and aimed itself for the crown of my skull.

"God. Mom." I rush to her side of the bed, to hold her, hug her, sing to her, and apologize, but she uses some kind of echolocation and her hand stings hard across my mouth. She wills the tears back into her eyes and her expression becomes marble.

"Get out of my house."

Marcel answers on the third knock. The light over his door is burned out and streetlights cast a golden pall. The bunny on his right foot is missing one ear and his left looks comatose. He regards me with leaden eyes and a grunt.

"I need an operation," I say.

His kitchen is almost as accommodating as his basement

surgery: cardboard boxes half-full of textbooks and home repair manuals line the perimeter, and a rainbow-river of wires runs across the chipped linoleum.

"Hazelnut?"

"What?"

"Do you like hazelnut coffee?"

I shrug and pull out a chair, moving a grocery bag of antiseptic mouthwash, grilling implements, dental floss and packs of wintermint gum to the floor.

"You know I'm not a brain surgeon, right? I mean, anything can go wrong." His words come in fits and starts, alternating warnings with counting scoops of coffee. "You've seen that yourself. It probably will go wrong."

"You're a doctor. You can do it."

"Henry," he pauses, laughing to himself. "Look behind you. Second stack from the corner, about waist-high. There's a box labeled head."

While he roots around in the fridge, I unstack piles, unearthing a box of neurological textbooks. He beckons with his hand, digs halfway down and grabs a book with a blank cover. Bologna sandwich hanging from his mouth, he leafs through two inches of pages, then spins the book to face me and jabs a finger on a diagram of the human brain.

"Right there, right there, and right there are where your memories are stored."

"I told you you could do it."

"It's not erasing a movie from a video tape, Henry. It's brain surgery."

"And?" On the counter, the coffee pot coughs and sputters.

"And those two spots, I could never get to. Not without turning your head into a skull-full of grits."

I get up and pour two cups of coffee. "So what are you going to do?"

"Nothing."

Fingers of steam rise from the coffee like smoke, like ropes of thick grey air that carry cinders and souls. I sip and expect to taste ash.

I point to another set of ridges. "What about there?"

He tilts his head, considering. "Well, yeah, but there's no guarantee. On any of it. I could do it and make you a drooling idiot. You could lose any memory you have. You could lose random ones and keep the ones you want gone. I could slip and nick another lobe, like this one."

He lays a gnarled finger on the next section. "That controls language."

"Okay."

"While I'd enjoy you not be able to argue with me, it might affect other aspects of your life. As in you and your—"

I swat away the idea. "Yeah, I get it."

We sip our coffee until it's only grounds scattered on the bottom of the cup. He offers half his sandwich, but I push it back to him. I try to stare a hole through his skull, to climb in and rewire his risk-assessment ridges. He won't meet my eyes.

Eventually, he stands and stretches. The edge of the sky bleeds pink, drop by drop, ray by ray. He tells me that he needs to take a shower and eat breakfast because there's a consultation scheduled in two hours. He pauses before going up the steps, turns and raises his gaze to mine. It's taken four hours for him to meet my eyes.

"I used to know a girl once, a singer, back when I was still fighting."

"So that wasn't a joke?"

"I didn't always look like this." He looks down at the buttons of his shirt, stretched tight and nearly popping free. "She had one of the most beautiful voices I'd ever heard—still, to this day—that could've taken her anywhere in the world. The only thing holding her back was the idea that things were always better on that other stage."

I flip back the edge of a box, pick at a veterinary surgery guide.

"You're going to do this regardless, aren't you?" he says.

"It's either you or drinking four gallons of turpentine." In a digging motion, I press a spoon to my forehead until white dots materialize like stars on the horizon. "Either way, he can't be in here anymore."

Marcel only nods. The spoon tinks on the tabletop.

"Go home and sleep." His footsteps echo in the hallway. "You can come in tonight."

The day passes in a breath, and as I kneel beside Mom, tucked under her covers as if she's sleeping, though I can tell from her breathing she's awake. I can't remember a single scene from my entire day. Marcel's voice echoed down the hall, then I was tiptoeing across the Mom's floor, a thief in my own house.

She rolls over and grunts, still pretending, and her hand falls on the edge of the bed next to mine. I lay mine over hers and sing in a voice barely louder than eyelashes blinking. I swallow bile and dig my fingernails into my thigh and sing the Hank Williams song she and my fuckface father loved. She manages to keep the appearance up and can control her breathing, but the tear welling in the crevice of her right eyelid gives it away.

I kiss her forehead and remove my hand, then slink away into the rainy night.

A pelican flies over water that looks like an ocean of sapphires while two palm trees sway in a gentle breeze that barely shifts any of the crystalline sand on the beach. A woman leans over a car from Smokey and the Bandit, the bandana she's using as a bathing suit disappearing between her thighs.

I've worked with Marcel for over two years, and I never noticed the posters he tacked to the ceiling.

"Nice touch," I say.

He nods, gives a half-smile. "I wanted to cover all the bases."

"It's only two bases." I sit up, leaning on my elbow. 'And that one's bordering on pornographic.'

He just shrugs and runs the edge of a knife over a tomato, testing the blade, then pours alcohol over it. Blotting it dry, he picks up a needle then sets it down, turns over a pair of tongs and replaces the Saran Wrap over the table. Three more slices in the tomato and I think he's stalling.

"You promised," I say.

His hand jumps, nicking the thumb. Hand to his mouth, he mumbles, "You're sure about this."

I just nod and lay down, close my eyes. A muted rainbow of dots float across the flesh inside my eyelids. I focus, try to rearrange them into a halftone print of a family portrait with only two people. Inhale. The smell of damp smoke floods my nostrils, and Marcel gave up cigarettes years ago when his wife died of cancer. Exhale. The sound of game-show audiences drowns out scratchy country guitars. Inhale. A fist of cheap cologne, vodka and the burnt baby laxative used to cut dope crushes my nose. Exhale. A whiff of ash, of baby powder, of Mom's shampoo from when I was younger that always reminded me of cut grass.

Inhale. Nitrous oxide and Marcel's liquid voice telling me to count to ten. Somewhere beyond my ears, past bloody eyelids and clenched fists and bruised legs and pipe-burnt chests, Hank Williams drags his voice over broken glass in the darkness.

✕

Static white. Fields of snow and the feathers of doves falling around me. A thousand rose thorns stab my fingers and feet. Marcel's voice sends the feathers into spirals.

I blink away the nauseating soot and see a brilliant blue swirl above me. Tiny fists reshape the inside of my head.

"Henry?" His voice is made of cotton and I can hardly hear it over the reverberations in my skull.

The air is tactile and claustrophobic. Hot metal, copper and antiseptic. I blink, tell my fingers to move. One trembles, or that could be my vision.

"Henry, can you hear me?" His snaps are cracks of thunder.

I hoist myself up to my elbows, swallow. An anchor must be tied to the back of my head.

"Do you know where you are? What's my name?"

He snaps his fingers to the left, right, left, up and down, testing my reactions.

"What's your mother's name?"

I clear my throat.

"Henry." Marcel takes my hand and looks me straight in the eyes. "Speak."

I open my mouth and silence devours me.

Nik Korpon

is the author of *Old Ghosts, By the Nails of the Warpriest, Bar Scars: Stories*, and the forthcoming *Stay God, Sweet Angel* (2014). His stories have bloodied the pages and screens of *Needle Magazine, Crime Factory, Shotgun Honey, Yellow Mama, Out of the Gutter, Speedloader, Warmed & Bound* among others, and he is a columnist for LitReactor.com. He lives in Baltimore.

THE ETIQUETTE OF HOMICIDE

TARA LASKOWSKI

11. On Introductions

A bove all, you must be patient.

It may take some time to get a full answer, so don't be afraid of a little bit of silence. Prompting, such as "go on," or "what are you thinking?" or "I'm going to beat your face into mashed potato pulp" will *not* help and will likely make them nervous. You should also generally avoid finishing their sentences when they pause for a moment. They want to articulate their thoughts in a particular way, so give them enough time to do so.

Listen carefully to their answers (but never write them down) and give positive feedback, such as, "You're doing a good job" or "That wasn't that hard now, was it?" Avoid threats if at all possible. Be sure to give sincere feedback between questions; if they don't think you mean what you're saying, it won't help you.

Express a positive impression of interacting with them. When it's time for you to part ways, smile and let them know that you appreciated talking with them. If you seem insincere, they may feel discouraged rather than uplifted. It is important to let them know this is nothing personal—it's just your job.

Appendix C—Recipe for Old Fashioned

2 oz bourbon whiskey
2 dashes Angostura® bitters
1 splash water
1 tsp sugar

1 maraschino cherry
1 orange wedge

Mix sugar, water, and Angostura bitters in a tall shaker. Dump in an old-fashioned glass, or if you are traveling, any glass will do. Drop in a cherry and an orange wedge. Muddle into a paste using a muddler or the back end of a blunt instrument (like a spoon, or the handle of a screwdriver). Pour in bourbon, fill with ice cubes, and stir. Drink in three gulps sitting down, shoes off, toes waving into the carpet threads. Repeat. Repeat.

Part 7—The Dance

There are no rules of protocol. The Client prefers you to use bullets. The gun is like your dick, The Client says. Hold it close, protect it. It makes you Who You Are, they say. A steady hand, scope, sniping away from a great distance.

Prefer something more intimate? A dance, then, with a partner who prefers to hover at the edge of the room, just in front of the floor-to-ceiling velvet drapes. Find him there, approach quietly from behind as not to startle. Put your arms around his and remember the waltz lessons Mrs. Kessel taught you long ago on that gym floor—*one two three, one two three*—and in Mr. Duncan's home economics class years after that, slicing through chicken quickly, efficiently—with confidence you get right through the bone. Trust the knife, silent like a goodnight kiss. Then pirouette your partner out, *one two three, one two three*. Thank you. Thank you.

Tip the concierge, but not too much. Too much will make him remember you; too little will make him remember you.

Part 10—Laundromats

Remove a bloodstain when it is fresh. Rinse the clothing in cold water. Then blot the bloodstain with some diluted Tide you buy for $2 in the vending machine in the back.

Laundromats are not glamorous. You never see James Bond in a Laundromat at 3:45 a.m., where the 24-hour fluorescent lights at the front entrance speak easy money for the enormous spiders and their webs. They know how to maximize their kills. Some of them you swear you can see breathing.

Ignore the bums sleeping in the corner or wandering through with wild eyes. Ignore the *thump, thump, thump, thump* of someone's bed sheets in the dryer. Ignore the smell of piss mixed with fabric softener. Focus on you, on getting through, on getting back.

If all else fails, try spitting on a bloodstain—especially if it's your own blood. Surprisingly, this may help.

On Dreams

Eating late at night makes for more vivid dreams. Eat as early as possible, and avoid drinking heavily right before bed.

Should you wake from one of the Terrible Ones, stand up immediately in the dark and jump up and down until your ankles start to hurt and the blood in your head feels hot. Remember you are here. Remember there is no God. There is just you and the dark and the carpet, the soft shaggy carpet you spent your first reward on that was worth every fucking penny because it is real and more money than your father would've spent on a car back in those days, back in New Jersey where all the houses squat sad and droopy and falling apart and fuck that, all that. Don't think about your parents either, those nights. Splash some cold water on your face and burn a fifty-dollar bill in the sunken marble tub.

When the fire dies out, eat the ashes.

Tara Laskowski

is the author of *Modern Manners For Your Inner Demons* (Matter
Press), a short story collection of dark etiquette. She is the senior
editor for *SmokeLong Quarterly* and has published numerous stories
online and in print.

DREDGE

MATT BELL

The drowned girl drips everywhere, soaking the cheap cloth of the Ford's back seat. Punter stares at her from the front of the car, first taking in her long blond hair, wrecked by the pond's amphibian sheen, then her lips, blue where the lipstick's been washed away, flaky red where it has not. He looks into her glassy green eyes, her pupils so dilated the irises are slivered halos, the right eye further polluted with burst blood vessels. She wears a lace-frilled gold tank top, a pair of acid wash jeans with grass stains on the knees and the ankles. A silver bracelet around her wrist throws off sparkles in the window-filtered moonlight, the same sparkle he saw through the lake's dark mirror, that made him drop his fishing pole and wade out, then dive in after her. Her feet are bare except for a silver ring on her left pinkie toe, suggesting the absence of sandals, flip-flops, something lost in a struggle. Suggesting too many things for Punter to process all at once.

Punter turns and faces forward. He lights a cigarette, then flicks it out the window after just two drags. Smoking with the drowned girl in the car reminds him of when he worked at the plastics factory, how he would sometimes taste melted plastic in every puff of smoke. How a cigarette there hurt his lungs, left him gasping, his tongue coated with the taste of polyvinyl chloride, of adipates and phthalates. How that taste would leave his throat sore, would make his stomach ache all weekend.

The idea that some part of the dead girl might end up inside him—her wet smell or sloughing skin or dumb luck—he doesn't need a cigarette that bad.

Punter crawls halfway into the back seat and arranges the girl as comfortably as he can, while he still can. He's hunted enough deer and rabbits and squirrels to know she's going to stiffen soon. He arranges her arms and legs until she appears asleep, then brushes her hair out of her face before he climbs back into his own seat.

Looking in the rearview, Punter smiles at the drowned girl, waits for her to smile back. Feels his face flush when he remembers she's never going to.

He starts the engine. Drives her home.

Punter lives fifteen minutes from the pond but tonight it takes longer. He keeps the Ford five miles per hour under the speed limit, stops extra long at every stop sign. He thinks about calling the police, about how he should have already done so, instead of dragging the girl onto the shore and into his car.

The cops, they'll call this disturbing the scene of a crime. Obstructing justice. Tampering with evidence.

What the cops will say about what he's done, Punter already knows all about it.

At the house, he leaves the girl in the car while he goes inside and shits, his stool as black and bloody as it has been for months. It burns when he wipes. He needs to see a doctor, but doesn't have insurance, hasn't since getting fired.

Afterward, he sits at the kitchen table and smokes a cigarette. The phone is only a few feet away, hanging on the wall. Even though the service was disconnected a month ago, he's pretty sure he could still call 911, if he wanted to.

He doesn't want to.

In the garage, he lifts the lid of the chest freezer that sits against the far wall. He stares at the open space above the paper-wrapped bundles of venison, tries to guess if there's enough room, then stacks piles of burger and steak and sausage on the floor until he's sure. He goes out to the car and opens the back door. He lifts the girl, grunting as he gathers her into his arms like a child. He's not as strong as he used to be, and she's heavier than she looks, with all the water filling her lungs and stomach and intestinal tract. Even through her tank top he can see the way it bloats her belly like she's pregnant. He's careful as he lays her in the freezer, as he brushes the hair out of her eyes again, as he holds her eyelids closed until he's sure they'll stay that way.

The freezer will give him time to figure out what he wants. What he needs. What he and she are capable of together.

Punter wakes in the middle of the night and puts his boots on in a panic. In the freezer, the girl's covered in a thin layer of frost, and he realizes he shouldn't have put her away wet. He considers taking her out, thawing her, toweling her off, but doesn't. It's too risky. One thing Punter knows about himself is that he is not always good at saying when.

He closes the freezer lid, goes back to the house, back to bed but not to sleep. Even wide awake, he can see the curve of her neck, the interrupting line of her collarbones intersecting the thin straps of her tank top. He reaches under his pajama bottoms, past the elastic of his underwear, then squeezes himself until the pain takes the erection away.

On the news the next morning, there's a story about the drowned girl. The anchorman calls her missing but then says the words *her name was*. Punter winces. It's only a slip, but he knows how hurtful the past tense can be.

The girl is younger than Punter had guessed, a high school senior at the all-girls school across town. Her car was found yesterday, parked behind a nearby gas station, somewhere Punter occasionally fills up his car, buys cigarettes and candy bars.

The anchorman says the police are currently investigating, but haven't released any leads to the public. The anchorman looks straight into the camera and says it's too early to presume the worst, that the girl could still show up at any time.

Punter shuts off the television, stubs out his cigarette. He takes a shower, shaves, combs his black hair straight back. Dresses himself in the same outfit he wears every day, a white t-shirt and blue jeans and black motorcycle boots.

On the way to his car, he stops by the garage and opens the freezer lid. Her body is obscured behind ice like frosted glass. He puts a finger to her lips, but all he feels is cold.

The gas station is on a wooded stretch of gravel road between Punter's house and the outskirts of town. Although Punter has been here before, he's never seen it so crowded. While he waits in line he realizes these people are here for the same reason he is, to be near the site of the tragedy, to see the last place this girl was seen.

The checkout line crawls while the clerk runs his mouth, ruining his future testimony by telling his story over and over, transforming his eyewitness account into another harmless story.

The clerk says, I was the only one working that night. Of course I remember her.

In juvie, the therapists had called this narrative therapy, or else constructing a preferred reality.

The clerk says, Long blond hair, tight-ass jeans, all that tan skin—I'm not saying she brought it on herself, but you can be sure she knew people would be looking.

The clerk, he has black glasses and halitosis and fingernails chewed to keratin pulp. Teeth stained with cigarettes or chewing tobacco or coffee. Or all of the above. He reminds Punter of himself, and he wonders if the clerk feels the same, if there is a mutual recognition between them.

When it's Punter's turn, the clerk says, I didn't see who took her, but I wish I had.

Punter looks away, reads the clerk's name tag. OSWALD. The clerk says, If I knew who took that girl, I'd kill him myself.

Punter shivers as he slides his bills across the counter, as he takes his carton of cigarettes and his candy bar. He doesn't stop shivering until he gets out of the air-conditioned store and back inside his sun-struck car.

The therapists had told Punter that what he'd done was a mistake, that there was nothing wrong with him. They made him repeat their words back to them, to absolve himself of the guilt they were so sure he was feeling.

The therapists had said, You were just kids. You didn't know what you were doing.

Punter said the words they wanted, but doing so changed nothing. He'd never felt the guilt they told him he should. Even now, he has only the remembered accusations of cops and judges to convince him that what he did was wrong.

Punter cooks two venison steaks in a frying pan with salt and butter. He sits down to eat, cuts big mouthfuls, then chews and chews, the meat tough from overcooking. He eats past the point of satiation on into discomfort, until his stomach presses against the tight skin of his abdomen. He never knows how much food to cook. He always clears his plate.

When he's done eating, he smokes and thinks about the girl in the freezer. How, when walking her out of the pond, she had threatened to slip out of his arms and back into the water. How he'd held on, carrying her up and out into the starlight. He hadn't saved her—couldn't have—but he had preserved her, kept her safe from the wet decay, from the mouths of fish and worse.

He knows the freezer is better than the refrigerator, that the dry cold of meat and ice is better than the slow rot of lettuce and leftovers and ancient, crust-rimmed condiments. Knows that even after death, there is a safety in the preservation of a body, that there is a second kind of life to be had.

Punter hasn't been to the bar near the factory since he got fired, but tonight he needs a drink. By eight, he's already been out to the garage four times, unable to keep from opening the freezer lid. If he doesn't stop, the constant thawing and refreezing will destroy her, skin first.

It's mid-shift at the factory, so the bar is empty except for the bartender and two men sitting together at the rail, watching the ball game on the television mounted above the liquor shelves. Punter takes a stool at the opposite end, orders a beer and lights a cigarette. He looks at the two men, tries to decide if they're men he knows from the plant. He's bad with names, bad at faces. One of the men catches him looking and gives him a glare that Punter immediately looks away from. He knows that he stares too long at people, that it makes them uncomfortable, but he can't help himself. He moves his eyes to his hands to his glass to the game, which he also can't make any sense of. Sports move too fast, are full of rules and behaviors he finds incomprehensible.

During commercials, the station plugs its own late-night newscast, including the latest about the missing girl. Punter stares at the picture of her on the television screen, his tongue growing thick and dry for the five seconds the image is displayed. One of the other men drains the last gulp of his beer and shakes his head, says, I hope they find the fucker that killed her and cut his balls off.

So you think she's dead then?

Of course she's dead. You don't go missing like that and not end up dead.

The men motion for another round as the baseball game comes back from the break. Punter realizes he's been holding his breath, lets it go in a loud, hacking gasp. The bartender and two men turn to look, so he holds a hand up, trying to signal he doesn't need any help, then puts it down when he realizes they're not offering. He pays his tab and gets up to leave.

He hasn't thought much about how the girl got into the pond, or who put her there. He too assumed murder, but the who or why or when is not something he's previously considered.

In juvie, the counselors told him nothing he did or didn't do would have kept his mother alive, which Punter understood fine. Of course he hadn't killed his mother. That wasn't why he was there. It was what he'd done afterward that had locked him away, put him behind bars until he was eighteen.

This time, he will do better. He won't sit around for months while the police slowly solve the case, while they decide that what he's done is just as bad. This time, Punter will find the murderer himself, and he will make him pay.

He remembers: Missing her. Not knowing where she was, not understanding, just wishing she'd come back. Not believing his father, who told him that she'd left them, that she was gone forever.

He remembers looking for her all day while his father worked, wandering the road, the fields, the rooms of their small house.

He remembers descending into the basement one step at a time. Finding the light switch, waiting for the fluorescent tubes to warm up. Stepping off the wood steps, his bare feet aching at the cold of the concrete floor.

He remembers nothing out of the ordinary, everything in its place.

He remembers the olive green refrigerator and the hum of the lights being the only two sounds in the world.

He remembers walking across the concrete and opening the refrigerator door.

More than anything else, he remembers opening his mouth to scream and not being able to. He remembers that scream getting trapped in his chest, never to emerge.

When the eleven o' clock news comes on, Punter is watching, ready with his small, spiral-bound notebook and his golf pencil stolen from the keno caddy at the bar. He writes down the sparse information added to the girl's story. The reporter recounts what Punter already knows—her name, the school, the abandoned car— then plays a clip of the local sheriff, who leans into the reporter's microphone and says, We're still investigating, but so far there's no proof for any of these theories. It's rare when someone gets out of their car and disappears on their own, but it does happen.

The sheriff pauses, listening to an inaudible question, then says, Whatever happened to her, it didn't happen inside the car. There's no sign of a struggle, no sign of sexual assault or worse.

Punter crosses his legs, then uncrosses them. He presses the pencil down onto the paper and writes all of this down.

The next clip is of the girl's father and mother, standing behind a podium at a press conference. They are both dressed in black, both stern and sad in dress clothes. The father speaks, saying, If anyone out there knows what happened—if you know where our daughter is—please come forward. We need to know where she is.

Punter writes down the word *father*, writes down the words *mother* and *daughter*. He looks at his useless telephone. He could tell these strangers what they wanted, but what good would it do them? His own father had known exactly where his mother was, and it hadn't done either of them any good.

According to the shows on television, the first part of an investigation is always observation, is always the gathering of clues. Punter opens the closet where he keeps his hunting gear and takes his binoculars out of their case. He hangs them around his neck and closes the closet door, then reopens it and takes his hunting knife off the top shelf. He doesn't need it, not yet, but he knows television detectives always carry a handgun to protect themselves. He only owns a rifle and a shotgun, both too long for this kind of work. The knife will have to be enough.

In the car, he puts the knife in the glove box and the binoculars on the seat. He takes the notebook out of his back pocket and reads the list of locations he's written down: the school, her parents' house, the pond and the gas station.

He reads the time when the clerk said he saw her and then writes down another, the time he found her in the pond. The two times are separated by barely a day, so she couldn't have been in the pond for too long.

Whatever happened to her, it happened fast.

He thinks that whoever did this, they must be a local to know about the pond. Punter has never actually seen anyone else there, only the occasional tire tracks, the left-behind beer bottles and cigarette butts from teenage parties. The condoms discarded further off in the bushes, where Punter goes to piss.

He thinks about the girl, about how he knows she would never consent to him touching her if she were still alive. About how she would never let him say the words he's said, the words he still wants to say. He wonders what he will do when he finds her killer. His investigation, it could be either an act of vengeance or thanksgiving, but it is still too early to know which.

Punter has been to the girl's school once before, when the unemployment office sent him to interview for a janitorial position there. He hadn't been offered the job, couldn't have passed the background check if he had. His juvenile record was sealed, but there was enough there to warn people, and schools never took any chances.

He circles the parking lot twice, then parks down the sidewalk from the front entrance, where he'll be able to watch people coming in and out of the school. He resists the urge to use the binoculars, knows he must control himself in public, must keep from acting on every thought he has. This is why he hasn't talked in months. Why he keeps to himself in his house, hunting and fishing, living off the too-small government disability checks the unemployment counselors helped him apply for.

These counselors, they hadn't wanted him to see what they wrote down for his disability, but he had. Seeing those words written in the counselor's neat script didn't make him angry, just relieved to know. He wasn't bad anymore. He was a person with a disorder, with a trauma. No one had ever believed him about this, especially not the therapist in juvie, who had urged Punter to open up, who had gotten angry when he couldn't. They didn't believe him when he said he'd already told them everything he had inside him.

Punter knows they were right to disbelieve him, that he did have feelings he didn't want to let out.

When Punter pictures the place where other people keep their feelings, all he sees is his own trapped scream, imagined as a devouring ball of sound, hungry and hot in his guts.

A bell rings from inside the building. Soon the doors open, spilling girls out onto the sidewalk and into the parking lot. Punter watches parents getting out of other cars, going to greet their children. One of these girls might be a friend of the drowned girl, and if he could talk to her then he might be able to find out who the drowned girl was. Might be able to make a list of other people he needed to question so that he could solve her murder.

The volume and the increasing number of distinct voices, all of it overwhelms Punter. He stares, watching the girls go by in their uniforms. All of them are identically clothed and so he focuses instead on their faces, on their hair, on the differences between blondes and brunettes and redheads. He watches the girls smiling and rolling their eyes and exchanging embarrassed looks as their mothers step forward to receive them.

He watches the breeze blow all that hair around all those made-up faces. He presses himself against the closed door of his Ford, holds himself still.

He closes his eyes and tries to picture the drowned girl here, wearing her own uniform, but she is separate now, distinct from these girls and the life they once shared. Punter's glad. These girls terrify him in a way the drowned girl does not.

A short burst of siren startles Punter, and he twists around in his seat to see a police cruiser idling its engine behind him, its driver side window rolled down. The cop inside is around Punter's age, his hair starting to gray at the temples but the rest of him young and healthy-looking. The cop yells something, hanging his left arm out the window, drumming his fingers against the side of the cruiser, but Punter can't hear him through the closed windows, not with all the other voices surrounding him.

Punter opens his mouth, then closes it without saying anything. He shakes his head, then locks his driver's side door, suddenly afraid that the cop means to drag him from the car, to put hands on him as other officers did when he was a kid. He looks up from the lock to see the cop outside of his cruiser, walking toward Punter's own car.

212

The cop raps on Punter's window, waits for him to roll down the window. He stares at Punter, who tries to look away, inadvertently letting his eyes fall on another group of teenage girls.

The cop says, You need to move your car. This is a fire lane.

Punter tries to nod, finds himself shaking his head instead. He whispers that he'll leave, that he's leaving. The cop says, I can't hear you. What did you say?

Punter turns the key, sighs when the engine turns over. He says, I'm going. He says it as loud as he can, his vocal cords choked and rusty.

There are too many girls walking in front of him for Punter to pull forward, and so he has to wait as the cop gets back in his own car. Eventually the cop puts the cruiser in reverse, lets him pass. Punter drives slowly out of the parking lot and onto the city streets, keeping the car slow, keeping it straight between the lines.

Afraid that the cop might follow him, Punter sticks to the main roads, other well-populated areas, but he gets lost anyway. These aren't places he goes. A half hour passes, and then another. Punter's throat is raw from smoking. His eyes ache from staring into the rearview mirror, and his hands tremble so long he fears they might never stop.

At home, Punter finds the girl's parents in the phonebook, writes down their address. He knows he has to be more careful, that if he isn't then someone will come looking for him too. He lies down on the couch to wait for dark, falls asleep with the television tuned to daytime dramas and court shows. He dreams about finding the murderer, about hauling him into the police station in chains. He sees himself avenging the girl with a smoking pistol, emptying round after round into this faceless person, unknown but certainly out there, surely as marked by his crime as Punter was.

When he wakes up, the television is still on, broadcasting game shows full of questions Punter isn't prepared to answer. He gets up and goes into the bathroom, the pain in his guts doubling him over on the toilet. When he's finished, he takes a long, gulping drink from the faucet, then goes out into the living room to gather his notebook, his binoculars, his knife.

In the garage, he tries to lift the girl's tank top to get to the skin hidden underneath, but the fabric is frozen to her flesh. He can't tell if the sound of his efforts is the ripping of ice or of skin. He tries touching her through her clothes, but she's too far gone, distant with cold. He shuts the freezer door and leaves her again in the dark, but not before he explains what he's doing for her. Not before he promises to find the person who hurt her, to hurt this person himself.

Her parents' house is outside of town, at the end of a long tree-lined driveway. Punter drives past, then leaves his car parked down the road and walks back with the binoculars around his neck. Moving through the shadows of the trees, he finds a spot a hundred yards from the house, then scans the lighted windows for movement until he finds the three figures sitting in the living room. He recognizes her parents from the television, sees that the third person is a boy around the same age as the drowned girl. Punter watches him the closest, tries to decide if this is the girl's boyfriend. The boy is all movement, his hands gesturing with every word he speaks. He could be laughing or crying or screaming and from this distance Punter wouldn't be able to tell the difference. He watches as the parents embrace the boy, then hurries back through the woods as soon as he sees the headlights come on in front of the house.

He makes it to his own car just as the boy's convertible pulls out onto the road. Punter starts the engine and follows the convertible through town, past the gas station and the downtown shopping, then into another neighborhood where the houses are smaller. He's never been here before, but he knows the plastics plant is close, that many of his old coworkers live nearby. He watches the boy park in front of a dirty white house, watches through the binoculars as the boy climbs the steps to the porch, as he rings the doorbell. The boy does not go in, but Punter's view is still obscured by the open door. Whatever happens only takes a few minutes, and then the boy is back in his car. He sits on the side of the road for a long time, smoking. Punter smokes too. He imagines getting out of the car and going up to the boy, imagines questioning him about the night of the murder. He knows he should, knows being a detective means taking risks, but he can't do it. When the boy leaves, Punter lets him go, then drives past the white house with his foot off the gas pedal, idling at a crawl. He doesn't see anything he understands, but this is not exactly new.

Back at the pond, the only evidence he gathers is that he was there himself. His tire tracks are the only ones backing up to the pond, his footprints the only marks along the shore. Whoever else was there before him has been given an alibi by Punter's own clumsiness.

He knows how this will look, so he finds a long branch with its leaves intact and uses it to rake out the sand, erasing the worst of his tracks. When he's done, he stares out over the dark water, trying to remember how it felt to hold her in his arms, to feel her body soft and pliable before surrendering her to the freezer.

He wonders if it was a mistake to take her from beneath the water. Maybe he should have done the opposite, should have stayed under the waves with her until his own lungs filled with the same watery weight, until he was trapped beside her. Their bodies would not have lasted. The fish would have dismantled their shells, and then Punter could have shown her the good person he's always believed himself to be, trapped underneath all this sticky rot.

For dinner he cooks two more steaks. All the venison the girl displaced is going bad in his aged refrigerator, and already the steaks are browned and bruised. To be safe, he fries them hard as leather. He has to chew the venison until his jaws ache and his teeth feel loose, but he finishes every bite, not leaving behind even the slightest scrap of fat.

Watching the late night news, Punter can tell that without any new evidence the story is losing steam. The girl gets only a minute of coverage, the reporter reiterating facts Punter's known for days. He stares at her picture again, at how her smile once made her whole face seem alive.

He knows he doesn't have much time. He crawls toward the

television on his hands and knees, puts his hand on her image as it fades away. He turns around, sits with his back against the television screen. Behind him there is satellite footage of a tornado or a hurricane or a flood. Of destruction seen from afar.

Punter wakes up choking in the dark, his throat closed off with something, phlegm or pus or he doesn't know what. He grabs a handkerchief from his nightstand and spits over and over until he clears away the worst of it. He gets up to flip the light switch, but the light doesn't turn on. He tries it again, and then once more. He realizes how quiet the house is, how without the steady clacking of his wall clock the only sound in his bedroom is his own thudding heart. He leaves the bedroom, walks into the kitchen. The oven's digital clock stares at him like an empty black eye, the refrigerator waits silent and still.

He runs out of the house in his underwear, his big bare feet slapping at the cold driveway. Inside the garage, the freezer is silent too. He lifts the lid, letting out a blast of frozen air, then slams it shut again after realizing he's wasted several degrees of chill to confirm something he already knows.

He knew this day was coming—the power company has given him ample written notice—but still he curses in frustration. He goes back inside and dresses hurriedly, then scavenges his house for loose change, for crumpled dollar bills left in discarded jeans. At the grocery down the road, he buys what little ice he can afford, his cash reserves exhausted until his next disability check. It's not enough, but it's all he can do.

Back in the garage, he works fast, cracking the blocks of ice on the cement floor and dumping them over the girl's body. He manages to cover her completely, suppressing the pang of regret he feels once he's unable to see her face through the ice. For a second, he considers crawling inside the freezer himself, sweeping away the ice between them. Letting his body heat hers, letting her thaw into his arms.

What he wonders is, Would it be better to have one day with her than a forever separated by ice?

He goes back into the house and sits down at the kitchen table. Lights a cigarette, then digs through the envelopes on the table until he finds the unopened bill from the power company. He opens it, reads the impossible number, shoves the bill back into the envelope. He tries to calculate how long the ice will buy him, but he never could do figures, can't begin to start to solve a problem like this.

He remembers: The basement refrigerator had always smelled bad, like leaking coolant and stale air. It wasn't used much, had been kept out of his father's refusal to throw anything away more than out of any sense of utility. By the time Punter found his mother there, she was already bloated around the belly and the cheeks, her skin slick with something that glistened like petroleum jelly.

Unsure what he should do, he'd slammed the refrigerator door and ran back upstairs to hide in his bedroom. By the time his father came home, Punter was terrified his father would know he'd seen, that he'd kill him too. That what would start as a beating would end as a murder.

Only his father never said anything, never gave any sign the mother was dead. He stuck to his story, telling Punter over and over how his mother had run away and left them behind, until Punter's voice was too muted to ask.

Punter tried to forget, to believe his father's story, but he couldn't.

Punter tried to tell someone else, some adult, but he couldn't do that either. Not when he knew what would happen to his father. Not when he knew they would take her from him.

During the day, while his father worked, he went down to the basement and opened the refrigerator door.

At first, he only looked at her, at the open eyes and mouth, at the way her body had been jammed into the too-small space. At the way her throat was slit the same way his dad had once demonstrated on a deer that had fallen but not expired.

The first time he touched her, he was sure she was trying to speak to him, but it was only gas leaking out of her mouth, squeaking free of her lungs. Punter had rushed to pull her out of the refrigerator, convinced for a moment she was somehow alive, but when he wrapped his arms around her, all that gas rolled out of her mouth and nose and ears, sounding like a wet fart but smelling so much worse.

He hadn't meant to vomit on her, but he couldn't help himself.

Afterward, he took her upstairs and bathed her to get the puke off. He'd never seen another person naked, and so he tried not to look at his mother's veiny breasts, at the wet thatch of her pubic hair floating in the bath water.

Scrubbing her with a washcloth and a bar of soap, he averted his eyes the best he could.

Rinsing the shampoo out of her hair, he whispered he was sorry.

It was hard to dress her, but eventually he managed, and then it was time to put her back in the refrigerator before his father came home.

Closing the door, he whispered goodbye. I love you. I'll see you tomorrow.

The old clothes, covered with blood and vomit, he took them out into the cornfield behind the house and buried them. Then came the waiting, all through the evening while his father occupied the living room, all through the night while he was supposed to be sleeping.

Day after day, he took her out and wrestled her up the stairs. He sat her on the couch or at the kitchen table, and then he talked, his normal reticence somehow negated by her forever silence. He'd never talked to his mother this much while she was alive, but now he couldn't stop telling her everything he had ever felt, all his trapped words spilling out one after another.

Punter knows that even if they hadn't found her and taken her away, she wouldn't have lasted forever. He had started finding little pieces of her left behind, waiting wet and squishy on the wooden basement steps, the kitchen floor, in between the cracks of the couch.

He tried to clean up after her, but sometimes his father would find one too. Then Punter would have to watch as his father held some squishy flake up to the light, rolling it between his fingers as if he could not recognize what it was or where it came from before throwing it in the trash.

Day after day, Punter bathed his mother to get rid of the smell, which grew more pungent as her face began to droop, as the skin on her arms wrinkled and sagged. He searched her body for patches of mold to scrub them off, then held her hands in his, marveling at how, even weeks later, her fingernails continued to grow.

Punter sits on his front step, trying to make sense of the scribbles in his notebook. He doesn't have enough, isn't even close to solving the crime, but he knows he has to, if he wants to keep the police away. If they figure the crime out before he does, if they question the killer, then they'll eventually end up at the pond, where Punter's attempts at covering his tracks are unlikely to be good enough.

Punter doesn't need to prove the killer guilty, at least not with a judge and a jury. All he has to do is find this person, then make sure he never tells anyone what he did with the body. After that, the girl can be his forever, for as long as he has enough ice.

✕

Punter drives, circling the scenes of the crime: The gas station, the school, her parents' house, the pond. He drives the circuit over and over, and even with the air conditioning cranked he can't stop sweating, his face drenched and fevered, his stomach hard with meat. He's halfway between his house and the gas station when his gas gauge hits empty. He pulls over and sits for a moment, trying to decide, trying to wrap his slow thoughts around his investigation. He opens his notebook, flips through its barely filled pages. He has written down so few facts, so few suspects, and there is so little time left.

In his notebook, he crosses out *father, mother, boyfriend*. He has only one name left, one suspect he hasn't disqualified, one other person that Punter knows has seen the girl. He smokes, considers, tries to prove himself right or wrong, gets nowhere.

He opens the door and stands beside the car. Home is in one

direction, the gas station the other. Reaching back inside, he leaves the notebook and the binoculars but takes the hunting knife and shoves it into his waistband, untucking his t-shirt to cover the weapon.

What Punter decides, he knows it is only a guess, but he also believes that whenever a detective has a hunch, the best thing to do is to follow it to the end.

It's not a long walk, but Punter gets tired fast. He sits down to rest, then can't get back up. He curls into a ball off the weed-choked shoulder, sleeps fitfully as cars pass by, their tires throwing loose gravel over his body. It's dark out when he wakes. His body is covered with gray dust, and he can't remember where he is. He's never walked this road before, and in the dark it's as alien as a foreign land. He studies the meager footprints in the dust, tracking himself until he knows which way he needs to go.

There are two cars parked behind the gas station, where the drowned girl's car was before it was towed away. One is a small compact, the other a newer sports car. The sports car's windows are rolled down, its stereo blaring music Punter doesn't know or understand, the words too fast for him to hear. He takes a couple steps into the trees beside the road, slows his approach until his gasps for air grow quieter. Leaning against the station are two young men in t-shirts and blue jeans, nearly identical with their purposely mussed hair and scraggly stubble. With them are two girls—one redhead and one brunette—still wearing their school uniforms, looking even younger than Punter knows they are.

The brunette presses her hand against her man's chest, and the man's own hand clenches her hip. Punter can see how firmly he's holding her, how her skirt is bunched between his fingers, exposing several extra inches of thigh.

He thinks of his girl thawing at home, how soon he will have to decide how badly he wants to feel that, to feel her skin so close to his own.

He thinks of the boyfriend he saw through the binoculars. Wonders if *boyfriend* is really the word he needs. The redhead, she takes something from the unoccupied man, puts it on her tongue. The man laughs, then motions to his friend, who releases his girl and picks a twelve pack of beer up off the cement. All four of them get into the sports car and drive off together in the direction of the pond, the town beyond. Punter stands still as they pass, knowing they won't see him, that he is already—has always been—a ghost to their world.

Punter coughs, not caring where the blood goes. He checks his watch, the numbers glowing digital green in the shadows of the trees. He's not out of time yet, but he can't think of any way to buy more. He decides.

Once the decision is made, it's nothing to walk into the empty gas station, to push past the waist-high swinging door to get behind the counter. It's nothing to grab the gas station clerk and press the knife through his uniform, into the small of his back. Nothing to ignore the way the clerk squeals as Punter pushes him out from behind the counter.

The clerk says, You don't have to do this.

He says, Anything you want, take it. I don't fucking care, man.

It's nothing to ignore him saying, Please don't hurt me.

It's nothing to ignore the words, to keep pushing the clerk toward the back of the gas station, to the hallway leading behind the coolers. Punter pushes the clerk down to his knees, feels his own feet slipping on the cool tile. He keeps one hand on the knife while the other grips the clerk's shoulder, his fingers digging into the hollows left between muscle and bone.

The clerk says, Why are you doing this?

Punter lets go of the clerk's shoulder and smacks him across the face with the blunt edge of his hand. He chokes the words out.

The girl. I'm here about the girl.

What girl?

Punter smacks him again, and the clerk swallows hard, blood or teeth.

Punter says, You know. You saw her. You told me.

The clerk's lips split, begin to leak. He says, Her? I never did anything to that girl. I swear.

Punter thinks of the clerk's bragging, about how excited he was to be the center of attention. He growls, grabs a fistful of greasy hair, then yanks hard, exposing the clerk's stubbled throat, turning his face sideways until one eye faces Punter's.

The clerk's glasses fall off, clatter to the tile.

The clerk says, Punter.

He says, I know you. Your name is Punter. You come in here all the time.

The clerk's visible eye is wide, terrified with hope, and for one second Punter sees his mother's eyes, sees the girl's, sees his hand closing both their eyelids for the last time.

284

OSWALD, Punter reads again, then shakes the name clear of his head.

The clerk says, I never hurt her, man. I was just the last person to see her alive.

Punter puts the knife to flesh. It's nothing. We're all the last person to see someone. He snaps his wrist inward, pushes through. That's nothing either. Or, if it is something, it's nothing worse than all the rest.

And then dragging the body into the tiny freezer. And then shoving the body between stacks of hot dogs and soft pretzels. And then trying not to step in the cooling puddles of blood. And then picking up the knife and putting it back in its sheath, tucking it into his waistband again. And then the walk home with a bag of ice in each hand. And then realizing the ice doesn't matter, that it will never be enough. And then the walk turning into a run, his heart pounding and his lungs heaving. And then the feeling he might die. And then the not caring what happens next.

By the time Punter gets back to the garage, the ice is already melting, the girl's face jutting from between the cubes. Her eyelids are covered with frost, cheeks slick with thawing pond water. He reaches in and lifts, her face and breasts and thighs giving to his fingers but her back still frozen to the wrapped venison below. He pulls, trying to ignore the peeling sound her skin makes as it rips away from the paper.

Punter speaks, his voice barely audible. He doesn't have to speak loud for her to hear him. They're so close. Something falls off, but he doesn't look, doesn't need to dissect the girl into parts, into flesh and bone, into brains and blood. He kisses her forehead, her skin scaly like a fish, like a mermaid. He says it again: You're safe now.

He sits down with the girl in his arms and his back to the freezer. He rocks her, feels himself getting wet as she continues to thaw all over him. He shivers, then puts his mouth to hers, breathes deep from the icy blast still frozen in her lungs, lets the air cool the burning in his own throat, the horror of his guts. When he's ready, he picks her up, cradles her close, and carries her into the house. Takes her into the bedroom and lays her down.

He lies beside her, and then, in a loud, clear voice, he speaks. He tries not to cough, tries to ignore the scratchy catch at the back of his throat. He knows what will happen next, but he also knows all this will be over by the time they break down his door, by the time they come in with guns drawn and voices raised. He talks until his voice disappears, until his trapped scream becomes a whisper. He talks until he gets all of it out of him and into her, where none of these people will ever be able to find it.

Matt Bell

is the author of the novel *In the House upon the Dirt between the Lake and the Woods*, published by Soho Press in June 2013. He is also the author of two previous books, *How They Were Found* and *Cataclysm Baby*. His writing has been anthologized in *Best American Mysteries 2010*, *Best American Fantasy 2*, and *30 Under 30: An Anthology of Innovative Fiction by Younger Writers*. He teaches creative writing at Northern Michigan University.

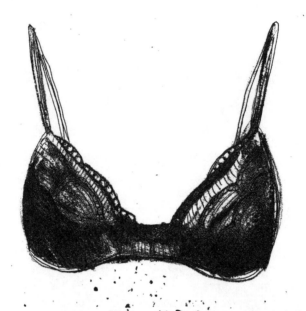

SUNSHINE FOR ADRIENNE

ANTONIA CRANE

The first man who raped her went blind. Her mom called with the news.

"That handsome football player you dated got eye cancer in both eyes," she said.

Adrienne heard chewing and the wet slurp of Nicorette gum. Her ma chewed two or three pieces at a time and when they lost flavor, she rolled the spit stones into grey balls and stuck them to the kitchen counter. Sometimes the cat knocked them onto the floor and batted them around.

"You mean Terry?" Adrienne's asshole clenched. Ma didn't know. All the girls at St. Julian's High School swooned over Terry's tanned wide receiver chest and tennis legs. She heard something being chopped on a cutting board with a steady whack, whack, whack.

"He's blind as a bat. His poor mother." The chopping got faster and faster and more precise. She could slice a carrot into paper-thin pieces in less than thirty seconds. She hated cooking.

"She's a whack job, Amy." Her father hollered in the background. A cupboard door slammed shut. Adrienne heard the refrigerator door make a sucking sound as it opened. She found her pre-work hit and bent spoon in the top drawer of her dresser, but no lighter, she thought. She rummaged around in other drawers where she last saw it and found ticket stubs from a show her father took her to when she graduated high school. It was the Della Davidson Dance Company's "Ten p.m. Dream," an interpretation of Alice in Wonderland. They'd nibbled calamari beforehand next door. Her football watching, beer-drinking father even sported a silky burgundy tie that matched her favorite maroon dress. She took her father's elbow as he led her to the front row, so close she felt the dancers' abdominal muscles vibrate and their snaky necks glisten and strain. She watched them as he watched the music pulse through her skin.

He liked to look at her pictures of birds too. She'd started drawing turkeys, doves and chickens when she was six years old with accidental skill. Her father couldn't draw an Easter egg if there was a gun to his head. Where he lacked imagination, she swelled with it. Her talents delighted him and bragged about her to his roofing buddies. "My daughter's a genius," he said, while ripping off grubby tiles. He collected her bird drawings and stuck them to the refrigerator door, where they were held in place by metal donut magnets he bought at the hardware store.

"Her only son. Can you imagine?" Ma's voice matched the sucking thud the refrigerator door made when it closed. The thing being chopped was gone and in its place, her father's voice: "Her loser son, still living at home at twenty-nine?" Her father grunted, which was the same as his laugh. Adrienne pictured him in his stretched white gym socks with a spaghetti noodle dangling from a fork, daring Ma to slap his hand away from her butt, which he pinched, when he wasn't yelling at the TV, drinking Coors light with their orange cat on the footstool near his feet. The skin on his hands matched his face: tanned, calloused and flaking off from working outside in the wind, rain, and dense fog that made roofs wet and slippery. He fell off a ladder and sprained his ankle last year. It swelled like a grapefruit so he managed the office and bid jobs, and farmed out the labor to his friends.

It was at St. Julian's High School where Adrienne got sneaky. She'd walk silently behind him on her way upstairs to her room. She'd been meeting Terry and getting high, staying out past curfew.

"Where the hell you been?" Her father didn't look at

her anymore. He held the TV remote in one hand, raised like an arrow, in the other, a beer. He was a channel surfer. There was a steadily growing gulf between them. Her curves brought popularity, lip-gloss, tampons and boys, but also self-righteousness and danger. She became reckless and reticent. He heard her whispering on the phone well after midnight. He smelled alcohol on her breath. She'd become too pretty for her own good, he sensed.

"Where?" He asked. He was made of sounds: slurps, moans, burps, and coughs. Startled, the cat leapt off the footstool and ran into the kitchen. She watched varicose veins on his chubby calves travel up to his thighs like a red river. She didn't have to hide her tiny dot pupils or her droopy, rubbery skin than hung on her face. He watched the football game on TV: "Olson, you pile of shit, you throw like a girl!"

She fingered a box of Marlboro's in her pocket.

"I was out buying smokes." She waved the box in the air so he could see it reflected in the TV screen.

"You're too young to smoke."

"I'm seventeen."

"It's eleven o'clock on a school night, Addy." Along with breasts, she'd sprouted a shitty new petulance. Her father disliked the distance between them. He gripped his Coors tighter knowing that if he didn't keep engaging with her, she will have slipped away and it would be too late. Perhaps it was already too late. The amount of rage he felt surprised him.

Adrienne shrugged her shoulders. She walked briskly into the kitchen where her ma buzzed around in slippers, gnashing her gum and talking on the phone aggressively like the women on *The View*.

The sun dropped into her tenderloin apartment like a dried,

rancid apricot, bringing night. She spotted her lighter on the floor next to the trash. She leaned over and grabbed it. It was out of fluid, but when she tried it anyway, a low flame appeared. A cat meowed.

"Terry's not a loser. He's ill. How would you like to be blind, hmm?"

"Wow, ma. That's awful," Adrienne said. The bathroom where she was raped was light blue with no windows. She reached for the soft brown belt on the floor, next to her Lucite stripper shoes. A gray pigeon stood on the single window ledge in her studio apartment. Her hands began to sweat.

"I'm going to bring them my famous broccoli casserole. You should come with me." Adrienne grabbed the belt and tied it around her forearm. She pulled it taught, gripping it with her teeth. Her best wormy vein surfaced inside her left elbow. The sweat from her hands transferred onto the worn leather where there were tiny dots of blood. She pictured diced sweet yellow onions and the hard shell of orange melted cheese on top. Terry would peel the hard cheese layer off and chew it with his bleached Chiclets. He would shake ma's hand with his tennis doubles grip. When he asked about Adrienne, her ma would lie. She'd tell him, "She's waiting tables and taking World Religions at City College." But that was four years ago. It was the story she liked to tell the neighbors. The needle hit the vein nicely and delivered the juicy black heat from Adrienne's belly up to her neck. She levitated from her chest to the top on her head. Butterflies came to mind. She took a dull pencil and drew some on a post-it.

"If you get on BART now, you can make it in an hour." Her ma's voice turned smoky and silver. The chopping sound was back but softer, like a slow finger tapping on water in a bowl. Tap. Tap. Tap.

292

"Adrienne, are you still there?" Her cheeks warmed and her eyes drifted like a plant leaning towards sunlight.

"I can't go to Oakland tonight, ma. I have to work." The space between them stretched far and wide as the Pacific Ocean.

"Come over for dinner tomorrow night. Spend some time with your father."

Her ma's breath was heavy and slow like hers. There was no more gum noise. She heard the oven door close and a timer tick. She felt comfort knowing the casserole was inside and the cheese would spread like butter and the chopped broccoli sizzled, as planned. She heard relief in her ma's mighty exhale. She exhaled too.

"I can't. I have to make rent for this shitty rat hole apartment."

"Okay, honey. We'll see you on Sunday."

Adrienne felt elegant and weightless in her tall, thick black motorcycle boots. They were heavier than she was. She chose a fishnet top to cover the purple red scars that lined her forearms. Her hair was pulled back in a neat, shiny bun. She hadn't washed it in days. When she was high, water felt like nails. Besides, the high rollers liked the tight bun. It read ballerina. Well groomed. Middle class. Her boyfriend, Dennis liked it too. "You look like a French lingerie model," he'd said. They lived together in a dinky apartment on Hyde Street where they listened to trance techno music, counted pigeons and slammed dope. Dennis looked at least forty, with crooked lines around his mouth and creased eyes. But he was twenty-eight, like her.

She checked her mailbox on the way out and found a red envelope from her father. She shoved it in her costume bag and walked the few blocks to Market Street Cinema, past the garbage that blew over the sidewalk and into the gutter. Fog drifted in and circled her like wet smoke. She gave a light wave to the homeless guy who always tried to sell her stolen perfume. Pigeons picked through the trash and carried off chicken bones in their beaks. Three pigeons in the trashcan; three grams of dope per day.

On the floor at the MSC, she saw her regular customer, the man in the white shirt, sitting in his usual spot. He was good for a hundred bucks. He sometimes brought her a single red carnation, which she thought was cheap and sad, but she smiled and thanked him and later tossed it into the gutter on Market Street. He glanced at his watch. She climbed over the crossed legs of a guy in a stocking cap, to get to the man in the white shirt. A familiar hand touched her bare stomach as she walked by.

"Sorry." She bent in half to lean in for a closer look. Dennis had a swollen, bruised eye that she could see, even in the dark and he was bleeding from one corner of his mouth.

"What are you doing at my work?" The white shirt customer now had a thick blonde gyrating on his crotch. Timing is everything.

"I was trying to bring you..."

"What?" Dennis uncrossed his legs. His fingers were long and graceful. He hid his face in his hands. Adrienne leaned in and hissed in his ear. He smelled like bleach, dirt and night. His eyes were badly swollen.

"You are never supposed to come into my work."

"I need..." Adrienne peeled his hands away from his face and remembered the birthday card from her father. She tore open the envelope and found eighty dollars. He'd written: "Hope Your Birthday is Ducky" on top of picture of a fluffy green duck she drew when she was about nine years old. It was her "duck phase" her father liked to remind her. She smashed forty crisp dollars into Dennis' sweaty palm. A leggy redhead whispered to a customer next to him, then glanced in her direction. It was obvious they were arguing, and it was making customers tense. The white shirt customer smiled at her. She smiled big. She smiled rectus. She smiled Cheshire. The vein in Dennis' neck bulged, the same way it did when he came. She moved her chest up to his bruised eyes, like she was about to dance for him.

"Get the fuck out of my work." The white shirt customer motioned to her to come over to him. She walked towards him and leaned in to kiss his cheek. Most nights, after work, Dennis took her money and met their dealer. Then they got high together and Dennis played guitar on their dingy brown sheets.

"Promise me you'll never come into my work," she'd said.

"Promise."

The numbers were good at the MSC. She gave five or eight hand jobs a night and left with seven or eight hundred bucks, enough for six grams. If she only did her share, she and Dennis could stay blazed for a couple days. The next night, she'd come back to work and do it again. And the next day the exact same thing. Never mind the bruises on the backs of her knees. She felt light and graceful on stage. Six years of ballet as a little girl kept her toes pointed and her arms loose. And there was her techno trance music where she got lost on stage.

She had three songs to get naked. The first one was frantic and unrelenting. She walked on stage slow as caramel, traveling to the side. Back and forth. When the beat got faster, she slowed down even more, pulling her shadow across the length of the stage towards the pole. She grabbed it with one hand and slid down the pole to the floor. She spread her thighs wide and gazed into the black space of the audience. Her chin dropped. Her eyelids closed. Her mouth went slack. Then she caught herself. That was the good thing about techno. It was a loop so she could start right where she left off. She used the pole as leverage to lift herself up to stand. The white lights could trigger a migraine, but this was no migraine. This was blindness.

She remembered Terry's megawatt smile and million crunches abs. He snuck her into the boy's bathroom after cheerleading practice. The plan was to make out and try his dope. "'Walking on Sunshine,' Addy," he said.

"What?" She asked with one hand on her hip. Terry pulled her into the blue bathroom stall and removed his smooth brown belt from his plaid shorts. They dropped down past his knees. He looked slimmer than usual.

"You should've used 'Walking on Sunshine.'" He wrapped the belt around her forearm. The dope was brown and gritty but when the fire heated it, it blackened like bubbling vinegar. Terry's arms were so veiny he didn't use the belt. He just flexed. "'Walking on Sunshine' is the best song for a cheerleading routine," he said.

He stuck the needle in her arm and it stung. The bathroom wasn't blue. It was mint green and freezing. She shivered. "'Walking on Sunshine' by Katrina and the Waves." The dope was a warm liquid kiss inside her skin. She nearly slipped back onto the toilet. He caught her. She laughed.

"No. We're using 'New Attitude' because it's slow enough for flips." He turned her around to face the toilet with her back to him. He yanked on her underwear.

"Wait," she said. She snatched a condom from her makeup bag and ripped it open with her teeth. She dropped the condom. It fell onto the floor. She reached down to pick it up but there was orange piss and curly black hairs where it landed.

The dope made her queasy. She threw up Diet Pepsi and

gummy bear bile and the sweetness mixed with the piss and soap smell. She tasted dope at last: burnt vinegar and warm ash. A dark shadow moved across the bathroom. The room turned blue. She flushed the toilet and the sound was so loud, as if monsters lived in the pipes inside the walls. Terry laughed. He didn't use spit when he put his cock in her ass. He didn't use lube. She didn't feel it or see the blood until later. Speckled lights twinkled behind her eyes. Prism zigzag lightening blurred the edges of the walls, of the toilet, of Terry. She saw her drool trickle from her open mouth.

"Don't."

"I don't want to get you pregnant," he said. Her thin spit was a rainbow thread hitting the toilet water, soft and certain.

Later she'd bleed on toilet paper. Sit on ice. Sleep on her belly. Buy more dope from Terry. He wasn't very good at shooting her up, but Dennis could find a vein in a garbage can.

On stage, at the MSC, the second song began. It was more manic and fast than the first. It was trance party music where a woman wailed about ecstasy and a little bit of you and me. Adrienne removed her slinky black dress. She stepped out of it like a spider discarding its skin. Her black bra was next. She tossed it to the one man sitting up front. Her pale skin and glossed red lips and sharp cheekbones shimmered under the white lights. She stepped on her dress and tripped. She fell down onto her knees. Her black thigh-high stocking covered the tracks on the backs on her legs but they were needle sore. She slid forward and felt the hot lights pierce her neck. Her tiny swollen hands touched her small breasts. Her chest was flat as an open road. Men loved that about her. She removed her black thong for the man in the white shirt and tossed it in his direction. He removed a twenty from his pocket and set it down on the stage, where she could see it. She crawled closer to him to let him know she saw the twenty. She removed his glasses and put them in his shirt pocket. She took his face in her fingers and wiggled it across her skin beneath her fishnet shirt. She felt his pointy nose and wet mouth brush against her nipples. She felt his slick forehead leave a greasy film on her ribcage. She loosened her bun and allowed her black hair to smack her cheeks. She watched the man's expression slide from guilt to anger as if she'd just become his eleven-year old niece.

"There's more where that came from," she said, tossing him her best pre-pubescent smile.

"You should have used the song I suggested."

He said, "You should come talk to me after this song." He placed a single red carnation on the stage in front of her. She didn't look at it, but she knew it was there.

"One more song and then I'll come," she said. Her fingers lingered on her abdomen but she wanted to scratch her arms. The itch was back.

"He said: "You have the best breasts." She stared up at the lights that opened her like a bone. She was lighter than air.

Antonia Crane

teaches teenagers creative writing in Los Angeles when she can convince them to log off of Facebook. Her work can be found in Akashic's *The Heroin Chronicles*, Soft Skull Press' *Johns, Marks, Tricks & Chickenhawks: Professionals & Their Clients Writing about Each Other*, *The Rumpus*, *Dame Magazine*, *Salon*, *PANK*, *Black Clock*, *Slake*, *The Los Angeles Review* and other places. Her memoir *Spent* is forthcoming by Barnacle Books/Rare Bird Lit in 2014.

FUZZYLAND

RICHARD LANGE

Big Mike insists I try on his ring. I tell him that's okay, but he's a pushy bastard. He bought it in Reno or won it, which makes it lucky or something. I wasn't listening; the guy's stories go nowhere. He wears the ring on his pinky, but it slips easily over my thumb. He laughs to see that and piles lox onto a bagel.

"You're going to miss me," he says to the waitress.

Upon his retirement next month, I'll inherit some of his accounts. It's supposed to be an honor. This deli, for example. I'll be stopping in once a month for the rest of my life, pushing flatware and dishes and, say, did I mention our special on toothpicks? Unless I screw up, that is. Which happens. Ask any salesman. Buy him a drink. Greek tragedies, man. One word too many, one wayward glance, and we are up shit creek.

The owner slides into our booth. My read is he's a little skittish coming out of the box. His hand is soaking wet when Mike makes the introduction. I'm cool though. I don't grab a napkin or go for my pant leg. He and Mike pick up where they left off last time, and I put it on automatic. Not that I'm missing anything: golf, golf, golf. It's a gift knowing when to smile or nod or raise my eyebrows without really having to listen, but I worry sometimes that it makes me lazy.

There's a movie star at the next table, some second stringer whose name I'll never recall. My wife's the one who's great with that stuff. The waitress gets the giggles pouring him coffee, and he smiles. She must be new in town. The flickering of the overhead light is killing me, the silverware clatters. I don't like where my mind's at. A bomb goes off in my stomach, and everything in it climbs back into my throat. I'm thinking about the movie star's money. With money like that you could hire people—a whole squad of detectives, bounty hunters, hit men.

"What do you say?" Mike asks me, darting his eyes at the owner, then giving me a look like it's time I jumped in.

"They raped my little sister," I reply.

"Whoa. Jesus."

That's not what I meant to say, but now that it's out—"Some motherfucker. Last night. Down in San Diego."

Rule number one is you do not bring real life into the sales environment; it's not about you. I know that, and I'm sorry, but I am going crazy here.

The bee man interrupts me while I'm shining shoes. Every pair I own, and all of Liz's, too, are laid out on the dining room table. I woke up with a wild hair this morning, and I've been at it since dawn. My fingers are black with polish. I'm so far gone, the doorbell gives me a heart attack.

The bee man's name is Zeus. His head is shaved, and he has a lightning bolt tattooed on his scalp, above his right ear.

"They let city employees do that?" I ask as I lead him down the side of the house to the backyard.

"We're contract workers. We don't have to wear uniforms either," he says. That explains the Lakers jersey.

The hive is in the avocado tree. I discovered it last week when I heard buzzing while watering the lawn. The gardener quit, so I've been doing all kinds of extra stuff around here. Bees were so thick on the trunk, they looked like one big thing rather than a lot of little ones. They shivered in unison, and their wings caught the sun. I didn't get too close. We have the killer variety now, up from Mexico. They stung an old guy to death in

Riverside last year, and, I think, a dog.

"Whoa," Zeus says.

"Are they Africanized?"

"Can't tell. The killers look pretty much like the others, except for they're more aggressive. I'll send a few to the lab when I'm done."

I thought I read in the paper that they relocated the hives to somewhere they'd be useful, but Zeus tells me that's too much trouble anymore. He has a foam that'll smother the whole colony, queen and all, in nothing flat. No sooner are these words out of his mouth than a bee lands on his arm and stings him.

"*Hijo de puta*," he says as he and I hurry away. "Those bitches are gonna pay for that."

Liz is drinking coffee in the breakfast nook. She uses both hands to lift the cup, wincing as it touches her lips. Her eyes are red and puffy. Neither of us slept much last night. It's been that way since we heard about my sister a few days ago. Guys laugh when I say Liz is my best friend. They think I'm pulling something high and mighty. Only Jesus freaks love their wives.

"Maybe it's time for a new mattress," I say.

She yawns and shrugs. "Maybe."

"The guy's here to kill the bees."

"What's that, lightning on his head?"

I have to eat something, so I scramble a couple of eggs and toast some bread. I smear mayonnaise on the toast and make a sandwich with the eggs. Liz has an apple and a slice of cheese. I get about three bites down before the phone rings.

It's my sister, Tracy, and she's crying. In our first conversations following the assault she was all facts and figures. Yes, it was horrible; yes, she was pretty banged up; no, the cops hadn't caught her attacker; no, there was no need to drive down, she already had a friend staying with her. This morning, though, she's a wreck. She can't get two words out without battling a sob.

Her ex-husband is up to no good, she says, using the attack as an excuse to press for temporary custody of their daughters. Her attorney has assured her it'll never fly, but she's worried all the same. She keeps apologizing for bothering me, which begins to piss me off. I throw the rest of my sandwich into the trash and pour myself another cup of coffee.

"We're on our way," I say.

"It's hard, all of this. I can handle it, but it's hard."

"Shouldn't take us a couple of hours, depending on traffic."

After I hang up, I grab the sponge and start washing dishes. It's one of those days when normal things feel strange. The soap smells bubblegummy, but when I get some in my eye, it hurts like hell. The window over the sink faces the avocado tree, where Zeus, wearing a beekeeper getup now, is spraying what looks like a fire extinguisher. The hive is soon covered with thick white foam. Liz comes up behind me and yanks on the waistband of my sweats.

"I'll drive," she says.

"I saw an actor at Canter's the other day. Big guy, dark hair. He was in *Private Ryan* and that Denzel Washington movie. Went out with Hiedi Fleiss."

"Oh, I know. Tom...Tom...."

She screws up her face and stares at the ceiling, folding and unfolding the dish towel. The grass is dying out back, even though I have watered and fertilized. A few bees trail after Zeus as he carries the foam dispenser to his truck. One of them veers off and begins bashing its brains out against the kitchen window with a fury that is truly humbling.

The freeway is clear until we get into Santa Ana, a few miles past Disneyland, then it locks up. I punch over to the traffic report. Whichever lane Liz chooses stops moving as soon as she weasels her way into it. She keeps humming three notes of a song she has stuck in her head. My mouth goes dry when I spot flashing lights.

"There's an exit right here," Liz says.

"I'm okay," I reply.

Car wrecks twist me all around. My parents died in one ten years ago now, out there in the desert, on their way back from Laughlin. Big rig, head-on, whatnot. It was an awful mess. My sister lost it. She'd just graduated from high school. She was arrested for shoplifting twice in one week. The second conviction got her a month in jail. I intended to visit, but I was working 12-hour days selling time on an AM oldies station where the general manager told everyone I was gay when he caught me crying at my desk shortly after my parents' funeral.

When Tracy was released, she moved to a marijuana plantation in Hawaii. I still have the one letter she sent. In it she asks for money to buy cough syrup and says she's learning to thread flowers into leis. She spends half a page describing a sunset. There's dirt on the envelope. The stamp has a picture of a fish. It made me angry back then, but envy can be like that.

I try to keep my eyes closed until we're past the accident, but the part of me that thinks that's silly makes me look. A truck hauling oranges has overturned, the fruit spilling out across the freeway. Two lanes are still open, and traffic crawls past, crushing the load into bright, fragrant pulp. The truck's driver, uninjured, stands with a highway patrolman. The driver keeps slapping his forehead with the palm of his hand and stomping his feet. The patrolman lights a flare.

Things clear up after that. We zip through Irvine and Capistrano and right past the nuclear plant at San Onofre, which looks like two big tits pointing at the sky. The ocean lolls flat and glassy all the way to the horizon, sparking where the sun touches it. At Camp Pendelton, the Marines are on maneuvers. Tanks race back and forth on both sides of the freeway, and the dust they kick up rolls across the road like a thick fog. The radio fades out, and when the signal returns, it's in Spanish.

We stop in Oceanside for a hamburger. The place is crawling with jarheads who look pretty badass with their muscles and regulation haircuts, but then I see the acne and peach fuzz and realize they're boys, mostly, having what will likely turn out to be the time of their lives. I convince Liz that we deserve a beer, so we step into a bar next to the diner. The walls are covered with USMC this and USMC that, pennants and flags, and Metallica blasts out of the jukebox. It's not yet noon, but a few grunts are already at it. I have the bartender send them another pitcher on me. They raise their mugs and shout, "To the corps." I can't figure out what it is that I hate about them.

A fire engine forces us to the side of the road as soon as we get off the freeway at Tracy's exit. I see smoke in the distance. The condo development she lives in rambles across a dry hillside north of San Diego, block after block of identical town houses with Cape Cod accents. The wiry grass and twisted, oily shrubs that pick up where the roads dead end and the sprinkler systems peter out are just waiting for an excuse to burst into flame. There have been a number of close calls since Tracy moved in. Only last year a blaze was stopped at the edge of the development by a miraculous change in wind direction.

We get lost on our way up to her place. There's a system to the streets, but I haven't been here enough times to figure it out. The neighborhood watch signs are no help, and the jogger who gives us a dirty look, well, better that than gangbangers. They keep a tight rein here. The association once sent Tracy a letter ordering her to remove an umbrella that shaded the table on her patio because it violated some sort of bylaw. I'd go nuts, but Tracy says it's a good place to raise kids. A lucky turn brings us to her unit, and we pull into a parking space labeled VISITOR.

Her youngest, Cassie, opens the door at my knock. She's four, a shy, careful girl.

"Hello, baby," I say.

Her eyes widen, and she runs to hide behind her mother in the kitchen.

"Cassie," Tracy scolds. "It's Uncle Jack and Auntie Liz. You remember."

Cassie buries her face in her mother's thigh. Her older sister, Kendra, who's eight, doesn't look up from the coloring book she's working on.

It's been almost a week since Tracy was attacked, and she still has an ugly greenish bruise on her cheek and broken blood vessels in one eye. She herds us into the living room, asking what we want to drink. The place smells like food, something familiar. "Cabbage rolls," Tracy says. "You loved Mom's."

"So how are you?" I ask. That's broad enough in front of the kids.

"Better every day, which is how it goes, they say. There are experts and things, counselors. It's amazing."

"You see it on TV, on those shows. I bet it helps. I mean, does it?"

"Oh, yeah. Sure. Time's the main thing though."

"Come sit with me," Liz says to Cassie. She's trying to draw her out of Tracy's lap, give Mommy a break.

"No," Cassie whines as she wraps her arms tighter around Tracy's neck.

My beer tastes funny. I hold the can to my ear and shake it. This big brother business is new to me. Tracy and I have never been close. We were in different worlds as kids, and since our parents died we've seen each other maybe twice a year. She came back from Hawaii, settled in San Diego, and met Tony. They married in Vegas without telling anyone. *Whew!* I thought. *I'm finally off the hook.*

But Tony's been gone six months now. Tracy used star 69 to catch him cheating. He was that stupid, or maybe he wanted to be caught. I notice that some of the furniture is different, new but cheaper. The couch used to be leather. Tony took his share when he left. Everything had to be negotiated. Tracy got to keep the kids' beds, and he got the TV, a guy who makes a hundred grand a year. It's been downhill since then. Battle after battle.

"You owe me a hug," I say to Kendra. "I sent you that postcard from Florida."

Exasperated, she slaps down her crayon and marches over. We scared the hell out of her when she was younger, showing up one Halloween dressed in a cow costume, Liz in the front half, me in back. She'll never trust me again.

She grimaces when I pull her up onto the couch. "What's the deal?" I ask.

"What?"

"What's shaking? What's new? How's school?"

"It's okay, but my teacher's too old. She screamed at us the other day, like, 'Shut up! Shut up!'" She has to scream, too, to show me how it went.

"Kendra!" Tracy says.

Cassie sees her sister getting attention and decides that she wants some. She leaves her mother to pick up a stuffed pig, which she brings to Liz, who soon has both girls laughing by giving the pig a lisp and making it beg for marshmallows and ketchup. There's a creepy picture of an angel on the wall. I ask Tracy what that's about. We weren't raised religious. We weren't raised anything at all.

"It was Kendra's idea. We saw it at the mall, and she was like, 'Mommy, Mommy, we need that.'" Tracy shrugs and shakes her head. Her fingers go to the bruise on her cheek. She taps it rhythmically.

"Angels, huh," I say to Kendra.

"They watch us all the time and keep us safe."

"Who taught you that?"

"Leave me alone," she snaps.

I walk into the kitchen with my empty beer can. Everything shines like it's brand-new. Our mother would wake up at four in the morning sometimes and pull every pot and pan we owned out of the cupboards and wash them. Dad called it her therapy, but that's bullshit. She'd be cursing under her breath as she scrubbed, and her eyes were full of rage.

Something is burning. I smell it. The fire must be closer than it seemed. I press my face to the window, trying to see the sky, while the girls laugh at another of Auntie Liz's jokes.

✕

Ash drifts down like the lightest of snowfalls, disappearing as soon as it touches the ground. It sticks to the hood of a black Explorer, and more floats on the surface of the development's swimming pool where the girls are splashing with Liz. The sun forces woozy red light through the smoke, and it feels later than it is.

I tug at the crotch of my borrowed bathing suit, one thing Tony left behind. My sister sits beside me in a chaise, fully clothed. To hide more bruises, I bet. The rapist got her as she was leaving a restaurant. That's all she told me. In a parking garage. That's all I know. "I'm lucky he didn't kill me," she said afterward. Her hand shakes when she adjusts her sunglasses; the pages of her magazine rattle.

"Come swim with us, Uncle Jack," Kendra calls. She can paddle across the deep end by herself, while Cassie, wearing inflatable water wings, sits on the stairs, in up to her waist. I make a big production of gearing up for my cannonball, stopping short a number of times until they are screaming for me to jump, jump, jump.

We play Marco Polo and shark attack. I teach Kendra to dive off my shoulders, and she begs to do it again and again. Cassie, on the other hand, won't let me touch her. Liz bounces her up and down and drags her around making motorboat noises, but every time I approach, she has a fit and scrambles to get away. "You're so big," Liz says, but I don't know. I'm not sure that's it.

A man unlocks the gate in the fence that surrounds the pool, and a little blond girl about Kendra's age squeezes past him and runs to the water, where she drops to all fours and dips in her hand.

"It's warm enough," she shouts to the man, who smiles and waves at Tracy.

"Hey, whassup," Tracy says.

She bends her legs so that he can sit on the end of her chaise. His hair is spiked with something greasy, and his T-shirt advertises a bar. I dive down to walk on my hands. When I come up, they are laughing together. He reaches into the pocket of his baggy shorts, and I swear I see him give Tracy money.

"Where are you going?" Liz asks as I paddle to the ladder.

"I want to swim, Daddy," the blonde girl yells.

"Not right now," the man answers without looking at her. He stands at my approach, smiles. A salesman. Maybe not for a living, but I've got him pegged. We shake hands professionally.

"The big brother," he crows, jokey jokey. My sister should be more careful.

"Philip's going to paint my place," Tracy says. "All I have to pay for is the materials."

"Unless we get burned out," he says.

She frowns and puts a finger to her lips, nodding toward the kids.

I scrub my hair with a towel and find that I'm sucking in my gut. It's sick. A flock of birds scatters across the smoky sky like a handful of gravel.

"You live in L.A.?" Philip says to me. "I'm sorry."

A real tough guy, going for the dig right off the bat.

"I like the action," I reply.

"I was down there for a while. Too crazy."

"You have to know your way around."

311

I adjust my chair, sit. Philip fingers the soul patch under his lower lip. I'm staring at him, he's staring at me. It could go either way.

"I. Want. To. Swim. Now," Philip's daughter wails.

"Your mother'll be here any minute."

The girl begins to cry. She stretches out face down on the pool deck and cuts loose.

"Go to it, Daddy," Tracy says, giving Philip a playful kick.

He stands and rubs his eyes. "This fucking smoke."

"Nice meeting you," I say with a slight lift of my chin.

He walks over to his daughter and peels her off the concrete. She screams even louder. He has to carry her through the gate.

"He know what happened?" I ask Tracy.

"What do you mean?"

I stare at her over the top of my sunglasses. After a few seconds she says, "I told him I was in a car wreck."

"So he's not like a friend friend?"

"Hey, really, okay?" she warns.

I throw up my hands to say forget it. She's right. I don't know what I'm doing, all of a sudden muscling into her life. The girls are calling for me again. I run to the edge of the pool and dive in, determined to get Cassie to play sea horse with me.

The kids turn up their noses at the cabbage rolls, so Tracy boils a couple of hot dogs for them. She's more accommodating than our parents were. Seems like a terrible waste of time now, the battles fought over liver and broccoli and pickled beets. And what about when Dad tried to force a lamb chop past my teeth, his other hand gripping my throat? Somehow that became a funny story, one retold at every family gathering to much laughter. Nobody ever noticed that I would leave the room so cramped with anger that it hurt to breathe.

Tracy pushes food from one side of her plate to the other as she talks about her job. She manages a Supercuts in a nasty part of town. The owner is buying a new franchise in Poway, and she once promised Tracy that when she did, Tracy could go into partnership with her. Now, though, the woman is hemming and hawing. The deal is off.

"I turned that shop around. She used me," Tracy says.

"Tough it out," I advise. "Regroup, then sell yourself to her. You have to be undeniable."

"Jack, I quit two weeks ago. I'm not going to take that kind of crap."

"Well, well," I say. "Man."

"Sounds like it was time to move on," Liz interjects.

"What I'd like to do is open my own salon."

It's not that I don't understand her disappointment. I made it to sales manager once at a Toyota dealership, but they put me back out on the lot after less than a month, saying I wasn't cutthroat enough. The owner's son took my place, and it just about killed me to keep going in every day. We had debts though. We were in way over our heads. It was a shameful time, but I didn't crack. Two months later Sonny Boy went off to rehab, and I was back on top. A good couple of years rolled by after that.

While Liz and the girls clear the table, I follow Tracy onto the patio. She closes the sliding glass door and retrieves a pack of More menthols from its hiding place inside a birdhouse. Placing the elbow of her smoking arm into the palm of her other hand, she stands with her back to the door so the girls can't see her take a drag. It's a pose I remember from when we were kids, a skating rink pose. That's where she and her dirtbag crew hung out before they were old enough to drive. Barely 13, and rumor had it she was already screwing some high school cokehead. Guys called her a whore to my face.

The backyard is tiny, maybe fifteen by fifteen, no grass at all. A shoulder-high fence separates it from the neighbors' yards on all three sides. I can see right into the next unit: a Chinese guy on his couch, watching TV. The sound of a Padres game curls through his screen door. I tried to talk Tony out of buying this place, but he wouldn't listen. His deal was always that I was too negative. Now Tracy is stuck with thin walls and noisy plumbing.

"You guys are still the happy couple," Tracy says. "Obviously."

"Most of the time, sure."

"The good part is you don't seem a thing like Mom and Dad."

"We got lucky, I guess."

Tracy's shoulders jerk. She turns her head and spits vomit into a potted plant. I'm not sure what to do. It would frighten her if I took her into my arms. We're not that kind of people. I'm sorry, but we're not. She wipes her mouth with the back of her hand and hits her cigarette again, then walks past me to stand against the fence, looking into the neighbor's yard so that I can't see her face. A gritty layer of ash covers everything now, and more is sifting down. The smell of smoke is stronger than ever.

"I still have some of the insurance money from the accident," I say. "What if you take it? You should get that salon going as soon as possible."

"Everything's up in the air," Tracy replies. "Maybe I'll go back to school."

"Use it for that then."

"You've got it all figured out, huh?"

"Hey..."

"It's funny, that's all."

She kneels to drink from a hose attached to a faucet at the edge of the patio. After the rape, she drove herself to the hospital. Nobody else in the family had that kind of fortitude. Our dad was a notorious hypochondriac.

Carrie slides the door open with great effort and says, "Mommy, what are you doing?"

"Watering the flowers," Tracy replies.

✕

We play Uno and Candyland with the girls, and then it's bedtime. Sundays are their father's, and he's picking them up early in the morning. Liz manages to get them upstairs without too much whining on the promise of a story. Tracy gathers the toys scattered about and tosses them into a wooden chest in the corner of the room while I go to the refrigerator for another beer.

"They love their Auntie Liz," Tracy says.

I hope she means that in a nice way. I think she does.

There's a knock at the door. Tracy looks worried, so I stand behind her as she answers. The police officer on the porch gives us an official smile.

"Mr. and Mrs. Milano?"

"Ms. Milano. He's my brother."

The cop scribbles on his clipboard. "Okay, well, we're out warning residents that they may be asked to evacuate if this fire swings around," he says.

315

"Oh God," Tracy sighs.

"Right now things are looking good, but you should be prepared just in case."

"God fucking dammit."

When the cop leaves, Tracy turns on the TV, but there are no special reports or live coverage. Liz comes downstairs, and I fill her in. She asks Tracy what she wants to pack, and Tracy says, "Nothing. None of it means anything to me." It's embarrassing to hear her talk like that. Liz treats the comment as a joke, though, and soon the two of them are placing photo albums into a plastic trash bag.

I decide to venture toward the fire line to see if I can get more information. Liz insists on coming along. We drive down out of the condos to pick up a frontage road paralleling the freeway. There's an orange glow on the horizon, and we make for that. A new squeak in the car gets on my nerves. I feel around the dash, desperate to locate it, and things get a little out of control. I almost hit a guardrail because I'm not watching where I'm going.

"Dammit, Jack, pay attention," Liz snaps. "Are you drunk?"

The road we're on descends into a dark, narrow canyon dotted with houses, the lights of which wink frantic messages through the trees. We hit bottom, then climb up the other side. As we crest the hill, the source of the glow is revealed to be a monstrous driving range lit by mercury vapor lamps. The golfers lined up at the tees swing mechanically. There is ash falling here, too, and the stink of smoke, but nobody's worried.

We pull over at a spot above the range and get out of the car to watch. It feels like something teenagers might do. Balls soar through the air and bounce in the dead grass. Liz drapes my arm across her shoulders. She really is great with those kids.

"Are you sure you don't want a baby?" I ask.

I watch her face. Nothing is going to get past me. When she wants to be blank, though, she's so blank. "I've got you," she says.

"No, really."

"Let's keep it simple. That's what I like about us."

We made a decision a few years ago. Her childhood wasn't the greatest either. A gust of wind rattles the leaves of the eucalyptus trees behind us, and the shadows of the branches look like people fighting in the street. When I close my eyes for a second, my blood does something scary on its way through my heart.

Tommy Borchardt hanged himself in his garage after they gave half his accounts to a new hire. No note, no nothing. Three kids. That's what I wake up thinking about after tossing and turning all night, waiting for another knock at the door.

We're in the girls' room, in their little beds. They're sleeping with Tracy. On a shelf near the ceiling, beyond the kids' reach, sits a collection of porcelain dolls. The sun shining through the window lights up their eyes and peeks up their frilly dresses. Their hair looks so real, I finally have to stand and touch it. Liz coughs and rolls over. Her clothes are folded neatly on the floor. She was in a rock band in high school. I wish I could have seen that.

Downstairs, I find some news on TV and learn that the fire has changed course and is headed away from any structures. They believe it was started by lightning. Tracy's coffee maker is different from ours, but I figure it out. It's fun to poke around in her cupboard and see what kind of canned goods she buys.

The kids sneak up on me. I turn, and there they are. I ask if they want me to fix them breakfast, but Kendra says that's her job. She stands on a stool to reach the counter and pours two bowls of cereal. I still remember learning to cook bacon. As far as I was concerned, I was ready to live on my own after that. Kendra slices a banana with a butter knife. She won't even let me get the milk out of the refrigerator for her. Tracy shouts at them to hurry and eat, their dad will be waiting.

"Is it fun at your dad's?" I ask as they sit at the table, shoveling Cheerios.

"It's okay," Kendra says like that's what she's been told to say.

"We have bikes over there," Cassie adds.

Hundreds of pigeons have occupied the shopping center parking lot where Tracy meets Tony to hand off the kids. They perch on the street lamps and telephone poles and march about pecking at garbage. Everything is streaked with their shit. When a car approaches, the birds wait until the last possible second to scoot out of its way. Tracy and Tony meet here because it's equidistant from both their places. He won't drive any farther than he's required to by the court.

I had to beg Tracy to let me come with her. She's worried that I'll start something. I like that, that she's worried, but I assure her that I'll hold my tongue. My hope is that when Tony sees me, he'll figure that she's pulled together some support and back off his custody demands. He's a hardhead though. We almost came to blows once over who was going to pick up a check at dinner.

The girls wait like little diplomats, wise in their silence. Carrie, strapped into her car seat, reaches out to touch the window of the minivan. Five minutes pass with just the radio playing. I watch the pigeons, the people pushing their carts out of the supermarket and filling their trunks with groceries. A cloud wanders across the sky, and I track the progress of its shadow.

After ten minutes I ask, "Is this normal?"

"He's very busy," Tracy replies, sarcastic.

There's a candy store next to the market. It's just opening up.

"Take the kids in there," I say. "You guys want candy? Take them in there and buy them something. Here's some money. I'll keep an eye out for him."

The girls are imbued with new energy. They screech and bicker and fight for the handle that slides open the side of the van.

"Look what you started," Tracy says.

I shrug as she flips down the sun visor and checks herself in the mirror there. The girls, already outside, practice tightrope walking on the yellow lines painted on the asphalt.

"Calm down," Tracy yells. "You want to get hit by a car just for some candy?"

Tony pulls up next to the van shortly after they enter the store. He's driving a new Volvo. He squints when he sees me, then gives a lazy wave. I'm all smiles as I hop out and walk around to his open window. He grew up on the East Coast somewhere and moved to California after college. Tracy cut his hair, that's how they met. He works in computers. I rest my palms on the roof of his car and bend over to talk to him.

"Yo Adrian," I say. I used to kid him that he sounded like Rocky.

"Jack."

"They should just be a minute. The girls were getting cranky, waiting so long."

Tony lights a cigarette. The ashtray is overflowing with butts. *Don't you sometimes see a chick and just want to tie her up and slap her around?* He asked me that once while he was still married to Tracy. We were camping in Yosemite, all of us. The women and kids had gone to bed. I remember looking up at the stars and down at the fire and thinking, *Whoops!* He pushes his sunglasses up on his nose and flicks ash out the window, between me and the car door.

"How's Liz?" he asks. "Good, I hope."

"You know us. Slow and steady."

"Are you still selling, what, restaurant stuff?"

"Why do you have to be that way, showing up late and everything?"

"Did she tell you to say that?"

I check to make sure Tracy and the kids are still in the store before continuing.

"She was raped, man, and you're coming at her with lawyers? Have a little compassion. Act like a human being."

"I said, did she tell you to talk to me?"

"I'm her brother. I took it upon myself."

I meant to approach this a bit more obliquely. Three years ago, two, I'd have had him eating from my hand, but these days I feel like all the juice has been drained out of me. We stare at each other for a second, then look away at the same time.

"She was wasted," he says. "Ask her. She was coming out of a bar. She barely remembers. Read the police report. There are doubts."

My vision flickers and blurs. I feel like I've been poisoned.

Kendra runs out of the store toward us, followed by Cassie. I push myself away from the car and search the ground for something—a stick, a rock. The pigeons make horrible fluttering noises in their throats.

"Hi, Daddy," the girls sing. They climb into Tony's car. Tracy watches from the store, half in and half out. I wish I was a gun. I wish I was a bullet. The girls wave bye-bye as Tony drives off.

"Can you believe that a-hole has a Volvo, and I'm driving this piece of shit?" Tracy says.

"He shouldn't smoke in front of the kids," I reply.

We pass an accident on the way back to her place, just a fender bender, but still my thoughts go to our parents. When they died I was almost to the point where I could see them as people. With a little more time I might even have started loving them again. What did they stand for? What secrets did they take with them? It was the first great loss of my life.

Tracy wants to treat us to lunch in Tijuana. We'll ride the trolley down and walk over the border to a steak house that was written up in the newspaper. That's fine with me. Let's keep moving. What Tony said about her is trying to take root, and I won't have it. She's my sister, see, and what she says, goes. I don't want to be one of those people who needs to get to the bottom of things.

We drive to the station. The crowd that boards the trolley with us is made up primarily of tourists, but there are also a few Mexicans headed for Sunday visits. They carry shopping bags, and their children sit quietly beside them. Tracy and Liz find two seats together. I'm at the far end of the car, in the middle of a French family.

We skirt the harbor, rocking past gray destroyers big as buildings. Then the tracks turn inland, and it's the back side of trailer parks and self-storage places. The faded pennants corralling a used-car lot flap maniacally, and there's always a McDonald's lurking on the horizon. Liz and Tracy are talking to each other—something light, if their smiles are any indication. I wave, trying to get their attention, but it's no use.

The young son in the French family decides to sing. He's wearing a Disneyland T-shirt. The song is in French, but there are little fart sounds in it that make his sister laugh. His mom says something snippy to him, but he ignores her. Dad steps in, giving the kid a shot with his elbow that jolts him into silence. There's a faded tattoo on Dad's forearm. Whatever it is has teeth, that's about all I can make out.

To cross into Mexico, we walk over the freeway on a bridge and pass through a turnstile. I did this once before, in high school, me and a couple of buddies. If you were tall enough to see over the bar, you could get a drink. That was the joke. I remember a stripper in a gorilla suit. Tacos were a quarter. The only problem was that the cops were always shaking someone down. The system is rotten here. You have to watch where you're going.

Tracy's got things wired though. Apparently she's down here all the time. It's fun, she says. She leads us to a taxi, and we head into town, passing ramshackle body shops and upholstery shops and something dead squished flat. Dirt roads scurry off into the hills where entire neighborhoods are built out of old garage doors and corrugated tin. The smell of burning rubber sneaks in now and then and tickles the back of my throat.

Calle Revolución is still the main drag, a disco on every corner. It looks tired during the day, like Bourbon Street or downtown Vegas. Hung over, sad, and a little embarrassed. It's a town that needs neon. We step out of the cab, and Tracy laughs with the driver as she pays him off. I didn't know she spoke Spanish.

I want a drink. The place we go into is painted bright green. Coco Loco. They sell bumper stickers and T-shirts. We get a table on the second-floor terrace, overlooking the street. Music is blasting inside, and lights flash, but the dance floor is empty except for a hippy chick deep into her own thing. The waiter is all over us as soon as we sit down.

I order tequila and a beer; Tracy and Liz get margaritas. Some poor guy in a ridiculous sombrero chachas around with a bottle of mescal in one hand and a bottle of Sprite in the other. For a couple of bucks he pours a little of each into your mouth and shakes your head, all the while blowing on a whistle. The sound of it makes my stomach jump. I'm startled every time. When my tequila arrives, I drink it down and guzzle half the beer.

"You guys wait here," Tracy says. "I have to run an errand."

"In Tijuana?"

"Tylenol with codeine, for a friend who hurt her leg. They sell it in the pharmacies."

"Wait a minute, Trace…"

"It's cool. I'll be right back."

She's gone before I can figure out how to stop her.

Everybody around us is a little shady. It hits me all of a sudden. Not quite criminal, but open to suggestion. A man wearing mirrored sunglasses and smoking a cigar gets up from his chair and leans over the railing to signal someone in the street. His partner is having his shoes shined by a kid with the crookedest teeth I've ever seen. The sombrero guy blows his whistle again, and a big black raven lights on the roof and cocks his head to stare down at us.

Liz insists that Tony is full of shit when I tell her what he said in the parking lot. I lean in close and speak quietly so no one else can hear. She says that men always cast aspersions on rape victims, even the cops. "You should know better," she says.

"I didn't mean anything like that."

"I hope not."

"She can do whatever the fuck she wants. Get her head chopped off, whatever."

"That's nice. That's just lovely."

It's the alcohol. It makes me pissy sometimes. Liz doesn't know the worst of it. Like the time I went out for a few with one of my bosses and ended up on top of him with my hands around his throat. He didn't press charges, but he also wasn't going to be signing any more checks for me. To Liz it was just another layoff. Quite a few of my messes have been of my own making. I'm man enough to admit it.

The bathroom is nasty, and there's nothing to dry my hands with. My anger at Tracy rises. She's been gone almost an hour. "Hey," I yell to a busboy from the bathroom door. "You need towels in here." He brings me some napkins. I have to walk across the dance floor to get back to the terrace. A kid bumps me and gives me his whole life like a disease. I see it all from beginning to end. "Fly, fly, flyyyyy," the music yowls. "Fly, fly, flyyyyyy."

They still have those donkeys painted like zebras down on the street, hitched to little wagons. I remember them from last time. You climb up on the seat, and they put a sombrero on your head that says KISS ME or CISCO and take a picture with some kind of ancient camera. Liz and I hug. We look like honeymooners in the photo, or cheaters.

There are those kids, too, the ones selling Chiclets and silver rings that turn your fingers green. Or sometimes they aren't selling anything. They just hold out their hands. Barefoot and dirty—babies, really. So many that after a while you don't see them anymore, but they're still there, like the saddest thing that ever happened to you.

Liz and I stand on the sidewalk in front of the bar, waiting. The power lines overhead, tangled and frayed, slice the sky into wild shapes. Boys cruise past in fancy cars, the songs on their stereos speaking for them. The barker for the strip club next door invites us in for a happy hour special, two for one. It's all a little too loud, a little too sharp. I'm about to suggest we have another drink when Tracy floats up to us like a ghost.

"You know, Trace, fuck," I say.

"What a hassle. Sorry."

A hot wind scours the street, flinging dust into our eyes.

The restaurant is on a side street, a couple blocks away. We don't say anything during the short walk. Men in cowboy hats cook steaks on an iron grill out front, and we pass through a cloud of greasy smoke to join the other gringos inside. It's that kind of place. I order the special, a sirloin stuffed with guacamole.

Tracy pretends to be interested in what Liz is saying,

something about Cassie and Kendra, but her restless fingers and darting eyes give her away. When she turns to call for another bottle of water, Liz shoots me a quizzical look. I shake my head and drink my beer. The booze has deadened my taste buds so that I can't enjoy my steak. Tracy cuts into hers but doesn't eat a bite. The waiter asks if anything is wrong.

We go back to Revolución to get a cab. The sidewalks are crazy, tilting this way and that and sometimes disappearing completely. You step off the curb, and suddenly it's three feet down to the pavement. Tracy begins to cry. She doesn't hide it. She walks in and out of the purple afternoon shadows of the buildings, dragging on a cigarette, tears shining.

"Must be one of those days," she says when I ask what's wrong.

We leave it at that.

She cleans herself up in the cab, staring into a little round mirror, before we join the long line of people waiting to pass through customs. We stand shoulder to shoulder with strangers, and the fluorescent lights make everyone look guilty of something. There are no secrets in this room. Every word echoes, and I can smell the sweat of the guy in front of me. Four or five officers are checking IDs. They ask people how long they've been down and what they've brought back with them. When it's my turn, a fat blond woman glances down at my license, matches my face to the picture and waves me through. We're all waved right through.

Tracy's mood brightens immediately. In fact, she laughs and laughs as we leave the building and board the trolley. Everything's funny to her, everything's great. The train is less crowded this time. We each get our own row of seats. Just some Marines at the other end of the car, talking about whores. "Oh, this little bitch, she went to town," one of them groans.

Tracy reaches into her purse and takes out a bottle of pills, opens it, and pops one into her mouth. She smiles when she catches me watching her.

The trolley clicks and clacks like it's made of bones. I stretch out, put my feet up. The reflection of my face is wrapped around a stainless steel pole dulled by a day's worth of fingerprints. Tracy dozes off, head lolling. Liz too. I watch the sun set through rattling windows, and all the red that comes with it.

The trolley lurches, and Tracy's purse tips over. It's one of those big bags you carry over your shoulder. A half-dozen bottles of pills spill out and roll noisily across the floor. I chase them down, mortified. Tracy opens one eye. I spread the bag wide. It's full of pills, maybe twenty bottles, all with Spanish labels.

"You've got kids," I whisper. "Beautiful kids."

"That's right," She grabs the bag away from me and hugs it to her chest.

"Tracy."

"Look, I didn't ask you to show up; I just didn't say no."

"I wanted to help."

"I fully realize that."

I try to talk to her some more, but she pretends to be asleep. Nothing I say means anything anyway because she thinks I've had it easy. Liz is suddenly beside me. She takes my hand in both of hers. The jarheads are rapping. *Bitch. Skeez. Muthafucka.* I could kill them. I could.

We can see the fire from the freeway. The entire hillside is ablaze. Tracy's condo is up there somewhere. Flames claw at the night sky, and smoke blots out the stars. I don't even know how you'd begin to fight a thing like that. Maybe that's what the helicopters are for. They circle and dip, lights flashing.

Tracy is still asleep. She could barely walk from the trolley to the car but wouldn't let us touch her. "Stop laughing," she yelled, so messed up she was imagining things. She's curled up on the backseat now, her arms protecting her head. We decide not to wake her until we're sure of something.

The police at the roadblock can't tell us much. The wind picked up, and everything went to shit. The gymnasium of a nearby high school has been pressed into service as a shelter. We are to go there and wait for more information. A fire truck arrives, and they pull aside the barricades to let it through.

"How bad are we looking?" I ask a cop.

He ignores me.

I back the car up and turn around, and Liz guides me to the school. We pass a carnival on the way, in the parking lot of a church. A Ferris wheel, a merry-go-round, a few games. People wander from ride to ride, booth to booth, swiping at the ash that tickles their noses. A beer sign sputters in the window of a pizza parlor. A kid in a white shirt and black vest sweeps the sidewalk in front of the multiplex. His friend makes him laugh. A mile away everything is burning.

My stomach is cramped by the time we get to the school. I can see into the gym from where I park. Cots are lined up beneath posters shouting GO TIGERS!!! Two women sit at a table near the door, signing people in, and further away, in the shadows by the drinking fountains, a group of men stand and smoke. That's about it. Most people have somewhere better to go. Tony must have told Kendra about angels. What a thing to put into a kid's mind.

328

A news crew is interviewing a girl who just arrived. She's carrying a knapsack and a cardboard box full of china. They shine a light in her face and ask about what she lost and where she'll go. She says something about her cat. She had to leave it behind.

I close my eyes and bring my fists to my temples. I have to be at work early for a meeting. I can see Big Mike sliding out of his Caddy, squeezing his gut past the steering wheel. He's my mentor, he likes to say. He's been married four times. He gets winded walking to the john. There's nothing lucky about him.

"I want a baby," I say. The words just get away from me.

"Jack," Liz says. I'm afraid to open my eyes to look at her. Tracy giggles in the backseat, and we both turn. She reaches up to scratch her face and grins in her sleep.

Richard Lange

has had stories in *The Sun*, *The Iowa Review*, and *Best American Mystery Stories*, and as part of the Atlantic Monthly's Fiction for Kindle series. He is the author of the collection *Dead Boys* and the novels *Angel Baby* and *This Wicked World*. He received the Rosenthal Family Foundation Award from the American Academy of Arts and Letters and was a 2009 Guggenheim Fellow. He lives in Los Angeles.

WINDEYE

BRIAN EVENSON

They lived, when he was growing up, in a simple house, an old bungalow with a converted attic and sides covered in cedar shake. In the back, where an oak thrust its branches over the roof, the shake was light brown, almost honey. In the front, where the sun struck it full, it had weathered to a pale gray, like a dirty bone. There, the shingles were brittle, thinned by sun and rain, and if you were careful you could slip your fingers up behind some of them. Or at least his sister could. He was older and his fingers were thicker, so he could not.

Looking back on it, many years later, he often thought it had started with that, with her carefully working her fingers up under a shingle as he waited and watched to see if it would crack. That was one of his earliest memories of his sister, if not the earliest.

His sister would turn around and smile, her hand gone to knuckles, and say, "I feel something. What am I feeling?" And then he would ask questions. *Is it smooth?* he might ask. *Does it feel rough? Scaly? Is it cold-blooded or warm-blooded? Does it feel red? Does it feel like its claws are in or out? Can you feel its eye move?* He would keep on, watching the expression on her face change as she tried to make his words into a living, breathing thing, until it started to feel too real for her and, half giggling, half screaming, she whipped her hand free.

There were other things they did, other ways they tortured each other, things they both loved and feared. Their mother didn't know anything about it, or if she did she didn't care. One of them would shut the other inside the toy chest and pretend to leave the room, waiting there silently until the one in the chest couldn't stand it any longer and started to yell. That was a hard game for him because he was afraid of the dark, but he tried not to show that to his sister. Or one of them would wrap the other tight in blankets, and then the trapped one would have to break free. Why they had liked it, why they had done it, he had a hard time remembering later, once he was grown. But they *had* liked it, or at least *he* had liked it—there was no denying that—and he had done it. No denying that either.

So at first those games, if they were games, and then, later, something else, something worse, something decisive. What was it again? Why was it hard, now that he was grown, to remember? What was it called? Oh, yes, *Windeye*.

2.

How had it begun? And when? A few years later, when the house started to change for him, when he went from thinking about each bit and piece of it as a separate thing and started thinking of it as a *house*. His sister was still coming up close, entranced by the gap between shingle and wall, intrigued by the twist and curve of a crack in the concrete steps. It was not that she didn't know there was a house, only that the smaller bits were more important than the whole. For him, though, it had begun to be the reverse.

So he began to step back, to move back in the yard far enough away to take the whole house in at once. His sister would give him a quizzical look and try to coax him in closer, to get him involved in something small. For a while, he'd play to her level, narrate to her what the surface she was touching or the shadow she was glimpsing might mean, so she could pretend. But over time he drifted out again. There was something about the house, the house as a whole, that troubled him. But why? Wasn't it just like any house?

His sister, he saw, was standing beside him, staring at him. He tried to explain it to her, tried to put a finger on what fascinated him. *This house,* he told her. *It's a little different. There's something about it . . .* But he saw, from the way she looked at him, that she thought it was a game, that he was making it up.

"What are you seeing?" she asked, with a grin.

Why not? he thought. *Why not make it a game?*

"What are you seeing?" he asked her.

Her grin faltered a little but she stopped staring at him and stared at the house.

"I see a house," she said.

"Is there something wrong with it?" he prompted.

She nodded, then looked to him for approval.

"What's wrong?" he asked.

Her brow tightened like a fist. "I don't know," she finally said. "The window?"

"What about the window?"

"I want you to do it," she said. "It's more fun."

He sighed, and then pretended to think. "Something wrong with the window," he said. "Or not the window exactly but the number of windows." She was smiling, waiting. "The problem is the number of windows. There's one more window on the outside than on the inside."

He covered his mouth with his hand. She was smiling and nodding, but he couldn't go on with the game. Because, yes, that was exactly the problem, there was one more window on the outside than on the inside. That, he knew, was what he'd been trying to see.

3.

But he had to make sure. He had his sister move from room to room in the house, waving to him from each window. The ground floor was all right, he saw her each time. But in the converted attic, just shy of the corner, there was a window at which she never appeared.

It was small and round, probably only a foot and a half in diameter. The glass was dark and wavery. It was held in place by a strip of metal about as thick as his finger, giving the whole of the circumference a dull, leaden rim.

He went inside and climbed the stairs, looking for the window himself, but it simply wasn't there. But when he went back outside, there it was.

✕

For a time, it felt like he had brought the problem to life himself by stating it, that if he hadn't said anything the half-window wouldn't be there. Was that possible? He didn't think so, that wasn't the way the world worked. But even later, once he was grown, he still found himself wondering sometimes if it was his fault, if it was something he had done. Or rather, said.

Staring up at the half-window, he remembered a story his grandmother had told him, back when he was very young, just three or four, just after his father had left and just before his sister was born. Well, he didn't remember it exactly, but he remembered it had to do with windows. Where she came from, his grandmother said, they used to be called not windows but something else. He couldn't remember the word, but remembered that it started with a v. She had said the word and then had asked, *Do you know what this means?* He shook his head. She repeated the word, slower this time.

"This first part," she had said, "it means 'wind.' This second part, it means 'eye.'" She looked at him with her own pale, steady eye. "It is important to know that a window can be instead a *windeye*."

✕

So he and his sister called it that, *windeye*. It was, he told her, how the wind looked into the house and so was not a window at all. So of course they couldn't look out of it; it was not a window at all, but a windeye.

He was worried she was going to ask questions, but she didn't. And then they went into the house to look again, to make sure it wasn't a window after all. But it still wasn't there on the inside.

Then they decided to get a closer look. They had figured out which window was nearest to it and opened that and leaned out of it. There it was. If they leaned far enough, they could see it and almost touch it.

"I could reach it," his sister said. "If I stand on the sill and you hold my legs, I could lean out and touch it."

337

"No," he started to say, but, fearless, she had already clambered onto the sill and was leaning out. He wrapped his arms around her legs to keep her from falling. He was just about to pull her back inside when she leaned farther and he saw her finger touch the windeye. And then it was as if she had dissolved into smoke and been sucked into the windeye. She was gone.

4.

It took him a long time to find his mother. She was not inside the house, nor was she outside in the yard. He tried the house next door, the Jorgensens, and then the Allreds, then the Dunfords. She wasn't anywhere. So he ran back home, breathless, and somehow his mother was there now, lying on the couch, reading.

"What's wrong?" she asked.

He tried to explain it best he could. Who? she asked at first and then said *Slow down and tell it again,* and then, *But who do you mean?* And then, once he'd explained again, with an odd smile:

"But you don't have a sister."

But of course he had a sister. How could his mother have forgotten? What was wrong? He tried to describe her, to explain what she looked like, but his mother just kept shaking her head.

"No," she said firmly. "You don't have a sister. You never had one. Stop pretending. What's this really about?"

Which made him feel that he should hold himself very still, that he should be very careful about what he said, that if he breathed wrong more parts of the world would disappear.

✕

After talking and talking, he tried to get his mother to come out and look at the windeye.

"Window, you mean," she said, voice rising.

"No," he said, beginning to grow hysterical as well. "Not window. *Windeye*." And then he had her by the hand and was tugging her to the door. But no, that was wrong too, because no matter what window he pointed at she could tell him where it was in the house. The *windeye*, just like his sister, was no longer there.

But he kept insisting it had been there, kept insisting too that he had a sister.

And that was when the trouble really started.

5.

Over the years there were moments when he was almost convinced, moments when he almost began to think—and perhaps even did think for weeks or months at a time—that he never had a sister. It would have been easier to think this than to think she had been alive and then, perhaps partly because of him, not alive. Being not alive wasn't like being dead, he felt: it was much, much worse. There were years too when he simply didn't choose, when he saw her as both real and make believe and sometimes neither of those things. But in the end what made him keep believing in her—despite the line of doctors that visited him as a child, despite the rift it made between him and his mother, despite years of forced treatment and various drugs that made him feel like his head had been filled with wet sand, despite years of having to pretend to be cured—was simply this: he was the only one who believed his sister was real. If he stopped believing, what hope would there be for her?

✕

Thus he found himself, even when his mother was dead and gone and he himself was old and alone, brooding on his sister, wondering what had become of her. He wondered too if one day she would simply reappear, young as ever, ready to continue with the games they had played. Maybe she would simply suddenly be there again, her tiny fingers worked up behind a cedar shingle, staring expectantly at him, waiting for him to tell her what she was feeling, to make up words for what was pressed there between the house and its skin, lying in wait.

"What is it?" he would say in a hoarse voice, leaning on his cane.

"I feel something," she would say. "What am I feeling?"

And he would set about describing it. *Does it feel red? Does it feel warm-blooded or cold? Is it round? Is it smooth like glass?* All the while, he knew, he would be thinking not about what he was saying but about the wind at his back. If he turned around, he would be wondering, would he find the wind's strange, baleful eye staring at him?

That wasn't much, but it was the best he could hope for. Chances were he wouldn't get even that. Chances were there would be no sister, no wind. Chances were that he'd be stuck with the life he was living now, just as it was, until the day when he was either dead or not living himself.

Brian Evenson

is the author of twelve books of fiction, most recently the story collection *Windeye* and the novel *Immobility*, both of which were finalists for the Shirley Jackson Award. His novel *Last Days* won the American Library Association's award for Best Horror Novel of 2009. His novel *The Open Curtain* (Coffee House Press) was a finalist for an Edgar Award and an IHG Award. He is the recipient of three O. Henry Prizes. Other books include *The Wavering Knife* (which won the IHG Award for best story collection), *Dark Property*, and *Altmann's Tongue*. His work has been translated into French, Italian, Spanish, Japanese and Slovenian. He lives and works in Providence, Rhode Island, at the school that served as the basis for Lovecraft's Miskatonic University.

ACKNOWLEDGMENTS

"FATHER, SON, HOLY RABBIT" BY STEPHEN GRAHAM JONES. FIRST PUBLISHED IN *CEMETERY DANCE* #57, 2007. COPYRIGHT © 2007 BY STEPHEN GRAHAM JONES. REPRINTED BY PERMISSION OF THE AUTHOR. "IT'S AGAINST THE LAW TO FEED THE DUCKS" BY PAUL TREMBLAY. FIRST PUBLISHED IN *FANTASY MAGAZINE*, 2006. COPYRIGHT © 2006 BY PAUL TREMBLAY. REPRINTED BY PERMISSION OF THE AUTHOR. "THAT BABY" BY LINDSAY HUNTER. FIRST PUBLISHED IN *EVERYDAY GENIUS*, 2010. COPYRIGHT © 2010 BY LINDSAY HUNTER. REPRINTED BY PERMISSION OF FEATHERPROOF BOOKS. "THE TRUTH AND ALL ITS UGLY" BY KYLE MINOR. FIRST PUBLISHED IN *SURREAL SOUTH 2007*, 2007. COPYRIGHT © 2007 BY KYLE MINOR. REPRINTED BY PERMISSION OF SARABANDE BOOKS. "ACT OF CONTRITION" BY CRAIG CLEVENGER. FIRST PUBLISHED IN *WARMED AND BOUND*, 2011. COPYRIGHT © 2011 BY CRAIG CLEVENGER. REPRINTED BY PERMISSION OF THE AUTHOR. "THE FAMILIARS" BY MICAELA MORRISSETTE. FIRST PUBLISHED IN *CONJUNCTIONS* #52, 2009. COPYRIGHT © 2009 BY MICAELA MORRISSETTE. REPRINTED BY PERMISSION OF THE AUTHOR. "DIAL TONE" BY BENJAMIN PERCY. FIRST PUBLISHED IN *THE MISSOURI REVIEW*, VOLUME 30, NUMBER 2, 2007. COPYRIGHT © 2007 BY BENJAMIN PERCY. REPRINTED BY PERMISSION OF THE AUTHOR. "HOW" BY ROXANE GAY. FIRST PUBLISHED IN *ANNALEMMA* #6, 2010. COPYRIGHT © 2010 BY ROXANE GAY. REPRINTED BY PERMISSION OF THE AUTHOR. "INSTITUTO" BY ROY KESEY. FIRST PUBLISHED IN *THE IOWA REVIEW*, VOLUME 34, NUMBER 3, 2005. COPYRIGHT © 2005 BY ROY KESEY. REPRINTED BY PERMISSION OF THE AUTHOR. "RUST AND BONE" BY CRAIG DAVIDSON. FIRST PUBLISHED IN *THE FIDDLEHEAD* #219 AS "28 BONES." COPYRIGHT © 2004 BY CRAIG DAVIDSON. REPRINTED BY PERMISSION OF W.W. NORTON. "BLUE HAWAII" BY REBECCA JONES-HOWE. FIRST PUBLISHED IN *NOVA PARADE*, 2012. COPYRIGHT © 2012 BY REBECCA JONES-HOWE. REPRINTED BY PERMISSION OF THE AUTHOR. "CHILDREN ARE THE ONLY ONES THAT BLUSH" BY JOE MENO. FIRST PUBLISHED IN *ONE STORY* #122, 2009. COPYRIGHT © 2009 BY JOE MENO. REPRINTED BY PERMISSION OF THE AUTHOR. "CHRISTOPHER HITCHENS" BY VANESSA VESELKA. FIRST PUBLISHED IN *ZYZZYVA* WINTER ISSUE, 2012. COPYRIGHT © 2012 BY VANESSA VESELKA. REPRINTED BY PERMISSION OF THE AUTHOR. "DOLLHOUSE" BY CRAIG WALLWORK. FIRST PUBLISHED IN *ATTIC TOYS*, 2012. COPYRIGHT © 2012 BY CRAIG WALLWORK. REPRINTED BY PERMISSION OF THE AUTHOR. "HIS FOOTSTEPS ARE MADE OF SOOT" BY NIK KORPON. FIRST PUBLISHED IN *TROUBADOUR* 21, 2009. COPYRIGHT © 2009 BY NIK KORPON. REPRINTED BY PERMISSION OF THE AUTHOR. "THE ETIQUETTE OF HOMICIDE" BY TARA LASKOWSKI. FIRST PUBLISHED IN *BARRELHOUSE* #10, 2012. COPYRIGHT © 2012 BY TARA LASKOWSKI. REPRINTED BY PERMISSION OF THE AUTHOR. "DREDGE" BY MATT BELL. FIRST PUBLISHED IN *HAYDEN'S FERRY REVIEW* #50, 2009. COPYRIGHT © 2009 BY MATT BELL. REPRINTED BY PERMISSION OF THE AUTHOR. "SUNSHINE FOR ADRIENNE" BY ANTONIA CRANE. FIRST PUBLISHED IN *THE HEROIN CHRONICLES*, 2013. COPYRIGHT © 2013 BY ANTONIA CRANE. REPRINTED BY PERMISSION OF THE AUTHOR. "FUZZYLAND" BY RICHARD LANGE. FIRST PUBLISHED IN *THE GEORGIA REVIEW*, VOLUME 56, NUMBER 3, 2002. COPYRIGHT © 2002 BY RICHARD LANGE. REPRINTED BY PERMISSION OF LITTLE, BROWN AND COMPANY. "WINDEYE" BY BRIAN EVENSON. FIRST PUBLISHED IN *PEN AMERICA* #11, 2009. COPYRIGHT © 2009 BY BRIAN EVENSON. REPRINTED BY PERMISSION OF COFFEE HOUSE PRESS.